Blackwing Rising

Volume VI in
The Saga of Magiskeep

By
Jean E. Dvorak

Cover art by
David Melanson

Printed in the United States of America

First Printing, 2015

ISBN-10: 1-942481-13-6
ISBN-13: 978-1-942481-13-3

Jean E. Dvorak
293 Deans-Rhode Hall Road
Jamesburg, NJ 08831
http://jedvorak.wix.com/magiskeep

About the Author

Jean E. Dvorak is a retired high school teacher. An avid horsewoman, she has competed and trained two horses to FEI level in dressage. No longer competing, she still trains her horses and those experiences are evident in the novels where horses play a significant role. From the author: "Fantasy writing is very liberating. It allows the writer complete control of the world. Where else can magic exist and anything at all can happen? The writer makes the rules and can take the story anywhere imagination allows." "The Magiskeep Saga" was "born" in 1984 as a response to a challenge from her students when she assigned them a writing assignment: "What would you do if you had a magic power?" Since then, encouragement from a group of gaming fantasy fans on "The Halfwittenberg Door" message board sparked more writing. The result is a total of four full novels and several shorter novelettes in the collection. Ms. Dvorak has also written a number of stage musicals, plays, and vocal musical pieces, all of which have been performed locally in New Jersey, where she lives.

Other Books by Jean E Dvorak

The Saga of Magiskeep

Kingdom Beyond the Rim

Honor's Way

The Wall Between

Silvrin Shards

White Wind

Romance Novels

The Loving Cup

Other Publications

Four Christmas

The Other Side of Stick River Road

The book is dedicated to

Ruth, Julius, and Walter Dvorak who always believed in me and taught me to believe in myself.

With special thanks to:

David Melanson

And

Eric Allen

Blackwing Rising

I

Though Edra had failed in every attempt to cure Prince Gareth of that peculiar "missing itch" in his breeches, he had ingratiated himself enough with Aberdeen's heir apparent to avoid the fate of many of his fellow Healers who languished in the darker recesses of the Palace's dungeons.

In fact, both he and Jyp, the young Sorcerer from Aberdeen's Cuver Street, had formed an uneasy, but practical alliance to keep them both safe from Gareth's rage. Neither man was particularly adept in Magic, a fact they kept from Gareth at every turning despite freely admitting it to each other. So they devised a plan to join forces whenever possible to keep up pretenses.

Letting Edra--who did proclaim himself something of a Healer--take on the master's role, Jyp, who had already used his Magic rather ineffectively to try to thwart Salene, Magiskeep's Mistress, pretended to admire the other Sorcerer's skills. He assured Gareth that, given time, he could learn enough from the Master Mage that it was likely the two of them together might have the skill and power to restore the Prince's stolen manhood.

"My Liege, that witch of Magic was indeed powerful, but she was a woman. Master Edra and I are men and it is well said the Powers of Turan pulse strongest in the male's line. Surely he and I can work together and reverse her spell."

Gareth, prone to whining whenever he was not in the public eye made no effort to hide his misery as he replied. "Male line? Men? How the words mock my suffering! Until Edra showed up, I had lost all hope. Then his failings near broke my heart." He clutched dramatically at his chest with his hand as if it would somehow hold back the pain. "Now you torment me again with empty promises? Or do you really believe what you say?"

"To a Sorcerer," Jyp answered, "the belief is all. I would not lie to you. Have I ever?"

Gareth considered this. "When you first came, you admitted you had little skill in Healing. And you did an admirable job of trying to stop that Sorceress in her tracks. And after, when she left me wearing the stinking skin of a bocart, you stayed at my side, struggling with all your will and pitiful talent to cure me. I do owe you some thanks in recompense. What, exactly, do you want?"

"Master Edra and I, as his lowly apprentice," Jyp said, offering Edra a deferential nod of his head, "wish to study together, here in the palace."

"Indeed, my Liege," Edra offered quickly. "My Magic is great, but I am a wilder of sorts, never having studied in this Magiskeep I've heard of so often from the lips of my young friend here."

When Jyp had first come to the palace, he had illusioned himself as an older man to satisfy the Prince's desires to be counseled by a gray head of hair, but since, he had let the illusion slide, claiming it was too great a drain on his limited power. In reality, he let it slip away at Will once Edra had arrived in order to appear more vulnerable and less of a threat to the more ambitious Sorcerer. By fawning on Edra's supposedly superior expertise and experience, he'd set the foundation for a truce and this eventual alliance. "I would be so honored to have his tutelage," Jyp said. "And of all, you, your Highness would reap the most benefit."

Gareth rubbed his chin thoughtfully. Already he had used Edra's skills to earn many a pleasure the mortal world could not offer without Magic. While the royal coffers could buy him nearly anything he wanted, Sorcery, he was discovering, had its uses. In Chillmonth, for instance, fresh surleps ripened by the Warmmonth sun were simply impossible to find. Certainly the sweet fruit grown in a Warmroom could fall easily into his Princely hand, but for some reason, despite being the same color and nearly as juicy, the flavor was simply not the same. But Edra could chant him a fresh surlep from the sun season with a wave of his hand, satisfying Gareth's craving in an instant.

So was it the same for a fine bolt of cloth for a new tunic woven from the superior wool of the Norreaches or even the tunic itself if Gareth were too impatient for the tailor to sew it. Crafts from the Sea Isles, a fine sword from Master Tyler's forge on FarIsle, or even the occasional heavy-breasted tavern maid could all be in his hands in an instant. He could touch, explore with his lean fingers every treasure of Turan at once with a single request to the fair-haired Sorcerer who had come to his court with an arrogant air he could actually back up with deeds.

As for Jyp? Something about the youth intrigued him. While he was not quite pretty enough to bed, he carried some kind of allure Gareth found hard to resist. He'd been gentle when Gareth had suffered the indignity of Salene's bocart curse, and each time his hand had touched the enchanted Prince, it was as if a current of deep understanding flowed between them. While still wary of the young and obviously untrained Sorcerer, Aberdeen's royal heir found him an easy companion and quite likely worth more alive than dead. "The west wing of the palace, behind the kitchens. There's a suite of rooms I will give you. You may study there with enough privacy to," he wiggled his hand suggestively, "do whatsoever you will with no interference from the rest of the royal household. Take your pleasures there, but you must at all times be instantly ready to answer our royal summons, for we may have great need of your Magic."

Jyp bobbed his head eagerly. "A private suite, your Highness. This is more than I could ever have hoped for." And, Jyp thought, *exactly what I wanted*. Left to his own devices, if he could ever find a way to extricate himself from Edra's presence, it gave Jyp the leeway he needed to pursue his true calling--to find out whether or not the Prince was trying to murder his father, Gailvarg the King.

*****

For months, Magiskeep lay in peace. And within the protection of its chanted bluestone walls, Jamus' little family was enjoying every moment of the rare and valued treasure such peace afforded.

Since their last battles with the Shadows and Jamus'
enforced separation from the Keep while he mastered the secrets of
the White River, the world of Magic had eased itself into a quiet
serenity. With Sarn still the designated Master of the Keep, Jamus
and Salene were free to spend all the time in the world learning how
to care for and love their little son, Jarien, who was already showing
some sign he had inherited his parents' potent mastery of the River.

When the baby cried, the heavens would open above with
showers. Jamus then, with his own well-practiced skill, would
command them to stop. And when Jarien threw a tantrum, if the
thunder rolled in response, all his father had to say was, "Enough, it
is enough," and the storm would still along with the wailing infant.

"Do you think you should control him like that?" Salene
asked. "Is chanting such a good thing when he's so young? I mean,
babies do cry."

Jamus shrugged. "But usually when babies cry the skies
don't tear themselves apart with every tear. I'm not trying to chant
Jarien, but I am trying to chant the consequences."

"And what if you're not here when he starts to fuss like
that?" Salene asked. "Does that mean Magiskeep will drown until he
gets whatever he wants to settle him back down? It seems to me we
need to find a better way to quiet our son's unruly calls to the River."

"I spoke to Sarena about it," Jamus replied, "but she insists
she's never quite heard of anything like it. Children don't usually
show a connection to the River until they pass seven circles or so.
That's why the Keep never tests them until they are eight."

"Well, it's pretty clear our son is a bit precocious now, isn't
it," Salene said. But she was smiling as she looked down on her son,
already showing sprouts of dark curls so like his father. "I'm not
surprised we have such a special little one."

"I shouldn't be either," Jamus told her, tickling the baby's
tummy until Jarien burst into giggles, setting the tarlets to singing in
the garden beyond the window." But I must admit it does pose some
interesting problems for his parents. Do you think you've mastered
my lessons well enough that I can leave the two of you alone for a bit
without fearing the lightning will sear the roofs off the village if he
starts crying for his dinner?"

"I can certainly supply dinner," Salene said, plumping her heavy breasts with her hands, "but the tantrum before?" At Jamus' scowl, she smiled. "Of course I can, my Love. You are a fine teacher and controlling the River in that small way, once I understood how to do it. It is really not as difficult as it may seem. I may not be the Rivermaster, but I am a mother, and learning to turn the heart of a wayward child is practically an inherited skill. I'll be fine if you need to go somewhere." She smiled again, "If you are so tired of your wife and son."

"By the Blood, no!" Jamus protested. Then he caught the mischievous sparkle her eye and grinned back. "I'd stay here forever if I had my choice, but I was thinking it would be worth a trip to the Great Library or Master Senital's vaults to see if there is anything of wisdom in Magiskeep's history or the Eldenlore itself that might help us with this young ruffian we've brought into the world."

"Do you think there's ever been another like him?"

Jamus shook his head, "Not really. He is our son, after all."

"Jamus!" Salene started to protest, but he cut her off with a wave of his hand.

"All joking aside, Salene, I find it hard to believe this has not happened somewhere before in all the Circles of Turan's past. All we need to do is find out when, where, and what in the name of the Hand the parents did about it."

As Jarien started to wail again, the skies rumbled. "I think he needs his diaper changed," Salene said. She bent over the crib and whispered, "Enough, it is enough."

Once more the skies quieted, and Jamus, with a sigh, gave her a quick kiss on the back of neck and slipped out of the room.

*****

Jamus was idly whistling an old tune he'd once heard Simen sing as he headed down the hall to the Great Library. It was the first time he'd been out of his and Salene's Chambers alone since Jarien had been born. Once he'd held the baby in his arms, he'd not wanted to miss a moment with the little boy or his mother. It was as if he was making up for his own lost childhood and the lack of a father's love in a month, each second more precious than the next.

The River would call him back, sooner or later, but for now his mothers, gold, silver, and white, had been generous to their son, perhaps they themselves making up for his lost childhood as well, letting him relish his son's. Kashar had never struck him as being particularly nurturing to her son, but he suspected she had taken charge of the situation for the Golden Waters were warm and embracing every time he reached for them, even in the smallest way.

When the crib Master Saraban had made rocked ever so slightly on one leg, Jamus had called the River to balance it. The waters had answered gently, bathing the beautifully crafted wood in a golden glow, but choosing instead to lift a stone in the floor beneath to resolve the issue rather than touch the master craftsman's handiwork, which needed no fixing at all. It was almost as if Magic were showing its own respect for the beautiful woodwork, trusting its perfection as much as Jamus wanted to.

"She answers my desire, not my command," Jamus told Salene when he pointed to the leveled floor. "I should have known in more than my heart that Saraban would never have made such a mistake with his wood."

Salene glanced over at the lopsided bookcase she had made for her husband and laughed. "You're right, Jamus, no Master carpenter would ever make such a mistake."

He laughed back. The bookcase had become a source of never ending humor between them as a symbol of the love they shared and of Salene's unfailing devotion to it. Though books might topple from its uneven middle shelf, Jamus steadfastly refused to even put a shim in to fix it. "Like our love," he said, "it might need a bit of tidying up now and then, but we always know we can find a way to fix it. Let it alone so we'll always remember that."

Now, as Jamus walked along, he took in the near perfection of every inch of the rest of Magiskeep and marveled at how hard everyone worked to keep it that way. Jeamel and his staff of housekeepers were meticulous at dusting and cleaning, and the staff of servants spent as much time tending the walls themselves as they did caring for the Magicians within them. Now and then, a little imperfection might have been worth something.

Then he stopped in his tracks, his eye caught by a flash of errant green and gold invading the upholstery of one of the hall's chairs. Modeled in his colors of royal blue and silver as had been the tradition of the Keep since the first Master had taken the seat, the Keep's furniture, at least on this, his floor, honored it. When Sagari had ruled, turquoise and white decorated every floor, but Jamus had let Salene and some of the other mistresses choose the décor for the rest of the Keep to avoid the monotony of his mark on everything. But this floor? His colors.

"My Lord?" a voice said from behind him. It was Sarn, the Keep's interim Master, his rule granted by Jamus until a Gathering or some other crisis might demand the Rivermaster return to duty.

Jamus turned. Sarn was dressed in an elegant green tunic decorated with gold vines and leaves along the front and sleeves.

Though little love was lost between the two Mages, each had a healthy respect for the other. Sarn both feared and resented Jamus' overwhelming power in the Magic, and Jamus respected Sarn's overwhelming self-love and the determination to protect Magiskeep at all costs in order to keep his own skin safe.

"My Lord?" Sarn questioned again. "Is there something I can help you with? I've not seen you out alone in some time. Does your wife need something the servants have failed to bring you?"

Jamus waved a hand of dismissal. "I'm on a quest, Sarn, and unless you are well schooled in the way of babies, I don't think you can help much."

Surprisingly, Sarn seemed actually concerned. "Is something wrong with your son? I can call Mistress Sarena."

Jamus answered quickly, his tone a little harsher than he intended. "My son is fine, Sur. I have kept at his side since he was born and intend to keep him as close as I can for as long as I can. It is a father's duty and a father's love to do so."

Sarn bristled, then shook his head. "I supposed I deserved that. I heard Jebe and his mother are well settled at Lord Delran's. I hope some day to go visit them." When he noted Jamus' scowl, he lowered his eyes. "I know I've been a selfish fool, and I always will be. But those months I spent in that sphere of yours made me reflect on more than just what spells I dared use. I'll never win love from either Lurela or my son, but I would like to see how he's doing. I hear he's quite a horseman."

Jamus softened a little. As self-centered as Sarn might be, he did have a good hand with the horses of the Keep, and at least in that aspect the two of them had a lot in common. "He is, Sarn. I would like to see him too one day. Shimmer will be nearly two circles soon. If I were a little as Jebe and if that colt were mine, I'd be putting the saddle on him soon just to give him something serious to think about."

"I hear the colt was Whim's son and a bit too much like him," Sarn remarked, daring a laugh. "When Whim materialized here in the hall ready to defend your honor against that imposter who'd tried to take your place, the whole Keep was talking about it for months after. I kept thinking what havoc a horse like him might cause in a stable if anyone tried to lock him in when he didn't want to be. If his son is like his father."

"Sons often are, Sarn," Jamus said softly. "It's a shame you never bothered to find out." But then he slapped his hand on his thigh. "But I didn't come out to lecture you on the duties of fatherhood, Sarn. I came on a quest for knowledge. If I don't find what I need in the Great Library, I'll need to search it out in Senital's vaults and I'd much rather visit them before dark."

Sarn shivered. "In that I don't blame you. Even going down into those dusky halls gives me a chill in Sowin's height. To think of going in the dark. Let me leave you then, My Lord, as long as you need nothing from me."

Jamus stole one more quick glance at the chair, the green threads wavering a little as if uncertain of their right to dominate the blue. "No, Sarn, nothing from you," he said. Then he added, almost as an afterthought, "But thank you anyhow. I do appreciate your concern."

The green threads stabilized--blue bordering green. Jamus decided it really did look quite nice, actually. The colors did, in the end, complement each other after all.

*****

Darkness, Tamor's greatest ally. Normally, the Dark Lord relished the last moments of Weswin when the damned sun of Turan dropped behind the eastern horizon and let the world fill with <u>night</u>. Then, his shadows could wander freely, needing no disguises. Many could walk the clouds, traveling at will through all of Turan, from Aberdal in the west to the shores of Arcula in the east. Only the Great Sea and its many islands denied them haven, for even the Black Magic was defied by the waters of the oceans.

He'd heard of the Sea Dragon, of course, but dismissed both its power and its purpose in his quest for the world. If his Darkness took Turan, it would take the whole at the close of the Great Circle, and the Great Sea mattered little. With the sun blotted out by his Shadows, the Black Dragon would rule all, and Tamor would be his surrogate in the pathetic world of men.

But for now, the Black Dragon slept and Tamor paced his own cave of darkness in growing frustration. It was not his nature to be thwarted much less defeated in a quest but this Jamus, this Kiselor, the Rivermaster—whatever name he chose to wear—had managed. Always, Tamor had wanted to take the Magician's life and his blood to close the Great Circle and plunge the world into his darkness. But now, a new flavor had been added to his desire— revenge.

It was a new sensation to this existence. He had gained a new sort of True Life to replace the body he'd worn when Jamus had Spellfired him in the inn at Wavering. By drinking enough Flesher blood to satisfy the Black River's demands, he'd earned a fresh shell of skin that was still a newborn in its waters. He knew and relished the feel of the world to his fingers, the taste of air to his lungs, and the warmth of his own blood pumping in and out of his heart, but these things coiling in and out of his brain were unexpected experiences. So was any emotion beyond the cold, empty hate of the Dragon.

The thirst for revenge was neither cold nor empty. It burned like the whitefire, threatening to consume the very flesh he wore if he would let it. But the painful thought of it served a useful purpose by inspiring him to put a plan into action instead of simply thinking about it.

He had already sent Gambel The Searcher, Melthus, and Grella to the far side of Turan, hoping to discover secrets useful to him as far away from the taint of Jamus' Magic as possible. Scrying the Dark Waters had told him where they needed to find the Flesher skins to wear in order gain advantage in the King's household. Then, even at distance, he would be able to at least control the world of ordinary mortals.

But Jamus and Magiskeep were another matter. For that, he needed an agent close to his enemy.

"Sorra, attend me," he called.

The Shadow woman hastened to his side. The reflection of a Sorceress he had nearly loved for her affection for the Black Waters, Sorra was still a fledgling in the Caves of Darkness. In True Life, before the Mirrors, she had been Sonya, as hated an enemy as Jamus had ever known. Now, Tamor hoped the reflection he had chosen from the hall of her mirrors had not been some weak-bellied image of that woman instead of the warrior-spy he needed.

As well, he hoped she had brought into his world some of the memories of the Keep, for she would need them.

"My Lord?" Sorra said, bowing ever so slightly. She was not one to bow to anyone, Flesher or Shadow, but she had accepted Tamor as Lord and felt at least a small obligation to show her respect.

"What do you know of Magiskeep?"

Sorra stiffened. "She once lived there. Her feet trod every stone a hundred times."

"And your feet?"

Sorra looked down at her own shadow form, billowing into an inky cloud where her feet would be if she had any. "My memory is keen. I was born of Sonya's rage the day the scum of a keep lord threw her out to fend for herself in a world of mortals."

So, Tamor, thought. I have chosen well after all. "Then, if you went there, you would have no trouble finding your way around?"

"I keep much of her memory if that's what you mean, My Lord. If you send me there on the wind, I will fill the corners away from the sunlight and do whatever you command."

"That was not exactly what I had in mind, my dear mistress. What I really need is a Flesher spy with a quick wit and equal courage to carry out a mission I shall set."

"Flesher? But I am not."

"We shall find you a body, a skin to wear," Tamor responded.

Sorra licked her lips. Already she was longing for the taste of blood. Jamus' would have been perfect, but for now any Flesher would do. "I will be pleased to do your will, My Lord."

"Come then," he said, illusioning her into more solid form. "Share the bed with me and when I am done with you, we shall go hunting."

*****

Since all his help to Jamus and Salene in their battle with the Shadows had gained him a bit of a reputation in the Keep, Senital was no longer the forgotten hermit of his vaults. He had grown used to visitors of all ages and status. But Jamus and Salene were still his favorites and when he saw Jamus this time his greeting was nothing short of enthusiastic. While still a bit eccentric, as was so often the way with scholars who spent too much time with their tomes and scrolls away from the company of others, he had learned the fine art of hospitality. In short order, the chubby little mage had set a fine table of snappies and oatmealers along with a fresh pot of sweetened keldherb. His little room had been transformed from a cluttered study to a neat sitting area with several comfortable chairs and a pillowed couch facing the fire. He even had a bouquet of fresh dalilies on the mantel. The soft glow of maglit lamps lent a welcoming glow to the place in every corner.

"My Lord, My Lord!" the Master of the Eldenlore said excitedly as he gestured for Jamus to sit. "I am so delighted to see you here. When that wee little one of yours was born, I was beginning think I was never going to see you again. New fathers find little hands and feet far more intriguing than a good book, I vow."

Jamus grinned. "There's a lot of truth in what you say, Master Senital," he said settling himself in one of the chairs. "My son and my wife have totally consumed me over these last two months or so. Why I don't even know how much time has passed since Jarien was born. I've been too fascinated to even notice the winds."

"Nigh on three months by my count," Senital replied. "The lad must have grown a far bit by now."

"He has indeed, Sur," Jamus said "and I suppose that's the very reason I've come."

"To see me?" Senital laughed. "My Lord, of all the Masters in the Keep, I am the last to know anything about babies--or their mothers for all that. I've never had neither myself." He paused, blushed a little, cleared his throat and then reconsidered. "Well, I didn't quite mean I had no mother, I simply meant a mother to a child…a woman…a wife…I mean," his voice trailed off helplessly.

Jamus smiled kindly. "Oh, Senital, I didn't come to you for personal advice, and even if I had, I would never pry into your personal life to get it. You are far too learned a man to need to know of such things. It's the wisdom of the Eldenlore I seek, not the wisdom of a man. The Hand knows I could use some now and then, but not this time."

Senital sighed audibly. "I often wish I were more schooled in the flesh of the world, Jamus, but every time I set my mind to do something about it, I find another Eldenscroll and end up burying my head in it. If it weren't for such lovely and kind ladies as your Salene and Mistress Jessa, I'd just be a lonely old bachelor who'd never even heard the sweet voice of a woman." He bobbed his head delightedly. "Mistress Jessa visits me often, you know. She's quite like a daughter to me, you see. And oh, so skilled in the Eldentongues. Why, she has translated nearly two dozen writings since she started coming. She puts the words into such poetry it nearly makes my heart sing." He laughed again. "Maybe that's why your Simen is so sweet on her, eh? All that poetry should well please his Follyman's heart. I'm waiting to hear them set the wedding date, you know."

It appeared Senital had learned the fine art of conversation and gossip as well, Jamus thought as he finished off one of the snappies. "These taste good, Sur. Have you learned to bake as well?"

"By the Hand itself, no!" Senital replied. "Those be from Mistress Ferna in the Keep's kitchens. She brings them fresh every day."

"Ferna," Jamus said thoughtfully. The woman was a fine cook and not too far from Senital in her time in the Keep from what he remembered. She had no husband of her own and reminded him of Becca in more than a cookie's dozen of ways. "She brings them every day?"

Senital nodded. "After Midmeal every day, once the kitchen's clean from all the food. She says she enjoys the cool of the vaults here and a chance to get off her feet."

"So, what do the two of you talk about?"

"Oh, everything, My Lord. She is quite curious about the Magic you see and loves the Eldentales nearly as much as I do. Her questions are always quite perceptive. She'll often stay for as many as two spans here by the fire. I do enjoy her company."

"I see," Jamus said, keeping a straight face despite an overpowering desire to grin at the little Mage.

"Why, ever since she heard I helped you and the ladies solve some of the troubles of the Keep, she said the felt the need to pay me back with some of her baking. She makes the finest surleycake I've ever tasted."

"I see," Jamus said, waiting for Senital to take a breath.

"We're going to share an evenmeal one of these days soon," Senital went on. "I don't often leave the vaults, you see, my Lord. Not that I'm a hermit, mind you, but aside from the snappies and surleycakes, I do most of my own cooking. Mistress Ferna says she's a better cook than I am and knows the healthy ways of the herbs." He patted his ample belly. "Now I could spell myself a more elegant frame I'm sure. A man like you wouldn't understand, My Lord, fit as you are, but me? Well, anyhow, the Mistress insists she can trim me up all with some good meals and a walk with her in the gardens."

"It would be quite pleasant, I should think."

"Aye, it is. I mean we've already been out. It's scant exercise, I know, but good for the body, or at least that's what Ferna says."

"She says that, does she?" Jamus said, a smile still tugging at the corners of her mouth. "She is a very wise woman."

"Oh, yes," Senital replied eagerly. "A fine woman, indeed. Why, if I spend some time with her in the gardens like that every day, I'll be able to fit back in my formal tunic in no time."

"I'm sure you will, " Jamus agreed, smiling now. "A daily walk with a lady like that would do most any man good, especially a man like you, Senital. Tell you what. I'll keep an eye out to the skies for you every day just past Midmeal whenever I'm here in the Keep. I'll do my best to keep the skies clear for you so you can enjoy the sunshine together."

"That would be a kind thing indeed, My Lord. The weather has been a bit fickle these last Sevenstins. Why just yesterday, the Mistress and I were caught in a sudden downpour and we both got a soaking. Of course I spelled the lady dry as soon as we reached the gazebo to shelter, but it was still a bit of a shock, you see."

Jamus nodded. "I'm afraid that's exactly why I'm here to see you, Master. Jarien, my son, seems to have acquired a bit too much of the Magic for one so young and some of his tantrums appear to be affecting the weather."

"As your nightmares used to?" Senital asked, intensely interested in the news.

"It seems so," Jamus said. "But he's just a baby and unless Salene and I intervene, there's no way he could calm the River on his own."

"A babe his age has no reason of it, My Lord. It takes no Eldenlore to tell a man that." Senital slapped his hands on the table, as he pushed himself up. "But that's just why you're here, isn't it. If the little tyke's showing such power now, before he can even understand it, he's a rare one indeed, and you've come to search the Lore to see if there's aught you can do about it."

"You are even more perceptive than Mistress Ferna," Jamus said, getting up himself. "As proud as I might be of my son's unusual talents for the Magic, I certainly don't want the world turned inside out because of it. Until he's old enough to learn how to control it, I'd like to find a way to do it myself without harming him."

"You've considered one of your spheres?"

"It's crossed my mind, but what kind of weaving? I certainly don't want to close him off from any part of the world at his age, and I worry that the Magic might be too potent for one so young. The River rarely flows to a child's hand until he's seven or so when reason starts to fill his brain. But if we wait that long, Magiskeep's walls might not even be standing anymore. He has some strong lungs and a will to match."

"Kept the two of you up a few nights, eh?" Senital laughed. "I thought I noticed some dark circles under your eyes."

Jamus rubbed his eyes self-consciously. "Nothing a few good nights of sleep wouldn't help, Sur. But it's not easy when every time he starts to cry the skies open. Salene and I do our best to keep him smiling, but with a baby, that's not always easy."

"So they tell me," Senital said opening the door to the room beyond. "Never had a babe of my own but that doesn't mean I can't offer a word or two of advice. Sometimes it takes a person with no stake in the matter to see the light."

II

Jyp tried hard to appear an apt student to Edra's tutoring, but the fact was neither Mage had the least idea how to use the other's Magic. Born, bred and trained in Magiskeep, Jyp saw Edra's nonchalant use of power as a wanton and selfish abuse of Rule and Vow. "The Magic in the power," he'd say to himself every time he saw Edra weaving a spell to satisfy his or Gareth's greed. "None other need be sought. If deeds for any other need be done, then deeds had best be deeds undone."

But neither the Prince nor his pet even considered such a thing. To both, Magic was there to serve their every desire with no regard for the consequences. Worse, Jyp could never quite comprehend for even a moment exactly how Edra was calling on the River. In fact, Edra's unbridled emotion when he used his power was so akin to Magic Unrestrained, it chilled Jyp to the bone.

For his part, Edra was just as puzzled by Jyp's skills. "Why do you always have to think so hard?" he said. "Just do it. Your determination is there, and when you do chant, you show some ability, but if you would just set your mind free from all those complications, how much simpler it would be."

"The waters do not rise unless I do," Jyp replied. His mastery of several of the Seven Arts he'd studied in Magiskeep promised the Golden Waters would always answere his command exactly as he wanted them to.

Not so for Edra. While Gareth might crave a fresh, juicy surlep, a green popple or some red dewberries might fall to Edra's hand instead. Thus he performed most of his Magic in private, hiding from the Prince the truth of its erratic nature. Used to the Silver Waters of Arcula, flowing freely under her soil, here in Aberdeen the tributary was leaner and less eager to answer him. But it did answer and as time went on he was learning little by little to let his desire grow--much more than it had ever needed to when he ruled the

Cauge—before he cast a spell. Rage and frustration, the two emotions he'd relied on most in his homeland, served him nearly as well in Aberdeen, so he was often in a foul temper when he was using his Magic.

Fortunately for Jyp, Edra's aggravation with him was often the source of the Arculan's better spells. As such, the two of them could make a formidable pair if everything worked out just right.

The truth that neither could understand was that they were each drawing on a different River. Gold to the Mage of Magiskeep, and Silver to the hand of the former Caugeman. There were many places in the palace where the waters mingled, giving both Mages equal power there, but except for the strange stream of silver which whirlpooled in one spot in the Royal Hall, Jyp generally had the upper hand.

But he was cautious to show it. He was not there to cast spells for the Prince or to learn anything from a poor teacher like Edra. He had come to the Seat of Aberdeen as a spy from Cuver Street, to find out just exactly was going on with King Gailvarg's health.

For several months passing, the King had been slipping in and out of one illness after another. The mortal Healers of the city did their best to keep him alive, but as time went on rumors were spreading around the streets that the noble Lord was on his deathbed.

This wasn't quite the case--yet. Gailvarg was thin, pale and often too tired to take on his Royal duties, it was true, but his spirit was still strong and his will unbending. Fortunately for Arcula, he was well able to keep his errant son in check for the more serious concerns even though he let the boy do as he might with personal pleasures and the more minor decisions of the Throne.

Gareth had longed for an army. He wanted fine soldiers dressed in silvrin breastplates to stand beside his throne ready to lay their lives down for him at his smallest command. He would have cavalry too. Hundreds of men mounted on the finest horses in Turan bred by Lords like Delran of Telma, who was reputed to own stock kissed by the Hand itself. And the men of foot would carry shining stelin swords and spears forged of Wemb's best metals by Tyler, the master weapon maker of FarIsle.

Gareth practiced with his own sword nearly every day, but Turan had been at peace for so long, he had no true weapon master to school him. His technique was raw, mostly moves he'd read about in a dusty scroll, or something he'd imagined in his reveries of his army.

Now, as he swung his sword in a great killing arc over his head, Edra saw him. Well skilled in swordsmanship himself as the first of the Cauge in Arcula, the Mage could hardly resist a word or two of advice. "Open yourself up like that, My Lord, and unless your enemy's already on his back ready to die, he'll slit your gut open and lay you out to the deathhawks."

Gareth dropped his sword to his side and glared at the Sorcerer. "Were you any other man, I'd kill you for speaking to me like that."

Edra shrugged. "If I had a sword in my hand, you'd have a hard time of it, Your Highness. I was a Master of the Sword in my homeland, and to be honest with you, as I always have been, you wouldn't stand a chance against me."

Gareth gestured at one of the practice swords hanging on the wall to his right. "Go on then, Sorcerer, I'll take your challenge. Show me just how good you are."

Edra selected a sword, hefting it experimentally in his hand. It was well balanced despite its crude construction and he was surprised and how good it felt to hold a weapon again after so long a time.

The two men squared off.

The battle was short. Two parries against Gareth's wild attacks, one attack of his own, and Edra disarmed his opponent and had his own sword at the astonished Prince's throat. "My Liege, do you surrender?"

"By the Blood," Gareth gasped, backing away from the blade. "Not only do I surrender, but I command you to teach me how to do that myself."

Edra grinned as he ran his hand along the side of his blade. "Get me a good sword, then, one I will enjoy using. It will take time but I can make a warrior of you if that's what you want."

Gareth nodded eagerly. He had always wanted to be a soldier.

*****

Lord Delran of Telma was claimed to have some of the best riding, carriage and draft horses in all of Turan. The highborn traveled Sevenstins from the more eastern cities and towns to purchase his stock. Wise in the ways of breeding, he had himself traded with Lord Sagari, Master of Magiskeep beyond the Rim for circles, sharing the blood of Sagari's powerful stallions and athletic mares to create mounts ideal for any rider. Now he and Magiskeep's new Master, Jamus, had bred a strain of elegant yet powerful dray horses to satisfy the titled carriages of Turan's wealthy. The creatures were sturdy, full of stamina, yet refined enough to suit the most discriminating lady while still having enough spirit to please a horseman.

Some months ago, Jamus had brought him the first lot of the new breed. Some months later, Simen, Jamus' brother, had returned with half dozen more and some new stablehands to care for them. Keep-trained by Magiskeep's head horseman Josep himself, Jebe and Nobby were two fine young lads ready, willing and able to do all the chores and some training as well under Joss's watchful eyes. Since Since Joss was Josep's son, the boys were already well used to exactly how things needed to be done in a well-run stable and equally ready to learn as much as they could from him.

Delran was eager to welcome the new arrivals into his home. As he and Jamus had agreed when the offer had come for Jebe to take on the new job, the Telman Lord had set aside rooms in the Main House for both boys and Jebe's mother, Lurela. As soon as the old man saw her, his heart melted, for she was a young slip of a woman who had worked hard all her life to support her young son and at once decided she would not have work in her new home as well.

"You don't have to lift a finger, My Dear," Delran told her. "Your son's labor and skill as a Beasttalker will more than earn keep here for the both of you. It's time you learned to rest your weary bones and enjoy the life of a Lady in my house. I promised Lord

Jamus I would see you as my daughter and so I shall. I would not make a promise to the Master of Magiskeep lightly."

"You are kind, Sur, and while I do appreciate your offer, I intend to work for my living no matter where I may be. Besides, your home needs a woman's touch." She looked around the main sitting room. Though it was comfortable, it was plain, without much color or real warmth. "Some drapes on the windows, perhaps? Pillows on the couch. A man's home needs a heart, My Lord."

"It had one once when my daughter was alive, and before her my wife," Delran replied sadly. "But now I am alone. Guests and my workers are all I have for company. If you really need a job, then offer yourself as a friend to a man in need. Sit at my table at Midmeal and tell me of your dreams. Share a cup of keldherb with me by the fire at night while you read to your son. Cook if you wish, sew and stitch to your heart's content, but know that just the sound of your voice and your presence will be payment enough."

Lurela's voice cracked as she put her hand on Delran's, "I am not your daughter, My Lord, but if I can stand in her place to cheer your heart to thank you for all you are doing for my son, I will do my best. It's been a long time since I heard a kind word from a man. Lord Jamus has vouched for your honor and I have trusted him already with my life. I can do no less for you."

And so a pact was sealed between them.

For Jebe, the whole experience was such an exciting adventure he couldn't even imagine how anyone could be anything but happy in this wonderful place. Crossing the Rim with Simen was even better than crossing with Lord Jamus. The difference was that even as he was sorting through the most dangerous of the mountains' illusions, Simen either sang or spouted Follyman's jokes to keep everyone smiling. Even Lurela, who had worried her way along from the moment she set foot in Pebble's stirrup, was hard-pressed not to laugh her way through most of the trip. By the time they reached Delran's Keep, they were more tired from grinning than from being in the saddle.

Once he had helped settle the other horses in the stable, Jebe led Shimmer to a stall at the far end of the barn. "Now you behave yourself, Shimmy. It won't do for you to pull any of your pranks here. This is not Magiskeep."

Joss, who had just finished filling the mangers with piles of good, sweet hay, came over to admire the colt. "He is a beauty, Jebe. I've not seen a finer animal since Lord Jamus' Whim."

"Oh, Whim is his father," Jebe replied proudly.

"Uh oh," Joss replied. "How much is he his father's son?"

"He's just like 'em, save fer his color. Ya see the gold? Flax was his dam, but I think he was more touched by his sire's Magic." Jebe's face screwed up into a frown. "I hope he's gonna behave hisself here. He can be a little devil when he wants somethin'. Master Jamus put a chanting on him fer me, but I don't know how much it's gonna hold this side o' the Rim."

"If Lord Jamus chanted him, I'm sure it will hold, but I can work a bit of Magic myself. I'll add a few weaves to make sure he stays where we want him to. I don't want him wandering about the property--or worse, getting into the grain and colicking." Joss waved his hands in the air towards the stall. Jamus had taught him how to chant winter blankets for his horses and Joss had expanded his skills since. Now he set an extra barrier of bars all around the stall walls to keep the colt well secured.

Shimmer snorted, tossed his head and pawed angrily.

Hate silverfall all round! Hate, hate. Make me mad. Want to go where want to go!

Jebe's brain ached with the colt's rage, but he kept his own voice calm. "No, Shimmy. You can't go wherever you want to go. I've told you that before. You must stay where we put you. We know better than you how to keep you safe."

Joss's brow lifted in surprise. "You know what he's saying?"

"Aye," Jebe replied. "Didn't you know I am a Beasttalker? I ain't the best at it yet, but Master Jamus told me if I practice I can be real good. That's one of the reasons he wanted me to leave Magiskeep and come here."

Joss frowned. "I would have thought Magiskeep would be the perfect place to learn your skill."

"Nope," Jebe said. "Master Jamus said the Masters there'd be pokin' and proddin' me to a worry jest to figure out how I was doin' the talkin'. He said a Gift like mine needed to learn its own way just by bein' round the beasties. He said nobody here would ever treat me bad or like I was a…a freak er somethin'."

Joss smiled now. To think the Master of Magiskeep had that much regard for him and Lord Delran nearly burst his heart with pride. And Jebe was right. As far as Joss was concerned, neither he nor anyone in Delran's Keep would ever treat this boy with anything less than respect. "I am delighted to have a man like you in my stables, Jebe."

Jebe puffed up a bit taller at the word, "man." "I'm gonna work real hard fer you, Master Joss."

Mean, mean, make silverfall all around. The colt lived up to his name, shimmering about the stall from one corner to another, shining first silver, then gold, over and over. Finally, frustrated at not being able to get his own way, he settled in the corner by his hay and began to eat. *Good greenstalk. Me like.*

"He likes the hay," Jebe said.

Joss laughed. "Even I can see that," he said. "He certainly has a good appetite. How old is he Jebe?"

"He'll be two circles by Warmmonth's end. Lord Jamus said I could back him a bit when he's two, you know. He said Shim's the kind of colt that would need the discipline sooner than most. And I'm light enough not to hurt him. I'm gonna be real careful."

Joss nodded. "I don't often hold with the idea of riding one so young myself, but his father has stamped him with the same solid bone and strong body he has. You hardly weigh more than a rimhawk feather yourself. If we take it one day at a time, I think we can do as the Lord suggests. But mind you, Lad," he wagged a finger at Jebe, "you will abide by my word all along the way. If I even think for a minute your riding him will break him down even in the least little bit, you will end up waiting until he passes his third circle and that will be that."

Jebe bobbed his head in eager agreement. "I'll do whate'er you say, Master Joss."

"Hey, Jebe!" Nobby called from the door of the barn. "Master Delran says we gotta get in the house now for Lastmeal. He says he wants you to come to table too, Sur Joss. He says the men what's take care of his horses gotta have a good meal in 'em for to do the work right. An' he says we gotta celebrate just 'cause it's a nice day. They put a big cavel roast on the table already."

Together, the three stablemen hurried towards the house.

In the stall, Shimmer chewed his hay quietly. But still, his coat flashed from silver to gold, silver to gold, over and over.

Outside, it started to rain.

*****

"It's hard to say exactly what this scroll means," Senital said, handing another dusty manuscript to Jamus. "The Eldentongue far too often hides its meanings in riddles."

Jamus sighed. "The bane of my life, I fear, Senital. I guess I shouldn't expect any less."

"Well, it says something about babes and silver streams, but whatever that implies, I can't say. Here," he pointed to a cryptic passage. "'Silver reigns in silver rains in silver miseries and pains. Tears from eyes, tears from skies need the silver, silver reins.' It's not often the Elds played with words like that you know. And not too many times a translation can bring the same wordplay to life. Those words, 'reigns,' 'rains,' and 'reins' all sound the same in our language, but they have completely different meanings. Strange to say the same is true in the Elden, you see?"

Jamus studied the writing. Though his knowledge of the Old Tongues was limited by lack of study, even he could see how similar the three words were. "Curious," he said. "Poetry rarely sings the same in more than one language. But this seems to. I wonder why?"

"It must be important, or perhaps even chanted somehow. But what could it mean?"

"To explain it in simple terms," Jamus replied shrugging, "it says, the silver rules and falls like rain when there is misery or pain. Sounds to me as if the sky cries too, all of which actually makes sense when I think about what's going on with Jarien. When he cries, as I told you, it does rain. But that part about the silver reins? You use reins to control a horse, but I can't see putting my son in a bit and bridle to keep him under control."

"Control? H-m-m-m." Senital considered. "Perhaps the 'silver rein' is something else? But why silver? Is it the water that looks silver?"

Jamus started to smile. "The water, of course. The Silver River. Why not? He is the Rivermaster's son, after all. When I was in Arcula I had to learn a new Magic."

"Ah, yes, I remember you told me a bit about that. Something about Magic Unrestrained."

"Exactly," Jamus said. He sat done on a stool and pulled the parchment over to him. "It would have all made some sense if I hadn't been too tired all these days to sort it out. Jarien has a natural touch to the river, but it's not the Golden River, not yet anyway. He can't think through the rational patterns needed to call those waters. But the Silver River's another story. He doesn't need to think. All he needs to do is feel. As long as he's happy, everything's fine. But as soon as he loses his temper or starts to cry because he's not happy about something, the Silver River leaps to his call."

"Can it be that easy?"

"Think about it this way, Senital. When a Mage of Magiskeep is driven to rage or fear beyond reason, doesn't the Spellfire leap to his hand? It's the only time the Golden Master would ever touch those waters. We've been trained since childhood to avoid them. The Hand knows not every Magician can ever touch them in the first place, but those who can never do--never dare to do."

"There's some in the Keep who never could," Senital agreed. "I'm one. When Sagari challenged me to take the Sorcerer's Crystal, I had no defenses at all to stop him. Spellfire wasn't even in my imagination, let alone my hand."

"There are hundreds like you, Senital," Jamus assured him. "It took me months of misery to learn how to touch Spellfire's waters myself. It's becoming clear to me each Magician has his own particular talents. You, for instance, have and amazing capacity to find secrets in the most obscure places. Why you found this scroll in less than a span. It's exactly the one we needed, and yet, when we came in here, you didn't even know what question I wanted answered. Then you admitted that in all your circles no one had ever asked you a question even remotely like it. But here," he slapped is hand down on the parchment, "is the exact text we needed."

"It would help if we understood it."

"I understand the better part of it. At least I have a pretty good idea of what's going on with my son. The problem is, I don't exactly know where to find those damned reins."

*****

Selecting Sorra's skin was proving more of a challenge than he expected. Tamor, bound to the limits of the flesh by the borders of Magiskeep, needed to choose carefully. He needed a body already east of the Rim and west of the Wall of Tears which separated Arcula from the Keep. Anything else would prove too hard to transport. Were Sorra to remain Shadow, it would have been no problem, for she could have ridden the clouds most anywhere. But mortal flesh was another matter altogether.

Magiskeep, though it had over twenty villages, was a close-knit world, well aware of the welfare of most of its citizens and, in light of past events, ever alert to the threat of Shadows. Sarn, the current Master of the Keep, had taken Jamus' warnings seriously enough to post watchers in nearly every town, ready to report the anything suspicious, especially violent deaths or missing persons.

It took the turning of a full two months before Tamor finally found a likely candidate. Natale, a widow, had moved out of the village of Tallridge nearly ten circles past. Still a fairly young woman, she had lost a husband and a child to an avalanche in the Norreaches while on a trip to see the mountain snows. She never recovered from her grief and finally moved away to live as a hermitess in a small cabin in the south, as far from the northern range as possible. She had lived off the land and a small garden, making no contact with any of the villages or her neighbors. She was, by all accounts, simply forgotten—invisible enough by now to almost be a shadow herself.

But she was a living woman, and a body of flesh and blood well suited to Tamor's purposes.

He waited for a particularly dark night, the second new moon of Warmmonth's season. The clouds were heavy, perfect for fast travel, and it was not even Norwin when he and Sorra arrived at Natale's door. Holding his finger to his lips to keep his companion silent, Tamor wove an even darker spell around the cabin and opened the door.

Natale was asleep on her cot. Tamor studied her for a few moments. She was thinner than he liked, but her breasts were full and rounded and her skin still supple. She would do. He whispered her name, "Natale, I have come."

Natale's eyes fluttered open. She stared into the darkness, confused by the total lack of light. Even the stars had been blotted out by Tamor's spell. Was she dreaming?

"Natale, I am here."

"Who are you? What do you want?" she asked in the darkness, trembling a little to hear the voice so close. If it was a dream, it was a realistic one.

Tamor reached out and lightly caressed her hair. He bent over her, and whispered again, this time directly in her ear. "I have come for you."

Natale tried to roll away, but something had bound her in place. Her heart began to pound. "What, what do you want?"

The fear makes the taste so much better, Tamor told Sorra in his thoughts. *Trust me. I will make her delicious.* "How long has it been since you have lain with a man, eh? How long since your breasts have felt a caress." He stroked her chest, working his fingers under the thin fabric of her nightdress. She cringed but lay silent. "Do you like the feel of my flesh on yours?" He dragged the sheet from her body and pulled her gown up, stroking her belly and searching lower and lower with probing touches.

Natale's heart was throbbing now, her skin burning under his hands, She writhed, arching up against the invisible bonds he'd thrown around her. "Leave me alone, please, leave me alone," she whimpered, tears starting to roll down her cheeks.

Tamor dropped down onto her, pressing against her bare body, rubbing himself over her again and again until she started to scream. Then he beckoned to Sorra. As much as he wanted this woman, Sorra needed her. He let her crawl onto the cot with him. The mattress sagged under their assault.

"Have you the dagger?" he asked aloud, assuring Natale heard every word.

Natale gasped, "Please…no, no."

Sorra traced a line along the woman's right shoulder, diagonally unto her breast, then she plunged it in.

Natale screamed. But there was no one around for spans to hear except the two Shadows, and it was exactly what they wanted. Sorra licked her lips, then dropped her face to the woman's body and began to drink.

Natale twisted in vain, Tamor's body heavy on her stomach, straddling her, and the terrible sensation of Sorra's black lips on her skin was too horrifying to bear. She would have fainted, but the Dark Lord denied her mind that escape, holding her consciousness captive with his Magic. "Dying is the only escape now," he hissed. "I will take you into the darkness as a woman so your ghost will remember me." He pushed between her thighs, forcing himself on her even as Sorra carved another gash in her bosom, letting the blood flow even more to her greedy appetite.

Natale screamed, and screamed again.

To the Shadows, it was a serenade.

*****

Jamus closed the door of their chamber as quietly as he could, but Salene woke up anyhow. Jarien lay on her stomach, still fast asleep. At least he had not wakened.

Carefully, so as not to disturb him, Salene sat up and picked the baby up, transferring him to his crib. Blessedly, he still slept, totally lost in the depths of infant slumber. He looked so peaceful Jamus couldn't help smiling. "He's so wonderful, I can hardly believe he's ours."

"Why? Because he sleeps?" Salene asked teasingly. "Lately the rest of the family seems to have lost the skill. Where do you think he inherited it?"

"The Hand only knows," Jamus answered. "Certainly not from me. But I must admit, the few time I have managed a few spans, I've not had any nightmares—not since he was born. It would be a gift indeed if that stayed true."

Salene poured herself a goblet of calidew from the tray the servants had brought a span before. She offered one to Jamus. "I hadn't thought much about that," she said. "But it is true. Ever since Jarien was born, the few times he has let you sleep, you've been nearly as quiet as he. Perhaps he's chanted you."

Jamus took a sip and pulled a chunk of bread off the loaf on the tray. "Considering what I've found out so far about our little tyrant here, that might not be so off the mark. We both know he has some considerable Magical ability already."

"What have you found out?" Salene asked eagerly. "Did you discover the answers to what's been going on with him? I've been so worried. Four times today I had to command the skies when he started to cry."

"It's the Silver River," Jamus told her. "Senital and I found an old scroll in the vaults. Apparently our son commands the Silver Waters already. They answer his emotions without a thought. He will probably command the Gold when he learns to reason, but for now, his cries touch the Silver."

"Already a Rivermaster, then?"

"The son of one," Jamus agreed.

"So how do we control him so the waters don't drown the world?"

"For now, I don't know," Jamus said. He sat down heavily on the window seat, idly toying with the goblet. "The scroll was a riddle of sorts." He quoted the text as Salene listened intently. "Silver reigns in silver rains in silver miseries and pains. Tears from eyes, tears from skies need the silver, silver reins."

"A poem with a play on words? This is the answer you found?"

"I'm sure you understand how it connects Jarien with the Silver Magic, and the havoc it raises when he cries.' Salene nodded. "But the last part, the silver reins—like the reins on a horse—that's the part that has me confused."

"Perhaps it's the commands we make to stop the storms?"

Jamus shook his head. "We call the Gold. It's the greater force of nature."

"Does it mean a sphere of protection? Some might call that silver."

"Silvrin, perhaps, but still the tool of the Golden Waters. Silver Magic is something quite different."

Salene shivered, "Well you certainly can't use Spellfire. Silver Mage or not, that would kill him—kill us all."

"Silver, silver, reins. Like riding the silver." Suddenly he smiled.

"Whim?" Salene asked.

"Another mount," Jamus answered. "The Dragon."

"Rath?"

"A perfect nursemaid, don't you think?"

"By the Hand, Jamus, you can't mean that. Even in human form that creature is still too much Dragon for me. She scares me, my Love. She likes her meat raw, you know."

"I trust her," Jamus replied softly, reaching for her hand. "When I was in danger, I called to her and she came here to watch over you until I could do it myself. She knows the Shadows and floats on the waves of the Silver River with ease. If any creature in this world would understand the talents of our son it would be Rath."

"A Dragon," Salene repeated hopelessly.

"Who better to watch over a child of the River?"

"Call her, then. I'll have to admit while she was here, I did get some sleep."

Rath, your Rider calls. I have need of your wisdom, need of your might, need of your knowledge in the Way of your Waters.

Best One?

I call.

Rath sleep.

But I do not. Give me your peace. I need you.

Have mate.

My mate needs you too. She calls. Her voice is mine.

Mate calls. She of Gold? Rath like. Kind heart. Still round?

Round? Jamus considered, then he understood. *The child is born.*

Kitling?

Yes.

Has he Dragon heart?
I think he may.
Son of River?
Yes.
Strong?
Yes. Would the interrogation never end?

But the rush of wings replied before Rath's voice this time. A great wind blasted in the wide double window, and a claw grappled for a foothold on the ledge. As it did it began to shimmer, then shrank, melting into a hand, and a moment later the silver haired woman climbed gracefully into the room. She brushed the stardust from her gown and peered at Jamus with her whirling silver eyes for a brief moment before striding over to Jarien's crib.

He was awake now, but as soon as Rath bent over to have a look at him, instead of wailing, he started to giggle.

"He is very small."

"Most babies are," Salene replied, hovering protectively beside her.

"Not Dragons," Rath said. "But you small too. I had forgotten how small these bodies are."

"You haven't been gone that long."

"Long enough. I am pleased you called. I am glad to see the kitling. I did not expect you would want me here." She looked into Salene's eyes as she spoke.

"I will not lie, Rath. It was not my idea. I'll be honest with you, you frighten me sometimes."

Rath tilted her head, "That is good, I think. It's wise for the twoleg to fear the Dragon. But I would never harm the mate of my master, or her offspring. Know that and you will know all."

"I am glad to hear that," Salene said.

"So why did you call if you fear me so?" The longer she wore her human form the more fluent her speech became.

"We need your help with our son," Jamus replied. "His name is Jarien."

Rath smiled. "The rider of the clouds, vision of all you lost, all you dreamed to be, a good name to use. Alran tells me you have learned to fly."

"In a manner of speaking," Jamsus answered.

"Your son already knows."

"I suspected as much" Jamus said, "But he is too small now. He needs to grow, to learn, to understand. He needs to Master the Golden waters first."

"That is wise. But already the Silver flows for him."

"That's why we called you. You, of all, understand the Silver waters and their power. Jarien doesn't, at least not yet."

"Dragonkit would."

"But he's not a Dragon. He's a boy and he wasn't born all-knowing. He can't even talk yet."

Rath stared at Jarien for a moment. Then she looked up, her brow furrowed. "He has no thought I can read. His head is full of hearing, seeing, but beyond that, no more. He cannot touch your River, can he?"

"No, he can't, not yet," Jamus agreed. "Babies take a while to discover the world and comprehend it."

"Not very practical. He would not last long in the Dragon's world."

"That's true, but he will not live in the Dragon's world for a long time yet. Perhaps when he is a man, circles from now. In the meantime, we need to assure that the human world does not suffer because the Silver Magic comes to his call."

"He makes the thunder then?"

"You know about that?"

Rath nodded. "He is like your dreams, Rivermaster. He was your dream, is your dream and will be your dream. I do not riddle this. You did not name him Jarien for idle reasons. He is the master of the clouds now and forevermore. Until he understands, we will need to hold the clouds for him."

"Salene and I have tried, but we're tired. We can hardly sleep for fear his misery will storm Magiskeep out of existence. Can you help?

"I have slept long enough. Now it is my time to wake and keep watch. Do not worry. I will keep him safe and with him, your world." She reached out and stroked Jarien's head, more gently than Salene could ever have imagined. "You feed him?"

Salene started. "Why, yes I do."

"He nurses well?"

"I suppose. He's my first…" she hesitated remembering the hopes of the daughter they'd lost. "He's my firstborn. I'm just learning to be a mother."

"I will help you. But already you have done a fine job of it, I think."

"You've had babies?"

"I am thousands of circles old," Rath replied. "I have had many kits—children. Dragons they may be, but to be a mother is little different. Food, love and," she sniffed, "a good cleaning. I don't suppose you used your tongue to wash him do you?"

III

Simen leaned back against the tree, tilted his head to the sunshine, closed his eyes and smiled. It was another beautiful day in Telma Province and he intended to enjoy every moment of it before heading back to Magiskeep. He'd safely escorted Jebe, Lurela, Nobby, and ten more horses through the illusions of the Rim three months before. Now, Jamus had sent him back with more horses and the request to check on the boy and his mother. He'd made the journey in less than a seventstin, earning him the right for at least short vacation at Delran's Keep. The Lord's hospitality was legendary and while Delran never asked for repayment from any of his guests, Simen had had the pleasure of singing for his supper nearly every Weswin simply because he wanted to. The music had flowed easily, full of happy tunes devoid of riddles for his brother or warnings of dire days to come. It was more pleasurable than he would ever have imagined.

And then there was Lurela, smiling herself and happy for the first time in long circles. Delran, despite protests, had finally allowed her to do some of the cooking and she had succeeded admirably. Simen figured he'd gained some girth feasting on her surlep and popple pies, two slices too much a temptation even after a sumptuous meal of roasted fowl and honeyed vegetables.

But, as good as her food was, her new blossoming beauty was even a better feast. Content in his own love for Mistress Jessa of the Keep, Simen noticed the same lovesick longing he suffered in Joss's eyes every time the young stableman looked at Lurela. They were not too far apart in age—perhaps Joss was a circle or two younger, no more—so the match was more than possible. All Simen needed to do was prod it along a little.

Jebe, he decided was the key. Already starry eyed at Joss's knowledge and responsibility with Delran's horses and stable, Jebe spent nearly every waking hour in the young Stablemaster's company. If he wasn't with Joss, he was doing Joss's bidding, or

trying to find some way to exceed Joss's expectations with the care
of his charges. The barn Jebe managed, full of mischievous foals just
weaned from their dams, fairly sparkled in the morning sun. The
foals themselves gleamed nearly as brightly as Jebe's own colt,
Shimmer. The feed and water buckets were so clean Simen would
have had no compunctions at all eating or drinking from them
himself. There was never a wisp of leftover hay or straw in the aisle
and the little halters and leadropes were hung in virtually perfect
symmetry on every stall door.

Joss spared no effort in praising the boy for his work,
admiring the foals' condition, and especially their unusually good
manners for horses so young. "I don't know how you do it, Joss," he
said. "But these are the best-behaved babies I've ever seen."

"I talk to them," Jebe replied, shrugging as if it were the
most ordinary thing in the world. "With the little ones, you gotta
explain things a lot, over and over. They're smart, but it's hard for
them to behave sometimes. When one of 'em starts to get too
rambunctious," he stumbled a bit over the big word, "I tell 'em to
hold on until I can get there. Then I take 'em out for an extra walk or
turn 'em out special with a friend so they can get rid of the urge."

"And they wait when you ask them to?"

"Oh, yes, Sur. They know I'm gonna keep my word and get
to 'em. Sometimes they paw a little and make some noise, but they
learn right quick that I'll be there sooner than later. It's important
with a horse that you do what you say yer gonna do, you know."

"Consistency is important for sure," Joss agreed. "And they
depend on us for most everything when they are here in the barns, so
we do need to keep our promises."

Jebe nodded knowingly. "Makes 'em behave a lot better
knowing we care." Then he shrugged again. "I wish Shimmer would
learn better. He's got a mind of his own and a temper about it when
he doesn't get his own way. He's too smart for his own good and
figgers he knows better than I do what's good for him."

"A horse like Shimmer can be difficult to train," Joss said.
"But once he starts to love you the way his father loves Master
Jamus, you'll have the finest mount and ally you'll ever need, Jebe."

"He trusts me already, and says he loves me. But sometimes what he wants is just too strong and he tries to follow his own mind steada mine."

"Then you'll just need to compromise now and then. Sometimes even Master Jamus lets Whim have his way, you know."

"I remember coming cross the Rim when Whim wanted to go one way and the Lord another. When they finally stopped arguing about is, Jamus gave Whim the rein and we found a good shortcut through a pass that took a span out of the trip. Whim was so proud of hisself and the Lord just let him gloat about it."

Joss laughed. "Lord Jamus is one of the finest horsemen I've ever seen."

"You ain't so bad yourself," Jebe said shyly, peering up at the taller man from under his shock of yellow hair. "I can learn a lot from you."

Joss tousled the boy's hair affectionately. "Thank you, Jebe. I may not be the trainer Lord Jamus is, but I know a thing or two. Why don't we take that colt of yours out into the pen and see how his lessons are going. It's about time he felt the girth and saddle, I think."

Jebe's eyes widend. "You think so, Master Joss?" His voice trembled with excitement. "You're sure?"

"Absolutely. He'll be two, as I recall, and he's ready to start realizing his life is going to more than running about the paddock and getting popple treats every time he sticks his pretty face over the stall door. Let's go out and give him some real lessons about what it means to be a horse in Turan."

Now, Simen was waiting to watch Shimmer's first lesson as a saddle horse while he considered the puzzle of Joss and Lurela.

The woman doted on her son and had given up every pleasure of her own life to make a good one for the boy. Joss's kindness and interest in Jebe's welfare would go far in attracting her attention. While Simen was certain of Joss's feelings for Lurela, what he was not sure about was whether Lurela had similar feelings towards Joss.

Like most woman who had lived hard lives, she was hard to read. Unlike ladies of leisure who wore their hearts on their sleeves and had the luxury of learning how to flirt, Lurela could mask her emotions with practiced ease, hiding behind a hard exterior ever wary and ready to take on whatever the world dished out. Despite the soft life Delran's Keep offered her, she had not softened much since her arrival. She was smiling more, and sometimes even joined Simen in a song, but every time he thought he was going to be able to read her heart, she would draw herself back and hide again.

Joss, ever mindful of his place as the Stablemaster, never dared to do more than speak to Lurela in company, and even then, he kept to the general conversation, avoiding even the smallest hints of personal interest. Yet, no matter where she was in the room, his eyes followed her, as if he were afraid somehow she might disappear and he'd never see her again.

He couldn't force them together, that was certain, but before he left Telma, Simen was determined he was going to get Joss and Lurela alone together where they might at least start to talk to each other about something besides how good the roast tasted.

Perhaps, he thought, this event, when Jebe first saddled Shimmer was the perfect time to put a plan into action. He'd sent Nobby to the house to tell Lurela she absolutely must come out to the stableyard, and now he saw her hurrying along the path to find out what was so important.

"Is Jebe all right?" she asked breathlessly when she saw Simen. "Nobby ran into the kitchen, tugged at my apron and pulled me to the door saying something about how I had to come out here right away. Did something happen to my boy?"

Simen took her hand reassuringly. "Jebe is fine, Mistress. He's fine. Nobby tends to get a bit too excited about things sometimes." She sighed in relief as he went on, "But it is important for you to be here. Today is the first day Jebe is going to put the saddle on Shimmer and I'm sure he'll want to you see him. He's done a wonderful job with the colt and Shimmer's the pride of his life. It's the kind of day his mother should share."

There were tears in Lurela's eyes as she searched Simen's face. "You are as kind as your brother to call me here for this," she said. "Thank you."

Simen smiled and pointed toward the pen, hoping to take her focus from his kindness to Joss's even greater kindness to her son. The last thing he needed was for Lurela to pay more attention to him than to Joss. "They're coming out now. Just watch how well behaved Shimmer is for Jebe. It's truly a wonder."

No sooner were the words out of his mouth, when Shimmer let out a huge buck and nearly broke free from Jebe's grasp, bolting against the lead rope and snorting wildly. Lurela caught her breath as she saw the horse drag her son halfway across the pen, his heels skidding in the sand as he hung on for all he was worth. Joss ran over, grabbed a hold of the boy and steadied him, taking the end of the rope in his own hand. "Talk to him, Jebe," he said, more calmly than seemed possible. "Tell him your mother's watching and he needs to behave now."

Jebe, finally able to stand still against the flailing colt, frowned.

Suddenly, Shimmer stopped dead in his tracks, lowered his head and stood quietly, his eyes fixed on his young master.

Mother be love for Jebe. Shimmer sorry. Be good now.

Jebe followed the rope over to the trembling colt and stroked his neck. "It's all right, Shimmer, it's all right."

Bad to make mother sad. I be good so she see Jebe be good too. Jebe be best in heart. Shimmer love. Do for Jebe.

"Something new for you today, Shim. You are going to wear a saddle for the first time. We will put it on your back and something around your tummy to hold it on. You've seen the big horses wear them. Today is the day you are going to start to learn how to be a big horse."

Wear Jebe too?

Jebe had to think about that one for a moment. "No, I won't get on you yet. First you have to learn how the saddle feels and get used to it. I will ride you soon, though. You'll have to be patient and learn your lessons first."

Shimmer stamped his foot once, then seemed instantly sorry to behaved badly again. *Hard wait for things want now. Be big horse like Whim some day.* There was a decided reverence in his voice when he mentioned his father. *Be loved by Jebe. Do good for Jebe. Windstep?*

"I hope so, Shim, I hope so. But first I will have to learn how."

I learn to wear Jebe. Jebe learn to windstep. We learn together?

Jebe started to laugh, but Joss was at his side with the saddle and girth and it was time to begin the lesson.

Some young horses buck and leap about when the first feel the girth and saddle. The strange sensation sends them into a wild frenzy. Prey animals by nature, that new thing on their backs might be a clawing tark seeking the killing bite. Some youngsters simply freeze in total fear and some simply accept the new feeling as part and parcel of trusting man instead of instinct.

Shimmer stood, curling his neck around so he could get a look at the tack, and then he snuffled Jebe's belt, looking for a surlep treat as a reward for his good behavior. The boy slipped a candy into the colt's mouth and as he chewed it thoughfully, he let his master lead him forward. The girth tightened at the first step and he hunched his back for just an instant before settling back down into a long strided easy walk beside his young trainer.

"Let the rope out a bit, Jebe," Joss said. "Give him his head a bit more so he can relax if he wants to. If he lowers his head just be ready. He'll either give a buck then or go to sleep over the whole thing. One or the other."

"Droppin' his head's a sign he's given in, isn't it?"

"Could be, if his back doesn't come up. Just be careful."

But there was no need for a warning because Shimmer behaved perfectly, not even starting when the wind picked up and blew a little whirlwind of leaves along the fence.

Feel funny, but Jebe say all good, so all good. Take time to get to like I think. Good not wear Jebe now. Later maybe.

"Some day soon," Jebe whispered in the colt's flicking ear. "Soon you and I will ride together. I just know it."

"Look at them," Lurela said proudly. "You'd think they were talking to each other."

Simen was a bit surprised that Lurela seemed unaware of her son's special talent. "They are, Mistress Lurela. Didn't you know? Your son is a Beasttalker."

Lurela sighed heavily. "I'd heard a rumor, one I didn't want to believe. Jebe's father…his father is of the Magic and I was hoping Jebe wouldn't be like him."

"Jebe will never be like Sarn," Simen replied quietly. "His heart is too big for that. Just look at how gentle is with that colt. He's nearly as good a horseman as Joss already."

"Master Joss is a good man for him to copy," Lurela said. "If even one man I'd met in Magiskeep were as good, I'd not have spent so much time alone."

Now Simen smiled for another reason. He had the answers he needed. Now all he had to do was try to capitalize on them. Somehow he had to get Lurela and Joss alone together.

*****

Sorra cupped her hands under her soft breasts and lifted them to admire their shape in the mirror Tamor had conjured for her in the little cottage. She smiled, not entirely pleased, but more than satisfied at their creamy skin. Then she stroked her thighs, letting her hand slide down to the graceful curves of her calves, her eyes watching in wonder as she wriggled her toes. She spun on her heel to face Tamor, throwing her hip out at him suggestively. "Do you like what you see, My Lord?"

Tamor grunted. Why were the Flesher bodies so full of vanity? She had only worn this one for half a span and already Sorra had started to worship it. He had Healed the scars from the knife, and wiped the little remaining blood away, marveling at how pale and soft the woman's skin had been. Now, seeing her naked before him, he felt a longing again to touch it, but he held himself back. Sorra was his for another purpose. He gestured with his hand, covering her bare form in a pale pink shaenis gown. "Look again, Mistress to see how the world must see you from now on. Unless I tell you, you shall be robed and covered. I have need of a noble woman, not a whore."

Sorra spun to look at her reflection again, this time letting her fingers stroke the silken fabric clinging to the curves of her body. The secrets it disguised were nearly as alluring as what lay beneath. "Will I have more skins like this to cover me? I like it."

"These skins are gowns, and I will give you enough to fill my needs, not yours. You are at my command, not your own. Best you remember that, or this skin and any other you choose to wear will forfeit any hope of True Life when I am done with them."

Sorra shrugged non-commitally. "If I drink my fill, you will, in the end, have no power over me."

Tamor stretched out his hand, curling one claw like finger at her. Sorra gasped and dropped to the floor, crying out in agony as she clutched her belly. "That is but a taste of what your disobedience will earn, woman of flesh." He crooked another finger and she began to scream, tears streaming down her face as she writhed in torment. He watched dispassionately, waiting until her throat was hoarse before relenting. "Get up," he commanded. She moaned. "Get up and face me. I want to you understand every word I say to you."

Sorra struggled to her feet shivering before her Lord and Master. "I am yours."

"Remember the pain. In this body you can feel it whenever I choose to remind you. Do not have ambition of True Life until the day I let you drink the blood of the Fleshers. I need you in half shadow until I am done. If you drink, it will bind you to that flesh you wear and you will not be able to walk the clouds at will. For the work we have to do we will sometimes need to travel quickly. I don't want you bound to the earth."

Sorra nodded numbly.

"The darkness will be your friend whenever you shed that skin to do as I tell you."

"I will leave this body?"

He nodded. "Sometimes, when there is need. Magiskeep is not an easy target for Shadows. Thus it is I let you wear the flesh. If you study carefully with me, you will learn to deceive their eyes and walk among them freely. No one will suspect your true nature."

"But if I leave this skin, won't they find out?"

"The darkness favors Shadows and if you are careful, they will never know. Fleshers sleep in the spans we Shadows cherish." When he saw the look of surprise and confusion on her face, he sighed. "This Sonya who bore your reflection must have been a fool in the ways of men to leave you so ignorant."

"She was too angry with the world to think of anything beyond her own hate for the Sorcerer when I was born," Sorra said. "It was the rage that sustained me."

Tamor smiled grimly. That hate was exactly what had attracted him to her in the first place. It made her the perfect one to take on his mission. But now it was also proving a detriment. Until he had taught her how to be a Lady of the Court, she could not be loosed in the halls of Magic. "You have much to learn."

"How? Here?" Sorra waved her hand taking in the little cabin's single room, spare and far from the world of men.

Tamor gestured to the mirror. "Behold," he said, "my schoolbook."

Sorra's reflection vanished as the mirror opened into the Way, its eye now focused on a room somewhere in Magiskeep. When he saw no one in the distant chamber, Tamor gestured again, this time showing her one of the Keep's main halls where servants scurried to and fro, dusting and carrying towels and sheets to rooms beyond. Another imaged opened in Joria's classroom where a tidy lot of Prentices bent over their scrolls trying for all they were worth to understand how to create an illusion to satisfy their mistress. Another gesture and for one brief moment she saw Jiala preening, her violet eyes staring intently at the glass as if there was nothing more important in all the world. And then, as that imaged dissolved, she saw Jamus, bending over to kiss Salene's cheek as she tended their baby in his crib.

Sorra snarled and leapt at the image.

Tamor's claw raked into her neck, pulling her back, snapping her head painfully against his chest. "You will have to learn to control that, My Dear," he whispered in her ear. She struggled, but a pain in her stomach seared through her and she fell limp against him. "As much as it pleasures me to see how much you hate him, this simply will not do." He gripped her by the shoulders and forced her to face the mirror's image again. Jamus had sat down on the edge of the bed next to his wife, and they were talking.

Sorra hissed to herself, but the pain stabbed through her, cutting her to silence.

"First lesson," Tamor said. "You will learn to smile when you see him. Then you will learn to bow, just so." He shoved her head down in imitation of a courteous bow to the Lord of Magiskeep. "The smile first, though."

Sorra gritted her teeth through the pain. But the corners of her mouth turned up, ever so slightly. As the image of Jamus faded, she could see her face again, wearing an ugly grimace that somehow resembled a smile.

Tamor's grip loosened. "That will do for a start, I suppose. We will practice again." He did not want to admit how pleased he was to have found the Way to Jamus' private chambers so quickly. There were hundreds of mirror in Magiskeep to search and finding this one so soon was more than he could have hoped for. Now he could spy on them whenever he wanted, and he was delighted to see them alone with the child.

What he did not see was a pair of whirling eyes watching the mirror from a corner of the room on the other side.

The Way worked in both directions, especially for Dragons.

*****

Rath said nothing when she saw a flicker of movement in the mirror in the Lord's chamber. Instead she watched, focusing her attention on the misty images revealed beyond the Way. She saw a woman lunge, just catching a glimpse of her face before she was yanked away by someone or something. Then it was dark, but a moment later, she saw the face again, indistinct and blurred as if it had no real substance. As keen as her Dragon senses were, she could not make it out clearly, but she memorized with most ancient care every detail she could see.

Something prickled at the back of her neck as she considered what to do. But Jamus and his mate were too consumed in their affection to bother with this now. Already she had learned to weigh the moments when it was right and proper to tell the truth in this world of the twolegs and when it was better to keep secrets.

She had never before seen the Best One so content, so…happy. The word rumbled in her brain as something new. But she realized the emotion was not foreign after all when she remembered how it had felt to fly for Jamus and use her fire against the Shadows below. It had been in a tapestry, of course, but the killing had been no less real for it. Then, she herself had been this happy thing and she recalled how pleasing it was. To see her Rider wear it on his face and in his heart stirred her in most unexpected ways.

And his mate, this woman, this Salene was happy too, fueling purpose to Rath's new role in their lives. She was in charge of keeping their kitling, their baby safe, and his safety would keep them in this happiness. She did not intend anything, especially anything spawned in the Way to threaten that. But until she was sure of what she had seen she decided not to tell the Rivermaster of it. For some reason, she decided he deserved this happiness and did not want to end it.

Not yet. Not now. Not before she understood.

"The day is fine," Rath said. "Perhaps the Lord and Lady might like to stroll in the garden, or go for a ride together? I will watch the little one in his nest."

"He might need changing," Salene said by way of protest.

"Though it is still strange to me, you have taught me how," Rath replied nodding to a pile of diapers on the bench. Curious how the twoleg felt about something quite as natural as waste, but she too liked a clean nest, so it did make at least a little sense. Still, it was such a bother when a mother's tongue could take care of it so easily.

It was almost as if Jamus had read her mind. "He is a human child, Rath. You must remember that. There are some wipes by the diapers and lotion if he needs it."

Rath flexed her fingers. "My hands work too, Jamus. I have learned well how to use them for your more curious customs. I will treat the babe as yours, not mine. Do not worry."

"I suppose a short ride would be nice," Salene said. "We haven't been out in quite some time."

"Since Jarien was born, actually, "Jamus replied. "I wonder if the horses will remember us."

"I've told Silvermane you are coming," Rath said. "He will not be pleased if you don't go soon. He is most impatient. Blackfur waits too."

Jamus and Salene quickly spelled themselves into their riding outfits and turned towards the door, just as someone knocked. "Yes?" Salene said. "You're welcome to come in."

It was Becca on one of her Sevenstin visits. "Oh, 'pears I be here at a bad time, eh?" she said when she saw how Jamus and Salene were dressed. "Ya look ta be goin' somewhere."

Salene smiled, "We are, Becca, but your timing is perfect. This will be the first time we'll be leaving Jarien in Lady Rath's care and I would be so pleased if you would sit with her." She saw Rath's eyes whirl. "Oh, it's not that don't trust her completely but she is still learning a few of the finer points of caring for a baby and it would be nice if she had someone more experienced standing by."

Becca bowed ever so slightly. "If she would have me here, I'd be right pleased to sit, My Lady." She drifted back into the common tongue a second later. "'Twon't interfere a mite lessen ya asks me to, Mistress. Ol' Becca's had enow work raisin' er own over the circles ta need ta change a dipy agin. Buts I be glad ta sit an' chat wid ya iffen ya wants my company."

Jamus' expression pleaded for Rath's assent. He knew Salene would feel much better leaving Jarien with Becca there too.

Rath nodded. "It will be a pleasure to have company. It can be lonely with a ki…babe that cannot carry on a conversation. I know Mistress Becca can."

Once out in the hall, Jamus whispered to Salene, "I hope the two of them will be all right together."

"Oh, Becca can take care of herself," Salene said.

"I wasn't worried about Becca."

Inside the room, Becca was already fussing over the baby who seemed to adore her as much as she adored him. She held him up in the air as he giggled. "There you go little man, you can fly!"

Rath arched her brow. "Do all men want to fly?"

"Some does, some don't," Becca replied, tucking Jarien back into her embrace. "It might be kinda fun to touch the clouds. I always wondered iffen they feel as soft as they look."

"Wet," Rath answered. "They feel wet."

"Don' spoil me dreams, Milady. I s'pose yer one o' them learned ladies, is ya? I know ya ain't Keep trained."

"I come from the Northlands. I have much knowledge."

"Book learnin's a good thing I s'pose. But whadaya know abouts little babes like this one? Have ya had any o' her own."

"A few," Rath answered. Then she remembered the manners she had learned since coming into the world of men. "How about you? Any offspring?"

"I had me four. Only one's still wid the world, the Hand be Blessed. Lost me twins to the fever afore we lived close ta the Keep. Me third son died in a cart accident. Me daughter moved off ta Lovental Province some ten circles past. Gots her a fine husband, but I don' see her much. How abouts you? Does ya see yer young'uns?"

"I too lost children but mine were to the spear."

"Warriors then," Becca said. "I ain't sure I could stomach sending one o' my babes to battle."

"It is the way of my kind," Rath answered. "It has been so for many hundreds of circles. Too many to count."

"Them northlands be hard country, I reckon," Becca said as she laid Jarien back in the crib and tucked the blanket in around him. "Ya done kept yer figger pretty good for bein' a mother." She put her hands on her own thick waistline. "Never did get all the baby weight offa me."

Rath considered some of the talk she'd heard among the women of the Keep when they'd been discussing their waistlines. It gave her something to say in reply. "I always eat fresh food and get plenty of exercise."

"Well now, I cain't make claim ta the exercise part, but as fer the food, I gots me a fine garden and Jeamel tells me I'se the best cook in the whole Keep."

"This Jeamel is your mate…your one love?"

Becca laughed. "One love? What a pretty way ta say it. Yep, that's me Jeamel. He works here in the Keep, ya knows. Prime Steward now. Been promoted season past. I'm right proud o' him."

"I think I know who he is," Rath answered. "I've often seen a fine looking man telling some of the other servants what to do. He's tall, with silver hair?"

"That's me lad!" Becca said. She wagged her finger at the other woman. "Now don' ya git no ideas about makin' a move on him."

Rath's eyes whirled, as she backed away from the admonishing finger in shock. "I would never take another's mate. It is not the way of my kind."

"Bory, Milady, don' take me all so serious. I was jest teasin' ya. Me Jeamel'd ne'er look ta another woman. Mind ya, he's had his chances. Man like him gots lots o' ladies lookin' to 'im, but he's too honest ta look back."

"You trust him."

"Wid ma life, ma soul, an' ma whole heart," Becca replied, smiling. "What about you? Ya gots a husband somewheres?"

"Husband, oh, you mean a one love? No. Not now. Once, perhaps. It's hard to say with my people. We do not always mate for life. Sometimes though…" Rath's voice trailed off. Once she had a lifemate. He was a great gray Dragon of the Winter Wind and they flew the skies together for nigh on five hundred circles. But, like so many of their kind, he had fallen in battle at the end of the last Great Circle and she had not found another to win her heart like that again. She envied Becca that, and Salene too now that she was herself walking on two legs, her wings folded in her heart. "It would be a pleasure to find one again."

"There's lots a good men here in the Keep. Ya bin lookin'?"

Rath coughed and collected herself before answering. It was not easy to balance the Dragon with the woman sometimes. "I have not, Mistress Becca. I have not. I'm here to watch for Jamus' son and don't have time for such things."

"Woman cain't live her life lonely alls the time," Becca said. "Next time the Lord and Lady takes care o' the lad theyselves, ya come visit me in the village. I knows a few fine fellers what'd love ta show a lady like yerself a good time, iffen ya knows what I mean."

Rath wasn't at all sure she did know what Becca meant, but before she could answer, Jarien started to cry.

Outside the clouds gathered quickly, covering the sun in a matter of seconds. Rath lifted her head and drew a deep breath. It was as if she were drawing in the sky itself as she spread her arms wide and closed her eyes.

Becca picked up the baby to soothe him. "He's wet."

But Rath did not say anything. Instead she seemed to be reaching up to the ceiling with her hands.

"I'm gonna change 'em,' Becca said, completely baffled by Rath's strange behavior. "Iffen that's how ya care fer a babe, I cain't fer the life of me figger why the Lord and Lady called ya here ta be his nanny."

The sky above quieted, the clouds parted, the wind died and the sun broke through the gloom.

Rath dropped her gaze back to the baby as Becca dried him before putting on a new diaper.

"He is strong," Rath said. "It is not an easy task to care for him."

*****

As soon as Jamus noticed the gathering clouds, he cast a sphere of protection over Salene and him. When Clouder, his big black dog who'd joined them for the ride, barked at him he laughed and added a spell to protect him as well. "I thought you liked to swim," he said when the dog seemed pleased to be included in the Magic.

For a moment, he considered commanding the storm to end, but decided against it. He was quite sure it was a result of Jarien's doing. But now Rath was with the baby and it was her first test at controlling the effect of his emotions.

"Is is Jarien?" Salene asked at the sphere closed above her, and the sky grew even darker.

"I think so, but I can't be sure," Jamus answered. "If the storm is natural, then I've no right to interfere, but if it's our son's,

Rath will have to be the reins as we'd hoped." Then, he felt a surge of command to the Silver River stronger than any he had ever attempted on his own. The demand pummeled against the surging waves, battered the clouds, and tore the rain from the wind before the first drop could fall. The River fought, bucking like a rebellious colt to the saddle. It raged to no avail for the command accepted nothing short of complete and utter obedience. The skies cleared and the sun broke through. Jamus was trembling and Whim danced fretfully under him. Never had either felt such power. "She is more than reins," he said, his voice shaking a little. "She is a stelin bit in the master rider's hand. I've never known anything like it."

Salene reached over to touch his hand. Born of the Golden Waters, she had felt nothing out of the ordinary. "Are you all right, My Love?"

He nodded wearily. "Rath has calmed the waters. I think she may have done even more with her command, but I can't tell for certain. Jarien's tantrums may have been thwarted for more than this one time. It may well be the River will be too afraid to answer him again for some time."

"Could that be? Could Rath have so much control over that River you speak of? I thought you were its master too."

"Nothing like that. She is the Silver Dragon, born of the waters, and their queen. I don't quite understand the Way of Dragons yet, but I can tell you I am most impressed. She may not be able to change a diaper, but she could turn the course of the ocean if she set her mind to it."

"The ocean is ruled by another sort, you said," Salene reminded him.

"The SeaDragon," he agreed. "And yet I would vow Rath might be more than a match for him. He may claim all four Rivers, but she...she is truly amazing."

"If I didn't know better, I would think you are enamored of the Lady, " Salene said, twining a lock of Flax's mane with her fingers. "She would be quite pleased to think that herself."

"Rath?"

"She loves you, you know. It's lucky she keeps her Dragon's heart in check for your sake. Otherwise, I fear she might try to fly off with you clasped in her talons."

Jamus laughed now, dismissing the sphere with an easy wave of his hand. "Whatever you may say, Rath would never take me from my chosen mate. She cannot love as men love, Salene, no matter how human she may appear. Her bond with me is as her Rider, and one day, her Master. She is beast to the core and Magic beyond comprehending. You have no reason to worry. She would lay down her life to protect you."

"I know she would and that's the most frightening think of all—to even think she might have reason to do so. Why, even when we are so blissfully happy, do we need to keep looking over our shoulders?"

Jamus sighed. He reined Whim over to the grove of brellums and let the stallion drop his head to graze on the sofferns. "Shadows," he said. "always the Shadows. There is only one River left to conquer and its waters are black."

IV

Gambel was satisfied. Melthus would have liked to be an inch or so taller, and Grella in inch or so fuller in her breast, but overall, the three Shadows were content with the bodies they had chosen to wear. Free of the kind of restrictions holding Tamor in Magiskeep, Aberdeen afforded them enough anonymity that it mattered little which Flesher's blood they had drunk to gain the skins they needed. In a city this large with so many comings and goings no one would notice.

They had selected their victims near the docks, choosing newcomers to the busy streets. That way they would not have to worry much about friends or family, and while they had not spent much time making sure they were right about that, a certain dark luck had directed them. It was the touch of Tamor's Magic, of course, but they preferred to think it was their own cleverness. Gambel had, several circles past, worn a skin before he had wandered back into the Way of Mirrors and gotten trapped again. Of the three, he was the wisest in the ways of the Fleshers and was quick to tutor his comrades in the basics of behavior. "You are a Flesher's reflection," he explained, "so you have your maker's wisdom already in you. Let your thoughts rely on that and keep your eyes and ears open to everyone around you. It is easy to wear a skin no one knows if you act as one of the living."

Grella knotted her long brown hair in a bun at the nape of her neck and pulled the laces of her bodice a little tighter. She looked to be a woman of some status, though not a Lady, and she decided to appear modest and proper despite Melthus's leering gazes. "I might even be welcome in a noble household if I speak the proper tongue," she said. "I've heard the blood of the rich nourishes well."

"The Master did not send us just to drink," Melthus countered flexing his arm muscles, relishing the feel of controlling such a strong body. "I wonder what craft this one did. He was well fit to the blacksmith's hammer. I am not keen to labor, but if it could afford me eyes in the houses of power, I am sure the Dark Lord would be pleased."

"Nothing would please the Dark Lord more than the knowing of how to inspire the mortals to raise an army in his name. If the end of time is coming, he will need bodies to fight for him and bodies to feed the lust of his Shadow army. He has given us the honor of planting the seeds while we are here," Gambel said. Athletic and tall, his body had once been a Knight of the Hand, no longer following the Vow, but still fit and capable nevertheless. "But we are also charged to learn how strong the hate is for the Rivermaster and his kin. It is said the Darkness will rise when the Rivers flow as one and the mortal world starts to drown in the waves of discontent."

"An obscure prophecy from some ancient scroll," Grella muttered. Reflection of a scholar, she had been caught in the mirror after a failed examination in the Halls of Learning and even now wore the skepticism of that reflection. "Men always think the Elden words are so important. Better they live for today instead of reading the past to guide their passage."

"Lord Tamor believes the Eldenlore, Mistress. It fuels his lust. He has waited long for the Black Dragon to fly. Anything we can do here to give it wings will please him."

"Pleasing myself is much better," Melthus said. "This skin feels better than I could ever have imagined. I would like to keep it."

"You will need to drink then. Is it safe to hunt in this city?"

"We need to be careful," Gambel warned, as eager to gain True Life as the others despite his loyalty to Tamor's cause. As much as he feared the Dark Lord's wrath, his own ambition ruled him more. Besides, Tamor had never denied any of them the right to take blood in pursuit of immortality. The Darkness needed an invincible army to ride against the Rainbow Dragon should the time come. Why should he not be one of its generals? It was the very reason he had chosen a warrior's skin to wear. "The city is vast and the Provinces beyond are full of Fleshers who will not be missed if they die by our hands. As long as we do not call too much attention to ourselves, we should each be able to find the twelve we need. But we must learn to be patient. We have a full season, and if the Darkness would grant, longer. If we please the Dragon the River will indulge us."

"How do you know all this?"

"I was The Searcher in my time before, Tamor's favorite and as close to True Life as ever Shadow could be before the Sorcerer and his kind defeated my quest. Why do you think The Lord sent me on this mission? I will not take this second chance lightly. I shall be The Searcher again and this time drink the blood of the twelfth."

"If your nose can find us some Sorcerers, we would not need to many," Melthus said. "While I respect your skills and the strength of your lust, it would please me greatly to reach my goal sooner than later."

Grella nodded, rubbing her hands along her hips to smooth her skirt. "I too would be pleased to taste the blood of Magic—the sooner the better."

"I am no blooddog, but I can smell the River," Gambel the Searcher replied. "If we work together, perhaps we can sate all our desires before the season ends and not need the Dragon. It would be good to be free of obligation to him."

"And Tamor?"

"How much power can even he have over three immortals?"

*****

Gareth paced the carpet of his sitting room. Things were not going according to his best wishes. His father seemed to be rallying again after getting some kind of herbal mix from Master Edra. Since the Sorcerers had come to court, Gailvarg had regained enough of his strength to spend at least a span or two each day sitting in the Great Hall to hear petitioners. And, as always, the people of Aberdeen were delighted with his every word.

The nobles, not so, again, as usual. Gailvarg had a well-earned reputation of siding with commoners over the wealthy and those with well-lined purses did not like it. They much preferred Prince Gareth's approach to disputes where a coin or two in the right hand would usually earn a favorable verdict.

Now, with the King back on his throne enough of the time to matter, the general populace was growing more and more content while the Lords were grumbling again of rebellion.

This put Gareth in an awkward position. While he wanted to make every effort to gain allies from the upper echelons of Aberdeen society, he also dared not cross his father. The King had more than once threatened to publicly disown him for much lesser offenses than disagreeing with his policy, and the Prince was certain the old man would follow through to full extent if he did. Until he had gained enough power of his own to combat him, Gareth had to bow to his father's will and at least appear to support his decisions.

Gareth's own little cupboard of herbs was nearly bare by now. Those he had used to rid himself of his meddling mother had long since lost their potency and it was becoming painfully clear that the ones he was using now simply did not have enough strength to do what needed doing.

He needed to find a new herblist.

And this led to the second element of his discontent. Greenmonth just passed, he had sent for his Aunt , the one member of the family whose love for Gailvarg was hardly worth a copper button. She had always been jealous of her brother-in-law and resentful of his taking the crown, when, as his elder, she believed it should have been her husband's instead. When Galan, her husband, died, she had left Aberdeen and sailed away to WorldsEnd, an island as far away from Aberdeen as any seaman had ever sailed. There, she had made a fine home for herself and reaped a fair bounty trading with the other islands of Turan, using her connection to the royal household to get goods shipped from the Mainland. While the practicality of it made no sense, merchant ships would sail all the way to her port, sell their goods to her for exorbitant prices, and then hire themselves out to take the same merchandise to trade with the nearer isles on her behalf. Everyone who had money to start out with always made more and those who had little paid far too much for whatever they bought.

Arista had always liked Gareth, for they were of the same mind about the King and Queen. Now, the Prince had sent for her on pretense of celebrating his father's fiftieth circle of reign, hoping, with her help, to make it his last.

The captain of *The Sea Eagle* had Arista listed on his passenger manifest. As far as he knew, she had reached port safely, unloaded half of her ample baggage and disembarked on the second day of the Sevenstin.

She had not been seen nor heard of since.

While Gareth really didn't care if she still lived, he was frustrated to not have more information about her whereabouts. Even a body would be better than nothing, for Arista always carried a pouch of particularly useful herbs on her person. In fact, this time he hoped she had more than usual since it was the very reason he had sent for her. He'd given her just enough information in the message he'd sent to fetch her to let her know it was time to dispose of her brother, and he was sure she would come to Aberdeen well prepared. Exotic poisons were her specialty.

So two frustrations plagued him as he paced and one more added was almost too much to bear. Despite somehow interfering in the plan to finish off the King, Edra had totally ingratiated himself to the Prince with the combat lessons. While learning to use a sword correctly delighted Gareth beyond expectation, at the same time it filled him with growing dissatisfaction. Edra was quick, talented, athletic, the sword easy in his hand. His opponent, though an intent student, was slow, clumsy and often too unfocused to manage sharp parries or sharp attacks. While Gareth's skill was slowly becoming passable, he was also beginning to realize that in a real war he would never be able to hold his own much less lead an army into battle himself.

He was the kind of warlord better suited to issuing commands with message birds and riders a good distance from the heat of the fighting. For that, he needed a strong battle commander and well trained troops to do his bidding. Though Edra seemed the perfect candidate, the Sorcerer declined the appointment repeatedly. "I am not a battle commander," he insisted.

"But you fought in a war in that Arcula you so often speak of." Gareth replied. "And to your account you were leader of the Cauge. You are the most experienced man I know."

"Aberdeen is not at war, My Liege," Edra said, trying to turn the tide of the conversation. He had never bothered to study the art of war in his homeland. Yes, he had mastered the weapons, but none of that required the book study of tactics or any of the learned skills a battlemaster needed. He'd hated books all his life, choosing to learn by observation or by using his hands rather than by reading anything at all.

"My heart is at war," Gareth said. Then his hand slipped to his crotch. "And my body longs to be—against those very Sorcerers who ruined me. I want revenge, Master Edra, and war against their Magic would suit me just fine. Think of it, you could carry my banner against our enemies!"

Edra shook his head. "I am unworthy, My Lord." The memory of his failure in the canyon of Arcula was still vivid in his brain. He had blundered into an ambush against the very force of Magic Gareth lusted to destroy. Even with the Dark Lord's Shadows on his side, he had sent his army into a trap and lost nearly everything. He looked at the stump where his left hand had been. Jyp had tried to heal him more than once, but the young mage's pitiful skill did little except ease some of the phantom pain. "I lost my war, My Prince. You should find a man who knows victory to lead your troops. I cannot."

"Where? In Aberdeen? All the soldiers here have gone soft with circles of peace. I could gather five hundred of them and find no more than two with half the skills of the blade you have."

"Wielding a sword is only part of battle, Your Highness. Where the soldiers march, how they position themselves on the field, when they charge and when they fall back all matter more than how the blades swing. Surely there is a battlemaster somewhere in Aberdal."

Gareth rubbed his chin thoughtfully. "Once the Knights of the Hand rode these lands. Legendary fighters. Now they march mostly for ceremony, but perhaps there is one of the old order around."

"Knights of the Hand?" Edra asked. Something was knocking in the back of his brain. While not a reader, he had always loved the old stories of Arcula before the Wall. In fact, at one time, according to Lore, all Turan had been one world. The Knights were, as Gareth had said, legendary. And they were the models for the Riders of the Cauge, the proud horsemen Edra had recruited to enforce his laws in the outlands of Arcuse. If he could find a Rider in Aberdal, he wouldn't hesitate to introduce him to the ambitious Prince, so why not a Knight? "Are there still such men around? With so much peace, men of war can fast become farmers."

"Some still serve as mercenaries to collect debts or settle border disputes in the other provinces," Gareth said. "What I need is one trained in the Temple. Even in the circles of peace the ways of war were well taught there."

"Master Jyp and I would be pleased to use our Magic to search for such a one," Edra offered, hoping against hope his young companion had some talent for scrying. If not, he suspected Jyp would know where to find a Seer adept in one of the more arcane skills of the Sight. Either way, another quest would solidify his position in the Court where he was learning again to enjoy the comforts of wealth and status.

"You will do this for us," Gareth stated, using the royal plural to accent his command.

Edra bowed. "As you command, My Prince." He knew enough by now to leave as soon as possible. Once Gareth started issuing orders it was better to be as far away as possible.

As soon as the Sorcerer left, Gareth cursed under his breath. "If I'd thought of it sooner, I would have told him to scry for my Aunt as well. I must have a portrait of her lying about somewhere."

*****

Jamus never expected it to be too quiet in the Keep, but with Rath's control over the Silver Waters, his and Salene's life with the new baby had settled into a peace neither had encountered in a long time. Their lives had been fraught with turmoil for so long it was almost unnerving.

"I feel as if I'm waiting for the next disaster," Jamus said one Easwin as he rolled over in bed after a good night's sleep. "Can I be mistaken, or did Jarien finally sleep all night?"

"S-h-h-h," Salene warned, giving him a quick kiss. "I think I'm still dreaming and I don't want to wake up." She turned her head to glance at the crib. "He's still there, sound asleep. If we don't make any noise, maybe he'll let us stay in bed for another span."

Jamus pulled her closer. "And whatever will we do with all the extra time in bed?"

Salene laughed and yawned. "I don't think you'll like my answer this time, My Love, but I want to take another nap."

He shrugged. "For once, I think I agree with you. I think I have a full season's sleep to make up myself. Where's Rath?"

"She's not here, if that's what you mean. When I first woke up and Jarien was still so quiet, I thought I was going to find her keeping watch. I think her eyes must have some kind of hypnotic effect on him. All she has to do is look at him when he starts to cry and he stops. It would worry me, but when he starts laughing at her I feel a lot better."

"She's not chanting him, if that's what you mean," Jamus replied. "It worried me too, at first, but I used my Sight when it happened and there was no Magic of any color flowing between them. I think he just likes her."

"Who would believe it? She is a beautiful woman but I wouldn't exactly call her warm and loving, at least not the way I see it."

"She is a Dragon, after all," Jamus replied. "I haven't met one yet I'd call particularly warm, or friendly for that matter. But they do have a curious capacity for Compassion, and the Healing touch of a Dragon is more powerful than any other Magic I've ever encountered."

Salene nodded. "Your Kisel has given life back more than once. Perhaps he and his kind no more about the Sixth Art than even we masters can comprehend. When I have some free time, I would love to talk to one of them about it. I'd like to learn some of their skills if I can."

"Ever the student, eh?" Jamus said, pulling the blanket up under his chin as he snuggled deeper into the down mattress. "I suppose it's just as well. One of the Eldenscrolls I found said that when there is no more to learn in the world, the Great Circle will close on its own. Then the world will plunge back into darkness and knowledge will have to begin all over again."

Salene shivered. "Could that ever be possible?"

"It's what the Black Dragon wants. He can only rule in a world of ignorance. Whether the Circle closes on its own, or because he wins the final battle, all knowledge will be lost and he will have the power."

Salene reached over and pulled his arm around her, seeking comfort in his embrace. "Even I will pray to the Hand that never happens." She said. "Just the thought of it makes me cold."

Before Jamus could answer, a blast of wind exploded through the window as Rath alighted on the ledge. Instantly, she transformed into her human shape and strode over to the mirror. She stood there for a long time, absently wiping the blood from around her mouth as she peered into the silvrin surface. Then she said, "One day I will teach Skyling to hunt. He will be good with the bow, I think."

Jamus, more used to the Dragon's comings and goings than Salene, pushed himself up to sit on the edge of the bed near the baby's crib. "Skyling? You mean Jarien?"

Rath nodded towards the baby. "You are Kiselor, he is Skyling, for one day when his wings grow long enough, he will ride the clouds."

"Astride your back. So he is destined to be a Dragonrider too?"

Now Rath shook her head. "At first, perhaps, until he learns his own wings. Did you learn nothing from Alran?"

Salene gripped Jamus' arm. "What is she talking about?" They both remembered too well the fate of Jarien's namesake when he had tried to chase the clouds.

But Jamus had another memory of the moment when Alran told him to fly to save his life and he had. "That was in a tapestry, Lady Rath," he said. "It was another place, another time, another world."

"Was it so with the boy? What time was that, Kiselor? How many times has the Way twisted your reality? How many times have you been born, eh? The Circle will never end as long as you do not know. Perhaps you will be the savior of mankind after all with all this unknowing."

Salene was shivering again. "What is she talking about, Jamus?" she repeated. "Is something going to happen to Jarien? Please, you have to tell me if you know something."

"Another riddle, Salene, that's all. If I solve it, according to Rath, the world is going to end. Maybe I shouldn't bother."

"Some of it you know already, Rivermaster. Some you suspect. And the rest? It will be for you to decide when the time comes, I think."

"And how will I know when it's time?" Jamus asked, noticing how intent Rath seemed on her image in the mirror. Was she looking for something?

"There is no time in the Way," Rath answered. Then Jarien whimpered. "The kitling is hungry," she said. She moved over to the crib, plucked the baby up and put him on Salene's breast. "He needs his mother."

Salene unlaced her bodice to let Jarien suckle, all the while keeping her eyes on Rath as if she feared the silver woman would pounce and snatch the baby away from her.

Rath's whirling eyes seemed to read her concern. "There is no need to fear Rath," she said. "I am sworn to the Master of the River and all he loves, I love too. As long as there is breath in my body, I will not let any harm come to you or your offspring. "

Jamus could feel Salene's breathing ease. He tried to lighten the mood. "So, you were out hunting, My Lady? Doesn't the food here in Magiskeep satisfy you?"

"You use too much fire on the meat," she replied. "And the growing things do not please my appetite much. I do like the drink of flame, but one day I downed a keg because Steward Jule said I could not drink it all before he did. I was dizzy hunting that night and Easwin next my head hurt."

Both parents stifled their laughter out of respect for the Dragon. "It's not good to drink too much," Jamus told her. "Trust me, I know. Ale, amberwine, either one can dull the senses and make a man do foolish things. It's a good thing you didn't crash while you

were flying in that condition. I've had a enough bad experiences
myself to know just how much I can drink before I'll be in trouble."

"Should I know for myself?"

"I can't quite say, My Lady. Were you in your Dragon skin,
I would think the anything less than a keg would be fine, but wearing
human form? I really have no idea how all that would work. If I were
you, I'd not finish off more than a goblet—two at the most, just to be
safe."

"The body is small," Rath agreed. "It will not hold as much.
I will remember." She glanced at the mirror again.

"Why are you so intent on that mirror?" Jamus asked. "Have
you seen something I need to know about?"

Rath considered for a long time before answering. She had
only once seen the woman and the Shadows behind her. And even
then the image had not been clear enough for her to be certain of
anything. "Every mirror opens to the way, My Rider. I must keep
watch, that is all. I must keep watch."

*****

Though ignorant of most aspects of human existence, Sorra
was, at least, a good student. Apparently the need for revenge which
had birthed her as reflection now motivated her to learn everything
she could about Magiskeep and its society. Unfortunately for Tamor,
the powerful emotions Sonya had worn when she seared her
reflection into the Way had blocked so much of her reason that Sorra
was more ignorant of that world and its knowledge than most other
Shadows the Dark Lord might have chosen for this mission.

It might well have been that ignorance attracting him to her
in the first place, for, like the Black Dragon himself, Tamor thrived
on men's stupidity. It was the very thing he and his Master desired
for it spelled the end of the Great Circle and the victory of Darkness
over Light. But when he learned she could neither read nor write, he
cursed his haste in taking her. The trouble was, the body he had
found for her was a learned woman, and if Sorra were ever going to
impersonate her in Magiskeep, she too would have to be learned.

It was not too difficult to teach her numbers and letters and
by using all his powers over her mind fill her brain with rudimentary

skills in reading and writing. So far she was able to make out the sounds of most words, but her accent was slow and her comprehension lacking of far too many of them. They had found Natale's diary in a small wooden box she kept under her cot. It proved a boon and a curse to his plans. Within its pages he was able to read the full story of the woman's life—her connections to Mudlake, the avalanche that killed her husband and child, and of some circles of study in the Hall of the Hand beyond the Rim in Lovental Province. Nearly a priestess before she met a man to love, she had mastered the Eldentongue and was a proficient and skilled writer.

If Sorra should run into anyone at all in Magiskeep who knew the woman, she would be hard pressed to keep up the pretense without being discovered. Worse, there was mention that she had visited Magiskeep's palace itself and once consulted with some Mage by the name of Senital to help translate an old text some time before her family had died.

"I cannot teach you everything you need to know," Tamor said, throwing up his hands in exasperation when Sorra once again failed to read aloud one of the diary's pages without stumbling over the words.

"I am sorry, My Lord. I am trying my best. Perhaps we could let them think Natale lost her mind here in the forest and forgot all she once knew?"

"Pah! In any place but Magiskeep, and in any other circumstance that might work. But the Healers in the Keep have unfathomable skill. And even if they could not cure your memory loss, Lord Jamus would never allow a madwoman anywhere near his wife and child. Either I must find a way to drum knowledge into your head, or I will need to find another Shadow to take your place and another body for it to fill."

Sorra shuddered at the threat. Wearing the skin was becoming comfortable and she liked the feel of the world under her fingers and was even finding the taste of food a pleasure. "My Lord, please. I will do anything for you. I would even face the Great Dragon himself and fall at his feet to let him to his will to me if it would please you."

The Dragon. Tamor smiled. Sorra may have been ignorant, but the panic driving her had somehow managed to make unexpected sense. Tamor had felt Kesel's power himself when he had taken his first skin. The Blackwing had burned knowledge of men into his head to allow him to trick many a victim into his caves. He remembered well how his head had nearly exploded as images and understandings poured into the corners of his mind. Why had he forgotten?

Perhaps it was because he had chosen to. Since his role as Dark Lord to the Dragon, he had gained power, prestige, True Life, and a will of his own. While he still dropped on is knee in the Dragon's presence, he no longer bowed his head but faced those dark eyes as a near equal. He would always have to submit, but now it was only because he chose to.

The Dragon knew this, and accepted him only because he had use of a creature like Tamor in his greater plan for the world. Together, they had nearly defeated the Rivermaster once already. And, now, although their enemy had gained power in the other three rivers and even some knowledge of the workings of the Black Waters, he was certain they could battle him again and win. While he knew little of Tamor's plan, he trusted his Shadowlord, not because he was worthy of trust, but because he knew Tamor's ambition was even greater than his own. Once the Darkness commanded the world of men again, it would take a man to rule it, not a Dragon. Tamor intended to be that man, and he had Kesel's blessing.

Yet Kesel was not going to make it easy, Tamor knew. The Dragon had pride and expected respect from his minions, no matter how powerful they might be. To ask for his help with Sorra would demand humility and Tamor's having to admit he himself had failed, needing the Dragon's help.

It was not going to be easy.

To make matters worse, he could not walk the clouds to Blackwing's lair with the woman. Had Sorra been pure Shadow, it would have been a small matter. But her all too mortal skin needed to learn as well and had to come with them to make their plea to the Master. "Pack whatever you think this woman might carry with her on a long journey," Tamor said. "I will conjure whatever else we need. You and I are going to see my King to ask for his help."

"I will do your will," Sorra replied, bowing as he had taught her. At least basic manners had stuck in her head.

"Prepare yourself," he said. "Neither this journey nor its end will be easy. Not easy at all."

V

Simen was packing his bag, getting ready to leave Delran's Keep when a servant rapped firmly on the door. "Yes?"

Nodding and bowing, but still determined to deliver his message, the young boy said, "My Lord, Lord Delran bids to come to the sitting room at once. He has guests and says you are to greet them."

"I'm nearly done packing," Simen replied. "I'll be down shortly."

"No, My Lord. The Master was very clear. You are to come at once, with me. He said if you refused, I was....I was to drag you." The boy squared his shoulders, trying hard to look taller.

Simen grinned. "Well, then, from the looks of those muscles of yours, I do believe I have no choice. Lead on, Sur. I will do exactly as you tell me to."

Proudly, the lad led the Follyman downstairs where, to Simen's absolute delight, he saw two familiar faces. He jumped down the last two stairs and swept Kala into his arms, hugging her nearly breathless. "Kala! Has it been so long already! What are you doing here?"

Kala wriggled out of his arms and laughed. "I go wherever I please, Lord Simen. Dale and I heard a rumor that some mad Sorcerer had invaded Delran's Keep, and we deemed it our duty to investigate."

"Dale!" Simen said as he grasped the other man's hand in the customary greeting of the gentry. "Wait, I still don't see a promise band anywhere—on either one of you. What's going on with you, man, that you haven't proposed to her yet?"

Dale smiled. "We've discussed it. Sometime, soon, I hope, when both of us have fulfilled our duties well enough that we can afford to leave them behind for a month or so."

"You're so busy you can't find time for love?"

"He didn't say that," Kala replied, blushing, despite herself. "Dale has been named Lord Counselor in Tulene, you know, and after all of Destan's failings there is still much to do in righting the city. He's done wonders, mind you, but circles of neglect take time to heal."

"If Jamus and Salene were here, they could right the city for you in a turn of the wind."

Dale raised his hand in protest. "I'm sure they could, but then, how would my people feel about their roads and walls? And how would my workmen feed their families? You know as well as I do that men thrive on hard work when they feel they are accomplishing something worthwhile."

"I seem to think I've heard a certain Master of Magiskeep say something just like that a few times myself," Simen agreed. "So it goes well, then. And what about you, Kala? What duties keep you from marrying him?"

"Not much more in Telma," she said. "Grandisite has given me more authority, though. In fact, the King himself has called me back to Aberdeen this very Sevenstin. He's finally well enough to sit in the Hall and he needs the advice of a Juris. I'm not sure how long I'll have to stay, but I can't deny his command….no matter how much my heart might want to." She kissed Dale on the cheek and took his hand in hers.

"So, you'll be leaving Tulene then. When?"

"My bags are tied to Silk's saddle. Dale and I will ride back to the city tomorrow, and then I'll be on my way."

"Alone?"

"I've traveled all the Provinces myself before, Simen. Nothing's changed."

"Oh, yes it has, My Lady," Simen replied bowing. "Before, you had no Sorcerers for friends. Now, as I recall, you have a Keep full of them. Jamus would never forgive me if he thought I'd let you wander off to Aberdeen alone. I would be most pleased to escort you." He winked. "I might even be able to make the journey a bit shorter if you'd let me."

"Not too short," Kala replied. "If I arrive in Aberdeen too soon after the summons, the King might grow suspicious. But Silk does love to fly and so do I. If you promise to keep it within reason, I would enjoy the company."

"Is it all right with you, My Lord?" Simen asked, fixing his eyes on Dale, searching the other man's face for any sign of concern.

"I've trusted you and your brother with my life before," Dale replied. "I think I can trust you with it again. I'd feel a lot happier about this whole thing if Kala had someone by her side. I thank you."

They had a wonderful dinner together, sharing stories of their adventures Lord Delran had never heard. Simen was pleased to see Joss and Lurela whispering together between courses. He had a feeling that part of his plan was going to work out just fine, but he did resolve to check on the couple now and then. With Delran's permission, he opened a mirror into the Way in the Lord's study, so travel between the province and Magiskeep was an easy journey if there were an emergency. Before the meal he had used it to contact Jamus in the Keep to tell him he would be delayed in coming home.

"If it's for Kala," Jamus said, "you can stay as long as you like. Just be careful in Aberdeen, though, brother. If the Prince recognizes my face in yours there may be trouble. And be sure you don't mention Magiskeep anywhere he may hear of it."

"I'll be careful," Simen assured him. "A Follyman wears many disguises in his life. Once I don one, even you wouldn't recognize me."

"Then enjoy the trip," Jamus said. "Keep in touch, though. I don't want to worry about you."

Though he didn't need it, Simen was happy to have Jamus' blessing. More and more, his brother was gaining power and status and he didn't even realize it. Simen felt the River's strength in his voice and saw it in his eyes. Jamus had become a man who demanded respect whether he wanted it or not.

"Jamus sends his best, "Simen told the party at the table.

"I hear he has a child," Delran said. "What a blessing it must be for him and Lady Salene. A man with a family is truly lucky." He smiled at Jebe. "I'd nearly forgotten how wonderful it could be until this young man and his mother came into my life."

"It's an honor, Sur," Jebe said, quickly checking his mother's expression to see if he'd said the right thing. Her beaming smile was all he needed. "I came to work here, though. I want to earn my keep and if I earn your love by doing it, I'll grow up to be a happy man."

Lurela's eyes filled with tears. Without thinking, Joss put his arm around her shoulders and reached up with his free hand to wipe a tear away. "I'm so proud to hear you say such a thing, Jebe," she said at last.

"You taught me, Maman," Jebe said. "Nobody never got anywhere good without workin' for it. You worked all your life outta love for me. I figure I oughta work outta love myself if I ever intend to be someone worth anything."

Simen smiled. Jamus had been so right in sending the boy and his mother here.

But then, Jamus was so right about most everything.

*****

"I want a warlord," Gareth insisted again, close to throwing a tantrum. He'd called Edra and Jyp to his private chambers, impatient to hear how their scrying had progressed.

"Nothing so far, Your Highness," Edra said, hiding his nervousness. He had misjudged the extent of Jyp's Magic this time, discovering too late that neither one of them had any kind of ability at all to See beyond their own noses. Now, Gareth as ready to call them to account and he had no answers.

"The weather has not been kind to scrying," Jyp improvised quickly. Edra's lie could cost them both dearly if he didn't find a way to fix things. "We've had little rain of late. When the Rivers run dry, the Magic often falters. It just means we need some more time to do as you command."

"How long?" Gareth asked. "My father has agreed to my plan to train an army. I don't want him to change his mind before I get what I want."

"If that's what's bothering you," Jyp replied evenly, "I can speak to the King on your behalf. He has allowed me private audience of late."

Gareth nodded. He had noticed how much time Jyp had been spending in the King's inner chambers. And he had also noticed that every time Jyp left, his father always seemed much stronger. As poor a Healer as Jyp claimed to be, he seemed to have some skill against Gareth's potions. He had heard the right combinations of herbs and tonics would work as countereffects against the brews he'd been using, however, so he suspected nothing beyond that. It was just one more frustration in what was becoming an avalanche in his greedy eyes. "We would be accepting of your speaking to our father for us," Gareth said. The royal "we" once again struck alarm clarions in Edra's head.

"I shall be glad to do so, My Lord." Jyp answered, bowing. "Is there anything more you want of us?"

Gareth did not notice the hint of sarcasm in Jyp's voice. "I want you, the two of you to scry something else as well. My Aunt, Arista has not yet come to the palace after making landfall here in Aberdeen. I want you to find out what happened to her."

"Do we know the woman?" Jyp asked, looking to Edra, who shrugged in denial.

Gareth pulled a locket from his pocket and thrust it at Jyp. "Here is her portrait. It's the only one I could find. She and our father have often been at odds and he did not keep many remembrances of her about the palace. You will find her for us."

Jyp studied the miniature carefully. "We will do our best, Your Highness. The city is large, searching for two may take twice as long."

"Speak to the King to earn your time," Gareth said sternly. "Whatever happens to the both of you will be up to the both of you."

Jyp wasted no time in seeking out audience with the King. His many successes at Healing had endeared him to the old man more than Gareth could ever have imagined.

"So, my fine young Sorcerer, just what do you need to tell me today?" the King said, waving off Jyp's bow and motioning to a chair beside him. Tall and leaner than he should have been Gailvarg was still a handsome man with sharp blue eyes, and a surprisingly ready smile. His hair was gray, but as he grew stronger with each of Jyp's Touches, he carried himself with elegance and an unmistakable bearing of authority quite intimidating to anyone who might not know his kinder nature.

"I've come on behalf of your son, Sire."

Gailvarg slapped his hands on his thighs and rocked back with a roar of laughter. "A Sorcerer in league with Gareth? I would have thought he would have thrown you to the tarks by now knowing what you are.' Then he looked hard at Jyp. "He does know what you are, doesn't he?"

Jyp shrugged. "Not entirely, My Lord. I have kept some secrets from him."

"You are a wise man, Sur Jyp. My son doesn't know much to start off with. I've always felt the less a fool like him knows the better."

"Harsh words about your own flesh and blood, Sire."

"If I could deny him, I would. To think I bred him often chills my very soul. How could such love between his mother and me go so wrong, I'll never understand. The Hand has a cruel touch sometimes."

"So it seems," Jyp agreed. Gareth was so different from his father it was hard to believe they were even related. But there had never been any kind of accusation or shred of evidence that the Prince's heritage was in question. Sometimes fate was a capricious mistress. "But I know you have hope for him, My Lord. Isn't that why you've indulged him in his efforts to train an army?"

"You are perceptive, Sur. The discipline of a military life might be exactly what my rash-headed boy might need. He's never had to work a day in his life. As much as I may grieve for the spell that Sorceress put upon him, as it will deny me my grandchildren, I cannot deny it had done Gareth some good. If it has helped turn his interests from bedding every woman in the kingdom to learning something about the history of battle in our kingdom, then I applaud the Magic for it." He laughed again. "To think, I am in league with Sorcerers. Once I was a warrior myself when it came to enforcing Wizardchase. Now, I wonder who the real enemies to Turan were. Did we really banish the right people after all?"

"Not all Magicians are evil, Sire."

"I have grown to learn that, lad. These gray hairs on my head have been well earned, I assure you. I've not been immune to rumors about you and your kind. Why some even say when Sagari went to

Tulene to stake his claim, there was other Magic there to help defeat him."

Jyp swallowed hard. He had heard the same thing and, having met the Lady Salene, he would not dismiss a single rumor about her. Clearly, even Gareth's disbelief had no effect on her power. Why should anyone with an ounce of sense think a Mage as powerful as Sagari could be defeated so easily by the denial of a bunch of farmers and merchants? Tulene was hardly the seat of learning in Turan. How did the people there even know what weapon to use when the Sorcerer came to demand their fealty? "As I said, not all Magicians are evil," Jyp repeated.

"Well then, as a Magician who is not evil, I suppose I should listen to you, eh? You think I should continue to encourage Gareth on this mission of his?"

"What can be the harm as long as you keep a leash on him? A well trained army could be a boon to Aberdeen. There are able-bodied men who would be happy to earn fair coin for service. As long as there is no war, a soldier's life is not so bad."

"It would keep some of the more energetic street ruffians busy. There are, I hear, some men who thrive on beating each other over the head with fists and sticks. I'm sure they'd love using swords and spears instead. What fun they'd have."

"I'd never quite considered learning to make war fun, my Lord, but there certainly do seem to be men who enjoy fighting just for the sake of it. And the countryside has never been short of mercenaries."

"My own father once rode with a troop of mercenaries to rout a hold of bandits who'd been terrorizing the merchant trains from the Norreaches. He always spoke fondly of those days. I never quite understood myself but there would be a gleam in his eye when he told me the stories. He had great respect for those men."

"I've never had the privilege of meeting a warrior myself," Jyp said. "We who practice Magic don't often need swords."

"I should think not," Gailvarg said, laughing. "When a mere woman has a weapon like--what was her name--Mistress Salene had against my son, what need had even she had of a blade? She gelded him quite effectively without one. I can't say I blame her. By the

Hand, I wish I'd been there." He made a grotesque slashing motion with the flat of his hand.

Jyp shuddered at Gailvarg's unexpected streak of cruelty regarding the Prince's misery. Perhaps father and son were more kin than it had first appeared. He resolved to be careful whenever he was around either monarch from now on. "She is most powerful. I would not want to cross her."

"Well, what's done is done. If you can't help my son, with his affliction, then I doubt anyone can. In the meantime, assure him I will support his efforts to raise his army. Perhaps it will take his mind off that other thing."

Jyp rose, bowing as he did, but Gailvarg was already consumed in reading one of the many scrolls on the desk by his window. He was humming tunelessly and didn't even look up as the Healer slipped out the door.

Jyp's head was spinning with the nagging suspicion that Healing Gailvarg's body was only half the problem. Some herbs poisoned the mind as well.

*****

When Simen had contacted Jamus through the mirror, it was Rath who first noticed him. She was always keeping an eye on the mirror whenever she was in Jamus' and Salene's chamber. "Brother of the Best One," she said as soon as she recognized him, "are you coming through the Way?"

"No, My Lady," Simen answered. "I am staying on here on the other side of the Rim. Is Jamus there? I need to talk to him."

It only took a few moments for the two Magicians to finish their discussion and as Simen's image dissolved back into Jamus' reflection, Rath stared again into the mirror herself, convinced she had seen the vaguest flicker of shadow fading with the Follyman. "You are certain that was your brother?" she asked as Jamus turned away.

"It was," Jamus assured her. "Why do you ask?"

"The Way has many dangers. As I guardian to your son, I must be watchful. You do not yet rule the Black Waters."

"I really wish you'd stop reminding me of that detail," Jamus
sighed. Salene had taken Jarien with her on an obligatory tour of the
Keep so everyone could fuss over him as was proper for babies and
their proud mothers. Rath had protested, but Jamus had woven a
Sphere of Protection around mother and child to satisfy her and
sworn it would keep them both safe. He would have gone with them,
but Salene had refused. "I've hardly been out of this room since
Jarien was born…by myself, that is. We both need to start living our
normal lives again trusting ourselves to be alone and apart now and
then. Give me this time to show off what a good mother I am without
you or Lady Rath hovering over me."

Now, alone in the room with his Dragon, Jamus was finding
it difficult to pass the time. He had a book to read and a scroll Senital
had carried up from the Vaults during one of his walks in the garden
with Ferna. He'd tried to read them both but the words keep blurring
and running into nonsense. At first, he thought it was because he was
simply too tired to concentrate, but now, after several good nights of
sleep, it was no better. He just could not read. He'd always been a
master scholar, full of curiosity ready to learn about everything.
Now, he didn't really want to know anything. "By the Blood," he
exclaimed, practically throwing the scroll across the room in
frustration, "if I didn't still think it was worth the battle for everyone
else, I'd just as soon let the Circle close and forget everything I ever
knew. I think my brain's too full to hold any more."

Rath's eyes whirled even more than usual at the
pronouncement. "Kisel would not be pleased. He waits for his
Rider."

"Well, he can damn well wait a while longer, a long while
longer then, for I'm done with it." He ran his fingers through his dark
waves of hair and dropped his head in his hands. "Do you know why
I've been hiding out here in this room for so many days? Everyone
thinks it's because I'm so besotted with my son and my wife that I
don't want to leave their sides. I'm a fraud, Madam. A fraud and a
coward. I haven't left because I'm afraid of what I have yet to do.
The Rivers mock me."

Rath shook her head and, for the first time as woman or
Dragon, tried to comfort him. "It is so with Dragons. Why do we

sleep? It is our way to run from the greatness of our purpose. We wait for the Rider to wake us and lead us to our destiny."

Jamus looked up. "The Dragons are afraid?"

"Fear is a man's word. Not wanting to do is the Scalewing's meaning. The Vows we must keep are heavy, even to our wings. Alran did not want you to fall. He had already grown to like you when he told you to fly. But it was not his duty or right to catch you if you failed. How much easier it would have been for him to sleep instead of waking when you called."

"Not wanting to do," Jamus repeated almost to himself. The phrase suited how he was feeling too perfectly. The Dragons had lived for hundreds of circles and witnessed the Closing many times. This was the only time for him.

Or was it?

"What do you know of the Way, Rath?"

"Whatever you need me to know," she replied.

Another riddle, Jamus thought. "I have seen Visions in the passages and met many who claim to be my mother."

Rath simply stared back at him, her whirling eyes steady and calm for once.

"How many times can a man be born? How many mothers can he have?"

"As many as he needs," she said.

"What if I am no more than a reflection myself? What if I am just the mirror of a man and nothing more?"

"The Way goes on to eternity," she replied. "There is no time in the Way."

"No time, no endings, no beginnings, like a circle."

"It is possible."

"And when I die?"

"Always you will be, somewhere," Rath replied, smiling ever so slightly. "You are nearly ready to seek the final tapestry, I think."

"If there is no time in the Way, then I am born always and die always. Is that what you are saying?"

"I am saying nothing," she answered. "You are doing all the talking, My Lord."

"So the story of my life has already been written? My destiny sealed? No matter what I do, it will happen as it has always happened and will always happen."

"Still you talk. Your Will commands the Rivers."

Jamus sank back into his chair, his shoulders sagging. "My Will. If I could Will it, I would be an ordinary man, perhaps," he looked over at Salene's bookcase, "perhaps a simple carpenter whose hands caress the wood to make it shine."

"Did you not like riding the winds? Did your heart not joy in the flying? When the waters rush to your bidding to bring breath back to the breathless, do you not laugh with the wonder of it? You have been tempered in the flame, like stelin, again and again, and yet you rise to fly once more. When the fire has made you strong enough, you will want to do."

"I'm tired."

"Sleep will come when you surrender. It will restore you."

"Riddles again, Mistress? I'm tired of them too."

"Kiselor is born to be born again, as many times as there are waters, as many times as there are reflections. He will fly the Rainbow into the sun after four Rivers call. Until then, you must let the waters have their way for they know where to flow."

"And the final tapestry. How do I find it?"

Rath shrugged, "It will find you."

*****

"Cuver Street" the sign read. Gambel, with Grella clinging to his side, had left Melthus behind in their hideout to go hunting. He would have preferred to be alone, but the skin he wore attracted too much attention from women no matter where he went. He was puzzled by it, unaware of how handsome he was or how his muscled chest and arms boasted of his manliness without a word. Nor did he know how the tunic he wore was even more attractive. Pale blue in color, it bore the crest of the Knights of the Hand—a great white eagle, with a bolt of white lightning in one talon and a rainbow in the other. So, unaware of why he was being noticed, he put Grella on his arm and fewer heads turned his way.

She looked older than he, just enough that she might be mistaken for his mother. Her brown hair had hints of silver and, at Meltus's orders she leaned on him to cross the uneven cobbles and let him open doors for her, always working to smile adoringly at him whenever he bent to whisper in her ear. Some even she suspected he was her lover, but most turned away when they passed, offering privacy to the couple as a sign of respect.

Gambel was seeking the remote streets of the city in hopes of finding prey. The three Shadows had decided to seek the True Life and for that, each needed the blood of a dozen Fleshers. Gambel, having done it all before, knew the need for secrecy. He was also hoping he might find a Sorcerer or two to ease his own transition along with only two or three victims depending on how strong their touch on the Rivers was. When he had heard a rumor in a local tavern about a "nest of Sorcery" in the southernmost alleys, he had pulled Grella from their bed and taken up the search.

In his last incarnation, Gambel had been called The Searcher, so named by Tamor for an unusual ability to scent out Magic wherever it might lodge. Now, though this Reflection's senses were not as keenly honed, it did have a vague memory of the skill. "I know I can find the Sorcerers," he told Grella and Melthus.

Once he'd told them of the rumors. He tapped his nose with his finger. "Their Magic stinks, you know. At least to a wise Shadow. The trouble is, in a city like this there are too many smells to sort before you can hone in on the right one. Rotting fish and gutter carrion cover the odor too well. I must get closer if I am to find it."

"So, do we roam the streets randomly in quest of sorceled prey? Tamor would not be pleased to know why we were hunting, but I supposed he would be pleased to know we are hunting."

"The Dark Lord wants to find allies, not enemies," Grella said.

"He wants an army of Fleshers to do his work," Gambel replied. "What better allies than Sorcerers cast out of Magiskeep? Why else would they be residing here when those enchanted walls beckon? You know how good it tastes to walk the clouds at will or benefit from Tamor's chantings. The small power we have now is but a drop in the River these Fleshers cherish. Why would they forsake the luxury of the Golden Keep and come here," he gestured contemptuously toward the squalid streets beyond their window, "to live in squalor like common rabble, afraid to use their power because of a King's decree?"

Melthus rubbed his chin thoughtfully. Though he was himself a reflection of common blood, his real self had often wished to be a Sorcerer, if only for a day. "Were I given the gift of the River, I would not live here. Give me rich gardens and full platters of fat cavel and fowl."

"Aye," Grella agreed. "This skin I wear is used to luxury. I would be a fool to want any less now that I wear it. Then you truly think this nest of Sorcerers is filled with rage for being denied the pleasures of Magiskeep?"

"I do," Gambel said. "They will welcome the Shadowlord's promises to give them back their kingdom when the Great Circle closes." He nodded to Grella. "You and I will hunt together. Melthus?"

"I will seek out the discontent. The poor and ignored make good foot soldiers for a price. The Dark Lord gave us purses ever full. I will use coin to lure and Blackwing's chants to snare. It will be a fine hunt for me."

They parted and now Gambel and Grella had finally made their way to Cuver Street where the Sorcerers were rumored to be.

Westportal lay far southwest of the main city. Its main focus was the race course which housed some of the finest horses in all Aberdal. Though the Course itself was a busy attraction, with many fine inns and taverns to satisfy the hoardes of fans who attended the races during the FullSeason, the surrounding streets and alleys had never benefited from the wealthy bettors and owners. Like Cuver Street to the north, the few modest homes were overshadowed by dozens more humble cottages and run down taverns which provided scant pleasure to those who worked hard for a living.

The Whispering Gardens, not far from the track and Gallops, was the only other jewel in the quarter of any note. There Jada tended the herbs and sold them to the local healers who had some reputation in Aberdeen for curing illnesses and injuries. But successful healings, even if they seemed to be accomplished by herbal remedies, always stirred rumors of sorcery and these were the rumors that led the two Shadows to The Forgetful Friend, one of Cuver's better taverns.

If Magic had a scent, the Darkness had a stench and Jada caught a whiff of it the moment Gambel and Grella reached the door of the tavern. But her full basket of fragrant herbs and a sudden breeze filled her nose almost at once and she dismissed it as nothing more than her imagination. Then, when Gambel pushed through the door behind his lady, she lost all suspicion. The visitor was a Knight of the Hand, a man she had seen many times at the Course losing his denerets on poor bets. Despite the Knight's reputation for being good horsemen, he had a terrible ability to pick a winner no matter what the odds. The old herbalist rose when she saw him and beckoned him over to her table, "Sur Dax, well met. I am surprised to see you here during the Sevenstin break in the racing. You don't usually visit without a pocket full of betting slips."

Gambel hesitated, but recovered quickly. He had chosen the body for its strength but had been under the assumption that, like the skin Grella wore, the Flesher had newly come to the city on one of the incoming ships. Now, faced with the consequences of his mistake, he had to quickly improvise. "I brought my Lady to see where I spend so many pleasant days."

"Pleasant?" one of the other patrons said laughing. "From what Mistress Jada tells us ya don't take too much pleasure when yer always losing yer money. I hopes yer Lady here don't mind havin' an empty purse now and agin."

"Don't mock 'em, Master Sim. Dax is bin a good lad an' I don't think he's e'er emptied his whole purse at the course, as bad as his luck is." She motioned to Grella to sit next to her. "Come, My Lady, sit here an' tell if iffen this big strappin' Knight's as good in the sack as he looks."

Grella felt a strange heat rushing up her neck into her face. "Do you think we are lovers?"

"If yer his Lady, like it be so," Jada replied, patting the chair seat again.

Gambel did not know what to say next, but he considered quickly remembering something he had once heard about the Knights. "I am her Protector only, Mistress Jada. She has hired me to escort her about the city."

"I'm here only for a short while," Grella said, hoping to add some credibility to Gambel's story. "I prefer not to wander about strange places by myself and Sir Dax was kind enough to offer me his services while I am in Aberdeen."

"Ah," Jada said, grinning. "A coin or three does inspire loyalty, I hear tell. I hopes ya bin payin' him what he's worth, Lady. Dax be a fine lad. Not too keen an eye for the runners, but good in the heart, I 'spect. He's always treated old Jada wid kindness an' I ain't always the kindest ya's wanna know meself."

"Thank you, Mistress," Gambel replied, bowing ever so slightly to the old woman. "I appreciate a good word from you on my behalf."

"So tell me, jest what do ya think o' our little place in the city, eh? From yer looks, Mistress, ya be from afar." Jada waited, hoping Dax might more properly introduce his companion. When he said nothing she went on. "I'm sorry, Milady, but lessen me ears been stopped up or something' I don't think I heard yer name.'"

"Grella," Grella said before Gambel's hiss of warning could stop her.

"'Tis her name for men to know when we need to use one. My Lady has come to Aberdeen for some, ah, delicate business and prefers to keep her true name secret until a more appropriate time."

Grella nodded quickly. "Ah, so. Grella was my maiden name. When I married, I took a new one. Sometimes it's most convenient to use the old one instead."

"Well, as I said afore, some sit and share a mug if ya've a mind. Yer escort's always been welcome in Cuver, so I figger you should be welcome too."

Gambel pulled out the chair for Grella and as she sat, he decided that even if they had not yet found any Sorcerers, at least he had learned some valuable information, and better yet, a potential ally.

*****

Jamus tossed and turned restlessly in the bed, jolting Salene awake. She reached out shaking his arm. "My love," she whispered. "are you all right? Is it another dream?"

He did not wake, but muttered something under his breath and rolled away from her onto his side.

Salene sighed, checked to see that Jarien was still sound asleep, and closed her eyes.

Jamus sighed in his sleep and clutched at the edge of the blanket.

The wind was rising, roiling the River's waters into heaving waves.

He raised his hand and the waters stilled, obedient to his command. But the wind rushed on, refusing to surrender. It was a dark storm, driven by forces beyond his ken and then he realized it was the beating of black wings overhead.

Dragon, he thought, and he ducked, almost without thinking as a great, dark form landed in front of him.

Darker than the darkest darkness. Blacker than black, the creature's eyes looked to be empty bottomless chasms opening into oblivion itself.

"Everending ever be, seek ye so to master me? Fool is ever seeking light, when the truth lies in the night."

"What do you want, Kesel?" Jamus asked, careful to use the Dragon's name, aware of the power it gave him.

"Name is nothing when you die."

"And will your name be nothing when you die, Blackwing? Will the world forget you too?"

"Dragon is immortal."

"That's not what I've heard. Men have killed Dragons before."

"Not of my clan. My brothers and sister own eternity. As long as our Waters run, so shall we."

"If I Master all the Waters, I will do as I wish with the Dragons, " Jamus said. "It is the prophecy of the Eld."

"Pah! Men's words, not Dragon's. In the Circles before, the Twoleg thought they knew the secret of the Dragon. May be they

were close to knowing, but when the Circles closed, the knowing was gone and the Scalewing ruled the knowing again. The Shadows will win against your light, Sorcerer, and again the almost knowing will be lost."

"I will win in the end," Jamus said. "I haven't come this far to do any less."

"Fool now, fool then, ever be fool." Kesel crouched and spit out a stream of black flame.

Jamus fell to his knees under the steaming onslaught as the Black Dragon laughed and then soared back into the clouds.

Jamus rolled over, the blanket soaked with sweat as he moaned, his body consumed by a raging fever.

VI

Simen and Kala had made such good time on the journey to Aberdeen that they needed to waste at least twelve winds before making their way to the King.

"We could visit some friends," Kala suggested.

"No one would be expecting us. Isn't it rude to just drop in on people like that?"

Kala laughed. "You may be wise in the way of many things, Simen, but I was not named Prime Juris of the Provinces without some special knowledge of my own. Tradition and the King's Law demands I be welcomed no matter whose house it is. Besides, these are my friends, and I have a feeling as soon as they see you they will be yours as well."

"Someone Jamus knows then?" Simen asked.

"The farm is about a span's ride to the north," she said. "I can't describe the road well enough for you to lift us there, so we'll have to try to enjoy the pleasure of each other's company for the time instead."

"I assure you, My Lady," Simen replied offering a little bow from the saddle, "the pleasure will be all mine."

Kala wagged her finger at him, "Don't flirt with me, Sur Follyman. I'm not one of your tavern conquests to fall at you feet in adoration of your golden voice. Besides, we've known each other too long for any kind of pretense. Now, tell me why you really wanted to come with me to Aberdeen."

"To be honest?" Simen asked, and when Kala nodded, he shrugged. "I did want to keep you company, and frankly, I didn't like the idea of your riding all unprotected, even if I know full well you're perfectly capable of taking care of yourself. But there was a more selfish motive. I've never been to Aberdeen and I wanted to see this King who could have spawned a rimsnake like Gareth."

Kala shook her head. "There's something more beneath even that reason, my friend."

"I'm not sure myself," Simen replied, "but ever since you showed up at Delran's something's been knocking at the back of my brain telling me there was something I needed to find out for Jamus' sake. It's almost as if the River were trying to tell me something. Do you think some of Jamus' kinship with your River may have rubbed off on me despite my every effort to be my own man instead of his reflection?"

"After what happened in Grandisite, nothing involving Jamus and his powers in my River or any River would surprise me. But a premonition? It is a Seer's skill some practice, I know, but not something I'd expect from you."

"Why? I was born of Jamus' imagination one day when he looked in a mirror. The way he told me, I was born from his desire to be happy in a world that denied him happiness. Don't you think the Hand may have somehow fated me to protect that dream in his life?"

"So you feel there's something in Aberdeen to threaten his happiness now?" Kala asked. "I would hate to think that myself."

"You've seen him smile when he holds that son of his. That baby and Salene are his whole world right now. And yet, he knows it won't last forever, as much as he wants it to. The Rivers make demands even their Master cannot deny."

"So no happy endings for him," Kala said, turning Silk up a new trail into the foothills of the Norreach Mountains.

"Not yet," Simen answered, "but maybe someday. I just keep feeling I have a part in the end of all this, as if I had been born for him, not just because of him. He gave me my life and I owe something in return."

"You've already done so much for him, Simen."

"The River still has plans for my brother and if he needs me, I intend to do whatever I can to help him."

Kala smiled, "Jamus has a way of inspiring loyalty from everyone who gets to know him. Dale and I feel the same way about him."

Simen grinned. "I was wondering when the conversation might come back around to Lord Dale. Are you two really too busy to get married, or are you both still trying to find excuses not to?"

"A little of both, I think. Every time we start to talk about it, something like this summons to Aberdeen comes between us. I'm not ready to give up my duties as Juris, even for his sake, and he's not ready to leave Tulene until the city is truly recovered." She sighed. "Sometimes I wish we both could just forget about everyone else and live our own lives locked away in some private hold somewhere."

"Like Jamus and Salene?" Simen asked. "The two of them have hardly spent any time out of their rooms since Jarien was born. Oh, they go out for rides once in a while, and occasionally a walk in the garden, but it's as if the walls are a fortress from the world and they want to stay locked inside."

"It's been just over a month since the baby was born. That's not so long to spend adoring him."

Simen nudged Magwin over to avoid a boulder blocking the main trail. "I think it's more than that, Kala. Frankly, I think they're both hiding. Jamus from the River and Salene from her fear of losing him to the River."

"They deserve more. So much more," Kala said. She steered Silk up one more narrow trail and pointed, "Just around the bend, up there, we're going to see a meadow. These mountain passes are deceiving. Beyond, the land flattens out again. If ever someone wanted a hideaway, this is the place."

They passed the last hill and Simen gasped at the beautiful view before them. The grass meadow stretched out before them like an beautiful green carpet. A half span from the trail's end, a line of rustic wooden fencing enclosed several acres. Magwin nickered and soon a little herd of long legged horses galloped over the gentle hill to greet them. Mostly bays and chestnuts the horses were lean and elegant, their coats shining in the Sowin's sun. "By the Hand, they are gorgeous. Runners, I take it from the looks of them? They remind me of Windstalker and the other two Jamus brought back to the Keep after his honeymoon."

"They're bred to race," Kala said. "I'm sure Jamus told you about Talia and Erlik."

"Of course, of course, I should have known." Simen remembered well Jamus' telling him the story of the young horse trainer from Wesportal and the young Silver Sorcerer he'd shared a prison cell with on FarIsle. They'd had a tumultuous adventure in Aberdal with, as it seemed a happy ending for everyone, except perhaps the Prince of Aberdeen. "Jamus said he hoped he'd assured Erlik his safety from Gareth's wrath by making himself the enemy. This looks like the perfect haven to assure it."

Magwin arched his neck and began to prance as they rode along the fence line towards the stables beyond. Simen patted the black stallion's neck and laughed at his antics. For at least these moments, the nagging unease in his mind dissolved in the sheer pleasure of the day and the beauty of the land.

The stable was sturdily built of ironwood logs. The ceiling was high with broad beams and the wide center aisle was lined with large box stalls on both sides. A young stablegirl greeted them, ready to take their mounts almost as if she had been expecting them. "The Master saw you cross the hilltop and said to expect company," she said, confirming Simen's suspicions at her welcome. "These are fine horses. I will take care of them for you. Skyland takes pride in our horses and will treat yours as our own. The Mistress and her Lord are up at the house waiting for your visit."

She took the Magwin's reins and led him to one of the well bedded stalls. Another girl mysteriously appears from the side and took Silk from Kala. "Can they be stabled next to each other, My Lord? We can keep the stallion isolated if need be."

"Magwin will mind his manners," Simen told her. "He likes to show off, but he's used to being stabled with mares and geldings. He's been well trained by master horsemen and knows his place."

"We'll keep him here at the end and put your mare in the stall next to him since he already knows her. Don't worry, though. We'll keep an eye on them, in case there's some fuss. They're in a strange place to they might bear watching."

But, as soon as he was unsaddled and given a quick rubdown, Magwin buried his nose in the manger of hay and hardly moved once he started eating.

Satisfied to see their mounts settled, Kala and Simen followed the gravel path up to the house's wide covered porch. A man and woman waited for them.

"In the name of all Turan, I greet you, Mistress Talia. It's been a long time."

"Madam Juris," Talia said, raising her hand in formal greeting. "I am pleased to see you in less arduous circumstances, As I recall, the last time we met was at a formal hearing disputing the ownership of one of the horses under my care." She paused, staring hard at Simen. "Your escort, My Lady. He looks…"

"Almost exactly like Lord Jamus," Erlik finished for her. "I hope this is his brother, Simen? Or am I mistaken?"

"I am," Simen replied extending his hand. "I'm a bit surprised you know."

"How could I not? When you're locked in shackles with another man on a ship for days, conversation is the only way to pass the time so you don't lose your mind. Jamus told me all about you. He bragged a lot about your Follyman skills and told me you were one of the finest men he'd ever known." He nodded to Kala. "Though we've never met, Jur Kala, I almost feel I know you too. Lord Jamus spoke fondly of you as well. He's a lucky Mage to have such a good ally in Turan."

Kala's heart lurched to hear that Jamus had spoken of her. What other secrets had the two men shared in their captivity? "It's good to know I'm well thought of. We came to ask for your hospitality for a few days. We're on the way to Aberdeen at the King's command. Magic brought us more quickly than expected so we need a place to rest for a bit before going into the city."

"While I am obligated by the honor of Turan to welcome you to my house," Talia said, "I would rather the two of you accept my invitation to stay on as friends. That way we can get rid of all the formal pretensions and enjoy some time together."

Simen laughed. "Jamus said you were a special woman. Now I see why."

"I've never been afraid to speak my mind, Sur. Come on inside. We have a cool pitcher of fresh calidew and some bread and cheese. I can have some fruit sent out, if you want it."

"Bread and cheese sound just fine to me," Kala said. "I like to skip the formal pretensions myself whenever I can. High language and Court manners have their place, but not in a place as beautiful as this. And your horses—they are simply breathtaking."

"Not good mounts for a ride like we've just had," Simen said, rubbing his back. "There finer boned that most of the stock in Magiskeep. Except for Windstalker, that is."

"How is he?" Talia asked. "Once I got to know Jamus I was really happy he'd bought that stallion, but I must admit, I do miss seeing him run. He was fast and determined."

"Josep, Jamus' horsemaster loves the horse. Jamus has been crossbreeding him with some of his draft mares and he's bred some really nice horses. I just imported a half dozen to Lord Delran's Keep in Telma Province."

"I've heard about those animals," Talia said. "Delran's reputation is growing in Aberdeen. Several of the better stables have bought teams from him. I saw a carriage drawn by some at the Course just last Sevenstin. They were powerful creatures but finer boned than most drays. So that's the kind of Sire Windy has become, eh? I was wondering why the team looked so familiar. Something about their heads, I think."

"They do resemble their father in looks and their dams in strength."

"We have a horse or two here Lord Jamus might like to add to his herd," Erlik said. "If you're interested we can look at them tomorrow. There are no races at Wesportal until next month, so our whole stable is here for the break."

"I'd love to see them," Simen replied. He settled himself in one of the cushioned chairs in the sitting room across from Kala and Talia, who were sharing the sofa. "I'm not quite the judge of horseflesh my brother is, but if you have stock to sell, I can certainly act on his behalf. I can at least recognize a good set of legs." He grinned over at Kala, who was wearing her tight traveling breeches, and Talia, who was dressed nearly the same.

"Put your eyes back where they belong, Master Simen."
Kala warned. "Talia and I are both Ladies and neither one of us
wants to be the victim of one of your Follyman jokes.

"I was talking about horses's legs," Simen protested, not
even bothering to hide his grin. "But I must admit, now that you
mention it, you do both look good in breeches."

"Perhaps, My Lady," Talia said sweetly, "we should have
stuck to formal pretensions after all. Master Simen seems a bit too
casual, don't you think?"

When Simen saw Erlik cover his mouth to hide his laughter,
he got to his feet, offered an awkward imitation of a formal bow and
said, "My apologies, My Dear Ladies. A Follyman is not often
known for his manners, but he is always known for his honesty. If I
have offended you with my compliment, I am most sorry."

This time, both Kala and Talia burst out laughing at his
antics. "You almost look like Gareth's Master Corm with that
fawning countenance, Simen." Kala said. "Are you sure you've
never been in the Court to be able to mimic him so well?"

"Let's just say I am a keen observer of people and seen
enough formal pretensions to know exactly how to mock them."

"Follyman's Art?" Erlik asked.

Simen nodded. "Some call it art, some call it a fool's
mission. Either way, it's a good basis for humor when man needs a
laugh. You do have to be careful of who's in the audience, though.
Usually those you mock don't find the jokes very funny."

*****

"What are we going to do?" Edra whined. "The time Gareth
gave us in almost up, and you still haven't found a scryer?"

"Come Weswin, and we'll take a little trip to Wesportal,"
Jyp said. I've contacted someone there who can help us. Actually,
she may have already found at least half of our quest."

"Which half?"

"The warrior. My friend says there's a Knight of the Hand
who might be for hire."

"A Knight. Would he help the Prince?"

"For money, most of the Knights I've heard of would do most anything. Since the order has fallen out of Power many have become mercenaries. This one still wears his tunic, so he still has some loyalty to the old crown. Gailvarg may have denied the Knights, but he never banished them."

"I've never seen one since I've been here," Edra said.

"Chillmonth Dawn brings a gathering of sorts. Last circle a squadron of about a hundred marched in Aberdeen Square to honor the coming snows. Their Keep was way up in the Norreach Mountains, spans from here. Not much is known about it, but from the looks of the way they marched and handled their weapons, they seem to be well-trained, even now. The Elden Tales say they were once fierce warriors defending the Law of the Hand long before the First Kings brought peace to the Provinces."

"How did they feel about the Magic? Where they involved in Wizardchase?"

"Wizardchase happened long before they fell out of favor, but again there are stories. Some say they supported the Sorcerers. Adoration of the Hand and Magic may well have had some kinship back then. Once the Sorcerers were driven out of mortal Turan, the Knights retreated to the mountains for the most part. They only marched in force when there was a rebellion against the RightKings. Now, with Gailvarg's peace, we hardly ever hear a thing, except for those who've taken up the mercenary life."

"Like this one we're going to meet?"

"My friend tells me his name is Dax and he's quite an imposing figure. We'll have to be cautious dealing with him. I don't want either one of us to have to Heal any sword wounds."

Edra shivered. He'd felt the blade twice when Jamus had bested him in Arcula and he still bore the scars on his chest as a reminder. And then he looked down at the stump of his left hand and shuddered. "I'll follow your lead, Jyp. You've been in Aberdeen longer than I have and know the manners of the city."

"Good," Jyp replied. "Some of my friends can be a bit strange at times, so don't be too surprised at their behavior. They are wary of strangers."

"Sorcerers too?" Edra asked.

Jyp shrugged. "Some claim so, and a few touch the waters. Nothing like mages from Magiskeep, though. No need to worry," he lied. He himself had studied in the Keep for seasons and some of the other residents of Cuver were Keep trained as well. Jada herself had walked those chanted halls circles well passed and had mastered four arts before leaving to seek adventure and a new life in Aberdal.

Something about being near the Sea had fascinated her and when Jamus had called the great SeaLord to bring Rafe safely back from his voyage, she'd never stopped talking about it. Some of the others who's witnessed Jamus' Magic were just as inspired, as if they had a special connection with the ocean none of them could quite explain. Had Edra been any other Sorcerer, Jyp would have told him that story too, but he kept it to himself, knowing his associate was far too ready to share every bit of information about the Magic with the Prince. Better to toss out just enough information to satisfy him if someone used Magic in front of him in Cuver, but no more.

He wouldn't normally have worried, but they were meeting Dax in a tavern, and every now and then someone drank a bit too much ale and forgot themselves.

The Seven Tables was one of the finer taverns in Wesportal, catering to the racing clientele during the day and the locals at night when the tourist crowds had left. Although its inn rooms were clean and pleasant, they were not as luxurious as most of the racing crowd preferred, leaving the tables bare of strangers most every Sowin change. That was exactly how Salli and the rest of Cuver's residents liked it. After dark she would lock the front door, pull the curtain to discourage unwanted visitors, and welcome members of the Counsel to sit, share a few pints and freely talk about anything they chose.

This night, she had warned everyone that Jyp was coming along with an outworlder friend, who, although he too plied the Magic, was not exactly the trustworthy sort. "He caters to the Prince," she told them, "and we well know anyone with such poor taste needs to be handled with care. The less he knows about us, the better."

"So why's Jyp bringin'im here?" Siton, one of the more outspoken Counselors asked. Here to sit as an advisor rather than a leader of the community, he often took it upon himself to ask the important questions before anyone else did.

"They need the Knight," Jada said. "I'm not sure I trust him either, or that so-called Lady of his, but I'd rather have him under Jyp's watch than wandering freely about the streets of Aberdeen."

"He's bin in Wesportal a fair piece," Siton said. "Never done nothin' bad I'se heard of. Somethin' ya know bouts 'im ya need to share, Mistress?"

Jada tapped her nose with her skinny finger. "Just a whiff of trouble methinks. Something's a bit off about him."

"You smelled Shadow?" Sim asked, leaning over his mug to meet her gaze directly. Touched himself by a little of the Sight, he hoped to read her mind.

"I'm not sure," Jada told him honestly, not bothering to put up a ward against his Search. "Some say Shadows wearing mortal bodies can hide from the Truth. I've ne'er experienced it myself, but it's always in my mind. We all know the River's been restless over the last seasons and just yesterday, I felt a new unrest in the waters."

Siton nodded. "They be roiling again, fer shure.... It's most like there be a storm rising in'em."

"The Rivermaster?" Salli asked.

"It's possible. With Lord Jamus anything is possible," Jada said.

"Why?" Ever since Jamus had brought her husband home from the sea she felt a certain affection for Jamus and often wondered how he and his wife were doing with the new baby. Now, she was worried that the River's unrest reflected some new misery in his life. "Do you think Lord Jamus is all right? He's a fine man, a fine man."

"So he is, and a powerful one too. Whenever the River cries, I have to think it's to his call." She closed her eyes and repeated a prophecy she had given Jamus when he'd first visited her in the garden,

> *"Warm and cold do flow as one*
> *Though Truth of two is known by none.*
> *One of none in the Darkness lies*
> *One of all describes the Skies.*

Only One in Mastery
Shall Lord be called
Of Land and Sea."

"The true Rivermaster," someone whispered in the too silent room.

"And Master of the Sea," another voice said from the bar. "If that prophecy is true then the Eldenlore warns us the End of the Great Circle may well be at hand. If that's so, then Jada is well right to warn us of Shadows in our midst."

"Some say the land will be covered in Shadow on the Day of Reckoning. I always thought it meant the clouds of darkness masking the sun, but maybe it means the Shadows themselves."

"Ain't held much ta prophesies much meself," Siton said. "Too much jibberish ta figger out. Always thought the Truth oughta be plain in yer face steada hiding behind words and rhymes, ya know? Makes it too easy fer them what stands ta gain to make up all kinds o' meanins jest to suit 'em."

"Siton's right like he mostly is," another patron agreed, "but fact is, I was here when Lord Jamus called up the SeaDragon, an' it t'were an awful thing ta see, I must say. Don't know what the rest o' that prophecy means but the last part sure is true."

"The rest is a riddle," Jada said. "Yet seeing that Dragon myself convinced me Lord Jamus is the true Kiselor, and if that's so, there are no riddles about in the Lore. The promise is crystal clear. Once Kiselor walks the earth men must prepare for the Great Battle against the Black Dragon and his army."

"The Shadows," Sim said. "Even I know that. So you think this Dax might be allied with them?"

"If he's not, introducing him to the Prince will do no harm, and if he is, then it will be up to Jyp to keep an eye on him."

"Is Jyp that good?"

"He's too modest to admit to more than four arts, Sim, but when he was in Magiskeep he was as close to being a Seven Arts Mage as this," she pinched her thumb and index finger almost together. "You'd be surprised at how good he is."

"He's just a lad."

"When he pretends to be," Jada replied, smiling. "He's at least as old as I am and in wisdom? Ten times more. We can trust him with our lives."

"I pray to the River we won't have to," Salli said, wiping off one of the tables and laying out a setting for four. It was the Eighth Table, the one reserved for special guests. While the other seven tables after which the Inn had been named represented the Seven Arts, this one represented nothing.

Nothing at all.

*****

Salene woke, brushed up against Jamus and cried out. The heat from his skin burned against her. Instinctively she reached out her hand to Touch him, calling to the River for a Healing.

There was no reply, only darkness.

She panicked, then took a deep breath, trying to calm back down. The River would not answer such emotion. She needed reason, the quiet practice of the Sixth Art. But it was impossible. Her heart was pounding, her own skin fired with his pain as he moaned under her hand. "I can't, I can't," she sobbed, despite every effort to take control. "I love you too much."

She got out of the bed, composed just enough to realize the illness might be dangerous to their son. She snatched Jarien out of the crib and ran to the door, holding him tight against her breast.

Once in the hall she cried out, "Someone, please, please get Sarena now! Lord Jamus is sick and needs her Touch!"

One of the servants dropped her cleaning rag and ran down the hall to the stairs, heading for the Prentice classrooms. Lila, one of the other maids, hurried over to Salene. "My Lady, Mistress Sarena will be here in a moment. Why don't you come over and sit down while we wait? You're all out of breath."

Salene shook her head, absently rocking the baby in her arms. "I can't, Lila. I'm too upset. Where is the Mistress? He's burning up with fever."

"The Mistress will Heal him," Lila said putting her arm around Salene's shaking shoulders.

"I couldn't," Salene sighed heavily. "I tried, I couldn't."

"They say sometimes the heart gets in the way of the Magic," Lila told her. She'd lived in the Keep long enough to understand something of the Power even though she had none of her own.

Salene gulped and nodded, her breathing steadying a little.

Just then, Sarena came running to them, "Salene, what's wrong?"

"Jamus, he's sick. Fever. He's burning up, Sarena. I've never felt anything like it. I tried to Touch, but I was so frightened the Waters would not listen. You have to do something. You don't love him like I do."

Sarena patted Salene's arm reassuringly. "Lila, please escort the Lady and her son to my private chambers."

"I want to stay here," Salene protested.

"No," Sarena replied firmly. "You've already admitted there was nothing you could do and Bless the Hand, if Jamus' illness is contagious, you and Jarien would be better off in my rooms than here. I promise, as soon as he's Healed I'll send word. Until then try to have some patience and trust in my Skill. Now go along with Lila."

Reluctantly, Salene let Lila lead her down the hall and as soon as she was gone, Sarena opened the door and went into the room.

Jamus lay in a tangle of bedclothes, his head flopping back and forth on the pillow as if he were trying to shake off the pain wracking his body. Sarena set her ward against his Magic, and hurried over, steeling her mind as she called to the River, and finally, Touched his brow.

Darkness. Nothing. No flow of Gold to her fingers. Emptiness.

She started back, breathing heavily. She focused her mind, calming her thoughts to the cold, logical reason of her Art, vividly Willing Jamus' blood to cool in his veins, his heart to slow, every nerve in his body to quiet and deny the pain. She reached out and Touched him again.

Darkness. Nothing. No flow of Gold to her fingers. Emptiness.

Caught now in her own despair, she moved away, staring at her patient, trying to find an answer.

A gust of wind beat at the window as Rath returned from her Norwin hunt. Before she could even alight, Sarena called to her, "Lady Rath, Jamus is fevered. My River will not answer. Please, call yours before he burns up."

Not yet full transformed the half Dragon scampered over to the bed. She took one look at Jamus with her whirling eyes and reached out a scaly paw to touch him. Her claw raked back an errant lock of dark hair from his forehead. His breathing eased just a little and his body relaxed, but the heat persisted.

"Cannot heal," Rath said, still speaking with her Dragon tongue. "Pain go a little, but not all. Too sick."

"What is it? Do you know what's wrong?"

"Blackfire."

"Blackfire, what's that?"

"Darkness."

"Can't your cure him? One of your brothers?"

Rath shook her head, her body slowly softening back to full womanhood. "Pain comes from inside, not out. We can do nothing."

"Who then?"

"Kiselor must cure himself."

Sarena grabbed Rath's arm and pulled her around to face her. "You know that's impossible. Even the Rivermaster doesn't have that kind of power. Tell me what are we to do?"

"As I said, he must do."

Sarena took a deep breath, trying to understand. What Rath was saying made no sense. "You have to explain this to me, Rath. I am not learned in the Ways of the Dragon. I need to understand. I can't just leave him like this. What if he dies?"

"One day he will die," Rath replied. "It will be his choice. This time, though, I do not think he will. Yet is is all up to him. We must not leave him alone. He needs a watcher."

"You and I can stay."

"No, he needs someone with deep love by his side. Someone to hold him to this world."

"Salene?"

Rath shook her head. "We cannot risk her or the little one. Blackfire denies a master and feeds on the helpless. Were Jamus not so strong in the River, he would be dead by now. He needs someone by his side who cares for him as much as Salene does."

Sarena thought for a moment. Kala, Simen—but they were far away, across the Rim. There was always the Way of Mirrors, but even that might take more time than they had. Who loved him so much? Suddenly she realized there was someone. "Becca," she said. "She's almost been his mother."

Rath nodded now. "Good woman. Strong in love. Strong in will too. Send for her. In the meantime I will do my best to ease his pain. Then it will be all up to him."

"Will he know how?" Sarena asked hurrying to the door to call for a messenger.

"He will know," Rath replied, stroking Jamus' cheek with her delicate fingers. "All he needs to do is solve the riddle."

Becca arrived before Sowin's change, hustled into the room by Jeamel, who had taken it upon himself to fetch her when he heard Sarena's call. "I brung my one love," he said to Rath as he hustled his wife along.

Rath smiled, pleased to know Becca had told her husband all about their conversation. It was good to know the two shared so much for it was a measure of love. And, according to her, Jamus' life depended on love. "It is good. The Lord of the Keep needs the comfort of her heart. I am pleased her One Love is willing to share it."

"Bory, MiLady, iffen Master Jamus needs augt from either one of us, he'd get it. We both knowed him since he was a little lad and think on 'im as a son. Besides, Becca's got the biggest heart in all the Keep. I'm right shure she's got more than enow to share."

Becca was already at Jamus side, her hand on his forehead. "He' so hot," she said. "Ya say ya tried ta Heal 'im?"

"We did, Mistress," Rath said. "Lady Salene and I have done all we can. The rest is up to him."

"An why be I here?" Becca asked.

"To watch over him. He has a hard journey to make on his own and he needs an anchor to find his way back to shore."

"He's gonna be at sea?"

"In a manner of speaking, Mistress Becca. It was a...a manner of speaking." Rath explained awkwardly. This human language often evaded her with all its nuances. She much preferred the plain and simple tongue of her people. Always the Dragon spoke only the essence of things. She tried again. "The Rivermaster must solve a riddle hidden somewhere in a tapestry of Magic. I could try to explain more of it, if you wish. Do you know anything of the Way of Mirrors?"

Becca made the sign of warding against evil, running her thumb along her cheek. "A dangerous place, Milady. Some say men go mad there. I gots me a mirror in me cottage gifted by the Lord here an' I keep it covered whener'er there be rumor of danger. I already near got killed by one Sorcerer from it, so's I know ta be careful."

"When a Magician crosses into the Way, he needs to know where he has come from even more than he needs to know where he is going. When Jamus takes this journey, he needs to be able to find his way back home. You must be his home, Becca—his anchor."

"And jest how am I s'posed to do that, eh? Hold 'is hand?"

"Love him as you do. Be here. Call his name if you think he is gone. Call with your heart if you must, but call. He will need to know where to find you."

Becca frowned. "I'll do as ya say, Milady, but in the meanwhile, I hopes some good common nursin'll do some good too. Do ya think ya can git someone ta fetch me a pitcher o' cool water an' some towels?"

Sarena, who had been standing quietly by the whole time, leaving Rath to explain things she herself did not understand. "Just a pitcher, Becca?"

"A coolin' bath'd do the lad good," Becca said. "But it'd take more'n ol' Becca her ta plop him in a tub. He's growed a mite since I usta be able ta pick 'im up inta me lap."

"Rath and I could help," Sarena replied, looking to the Silver Woman for her assent. Rath nodded, and she went on, "I'll need to hold on to someone's hand myself, though. Lord Jamus has always had a rather peculiar effect on me."

"Ya needs an anchor ta tech him?" Becca asked.

"Exactly," Sarena replied. "Come on then, let's get that bath going." She gestured once, conjuring a copper bathtub filled with cool water in the center of the room. Then the three woman stripped off Jamus' damp sleeping gown and lifted him gently into the bath.

The waters closed around him, whispering his name. For the first time since the fever had struck, Jamus' mind cleared as the soft, cool currents eased his pain. His head stopped pounding and his heart began to beat a steady rhythm again.

He longed to sink beneath the surface to surrender to the water's caress, but strong hands kept pulling him up. He struggled against them in vain for the sickness had left his body too weak and his Will too fragile.

Why wouldn't they let him go? The River was calling him home, wrapping him in an irresistible embrace. It would be so easy, so quiet to just drown in the flow to let the Waters carry him wherever they wanted.

"You be Kiselor," a voice sounded in his head. "River does not command you. You command River. Let be. For now, it is enough."

He broke from the trance, his eyes meeting Becca's. "That feels good," he mumbled hoarsely. "Good."

"So, you've come back to us," Salene said, pulling her hand away before his Power took hold again. "Are you planning to stay?"

"If I can," he said. "If I can." Then he closed his eyes again and the women pulled him out of the tub and put him back to bed.

*****

They needed horses to ride to the Norreaches to meet the Dragon. Tamor wanted good mounts, with speed and stamina. They also needed some courage as he would lift their strides once they left the more civilized lands of Turan. Until then they would have to depend on grounded gaits and mortal travel.

The stables near Mudlake were full of shaggy mountain ponies and draft beasts, none fast enough for the journey. There were horses in the Keep for certain and it was only a wind away even on the backs of ponies.

Tamor laughed at the notion of stealing two of Jamus' precious animals to take Natale and him to Blackwing's Lair set his plan in motion. It was a pleasing thought.

He offered the stablemaster a full purse of gold for two of his best mounts, but when he went into the barn to select them, the ponies would have none of it. Scenting Shadow, they screamed and plunged so wildly in their stalls no one could get near them. He finally had to settle on two old drays too lame with ringbone to bother much with fussing. The horses switched their tails in obvious displeasure with their new master, but circles of hard work had made them docile and insensitive to so much of the world, even the Shadows did not did not keep them from letting them ride.

It took them nearly three winds to reach the Keep's northern borders. There, they camped until dark before Tamor took to the clouds to search for the horses he wanted. As luck would have it, there was a good sized herd in the first pasture he found. He stepped down into the midst of them, pleased to find his Shadow form did not seem to bother these animals. Well used to Magic, its color did not matter to them. They would make good mounts. Sorra's body was not a good rider, so she needed a docile mare or better yet, a gelding. He spotted a small bay at the edge of the herd, standing a bit to the side as if he was too shy to challenge the hierarchy. Such creatures were usually quiet and cooperative under saddle, so he was the first Tamor chose. A long-legged chestnut caught his eye as it vied with a large black mare for a particularly tasty spot of grass and Tamor decided he would take that horse for himself.

All he needed to do was capture the ones he wanted and then break the fence so the others would escape. That way, no one in the Keep would be any the wiser if a horse or two had strayed away during the night trough the broken rails. Tamor walked over to the chestnut and bent over to see whether he had picked a mare or gelding when the night burst forth in blinding silver light.

The Dark Lord bolted upright to find himself face to face with a huge silver stallion, challenging his presence. "Damn you, Sorcerer's horse. I've seen you before. You think you'll keep me away from your herd, do you?"

Whim snorted, tossed his head and stamped his hoof into the ground.

"Then we'll see how you like the taste of my Magic," Tamor spit, raising his hand to loose a bolt of Blackfire.

The split second before it hit, Whim vanished in a swirl of silver only to appear again, charging at Tamor's right side.

The Dark Lord spun, raising his hand again, but the stallion disappeared and now charged him from behind.

The two danced the deadly game over and over, Tamor spinning into Shadow if the horse got too close and Whim spinning into silver to press the attack from a new direction. It soon became all too clear to Tamor that the horse had the advantage. Not only was he quicker on his feet, but he seemed to be able to anticipate the Dark Master's every move as soon as he thought it.

Gasping for air despite his powers, Tamor soon had to admit defeat and he leapt into the sky to step across the clouds and escape the furious stallion.

When he landed back next to Sorra and their poor mounts, she reached out to grab his arm as he staggered and nearly fell. "My Lord, are you all right? Where are the horses? You said you'd bring them."

"I ran into some unexpected opposition," Tamor growled, shaking off her hand. 'We'll just have to ride these."

He rubbed his clawlike fingers over the legs of the two drays, using his limited skill at Compassion to Heal them enough to they might offer a canter now and then instead of just an unsteady walk or shuffling trot. They had accepted some lifting of stride, but the going south to the Keep proper had been hard going and heading back north to the mountains would be even worse. Never having traveled there by land, Tamor did not know any of the trails. Lifting strides needed knowledge and he had none. He wouldn't have cared if he were by himself, but accidentally landing in a canyon or toppling off the edge of a cliff due to a mistaken stride would surely kill Sorra's borrowed body and he would have to start all over again with a new one. Better to try his patience and take the time to do it safely than risk her.

Curse the Fleshers anyhow. He never did understand why they clung to life so desperately. He hardly remembered the True Life he had first owned hundreds of circles before. He knew he'd had a mother and father, but there was no memory of love from either and no tender promises echoed even in the remotest part of his brain. Fleshers seemed to cherish families, and he had often heard them talk of the overpowering treasure of a parent's love for children. While he had never known it, now it was his total inspiration. It was the very reason he needed Sorra.

"My Lord, you are being very quiet," Sorra said, interrupting Tamor's reverie. "Have I displeased you somehow?"

"Not yet," he replied. "Our beddings have been satisfying and despite the fact that you are rather dull, you have learned what I have taught you."

"My body is yours to do with as you will," she said, once more trying out a smile and her skills at flirting. "I ache to think of the two of us under the blankets. You are a good lover."

"Lover?" he spat. "Do you think that's why I use you? You are but a vessel to ease my lust when my body needs release. It is not love between us, merely my need."

"I am at your service, My Lord."

"You'll need to temper your sex when you go to Magiskeep, Madam, so enjoy my use of you while you can."

"You haven't told me what you want me to do in the Keep. Why am I so important to you?"

"Suffice it to say you will play a significant role in the defeat of the Rivermaster, Mistress. You will have your revenge on Lord Jamus, and I will lead the Black Dragon's army to victory in ending the Great Circle."

Sorra pulled her cape around her body as the mountain winds picked up. "It will be both and honor and a pleasure, then," she said. "But, My Lord, I would ask one small favor in return for my service."

"What?" Tamor asked brusquely, annoyed by her boldness.

"I would like, My Lord, to drink Kiselor's blood."

Tamor threw back his head and laughed.

Then they spurred their horses on, up into the mountain passes.

VII

The tavern grew silent when Gambel and Grella came in. For a moment everyone simply stared at them, but Salli quickly showed them to the vacant table and soon conversation resumed as if nothing unusual had happened.

"Ale for you and the Lady, Sir Dax?" Salli asked.

"Fine, fine," Gambel answered, hardly noticing Salli's use of his name. "I am expected someone."

"I know, My Lord," Salli answered. "Mistress Jada, over there, was the one who arranged the meeting for you. It's her friend who's coming to meet you. She asked me to show you every hospitality. We've a fine joint of lamb tonight if you'd care for a bite to eat."

"I'm not hungry for lamb," Gambel said.

"Mistress?" Salli asked, looking at Grella who was still taking in the other people in the room. The hair on the nape of her neck was prickling as if there were Magic somewhere, but she could not pinpoint it.

"Oh," Grella answered, "a serving of meat would be fine, if you have some rare."

"Aye, indeed I do," Salli said, filling their mugs with frothy ale. "My cook always sears the meat to order. I'll tell her to keep the blood on yours if you'd like." When Grella nodded, she turned back to Gambel. "Are you sure you won't have a plate too?"

"Rare," Gambel grunted, taking a sip of the ale. It fizzed on his tongue, another new experience of this Flesher skin and one he decided he really liked. Perhaps there was something to more to this longing for True Life than he'd realized. The body was beginning to please him and he decided he would accept the name as well as the flesh. "Dax," he said softly, letting the word roll off his tongue. "Dax."

"Stop your mumbling, Gambel," Grella hissed in his ear. "Someone will notice."

"Dax," he said again. "When you have a name, we will use it too."

She shrugged in disgust and tried the ale. It was bitter, but somehow refreshing. Curious how the body craved things she herself did not. It would be hard deciding which to listen to. Then as she watched Dax down the mug and ask for another, she knew he had already decided. She wondered whether he was right after all.

One of the serving girls opened the tavern door to admit two men. One was a youth and the other? Dax, still The Searcher, recognized him from his time in Arcula. He nearly started, then remembered that Edra would not recognize him in his new skin, so he relaxed. What, in the name of all darkness was the Caugeman doing here?

Edra and his companion made their way over to the eighth table and nodded to Dax and Grella.

For a brief moment, although only the two Shadows noticed, the air grew heavy with the weight of Tamor's Dark Magic, stirring the waters of fate to meet his needs. The skins were perfect. The weight lifted, the air cleared as Grella and The Searcher awaited the consequences.

Neither was fully prepared when Edra's companion spoke, "Well met, Sir Dax and, if I am not mistaken, Lady Arista. This is more fortunate than we could have ever hoped. My name is Jyp and I come as a representative of your nephew, My Lady. Master Edra and I had requested to speak to Master Dax, here, but now that we've found you with him our joy has been compounded."

Edra took Grella's hand in his and kissed it. "My Lady, I am so relieved to see you well and in such good company. Prince Gareth has been worrying himself sick over you. He'd heard you'd landed safely here in Aberdeen and then just simply disappeared. I do hope it was for good reason."

Now Grella found herself forced to improvise. How had they recognized this skin? Could they be mistaken? "How do you know me Sur? We have never met."

Edra pulled a locket out of his purse and showed it to her. "The Prince gave us this portrait of you and bid us search the city. I must admit the picture does not do your beauty justice, but the likeness is remarkable, nonetheless." He was smiling broadly, his delight in solving both of his problems with Gareth at the same time and enormous relief. That is, if he and Jyp could convince Dax to come to the palace.

Grella blushed at the compliment, finally letting her body do as it willed. If she had a masquerade to play she would have to surrender sooner or later. Besides that name, "Arista," felt good to wear. "I would have come to the palace at once," she said, "but the ship lost some of my baggage, and Sir Dax here, came to my rescue." She lowered her eyes coyly and looked at the Knight from under her heavy lids. "We have been companions since. I am not usually so forward, but he is a fine figure of a man."

Though Jyp was taken aback, Edra, well used to bedding women himself, grinned and slapped Dax on the back. "Well done, well done, my friend. To turn such a fine woman's head in but a Sevenstin is quite a feat. To bed her is one thing, but to earn her praise in public like this is a triumph."

Dax coughed, choking on a too big gulp of ale. He recovered quickly and laid his hand possessively on Arista's knee. "She is a tarkess between the sheets, My Lord. Quite the pleasure for a man who knows women like I do. We have had a pleasurable time together."

Now it was Jyp's turn to cough. Even in the tavern, he was not used to such forward talk. The men of Cuver Street usually kept their personal lives to themselves out of respect for the women. He glanced over at Jada, whose shoulders were shaking with laughter behind her napkin, and decided it was time to change the subject. "Well, now that we have found you both, the Hand be Blessed, perhaps we should get to the business of it all."

The serving girl brought over the two plates of meat and set them on the table. Jyp felt his throat catch when he saw the blood running out of the mutton, but he checked himself enough to go on, "Prince Gareth is seeking to hire a man to train and lead his army."

"Aberdeen is at war?" Dax asked, straightening in his chair.

"No, not yet. But the Prince has concerns and wants to be prepared. There is no one in his Guard capable of teaching tactics and maneuvers. We…he thought hiring a Knight such as you would be a wise move."

Dax considered. He had only been at war once himself, in Arcula, and there his allies has suffered a stinging defeat. But that did not mean he was incapable. He'd spent his time once more lost in Shadow to consider the mistakes Edra and the Dark Lord had made, noting well how the enemy had used the terrain and a careful placement of troops to turn the tide of battle. While it was true that in the end, the Silver Dragon had been the deciding factor, he was sure victory would have been lost anyway. The opposing army was just too well organized. "Would I teach the men to fight as well?"

Edra flexed his good hand. "I am a master swordsman myself, but limited in my skills as a tactician in the field." He too remembered the defeat but had learned nothing from it. "I am sure you have many weapon skills I lack. I would think between the two of us, we could build a force able to stand against any foe Turan might offer."

An army, Dax thought. Exactly what the Dark Lord wanted. How perfect. They could march under the royal banner and no one would be the wiser as to who their true master was. "I would be honored to accept the position," he said. "I will be paid well?"

"In gold, lodging and anything you may need. The royal coffers are open for this endeavor. I'm sure we can agree on suitable arrangements."

"When do you want me to start?" Dax asked.

"Tomorrow," Jyp said. "If you would escort Lady Arista to the palace at Easwin, I am sure the Prince will reward you handsomely with his thanks and a good purse. For now, let us enjoy the hospitality of the Seven Tables to celebrate our pact."

Edra beckoned to Salli. "Tell me, mistress, if you have any more of that fine rare lamb in your kitchens. It looks delicious."

Jyp quickly excused himself from the table and made his way over to the bar where he ordered a goblet of herb blended amberwine to settle his stomach.

*****

Jamus opened his eyes in the darkness of Norwin. Moonlight streamed in through the window, making lacy patterns on the curtained wall across from the bed. Becca, sitting in the big chair pulled up next to the bed was snoring softly.

Feeling a little better despite his fever, Jamus tried to focus his eyes on something, but he was dizzy and his head still hurt. He rolled on his side and thought he saw the curtain move. Was it real, or just a figment of an imagination corrupted by delirium? The moonlight was dancing.

He frowned, squinting hard to see. There was a face, then another, grotesquely outlined in the silver light, first smiling, then leering at him with open mouths and twisted chins. "Stop it," he said aloud. Becca stirred but did not wake.

The faces began to laugh and in his head he heard them jeering. He pulled himself up from the pillow, "Stop it. It is enough" His dry throat betrayed him and the raspy whisper had no effect on the images. They still danced, still grinned, and still jeered.

He grabbed the bedpost and dragged himself to his feet, stumbling over to the curtain, reaching out as if to chant a spell against the vision, but instead he tumbled forward, his hands grabbing at the curtain to break his fall. The fabric tore from its hangings and fell on top of him.

Collapsed and almost too weak to move, he managed to pull the curtain away from his body and clamber up onto his knees.

The wall behind the curtain was not bare. It was covered with a tapestry.

The same grotesque faces were embroidered in it in muted colors, attached to twisted bodies seeming to writhe in pain before his eyes. In the very center of the tapestry were loose threads where the weave was broken.

His head spun as he looked at it, lost in the meaning, confused by the fever, and drawn into the images by some undeniable force. Unable to help himself, he reached up his hand to the broken pattern and felt his fingers slip through. It was blessedly cool on the other side, soothing, alluring. He opened and closed his hand in the refreshing air, longing to feel it on his face and burning skin. He was almost too weak to stand, yet he clutched at the edges of the tapestry and staggered up. He turned to take one long, lingering look at Becca and stepped forward.

The wind caught him, lifting him upright, supporting him, caressing him with its cool, comforting breath. Strength surged into his limbs, his head cleared and he found himself standing on a street in Magiskeep not far from the palace itself.

He squinted in the bright sunlight. Turning back again he saw the darkness he had left and Becca, now a misty vision out of reach. Never before had a tapestry taken him into a world he knew this well. Merchants and workman busied themselves in the street and when he looked up, he could see the spires of the Keep, turquoise and white, shining in the sun.

Turquoise. Sagari's color.

He was in Magiskeep, but when?

Sagari had been Master of the Keep some forty circles before he had rescued Jamus from the Rim. And he had ruled for nearly twenty after until Jamus had killed him. The tapestry could have taken him anywhere within that sixty circle span. Before he did anything to solve whatever riddle awaited him, he needed to know just when it was. Either way, he needed to be careful. Using his own name and even his own face could spell disaster. The real Magiskeep would know him. He wove an illusion of Master's Art to disguise himself, darkening his eyes and lightening his hair. Subtle differences sealed by a complex weave rooted in the Way's reflections. Only another Master of the Way could unravel it, and he knew few of them had ever trod the stones of the Keep.

But the riddle remained. What Magiskeep was this?

There were few clues in the streets themselves. The shops were familiar in some places, but when he did not see Doria's bakery across from the fountain, he knew he had somehow stepped into the past. Doria had opened her shop a circle after he had been Prenticed. He remembered because she had celebrated by giving all the students in the Hall round cookies covered in sweet sugar power and layered with raspberry jam. Even now Jamus' mouth watered as he recalled how good they had tasted.

Suddenly he realized how hungry he was. Since he'd caught
the fever, he hadn't eaten a thing and now his stomach started to
rumble in protest.

Carefully he flexed his fingers, testing the water to see if
Magic worked for him in this world. To his relief a pouch full of
coins appeared in his hand. At least he was not denied his power. It
made him feel a lot better.

He headed for East Village, hoping The Dancing Flame,
Merth's tavern, was where it belonged. The food was delicious, and
sitting down to a meal would give him time to think. Besides, a
tavern was always a good place to learn the gossip of any town.

Sure enough, though it didn't looked exactly as he
remembered it, the tavern was in place, with its great wooden door
and shuttered window open to welcome both the sunlight and
patrons.

Jamus walked inside, his eyes taking in the dark wooden
beams and so familiar cream-colored walls. A pretty little barmaid
escorted him to a table. "Master Markus offers a fine menu, to our
guests, Sur. Today our special is a tasty taroot soup and braised
waterfowl. Our cook is a master of spices, so I'm sure you will like
the flavor. Can I get you a mug of dark ale to start your meal?"

"Master Markus is the proprietor?" Jamus asked. "I thought I
heard someone in the village mention a Merth? Does that name
sound familiar to you?"

"Merth? Oh yes, My lord. That's the Master's son. He's but
a wee lad, but he struts about the town telling everyone how when he
grows up he's gonna take over the business hisself an' earn more
gold than even Lord Sagari holds. Clever little mite, but a bit uppity.
Still his Pap loves him and so does the whole village. If he ever does
take over the Flame he won't be lacking fer customers, that's fer
shure."

The maid's accent was not quite the common tongue he was
familiar with, but that didn't matter as much as what she said. If
Merth were a boy then, by his reckoning, he was close to fifty circles
in the past, in the early part of Sagari's reign.

"I'm new to Magiskeep proper," Jamus said. "I've just come in from the Farreaches. My father sent me to the Keep to see if I could learn something more of the Magic to help with the farm."

"Yer a bit old ta be a Prentice, but I hear tell the Masters in the Keep are generous with their learning to them what wants to know the Way of the Waters."

How curious to hear a someone speak of the Magic using those words. But this was not a familiar time, so there was no reason to be surprised. He was certain he was going to find many more strange expressions and customs. Education and the Magic itself had flourished under Sagari's hand, and until his ambition had clouded his better instincts Magiskeep's knowledge had grown by leaps and bounds.

"Do I just go to the Keep and ask?"

The barmaid shrugged. "Most petioners I know had sponsors. Tell ya what. There be a little mage who comes in here near every Sowin fer one o' our meals. His name's Senital, and he's a sweet one. He should be in soon if he's comin' today. The wind's near change an' he loves the taroot soup. If ya'd like, I'll introduce ya and ya kin ask him yer questions."

"I'd appreciate that," Jamus told her, breathing a sigh of relief. Senital had always been a good friend. If this was indeed the real Magiskeep of a time gone by, he would be the same kind and wise man he had always been.

The real Magiskeep. That is always the question in a tapestry. Although he had already solved many, he never did quite understand how they worked. Within their threads, time warped and sometimes, their reality was actually reflection. There was some connection to the Way of Mirrors, he was sure, but the explanation eluded him. Meeting Senital would tell him what he needed to know for this part of the riddle, at least.

Just as the wind changed, the little mage strolled through the tavern door. The barmaid intercepted him and pointed at Jamus. Senital smiled and came over to the table, extending his hand in the sign of greeting. "Welcome, welcome, lad. Missy Gina tells me you touch the River. Is it so?"

"I have the Magic, Sur. Not as much as my father would like, but I can work a spell or two."

"Few fathers expect less of their sons. Most expect more. I take it he sent you here, then?"

Jamus nodded. "He wants me to learn more about the Magic so I can help with the farm."

"The Farreaches, Gina said. What crops?"

"Fruit trees, grapes for wine," Jamus said, careful to only mention the plants he understood well enough to offer some expertise in case anyone questioned him further. "Father hopes to plant some new kind of corn if we can get water to it." Lord Sarkem's fields were coming in handy now as he embellished his story. "Sweetling corn, Father calls it. He thinks it might make some money in the taverns like this one."

"A wise man to think ahead like that, your Father. Wise to send his son here too. There is much to learn in the Keep proper."

"Do you think you could help me?"

"Sponsor you? Of course, of course. Did you tell me your name? I suspect you already know mine. I'm Senital master of the First Art. I practice most of my skill in the Great Library, but I hope one day to rule the scrolls and ancient rune."

"My name is Jarius." As he said it, Jamus thought he saw a flicker of confusion cross Senital's face. Had he made a mistake? The name was of a minor mage in a story of little consequence in the Eldenscrolls.

"Jarius," Senital said thoughtfully. "Well, as I said before, welcome to Magiskeep, Master Jarius. Let's share a meal, talk a bit more and then head back to the Keep. I'm sure we can find a room for you in Prentiscape. Most of the students are much younger than you, but we do have private quarters for older mages who come to seek wisdom in our halls. You won't be alone in your quest."

As Gina had predicted, the soup and waterfowl were delicious, and Jamus' pleasure in filling his belly was added to by finding Senital to be the same kind and wonderful man he had always known.

This indeed was Magiskeep in the past. Now all he had to do was find and solve the riddle.

He hoped it would be enough to cure his fever.

*****

Becca's eyes fluttered open. For a moment she thought Jamus' bed was empty, but then she woke up the rest of the way and saw him lying there. She put her hand on his still hot forehead, then dipped a towel in the bowl of water on the bedstand and put mopped his brow. His breathing was shallow, but even and steady. He was no better and no worse than he'd been when she'd fallen asleep.

"Poor, poor laddie," she crooned. "I seen fever like this afore ya know. T'was what killed ma little babes. Twins they was. Did I ever tell ya? Girl an' a boy. Sira an' Jeb. Jeamel said they was teched by the River, so we named 'em as such. Weren't no way o' knowin' fer sure, 'cause they was too little. Jest babes, jest babes." Tears filled her eyes as the wet the towel again and put it on his forehead. "Babes no bigger the your'n. Fever come ta Tallridge, northwest o'here. Ya bin there. Nice village, but far from the Keep. Dint know nothin' about the Healing back then. Some, let me think, near some fifty circles past. I was a lass of eighteen myself, fresh married to ma One Love."

Becca got up to stretch her legs. When she saw the curtain lying on the floor, she frowned. "Now when did that fall down? I swear, Becca, onct ya falls asleep yer like a rock." She picked up the curtain, folded and put it on top of the dresser." She studied the tapestry for a moment but in the dim light, its faded images didn't make much sense. Shaking her head she went back over by the bed and sat down again.

"Now, where was I? One Love. That's ma Jeamel case ya don't know. That's what yer Lady Rath called 'im when we was talkin' an liked the name jest fine. Yer silver Lady's kinda strange sometimes, but I gotta say I likes her. Any soul what cares about Lady Salene and yer little Jarien like she does has gotta be a good person, ya know? 'Course who wouldn't like that babe. He's cute as a duskit's tail now and I can already see e's gonna be handsome like 'is Pap. Yer gonna have ta teach him good when he grows up so he'll know how to treat the ladies proper, 'cause they're gonna be fallin' at his feet."

She pulled down the blanket and sponged Jamus' chest, checking again to assure herself he was really breathing. Then she laid her head on him to listen for his heartbeat. It was faint but steady. She took a fresh sheet from the dresser drawer, stripped off the one covering him and put the new one in its place. "There now, that should be a bit better. Clean bed makes a good sleep, eh? Lessee. I was tellin' ya about ma babes afore I got kinda lost there. Tallridge, an' no Healer. The fever done hit the whole village, but mosta the ones what died was the babes. Mistress Sarena tole me circles later there weren't much I coulda done anyhow cause they was jest learnin' the Healing back then. Well, she said they knows about it, but t'warn't till like ten circles more afore they unnerstood how ta fix a fever." She laughed sadly. "'Pears from the likes o' ya they still ain't got it right. Makes it a might easier knowin' that. I always blamed maself fer losing those babes. Kept thinkin' there musta been somewhat I coulda done. Broke ma heart, ya know?"

She patted Jamus' arm. "Not that I'd want ya ta ever really know. Yer Lady an' ya lost that babe afore she were born, sure, but that ain't near the pain ya feels losin' a child what's already learned ta laugh." She had to stop, her voice choked with renewed sorrow from the memory. "Lost me boy, Solly ta a cart tippin' but even that dint hurt like losin' those babes. They were ma first."

"Well, ya gots me talkin' din't ya. Ya always was a good listener, Jami. Even when ye come ta the cottage all tears 'cause o' one o' them nightmares, ya always wanted ta listen steada talkin' yerself. Ya havin' a nightmare now? Don't look like it, but ya never know. I'd like ta think yer off in some sunny land somewhere jest having a good day. Good dream like that'd be nice fer a change. Might be better if ya was in the Norreach mounts where it'd be nice an' cool fer ya, though. Jest hope it's a good dream. Ya deserves a good dream now and agin."

*****

"We'll be off again tomorrow," Kala said as she watched Talia lead one of the mares out into the paddock with her new foal. The little filly, lanky and leggy had been born the night before. It was the first time Kala had ever been there to see a foaling and was surprised to see how fast the little one had gotten to its feet and started nursing. According to Talia, it had been a perfect birth and the foal an exceptional example of a potential runner. Now, just a day later she was out trotting alongside her mother as if she had been on those four little feet for circles instead of just two windchanges.

"I hope you come back to see this little girl again before she stops being so cute. They grow fast and get all sassy in a few months. Then there's an awkward stage where most foals look like they don't even know where their legs are going half the time. They run around a lot, and play, but I swear I don't know how they manage. Nothing seems to fit together quite right."

"I'll make sure I do," Kala said, laughing as the filly nudged her mother's teat and insisted on having a drink before she frolicked off again to explore the world. "You are naming her Dreamer, aren't you?"

"Kala's Dreamer," Talia said. "A horse like her needs two names. And I told you she wanted to be born when you could watch, so you deserved a part of her. We'll share the purse when she wins her first race."

"You didn't have to give her my name."

"Why not. I have a whole pasture full of beasts with no name at all yet. Do you know how hard it is to think up good ones? When you suggested Dreamer for her, you made my life so much easier. I think you earned a little bit of her."

"When will she be ready to run?" Kala asked. "I don't know too much about racing."

"Most babies run at two, but I like to wait until they pass at least three circles. Even then they're really too young, but if you're careful with their training and you don't run them too often or too far at first, you can keep them sane and sound. I'll wait an extra year with some of them all depending on how well they mature."

"Body or mind?"

Talia laughed, "Both matter to me. You won't find a broken runner in my stables if I have anything to say about it. Trouble is, you can't make a deneret on a colt until he's old enough to run unless you sell him. Most breeders can't afford to wait until their young stock is older the way I do. So the babies take to the Course before they're strong and get hurt trying to run for their board and keep."

"And how do you manage the finances?"

"Oh a rather large inheritance from my father and the money I earn training other owner's racers. I have a good reputation and can charge ridiculous fees because my horses win."

Kala smiled. "A tribute to your good care, I take it."

"I keep them well fit and well fed, so they stay happy. It just seems that when a horse goes out to the track from my stable it's having fun."

If Kala had been able to use her Gift to do some Beasttalking, she would have heard some interesting conversations in the barns. Talia's runners and all the rest of the horses at the Course adored the petite trainer and her utter kindness to any animal in her care. They had made a pact to assure Talia's success by giving her at least two winners every day. And the horses themselves decided just which runner it would be.

Silk and Magwin both danced along the trail, practically begging to take to the air, but Simen had decided the only safe way to reach Aberdeen at the expected time would be if they stayed grounded, spending most of the ride at the walk. "We should reach the city gates by Easwin tomorrow," he said.

"Another night on the trail, then?" Kala said. "I must admit camping with a Sorcerer is quite a pleasant experience with all the luxuries you conjure to keep us comfortable. But we are close to too many farms and villages now. I think we can find accommodations on one of the little inns along the way this time."

"You spoil all the adventure with practicality, Mistress," Simen complained. "I was hoping to impress you with a roaring blaze and a huge silken tent to shelter you. I guess I'll just have to settle for a lumpy mattress and some hot country stew instead."

"So, did you and Erlik pick out any horses for the Keep? I never did ask," Kala said, changing the subject to keep from laughing at what would surely be a round of teasing from the Follyman.

"Erlik is a curious fellow," Simen said, holding Magwin back to he was even with Kala. "He is a Sorcerer, I'm sure you know that."

"I do."

"And he's from Arcula. Seems he ran afoul of the Cauge and was tossed out to sea."

"I heard a bit of the story from Jamus."

"I mean, I heard the story from Jamus too, and he told me about that Silver Magic but hearing a story and meeting someone from that world is really quite amazing to me. It's as if the power just flows from his fingers without a thought. But when I ask him about it, he has absolutely no idea how it all works. Arcula's not like Magiskeep at all or even your Grandisite. Magicians have no training and little education. It's quite remarkable, really that all that potential exists with no control whatsoever."

"Jamus has mastered the Silver River. I doubt his touch of it lacks control. How did he manage?"

"Jamus is Jamus, Kala. How does he do anything? His mind is so keen, he can understand things it would take a lifetime for any ordinary man to master."

"My Masters in Grandisite were certainly impressed by him." Kala agreed. "Once he found out how the Sight and its Light could be mastered he perfected his Art in a matter of days. Even I was amazed and I've known him long enough to always expect the unexpected from him."

"Strong confession from a Seer."

"Magic and the Sight have ever been at odds, Simen. And Jamus represents everything the Seers have feared since the Eldentimes. His Power is pure, and his ability to create reflections can defy even the greatest Seer from perceiving the Truth of them. Most Sorcerers really can't lie very well in the face of the Light like he can. Their illusions, no matter how good, usually falter in a Sifting. But Jamus…"

"He is the Rivermaster, Kala, unique and incomprehensible, even to himself sometimes. I, of all people, should understand him, and yet who he really is constantly eludes me. He's suffered as no man should ever suffer and always he rises above it, forgiving when he can and meting out unquestioned justice when it's needed. It's as if every misery just makes him stronger."

Kala nodded. "I know. At least we have the comfort of knowing he's happy now, safe with Salene and his son. I can tell he's enjoying his fatherhood."

"He is. Over these last few months, I've hardly ever seen him without a smile."

"May the Hand Bless him then, with many more such months. I've never known anyone who deserves it more."

*****

Gareth was pacing the Hall again. It was becoming an annoying habit with those two Sorcerers around, he thought as he started to count his footsteps. Forty paces to the far wall, forty paces back. He could vary that, taking sixty if he shortened his stride, pretending to be escorting a Lady of the Court in her long trained gown. As a warrior, it could take twenty-seven or twenty-eight, but it was hard to keep the long steps as even as the shorter ones. He decided to practice, until he could get it right every time, wondering if measuring his gait with such precision was part of a soldier's training. His father seemed to think military discipline would do him good and while he usually didn't agree with the King, the idea intrigued him now.

He leaned his back soldier straight against the left wall, closed his eyes and made a march across the room. "One, two..." he counted aloud. At "twenty-six," he crashed into the bench on the far side. Cursing and rubbing his bruised shin, he opened his eyes to find out that not only had he misjudged his length of stride, he had veered badly to the right. His objective was harder than it first appeared.

He turned again, focused his gaze at a point in the center of the opposite wall, closed his eyes again and marched. This time he stopped with his nose a hand's breadth from the wall, but it had taken him twenty-nine strides. Once more, he had miscalculated, but he had walked nearly a straight line.

"One step at a time," his father had always said when he'd tried to teach Gareth how to handle a sword. Again the boy had not listened, swinging wildly instead making useless attacks and never parrying . When Gailvarg had given up in exasperation, the Prince had gone off on his own to fight imagined foes in front of his mirror, quite content to see himself as a mighty warrior and swordmaster.

Edra's training had taught him how foolish those childhood fantasies had been. His father had been right. "One step at a time."

He turned around and tried his march again. This time he was interrupted by Edra who burst in the door and fell on his knee, gasping for breath. "We found them, Your Highness. Both of them."

Still lost in the puzzle of his march, Gareth asked, "Found who?"

"Your lost aunt and your general."

Gareth did not respond. To Edra's surprise, he muttered under his breath and started marching again, counting aloud, "Twenty-four, twenty-five, twenty-six, twenty-seven, twenty-eight." He threw up his hand in a triumphant fist as he stopped just short of hitting the far wall. Only then did he acknowledge Edra. "When will you bring them?"

Taken aback by the Prince's apparent disinterest, the Sorcerer hesitated, not wanting to displease him. "Tomorrow, Your Highness? It's late now, past Norwin. I've just left the tavern where I met them. After a good night's sleep...."

"Now," Gareth said. "Not tomorrow. I want to know how many paces I should be taking."

"My Lord?"

"Now. I need to know now. Bring my General."

Edra rose and backed towards the door, his legs having a hard time of not breaking into a run. "As you wish, My Prince. At your command." As soon as he was out of the Hall, he took a deep breath to steady himself. Then he did run, out of the palace and into the courtyard where he leapt into the saddle and galloped out into the streets heading for Wesportal.

As he spurred his horse along, his mind raced with the clatter of the animal's hoofs on the cobbles. Dax had said something about the Copper Kettle, an inn not too far from the Course. Maybe he and Arista were staying there. At least is was a place to begin looking. While they had made plans to meet at after Easwin's change, Gareth

had made it clear he wanted an instant response, and Edra intended
to obey no matter how many inns he had to search.

The Copper Kettle's front door was locked. Edra pounded on
it with his fist. "Open up, in the name of the King!!" he shouted.

Just as he was ready to cast a spell on the lock, the door
opened a crack and the sleepy-eyed innkeeper peered out at him.
"Who be ye at this hour?"

"A royal summoner," Edra replied, pulling himself up to his
full height as he fingered the hilt of his sword. "I've come to take the
Knight Dax and his Lady to the palace.....now."

"They be in for the night and don't wish to be disturbed."

"Well, they will just have to wake up and come with me. It is
the Prince's command." He pushed the door open, knocking the
innkeeper out of the way. "Which room?"

The innkeeper pointed a shaking finger at the staircase.
"Second door on the right."

Edra strode past him and ran up the stairs. He grabbed the
door handle and shoved the door open without a word.

Dax lay sprawled on the bed naked, half on top of Arista,
snoring loudly. His hand was tangled in her long loose hair and she
had her arm draped over his buttocks. There was another bed in the
room, its blankets and sheets rumpled. A pair of boots was set beside
it along with a traveling sack.

Curious, Edra thought as he looked around to see if there
was any sign of another boarder in the room, but aside from the open
shutters of the window, nothing seemed amiss. "Wake up!" he
shouted. When there was no reaction he went to the bed, grabbed
Dax's shoulder and shook it roughly.

Dax bolted from the bed, pulled his own sword from its
scabbard hanging on the bedpost, and attacked. Edra darted to the
side, drew his own sword, and parried the other man's blows. "Sir
Dax, stop," he cried dodging the Knight's blade and once again
defending with his own. "It's Edra, from the Prince. Edra! You know
me."

Dax backed off, glared at Edra and then let his weapon fall
to his side, dangling loosely in his hand. "What the blazes are you
doing waking a man like that? It's the middle of the night."

Edra's voice caught. The contours of Dax's muscles were melding with the shadows in the room, giving him an almost beautiful allure. How could a man look so powerful, so strong? No wonder the woman let him bed her. He snapped his mind back to the business at hand. "The Prince commands you and the Lady Arista to come with me to the palace at once. He does not want to wait for the sun to rise."

Dax growled, as Arista, wakened by the fight, pulled herself up to stand behind him. She had not bothered to cover herself and again, Edra found himself gaping. How long had it been since he had bedded a woman? She was older than he preferred, but her full hips promised much. Dax was a lucky man. "Dress for riding, My Lady," he said at last after his eyes were satisfied. "We need horses."

"There's a stable for the inn," Dax said pulling on a pair of leather breeches. "Come on, then. We need to hurry."

Edra sprinted down the stairs and grabbed the still stunned innkeeper by his nightshirt. "Horses. You have some for hire. With his free hand he dangled a money pouch in the man's face. "I'm hiring two. I'll take some tack too. King's business, but even the royal household pays its bills." He dropped the pouch into the innkeeper's hand and headed out to the stables.

There were six horses dozing in their stalls. Two appeared to be driving beasts and the other four seemed suited to the saddle. He chose two of the riding horses, and after looking around to make sure no one was watching chanted the saddles and bridles on them.

Dax and Arista arrived a fraction later. As soon the Knight reached for his horse's reins the horse reared, its eyes rolling in fear. "Wretched beast," Dax cursed, yanking hard to pull the horse back down. "You could have picked a better one for me."

Without thinking beyond his frayed nerves, Edra cast another quick spell on both horses, settling them down so Dax and Arista could mount. Then he collected his own horse from the hitching post in the street and led the other two on at a gallop, careening through the streets.

To Edra, the palace seemed spans away. Already the sky was graying, hinting of the first breath of Easwin's change. He hoped

Gareth would understand that no one could travel on the wind, not even a Sorcerer.

VIII

"Now remember, Jarius, I am just your sponsor," Senital explained as they neared the steps up to Magiskeep's Halls. "The Lord of the Keep, Master Sagari has the last word as to whether or not you can stay here to study."

Sagari. Nervously, Jamus checked the pattern of his weave, assuring himself his illusion was impenetrable. The last thing he wanted was for the Golden Sorcerer to see his true face and remember it circles later when they met again. His head spun at the thought. By now he should have been used to the twisting times in the tapestries, but this was almost absurd. Here he was, a grown man, preparing to face his nightmares again and his hands were shaking. Sagari was dead, and yet here, he was alive again.

"You'll like the Master," Senital said, pulling Jamus' arm to hurry him along. "Dear me, we stayed a bit too long in the tavern, I'm afraid. I should have been back a long ago. I had a class to teach. Lord Sagari will have taken my place, of course, but those Prentices are, well, a bit challenging when I'm not there to check their behavior. I do hope the Master has kept them in line. They know just enough Magic to pull a few pranks on a substitute instructor, I'm afraid."

Jamus nodded numbly, memories flooding his mind as they made their way up the familiar staircase to the classroom floor. Every detail in the stone floor kicked another recollection into his head, for as a boy he had often walked this very hall, his eyes fixed on the floor, hoping no one would notice him. A new pain stabbed at his heart as the old anxiety nagged at him. He had been bullied, rejected, and in the end even hated here. Why had the tapestry demanded he come back? With every step he was more and more certain this was truly Magiskeep, not some illusion of the weave to trap him into thinking it was just to make him solve a riddle so he could escape back to reality.

Senital opened the door of a nearby classroom—Jired's, the Master of Comprehension. Of course, it made sense. Of all the mages in the Keep, Senital would have once taught this art himself before he became Master of the Vaults.

They stopped at the door.

One of the young Prentices, a fair-haired boy was desperately trying to weave a warding to hold off the very waterball he had conjured from splattering in his face. Its target had been the back of his teacher's head when Sagari had turned away from the class to point to one of the many colorful illustrations on the wall. But now, the gleeful grin on the Master's face clearly showed he had turned the tables on the little prankster and was enjoying every moment of it.

The boy's hand trembled as his fingers wove the spell, and Jamus could see it was a futile effort. The child had neither the skill nor strength to win the battle. Yet he also saw that Sagari was holding the little sphere back himself, just enough that the boy's weak efforts were having some effect.

And Sagari's grin was not nasty. He was actually having fun. "Well, now, my young Sur, it seems you have a bit of a dilemma there, although I must admit you are doing a fine job of solving it on your own." He laughed, his eyes sparkling with amusement. "Let me give you a bit of help."

The boy flinched and Jamus did too, fully expected the ball to slam into the boy's nose, soaking him. Instead, it dropped with a splat on the study tabe, water dripping down the sides of the tall narrow desk, making a puddle on the floor. One more wave of Sagari's hand and the floor dried along with the boy's tunic where some drops had hit him.

"A good lesson for you all, My Prentices. Never, never underestimate the Masters of this Keep. We were all once fresh-faced Prentices like you are, and not a one of us has forgotten the tricks we used to play on our teachers. Once learned by a Master, a lesson is never forgotten, in fact." He looked over at Senital. "I see Master Senital has come to rescue me."

"It does not appear you need rescuing," Senital replied, smiling.

Sagari gestured toward the group of twelve gray tunicked children and smiled again. "These little sweet babes? Why, they wouldn't hurt a duskit, let alone a Master of Magiskeep. They do make mistakes now and then," he cast a knowing glance at the little boy who bowed his head in obvious shame, "but mistakes are easily forgiven in young lads and lasses. I'm sure they have had enough schooling for one day. If I recall, I do believe the cook in Prentiscape was going to make a few batches of cinnisnaps today. They should just about be cooled off enough to eat by now. Why don't you dismiss your class so they can go get some."

"Class dismissed," Senital replied, pulling Jamus to the side so neither one of them would be trampled by the scurrying students.

Once the children had gone, Sagari reached out a hand in the customery greeting. "Welcome to Magiskeep, my friend. Your presence explains why Master Senital was late to his class. Are you here to see me?"

Senital spoke before Jamus could answer. "This is Jarius, My Lord. He is a young Magician from the Farreaches. He has come to learn the Arts and I have taken on his sponsorship."

"Ah," Sagari said warmly. "Welcome, again, then Jarius. As Master Senital has told you, I am Sagari, Master of Magiskeep and whether you can stay all depends on my decision. Tell me a bit about yourself."

Taken aback by Sagari's kind and generous attitude, Jamus was nearly at a loss for words. This was not the man he had known when he was a child. That Sagari was hard and unforgiving—a harsh taskmaster in lessons and sometimes even cruel. He swallowed hard, returned Sagari's gesture of greeting and finally said, "I do ask to study here, My Lord. My father has a farm far south of here. His crops grow well, and our vineyards are wonderful, but he has hopes of expanding and believes my Magic will help. There's a stream that needs to be diverted, and some land to be leveled, just basic things like that."

Sagari wagged his finger at Jamus. "Nothing is basic about using Magic to change the world, my young friend. If you learn anything here, that will be most important. Can you show me a simple spell so I can judge your skill?"

This, Jamus had anticipated. Careful to make a great show of
wiggling his fingers and muttering a chant, he created a crude, but
solid looking illusion of a bunch of grapes in his hand and offered it
to Sagari to examine.

The Golden Sorcerer took the cluster of fruit and examined
it. Even as he did, its outline started to shimmer. His eyes caught
Jamus' hand moving again to correct the faulty weave before the
grapes vanished, and he smiled. "Well done indeed. Your Skill needs
work, but the grapes had all the quality of real ones, and I was
pleased to see you noticed the error in your chanting and fixed it
before I said anything. It was smart of you to pick something like
grapes to show me. The wise Mage would only illusion something he
was completely familiar with. I do think you show some promise."

Jamus was stunned. In all the time he had been in the Keep,
Sagari had never complimented him like that, nor been as kind. He
was beginning to question reality again, though everything else,
except for this Sagari was perfect. "Thank you, My Lord."

"Master Senital. I do think your young man is lacking in
knowledge if he lacks in anything. He wove that illusion most
effectively, but the grapes were still a bit unbalanced. I would like
you to take him into your private tutelage. Comprehension is the first
and most important Art a good Magician must master. Until he
understands how to sift to find the true nature of things, his talent
will be limited by his ignorance." When the little Mage nodded,
Sagari turned his attention back to Jamus. "We have private rooms in
Prentiscape where you will be quite comfortable and safe, I think,
from waterballs." He laughed again. "I can't promise those little
rascals won't find some other way to torment you, but you look to be
a man who can take care of himself. They're really sweet little ones,
but I wouldn't turn my back on them. Come along, I'll show you
where you'll be staying."

They were only in the hall a moment when a voice called out
from a nearby door. "Papa! Papa, I made something for you!" A
towheaded little boy ran up to Sagari, tugged at the sleeve of his
turquoise tunic, and stuffed a piece of parchment into his hand. The
Master of Magiskeep smoothed out the crumpled page revealing an

indecipherable blob of red set against a green and blue background. "Why, it's wonderful, Sagin."

"It's a tarlet, Papa! I seed one out the window when I was with Mistress Nara and I drawed it for you so you could see it too!"

"Indeed, indeed," Sagari said, studying the parchment carefully. "This is by far the best tarlet I have ever seen. Why I almost feel as if it's alive. Gentlemen," he held the boy's drawing up so Senital and Jamus could have a look.

Senital smiled benignly but Jamus peered at the work with Master's eyes. He could see the tarlet as clearly as the one he had remembered from the Keep garden so far into the future. It had hatched, he later discovered, from an egg he had conjured for Sagari as an apprentice exercise, and the little bird had proved the beginning of his own undoing. Now, he saw a beautiful little songbird in full flight on the parchment, as if he were seeing it through little boy eyes once again. "My goodness, Master Sagin, but that is one of the most beautiful tarlets I have ever seen. Why I do love the way you have him spreading his wings just as he's about to take off from the tree branch."

Sagin nearly jumped for joy. "He were gonna fly right off, but I asked him to stay so I could draw him just right and he sat there for me a long time, flapping his wings. I think he liked me painting his picture."

Sagari turned the picture back around to stare at it again himself, but it still looked like a blob of red to him. His son had a vivid imagination and so, apparently, did this young Magician he had just welcomed to his hold. "He almost looks alive," he lied, much to the delight of his son.

Jamus nodded. "Your father is right," he said. "I think he'd better hold on tight to that parchment so that bird doesn't just take wing and fly right off the page. I'm sure he's going to hold on to it forever."

Sagin grinned broadly and snuggled against his father's leg. Sagari could not resist and scooped the little boy into his arms.

As Sagin giggled in his father's embrace, Jamus heart started aching again. Sagari had never held him like that even though he'd adopted him and claimed him as his son. He could not even remember a single truly kind touch from the Master of Magiskeep. Was this part of the riddle? Something he needed to learn? "Perhaps Master Senital can show me to my rooms, My Lord. I think you and your son have far more important things to talk about than bothering with me."

"You promised me I could ride my pony, Papa," Sagin said breathlessly between his laughter. "Can we go now? Can we?"

"Of course we can, Sweetling," Sagari said, tossing the boy up onto his shoulder. He turned to Jamus and smiled. "Thank you, Master Jarius, for opening my eyes to the tarlet. I might have missed some of the marvelous detail were it not for you." Then he winked and trotted down the hall, Sagin bouncing on his shoulder.

"The Master loves that little boy more than life itself," Senital said as they watched them go. "His mother, Jodia, closed her circle giving life to the wee lad. Sagari loved her dearly, and I think he's put all that love into the child now. Rumors are he'll marry again—he's been spending a fair bit of time with Mistress Salecia of late, but I don't know if he will ever fully get over his first love."

Salecia, Salene's mother. Everything was so right and still so wrong. "Master Sagari seems to be a kind and generous man," Jamus said.

"Oh, he is, he is," Senital agreed. "He is well loved in the Keep. Now, come along, let's get you settled in, and then we can go to my study to start your lessons."

"Today?"

"Why not, lad?" Senital replied, reaching up to clap Jamus on the back. "The sooner we start your lessons the sooner you can be on your way home."

*****

Simen yawned and stretched in the first light of Easwin. The inn's bed, despite his prediction, had been almost too soft, making it doubly hard to get up after a good night's sleep. The ride to The Mother's Love, the little inn nestled by a hillside in the western suburbs of Aberdeen, had been long and hard since they had not dared to lift strides. He'd kept a sharp eye to the sun's journey across the sky to make sure they were not going too fast, so their eventual arrival in the city would not arouse any suspicions. When they found the inn, they both agreed it would be the perfect place to stop, refresh themselves, and spend the night before riding to the palace in the morning.

The food at evenmeal had been wonderful and Simen had entertained the small group of guests who were overnighting as well. Apparently the inn had earned a good reputation and most travelers who journeyed to or from the city stopped there for meals or beds. After spending the night, Simen understood why.

He dressed quickly, packed his bag, and knocked on Kala's door to see if she too was awake. "I'm nearly ready, Simen," she called from inside. "Go downstairs and start firstmeal. I'll be right there."

Surlep pudding with cavel milk, plates of griddlecakes, and all kinds of fruits lay out on a wide buffet table, awaiting the hungry early risers. There were only two other guests in the dining room ahead of him and they smiled as soon as they saw him.

"By the hand, if you just aren't the best Follyman I've ever heard sing," the man said. "My wife was laughing so hard at your jokes even after we went up to bed that she could hardly fall asleep."

The woman started laughing again. "That story about the Prince and the bocart...I don't know where you get all those ideas for such funny tales, but that one had my sides hurting, I was laughing so hard."

Simen offered a Follyman's bow of appreciation. "I often take my tales from life," he said, "then add a bit of my own color and decoration." He didn't dare tell her that most of that story was exactly the way Jamus and Salene had told it to him after they returned from their honeymoon in Aberdeen.

"Well no matter where your talent comes from, we just wanted you to know you made our stay here the best time we've spent anywhere in Aberdal."

"You've been in the Province long?" Simen asked as he filled his plate with griddle cakes and surlep syrup.

"A month," the woman replied. "We attended the races for the first two Sevenstins and then, when they closed for the break, we toured Aberdeen. We swam in the sea, visited all the monuments and

toured the gardens. We even got to see the King himself! He drove
through the square in a magnificent carriage drawn by a team of the
finest horses I've ever seen. They were as beautiful as the racers, but
bigger, and much stronger."

"After we get back home to Lovental, I've planned to go
visit a Lord Delran near Tulene in Telma. I was told that team came
from his farm. I'd cherish a team like that myself. Might be a bit rich
for my purse, but they would be well worth it."

Simen nodded. "I know the Lord, and I can tell you the
horses would be well worth it. They are well bred and well trained. If
you do go to see the Lord, be sure to tell him you met his Follyman. I
can't promise anything, but it might just save you a soverin or two."

Just then, Kala skipped down the stairs carrying her travel
bag. Dressed now in the traveling gown of the Prime Juris instead of
her breeches and tunic, she still managed to take two stairs at a time.
"What's on the table?" she asked, as the husband's and wife's
mouths gaped open to see her attire. The green and gold dress was
embroidered with a royal emblem on the bodice and there was hardly
person this side of the Rim who did not recognize its significance.

The husband rose to his feet, and bowed, "My Lady. Madam
Juris. We had no idea. I hope we did not offend you last evening
with our informality."

"By the Hand, Sur, don't even think once on it let alone
twice. I was having so much fun I wouldn't even have noticed an
insult if you'd offered one. My title will never deny me the pleasure
of spending time with good people like you and your beautiful wife.
Now do sit back down and fill up on some of this wonderful food. I
know I will." With that, she filled her plate with fruit, took a bowl
and spooned a generous portion of the pudding, and pulled up a chair
across from Simen. "We'd better enjoy this while we can. The royal
cook is fair, but never sets a table like this. This pudding is
delicious."

"Cooked with Mother's Love," Simen said, pointing to the
sign just outside the window.

"My mother was a good cook, but not this good," Kala said.

"The only place I've eaten like this was at Mistress
Becca's."

Kala laughed, "She won't let anybody leave her cottage without a full stomach from what I hear. Jamus told me he was sure one day he wouldn't be able to fit back out through her door after one of her meals."

"We haven't seen the innkeeper, you know," Simen whispered. "Maybe Mistress Becca slipped out of the Keep?"

Kala laughed. "Hedra, the barmaid told me the innkeeper was an old man who was planning to sell the inn soon. The cook's his daughter, Maggie. Hedra says when the inn is sold she won't stay on. It's a pity, really. It's such a lovely place."

"Things change," Simen said between bites of his griddlecakes. "Time passes and men grow old."

"Sorcerers don't," Kala said, sighing.

"Unless they want to," Simen replied. "Some do, you know. Some even choose to end their circles when they think they've lived too long."

"A blessing to have the choice?" Kala asked.

"A blessing, or a curse," he said.

*****

The journey north was wearing thin on Tamor's patience. The horses were pitiful creatures compared to the fine steeds he had hoped to steal. The wind, even with his chants of protection, seemed to bite through his weaves, and Sorra was shivering so badly she could hardly speak when he asked her if she needed to stop to rest. At least she wasn't complaining, and while that did please him, he didn't want the body they had worked too hard to prepare to collapse. He had no idea how strong a Flesher woman might be but since the cold was attacking his immortal bones, it certainly must be doing the same to her.

Ahead, he spied a cave in the cliff, and he hauled on the reins, turning his reluctant horse towards it. It had once been the den of a mountain tark and smelled of cat and carcasses, but it offered shelter and he forced his horse inside. Once under cover he dismounted and, when he saw Sorra was too stiff to throw her leg over the saddle to get down, he pulled her off her horse and plopped her down on a nearby boulder. She wrapped her arms around her shaking body and sat quietly, waiting for his next demand.

The Dark Lord wasted no time, gathering a pile of firewood with his Magic and then lighting it into a blazing fire with bolt of flame from his fingertips. Sorra shifted closer to the fire, rubbing her hands in its warmth.

Tamor chanted piles of hay for each of the horses after tethering them to some roots hanging on the cave wall and then sat down by the fire himself. He was surprised at how good the warmth felt as it curled around his limbs. "Sustenance?" he asked.

"Something hot," Sorra answered, her teeth chattering. "I did not know how cold this skin could be."

"I can see that," Tamor said. He was almost feeling sorry for her, a reaction long forgotten in the circles of his existence in Shadow. Once, hundreds of lifetimes before, he had been a man. He'd sold his allegiance to the Black Dragon for what may have once been a noble cause, but that too was forgotten along with the rest of his humanity. Now, having gained True Life after drinking enough blood to satisfy the River's demand, he was always discovering something of his ancient identity creeping into his thoughts. For some reason, Sorra's company was reminding him of how men felt about women in more ways than just physical lust. He conjured a cup of hot keldherb, some warm bread, and a bowl of broth, not at all sure of what her skin needed for nourishment. He had remember those foods from Natele's little kitchen and thought they might suit.

Gratefully, Sorra sipped the hot keldherb, pulled off a chunk of bread, dipped it in the broth and ate, chewing thoughtfully. Like so many things, her body did this instinctively but like Tamor, she too had inkling of memory, even though most of it was blocked by the savagery of Sonya's rage. "Even the Sorceress had appetite, I suppose," she said, dipping another piece of bread. "I am not a complete fool in the ways of the Flesher."

Tamor was surprised to find his hand reaching out to comfort her. "You are not a fool, Sorra. Far from it. You worked hard to learn all I could teach you. But it was not enough. My fault, not yours. The Black Dragon will know what to do. We've come too far together to give up now."

"I will never give up, My Lord. You have promised me vengeance against the Rivermaster and it consumes my being. I will do whatever you or your Master commands to get it."

"You're not afraid of the Dragon?"

She shook her head. "I am already Shadow, his kin. As long as he knows the purpose in my heart, he will see me as an ally as you have. We are all of one mind."

"As I said," Tamor repeated, "you are not a fool." He moved closer to her, his hand moving from her hand to her breast.

She shivered again, but not with cold this time. Instead she leaned into his touch, sighing. "That feels good, My Lord. Flesh to flesh is most pleasant."

For the first time in forever, Tamor reacted as a man and pulled her into his embrace, his hands groping under her clothes as she responded to his caresses.

They tumbled together to the floor of the cave, using their capes and clothes as a bed and joined in what men might have called love but to them was a mutual physical need neither one could ever begin to understand.

*****

At Windchange sunrise, Edra, Dax, and Arista had finally reached the palace courtyard. Even with Edra's enchantments, the horses had been balky, slowing the pace over and over as they shied at cats in the street and sometimes simply refused to move at all. But they had arrived and, breathing a sigh of relief, Edra hurried the couple up the steps and into the main Hall.

Prince Gareth, his eyes red-rimmed and bleary was, to Edra's surprise, still pacing the floor with nearly the same intensity he'd had when Edra had last seen him. "Twenty-eight!" Gareth cried triumphantly as he met the wall. "By the Blood, I have it now. Do you see, Edra? I have mastered the length of stride perfectly. Do you know I've done it twenty seven times in a row now without a mistake. I'll make it twenty-eight to match the count, and be happy. Don't disturb me now, I have to concentrate. If I err, I'll have to start

all over again." He started his monotonous march as the three
visitors stood in stunned silence, watching his obsessive exercise.

Much to Edra's relief, Gareth reached the wall again in
twenty-eight paces and raised his fist in victory. "I had to start over
at least a dozen times," he said. "It took me all night. I think you
brought me luck Edra. Luck."

"What I did bring was your General, My Lord, and, of
course, your Aunt."

"My dear Arista!" Gareth exclaimed when he finally noticed
her. "I do hope you brought your herbs and potions as I asked. Father
has been so ill. I thought perhaps you could do something about that
for me."

Grella started to shake her head, but then she remember the
leather pouch she had found in the woman's luggage. "Ah, yes, My
Lord, as you requested. They are in my bags. I'm sure we can find
something suitable for your Father."

"Your brother," Gareth corrected, pointing an admonishing
finger at her. "I know there is little love between you, but blood
makes a strong bond. I am confident you will not forget that."

"Blood," Grella repeated. "Yes, blood does make a strong
bond, indeed."

Gareth turned his attention to Dax. "So, you are my
general?"

"If you so will it, Sire."

"You wear the Knight's crest, I see. A trained warrior then.
Did the order teach you tactics as well? I already have a
swordmaster," he nodded to Edra. "What I need is a man who
understands the ways of war. Have you ever been in a real battle?"

"I have, My Lord."

"Did you win?"

"Let me say we were not truly defeated. Though some might
dispute it, in the end there was no victory for either side."

Gareth clucked his disapproval. "I would rather you had
won. I don't like losers."

"I was not the general in charge Your Highness. My
commander's tactics had some flaws, I fear, but as a good soldier I

followed orders. Sometimes a man can learn a great deal from another's errors."

"Quite so, quite so," Gareth agreed. "I too have learned from my mistakes. That's the very reason I want to hire your services." He blinked, and rubbed his eyes. "Tell me, Sir Dax, when you march, how long is your pace?"

"My Lord?"

"Your pace, your stride...how long? How many steps would it take to cross this Hall in a proper marching pace?"

Dax looked at Edra in confusion. "You heard the Prince," Edra said, hoping Dax would pick up the hint. "You heard him, I'm sure. Answer the question."

Dax, considered, and smiled. "Twenty-eight, My Lord. Exactly twenty-eight. A soldier trained to march would do it in exactly that, no more, no less."

Gareth smiled. "I am right again. A gold coin for every man you recruit, Sir Dax, room, board, and a purse of twenty silver every Sevenstin. If you please me, I will give you more rewards. Train my army to march to twenty-eight and to fight to a hundred."

"I will do as you require," Dax agreed. "But, My Lord, an army motivated by an enemy will train far better and more quickly. Is Aberdeen under threat?"

"Not yet, at least not now. But I have been in the past and I will not stand alone again. This time, I will not let the enemy come to me. I intend to go to the enemy with my army at my side and I will have my revenge."

"And who is this enemy?"

Gareth walked to the wall again, put his back against it and prepared to march. "The Sorcerers across the Rim," he said. Then he stepped off and started to count.

*****

Sarena felt Jamus' brow. "He still has a fever."

"I bin spongin' 'im, Milady. He's bin breathin' kinda funny sometimes, an' I think I kin feel his heart flutterin' but he's still here, so that's a good thing," Becca said. " I knows Lady Rath says it's Magic, but I remember when the fever, somethin' jest like this hit

Tallridge. Los' ma twins—may th' Hand giv'em peace--to it. Told Master Jamus all about it jest t'other day when I was sittin' here wid 'im. Anyhows, that fever done kill some ten little 'uns in ma village. 'T'weren't no good Healers like we gots now, but when the ol' folks got sick, they gots better. Took a while, but they gots better. Lost the littl'uns we did. Jami's a strong man now, all growed up. Jest like in Tallridge, he's gonna get better. He's gotta, ya know? I already's lost too many o' ma babes. I ain't gonna lose another one."

Sarena put her arm around Becca. "I'm sure he heard you, Becca. Remember, you are his anchor. He'll always come back to you no matter where he goes."

Becca leaned her head on the Healer's shoulder. "I had me a dream t'other night. I knowed I was still asleep cause I looked here at the bed and Jami weren't in it. It was like he done jest got up an' walked off somewheres. Dang tapestry, over there on the wall was kinda all misty fer jest a bit. Don't know how that curtain fell off that was over it, but when I looked back at the bed, he was there agin, jest like he is now."

Sarena got up. She had not noticed the tapestry before. "You say there was a curtain here?"

"I put in on the dresser. Musta fallen er somethin'. Things get old, they kinda droop by theyselves, ya know."

Sarena studied the tapestry, fingering the hole in its weave. Could it be? Jamus had told her once about tapestries, but it had not made much sense to her then. It all had something to do with riddles and being the Rivermaster. The images in the fabric were too faded and dirty to decipher. She considered using her Magic to refine them but she hesitated. If this hanging had anything at all to do with Jamus' illness, she couldn't risk it. Now she wished she'd asked him more questions and tried to understand. Somewhere in Magiskeep, there must be someone who might know. "Has Salene seen this?"

"The Lady ain't bin in here since ya sent her off with little Jarien. I'd be scairt ta have her anywheres near Jami till he's all better agin. Like I tole ya, fever kills the young'uns an' if it's catchin' we don't want her or her babe here."

Sarena nodded. "You're right, Becca. You still feel well, don't you?"

"So far so good, but I had me a tech o' the sickness back in Tallridge an' some says onct ya got better 't'weren't like ta git sick agin."

"If Rath is right, there's no need to worry about that." She looked again at Jamus' flushed face, stole another uneasy glance at the tapestry, and sighed. "Still there's no reason to take any chances. You call me at once if you start to feel sick. Don't wait. Promise me."

Becca held up her hand. "I swears I will, MiLady."

"Good. Your dream made me remember something Lord Jamus told me a while ago. I need to talk to someone about it. I'll be back to check on the two of you before Weswin's change." She left the chambers and hurried down the hall, heading for the gardens and Senital's vaults beyond. If anyone in Magiskeep knew about tapestries, it would be the Mage of the Vaults.

Sentinal was lost in reading a little leather covered book in his study when she found him. He jumped when she said his name, then broke out in a broad grin. "Mistress Sarena! What a delight! It's not often I see such sunshine down here. Do sit down. I can brew some keldherb for you and we can have a nice chat."

"As nice as that sounds, Master, I really didn't come for a social call. I'd rather just like to get some questions answered."

"That's why most people come down here, " Senital said, motioning to a stool and waiting for Sarena to sit before sitting back down himself. "So ask, Mistress."

"You know Lord Jamus is ill."

"Indeed I do. As a matter of fact," he waved his hand over the scattered scrolls and books on his large research table. "When I heard you had failed to Heal him, I started trying to find out about what might be going on. If I wasn't misinformed, Mistress Joria said you told her your Touch was blocked by some kind of darkness?"

"Joria's already been here?"

"Just to fill me in on the basics," Senital replied. "I should have been expecting you too."

"I take it you haven't found anything useful."

Senital held out the little book he'd been reading. "This is a diary from one of the Healers who was here in Magiskeep about sixty circles ago when a strange fever struck the Keep villages. The trouble is, there are a number of pages where the ink is too faded and blurred to read. I can almost make out a word or two now and then, but it's almost as if the pages are chanted."

"Let me see," Salene said as she took the book in her hand. When she opened it, her fingers tingled, almost exactly as they did when she started to call to the River for a Healing. 'I think you are right, Master. There is some kind of chanting on this diary. Do you know who wrote it?"

"Jada, from what I can tell. She was one of the Healers who left Magiskeep some twenty circles after Sagari became Master here. I'm not sure what happened, but there were a number of Mages who left then. There's just a little in here about it. Right before she left she wrote something about how the…wait, here, let me read it to you." He took the book back, thumbed through the pages and began to read aloud, "Times have changed, and will change again as is the way of the world. With the changing of times, men must change as well, some for the good and some the bad. I must leave here and that will be my change. The Golden Master has tarnished. I cannot stay. I leave this here for those of new times to read, to learn the lessons wisdom has granted me. When the tapestries are mended, then these pages will be full and Turan's Way made clear."

"Tapestries," Sarena said. "How strange. That's exactly why I came to see you."

"It's not at all clear to me what she's talking about," Senital said. "If you can make heads or tails of it, I'd be most grateful. I don't like riddles."

"Well, I do know Sagari was called the Golden Sorcerer, but you know that already. So we can guess that reference to his being tarnished is really quite clear."

Senital shook his head sadly. "Ah, yes. Now it makes sense. Sagari never got over the death of his first wife and son. He was a kind, gentle man before the lad died of the fever. I was still a young Master then. Wise in the ways of the children I was teaching, but foolish in the ways of men's grief. Well, I don't think there was anything I could have done anyhow, but over time Sagari became harder and harder. I buried myself down here in the vaults,

pretending I didn't notice. By the time he adopted Jamus, he was a
cruel, unjust man with all those ambitions driving him to his end. He
blamed Turan for his son's death, you see. He claimed the fever had
come from across the Rim with one of the traders who'd come here
through the Norreaches. I think he believed if he conquered the
world of mortals he could somehow get rid of his pain."

"I've never heard any of this, even from Joria."

"She won't speak of it. No one who knew Sagari back then
would speak of it freely. I wouldn't even be telling you now if Lord
Jamus weren't ill. I think we were all too ashamed that we hadn't
tried to do anything to stop him."

"What could any of you have done? Sagari was a Seven Arts
Mage and more dangerous than even I care to admit. Once he set his
mind to something only another Master of greater power could have
stopped him."

"Like Lord Jamus," Senital said, nodding. "Still, if we'd
united...."

"Joria and I tried more than once and failed, Senital. I feel
guilty myself, if it makes you feel any better, but I've resigned
myself to the fact that there was really nothing I could have done.
Besides, I don't think it was part of Turan's Way for us to stop him.
I'd wager your books of prophecy would prove it was the
Rivermaster and the Rivermaster alone who would right those
wrongs."

"You are right, of course, Sarena. Turan's fate will always
be in Jamus' hands. It's a heavy burden he bears." He sighed. "I wish
I could help ease it. I always felt so sorry for him when he was a lad.
Sagari was a poor father for a boy like him. I think Jamus always
thought it was his fault he was treated so badly."

"It would be a gift to be able to go back in time and change
what we've done in the past, but we can't. There's no reason to
torment ourselves about it."

"There is no time in the Way, Mistress."

Sarena shivered. "And men go mad in the Mirrors. Jamus
may travel them, but I never would. It'a hard enough dealing with
today let alone wandering about in all the confusion of yesterdays
and tomorrows."

"If I'm correct, the tapestries you're asking about and the
Way are not so different."

"How?"

"Time," Senital said, unrolling a scroll from his pile. "The
Eldenlore." He pointed at some runes on the parchment. "The Hand
weaves the tapestries of time. Threads broken, threads mended by
those who pass the weaves. Only one in the Circle can mend them,
only one can mend the path of Turan's Way, only one can mend the
past, mend the present, mend the future make the image whole to
fulfill the promise made."

"Another riddle," Sarena sighed.

"At least this one has some explanation in the other histories.
I've had to piece things together, but I did find mention that the
Rivermaster needs to assure Turan's Way by righting wrongs and to
do that he needs to travel into the Way to seek out the past. Here," he
pointed again at the parchment, "it says…'the tapestry is but a mirror
of memory. He who walks its story has the power to join the rivers
and one day, answer all the questions.'"

"I wonder about all this talk of mending the threads in the
past, suggests that by changing something in one of those tapestries,
the Rivermaster could change the future?"

Senital shrugged. "I'm still finding those answers myself,
but it would seem so. One new deviation could change the path of
Turan's Way."

"What would that be like?" Sarena asked, as much to herself
as to Sentinal. "To think, one moment something you had known all
your life was true as no longer."

"It is a curious thing to think about," Senital agreed. "All
these chronicles and scrolls I've been reading all these circles would
be new texts. Would I be aware they had changed, or would I have
read them already in their new incarnations?" He rubbed his chin
thoughtfully. "Would I even remember how they had been?"

"How could you? Their old meanings would have never
even existed."

Senital was starting to bounce with excitement. He got up
from his stool and started to pace his study. "I suppose it might be
like a dream you've had in your sleep—one of those dreams that

seems positively real when you are in it, but when you wake up, you can't remember a thing. Why, you think you may have had a dream, and there might even be a fragment of it left in your head, but the whole of it that had so captured you was gone. Fascinating."

"People you knew, days you'd spent walking in the sunshine, moments of joy or sorrow could be wiped away. I'm not sure I like that idea."

"They say when the Great Circle closes, that's exactly what happens, My Lady. All knowledge is lost and those who live through the closing, as most men do must start to learn everything all over again." He paused in his pacing and laughed a little at the idea. "To think, I'd have to start reading all this from the beginning."

"But first you would have to learn how to read, Senital," Sarena reminded him. "It's no wonder the wise Mages fear the Circle's Close so much. They would have to sacrifice a lifetime of learning."

"Ah yes," Senital agreed, "but if the rest of our theory is correct, they wouldn't even know what they'd lost. Now, you came to ask about tapestries. Did you ever tell me why?"

"There is a strange tapestry in Jamus' chambers. It been hidden by curtains for circles, but just the other night, somehow the curtains fell away and the tapestry was revealed. Its images are faded and blurred, much like the pages of that diary. And it's frayed in the middle as if it could use a good mending."

"There's more," Senital said, not questioning.

Sarena nodded. "Becca's been watching over Jamus and she told me she woke up and thought he was gone from his bed—the very night that curtain fell. She thinks it was all a dream because she turned back and he was there, still asleep. But I'm not so sure. When I put my hand on his head to feel for the fever, aside from the heat, I felt nothing."

"Joria said your Touch was being blocked by some kind of darkness."

Sarena shook her head slowly. "No, it's not the darkness. You see, Senital, ever since I first met Jamus every time I touched him I would feel his power. It was like an irresistible force drawing me to him. I will not tell you all the embarrassing details, but suffice it to say it was quite intoxicating. Today, when I touched him, I felt nothing. It was almost as if he were someone else entirely."

"Reflection?"

"Perhaps. It looks like Jamus and if he is reflection, he is solid flesh and blood. I thought perhaps there might be something in your Vaults to explain it all."

"Come, Mistress, I would like to see this tapestry for myself and our sleeping Lord. Not all knowledge comes from books. Sometimes you have to see things for yourself."

IX

Tamor reached out, grabbed Sorra's hand and pulled her up the last several feet into the Dragon's Cave. They had left the horses tied to a tree some thirty feet below and come the rest of the way on foot up a steep, icy trail. Again, had he been alone, the Dark Master would have flown here on the night wind, so this was another new experience for him and when he stood beside the stalagmites shimmering around the Dragon's nest, he was out of breath and could hardly speak. "My Great Lord. I have come to ask your help."

The Dragon uncoiled one of its sinuous tentacles and seemed to stretch as it opened its dark, impenetrable eyes to look at his visitors. Unlike his brothers and sisters, whose clean lines and leathery wings gave them an almost beautiful grace, he was grotesque and misshapen. His huge head was dominated by massive jaws with teeth sticking out on top, bottom and both sides. His snout best resembled a pig's and his eyes, though huge, were empty caverns of inky black. Long tentacles flicked from his chin and replaced what would have been claws on a better Dragon, and his wings, folded now around his giant mound of a body, were covered with mostly dark feathers instead of scales. His back was feathered too, making him appear to be a hellish cross between bird and lizard, a creature born of nightmares instead of Magic's River. "Everendings, ever be, why does Dark One seeketh me? Need for power given still, any more is Dragon's will."

Tamor pushed Sorra forward. She had been cowering behind him. "I bring this woman, part of my plan to bring the Rivermaster to his knees before you. But she is weak of mind and learning. Give her your great knowledge of Kiselor's world so she may walk it with her deception."

The Dragon fixed his eyes on Sorra and she let out a little scream as one of the ebony tentacles licked at her cheek. "Soft one this," the Dragon said, "take Dragon kiss. Why you be here to aid the Dark Lord?"

Sorra glanced over at Tamor in confusion.

"He wants to know why you want to help us. Answer him, woman, or he will do more than just kiss your cheek."

"I...I hate Lord Jamus," she replied.

"Ah, hate be good reason. Blackwing taste Shadow in Flesher skin."

"I am a Reflection Lord Tamor freed from the Way," she said, gaining a little confidence now. "The Sorceress who birthed me was wronged by the Rivermaster."

"Have plan?"

"Lord Tamor has a plan, My Lord Dragon, but I do not yet know the whole of it. I do know I am to go to Magiskeep wearing this skin to do his bidding. He promises me it will give me the vengeance I desire."

"Good. The best soldiers battle for selves, not masters."

"Mistress Sorra will do as I tell her because she hates the Sorcerer as much as you and I do, Great One. We can have no better ally."

"She needs much from me?"

"The skin...the Flesher she impersonates was an educated woman, well schooled in the reading and writing of man's language. I have taught her some of the customs of men, but this learning is not an easy thing to master. She was not unknown in the villages of the Keep and it's important to my plan that she be trusted, so she needs to know what to do with a quill and book."

"Foolish tools of mortals," the Dragon scoffed. "Ignorance is Blackwing's friend."

"But you do have the knowledge."

"Must know enemy to gain victory. I have what you need. Come, woman. Come close. Need Dragon's breath."

Reluctantly, Sorra walked towards the Dragon. His breath was rank, nauseating, smelling of rotten carrion. It was all she could do to keep her stomach as his tongue licked her mouth. A slimy tentacle wrapped around her thigh, pulling her close to his breast as another probed between her legs, sending new shivers through her body as he pulsed within her, seeking, always seeking. She felt herself go limp, surrendering, unable to do more then let her body respond to the invasion. Then, the world exploded, pain searing up through her loins, into her breast and finally into her mind. She arched back, screamed, and fainted.

"Is done," the Dragon said. The creature's lips curled into a grin. "Was good for Blackwing. Good."

Tamor gritted his teeth fighting to keep silent in the face of this hideous beast he had to obey. He did not know this new feeling filling his mind, driving him to rage against his master.

Jealousy.

He picked Sorra up in his arms and stumbled out to the trail, sliding down the rocks to the horses. Gently, he lifted her up on his own horse, mounted behind her, and leading her horse, headed down the trail.

The cave where they had spent the night before was two spans farther down and Sorra's eyes did not flutter open until they were halfway there. "My Lord?" she whispered hoarsely, barely aware she was in his embrace.

"I have you," Tamor said, holding her even tighter so she would not fall. "I did not expect it to be so hard for you."

She snuggled up against his chest. "You are a much better lover."

He would have laughed, if he'd known how, but his body had not yet mastered the skill, so all he did was cough instead. "You are feeling better then?"

"Now that I am with you, I am, My Lord. This skin was not unknown to men before I wore it."

"He did not need to take you like that to teach you. It was his lust driving him. I am sorry. Even I did not expect that."

"How much farther to our cave?"

"Just around the next bend. I'll build a fire and make more broth if you wish."

"That's not what I want from you, My Lord. 'The heart is hollow that does not seek the touch of a lover. The night is empty that does not fill with the touch of another's hand. The soul is barren that does not seek the comfort for the heart,'" she said, quoting the text of an Elden lay.

Tamor stiffened, "How did you know those words?"

"I just know them," she replied. "My head is full of words like that—poems, songs, stories. I can see them in my head. It's truly wonderful."

"He did it, then," Tamor said.

But what a terrible price to pay.

*****

King Gailvarg was sitting on a cushioned bench staring out the window when his manservant admitted Kala to his conference room for an audience. "My Liege, I have come at your request," she said. "I understand you need my advice."

"Ah, Madam Juris, Mistress Kala, my favorite Seer. Welcome, welcome. Do come and sit down. You say I sent for you?"

"You did, My Liege. Your messenger said it was important. Is there some case you are deciding which needs the advice of my Sight?"

"Let me think, let me think. My mind's been a bit befuddled of late. You know I have been ill."

"Yes, I do know. And I am glad to see you up and about again. We have all been worried about you."

"Worried that my scamp of a son would be taking over the throne?" Gailvarg asked. "He is a bit of a scalawag, but he is my son, after all. He can't be all bad, can he?"

"I wouldn't know, My Lord, I have never Searched him."

"Ah, yes, you Seers do judge men differently than most. You, of all, can see the color of their hearts. I cannot....oh, that's what it is. Now I know. Borders, that's it. Something about borders. Two lords are claiming the same piece of land in Lovental. It is a fertile tract between them. Each seems to have a valid claim, but one of them is lying."

"Are there witnesses?"

Gailvarg nodded. "On both sides, equally persuasive. The Lords have troops of their own, well armed and trained. If I cannot settle the matter once and for all they threaten war to do it for me. I do not have the troops myself to suppress an uprising." His eyes drifted back to the window. "Gareth has petitioned me to build an army, did you know? Edra says it's a good idea...no, was it Jyp? Or maybe I said it myself…it would be a good project for the Prince, you see. The military demands discipline and he could use some. So I told them I approved. We've been at peace so long, I never needed an army, you see. That field over there," he pointed, "they could practice out there and I could watch from this nice bench. It was my wife's favorite place to sit on sunny days, you see, so I would like to sit here and watch the soldiers marching back and forth, back and forth."

Kala nodded, her heart lurching as she listened to his rambling. This was not the wise and competent ruler she had once known. "It is a lovely view, Sire."

"Well, why is it you are here again? I've forgotten."

"The land dispute, My King. You needed my advice."

"Maybe I should just let them fight it out. That would teach them a lesson now, wouldn't it."

"It's never good to fight if it can be avoided. It would be much better if we could find an acceptable settlement instead."

"Wouldn't a war be beautiful though?" the King asked, his face clouded over with a mist Kala's Sight perceived without even trying. It was as if he were behind a veil. "Shining armor, the clash of swords ringing through the air, and the bravery. Oh, the bravery."

"The Seers are people of peace, My Lord. We do not condone war, for any reason."

"You're wrong, My Juris. It was your people who drove the Sorcerers out of Turan in Wizardchase. The King had an army then." He grinned, and tapped his nose with his finger, "I have Sorcerers in the palace now, you know. My son has found them quite useful. He's a good judge of men, you see. A good judge of men. Don't you agree?"

For one of the few times in her life, Kala broke her Seer's oath and lied. "Yes, My Liege, I do."

*****

Simen was waiting for Kala in the King's antechamber. Jyp saw him there as he was passing and stopped in his tracks. Was it Jamus? Here in Aberdeen. He took a better look, shook off the thought and entered the room.

"Sur," he said, "I hope you will excuse my intrusion, but you look so much like someone I know I had to assure myself. Now that I can see your face, I know you are not Lord Jamus, but the resemblance is uncanny."

Simen rose and extended his hand in greeting. "I am his brother, Simen. And your name?"

"Jyp," he replied, returning the gesture with one more familiar to the Keep. He noted Simen's reaction and continued, "I met Lord Jamus' wife some time ago. I hope she spoke of me."

"She did, Master Jyp, and most kindly, I must admit." His gaze darted to the hall to make sure there was no one around to hear. "I'm not sure we should talk much more here in the palace."

"What? About the fact that I am a Sorcerer? No, no, it's fine. I am still here in Prince Gareth's employ and even the King himself has accepted me." He lowered his voice. "While there are secrets I keep from them, they do know I am of the Magic."

"We should talk," Simen replied. "I am here with Jur Kala."

"The Seer. Another strange alliance in times like these. The King has been ill, you know. Bless the Hand I have managed to Heal him, at least to some degree. He is not fully recovered, but I hope my herbs and the River will grant him better health soon. It is not yet time for the Prince to inherit the throne."

"So I have heard," Simen said. "The King is a fine man."

"The King is mad," Kala said as she emerged from the inner room. "He is really quite distracted and I could not read through to his reason."

"My Lady," Simen answered quickly, 'This is Master Jyp, advisor to the King."

"And Sorcerer," Kala finished. "You are a Healer of some skill, Sur. Have you Touched Gailvarg? What's wrong with him?"

Jyp sighed, "Not here, My Lady. Master Edra and I have private chambers where we can talk. He is giving the Prince his lesson in arms. We'll have a span or so undisturbed if you would like to come with me now."

Kala nodded and the three of them headed for Jyp's rooms.

The walls of the Sorcerers' study were covered with all sorts of charts and illustrations, the large counter by the far wall had flasks and jars full of herbs and potions. Even with his limited knowledge of Magic, Simen recognized a fraud when he saw one. Most of the paraphernalia and materials were useless to a true Master.

"Posh and nonsense," Jyp said looking around the cluttered room. "I spend more time trying to find ways to pretend I know what I'm doing than I do actually doing anything. The Prince is always impressed and Edra…well, Master Edra can cast some fairly effective spells, but he has absolutely no idea how he does it."

"I do," Simen told him. "And if the Silver River runs as does the Gold, there is only one Edra. If he is the man I believe him to be, he is not to be trusted."

"I knew he was a fool, but no more," Jyp said.

"Edra," Kala said. "Wasn't he the leader of the Cauge in Arcula Jamus told us about?"

Simen nodded. "Sounds like it. As for his Magic, Jyp, the reason you don't understand it is because he draws on another River. His power depends on pure emotion, not logic. It's alien to the Mages of Magiskeep."

Jyp seemed excited by the prospect. "That explains everything. Every time he does cast a spell, I can't understand how he does it, and he certainly can't tell me. We've been at odds for months over this. I was beginning to believe one or both of us were just dolts."

"You are no dolt, Master," Kala replied, "and I need no Sight to see that. Frankly, while your relationship with Edra is certainly important, I am far more interested in what you know about the King."

"Gareth has been poisoning him," Jyp said.

"You're sure of this?"

"I am a Healer of considerable skill, My Lady. Keep trained nearly to Master's Art. Had I stayed in Magiskeep I would have been so named in at least three Arts, perhaps four. The first time I Touched Gailvarg sensed the taint of poison. Since then I've done a bit of my own kind of searching and discovered some disturbing truths. Gareth had a large collection of herbs and brews stashed away in some of the deeper chambers of the palace. It's been all I could do to keep my eye on him since I've been here and on no less than five occasions I've caught him slipping something noxious into the King's food or drink. I've countered every effort so far and the King is rallying, but I'm afraid some damage has already be done that even Master's Art cannot reverse."

"It's affected his mind?"

"That's only the half of it, I'm afraid. His heart is failing and I'm sure there's more weakness inside him. With good care, he will still live a long time, but without someone who knows what's going on watching over him, I don't know what might happen. I've been leading Gareth along as best I can to convince him to keep me here in the palace. So far it's worked, but I have to be careful how I behave around him. I hope you'll understand while you're here in case you hear me say something outlandish."

"It's a good thing you're telling me this," Kala told him. "I am honor bound to speak the Truth to the King and public in all things. I must admit, having Sorcerers for friends has pressed me to go back on those vows more than once. I guess I'll just have to resign myself to it again."

"Thank you, Madam. I know how important those Vows are to you, sworn as you are to Grandisite. But some of the Seers about the city have already started to join our Counsel to keep watch over the Royal Household's abuse of power under Gareth's hand. I think your Lady Salene had a lot to do with that. Her rather unique cure for some of the Prince's rather offensive behaviors did rally some of our women to the cause."

"The Vision does pass down through the mothers," Kala told him. "The best Seers are often women. I would think they would find Salene inspiring."

"Her weave is very clever, actually and it's what brought me here to the palace in the first place, at least in Gareth's mind. He wants me to cure him."

"Salene's spell is Master's Art," Simen offered, "not easily undone even by another Master."

"That is true, but I've studied it often enough to sift its secrets. Gareth has a terrible habit of dropping his pants nearly every time he sees me…well, in private at least…asking me to try again. I make all kind of gestures and screw up my face just so." He twisted his mouth, furrowed his brow and grimaced. "Then, I tell him I failed again but I was so much closer. Someday, he's either going to kick me out of the palace on my backside, or I'll have to loosen at least a thread or two."

Simen laughed. "Too bad I can't use that story in my act. The audience loves the tale of the Prince and the bocart already. A version of this one would be priceless."

"The bocart enchantment was quite public," Jyp agreed, "and it was all I could do myself to keep a straight face looking at Gareth after Jamus cast that spell on him. He made a good bocart, I must admit. It was a perfect transformation and a masterful illusion. I had to set the Prince free, of course, but it was fun while it lasted."

"The trouble is, none of this is Follyman's pranks anymore," Kala said. "If Gailvarg dies and Gareth has his army, who knows what kind of havoc he'll wreak."

"He wants to make war on Magiskeep," Jyp said. "Revenge for what Salene did to him. Even if I do cure him, I doubt it would stop him."

"So what do we do, then? Gailvarg has approved the army. Once Gareth has forces, there'll be no stopping him."

"Magic has friends in Turan, My Lady. The Sorcerers are not as hated as you may think."

"You yourself know even Grandisite was willing to take Lord Jamus in once your masters recognized his virtue," Simen offered. "The Seers have a great deal of influence."

"And there are others," Jyp said. "We all—as I am already doing—simply need to keep watch. If the need arises, we should have ample warning to put out a call to our allies to raise an army of our own. Remember, we will have the River on our side."

*****

Lacking even the smallest clue to the riddle, Jamus had decided studying in Magiskeep would at least be a pleasant diversion in what was fast becoming a confusing tapestry. Everything except Sagari fit perfectly into the Magiskeep he knew. The cast of characters varied, of course, since so many circles separated this world from the one he lived in, but the rest? It was still Magiskeep.

So, he would simply let the River take him along on its currents without trying to swim. Sooner or later something would happen of note.

Senital was a patient teacher, well versed in Comprehension with a facility for explaining complex ideas in simple, clear terms. While Jamus himself was expert in the Art, he was actually learning a great deal about how to communicate its finer aspects so even the youngest Prentice could understand. If anything, when he returned home, he could always take up teaching himself, or even convince Senital to return to the classroom.

All was going well by the end of the first Sevenstin. Senital had a wealth of scrolls Jamus had never seen before, and he found himself continually delving into them to the point of distraction. It would soon prove his undoing. Senital had just brewed a fresh pot of keldherb and poured Jamus a mugful. He took a sip, realized it was too hot to drink, and without thinking tossed a cooling sphere into it with a casual flick of his finger while he kept on reading.

Senital noticed. "All right, Master Jarius, the time has come for you to tell me the truth."

Still lost in the text of a story about The Closing of the First Great Circle, Jamus reacted. "Master?"

"I said, it's time for you to tell me the truth."

Jamus finally broke from his reading and looked up to meet Senital's stelin gaze. "What do you mean?"

"Don't think I haven't been suspicious these last few winds, lad. You learn things too easily for someone who claims to have no schooling--try as you might to convince me otherwise with your pretended ignorance. And now, I see you using Master's Art to cool your drink with no more effort than it takes you to breathe."

Jamus frowned. The spell had been simple and he'd done it without a thought. It had been a foolish move, but Senital was a man to be trusted, so at least he had made the mistake in the right place. "I am a traveler of the Way," he said. "To explain any more might take till well past Norwin."

To his relief, Senital smiled. "Ah, so I was not mistaken about you. We are not in the mirrors, though. Surely you know that."

"I am in a tapestry, if that means anything to you, Master Senital. I am here to solve a riddle."

"By the Blood, the Rivermaster? From which circle?"

Jamus was taken aback by Senital's question. Apparently this Master was far better informed than he thought, even so long ago.

Jamus replied. "As near as I can tell, this is some fifty circles into the past for me. I haven't found the riddle yet, let alone the answer, so the weave is still broken."

"Makes sense, makes sense," Senital muttered. "I've been feeling uneasy for the last month or so as if there was something wrong on Turan's Way. It is said all the tapestries must be mended."

"So the legends go," Jamus told him.

"This tapestry of yours," Senital asked, "what did it picture?"

"I'm not sure," Jamus replied. "The image was faded and I was feverish when I first saw it. Faces are all I remember. In my delirium, I thought they were crying."

Senital leaned forward, intent on every word. "You were sick when you entered the weave? You don't seem sick now."

"As soon as my feet landed on the streets of the Keep, I felt fine.To be honest, if I didn't have to face some damned riddle, I'd almost be happy to stay." As he said, it, he realized a part of him would be happy here. Just meeting the Sagari he had always dreamed of had somehow started to heal some of the pain of his own childhood. Maybe that was why his fever and headache were gone. Could that be the riddle? "Tell me about Sagari," he said. "He is not the same man I knew."

"There is not much more to tell. You met him and saw him with his son. He is a doting father a good Master, powerful in Magic, and generous to a fault. Does he change so much?"

"Perhaps he's part of the riddle," Jamus sighed. "So far, he's the only thing out of place in the Keep. You are the same, a bit older, perhaps."

"Will I be here or in the Vaults?"

Jamus laughed, "So now I have the power do scry the future do I? Suppose something I do while I'm here changes it? I might send you off to Aberdeen to work as the King's Librarian."

"That wouldn't be bad, although I do like Magiskeep."

"Suffice it to say I will know you, Master Senital, and be privileged to call you my friend, as I hope I can now."

"You have another name too?"

"I won't tell you that either," Jamus answered. "Here I am Jarius, a mage of modest skill trying to learn how to grow corn for his father. I would like to keep it that way. I've traveled enough tapestries to realize the River guides me and the less I swim against its waters, the better."

"Well, then, let us search the Elden texts to see if there is anything here about tapestries and riddles to help you along. I see no point in wasting time giving you any more lessons in Comprehension. We'll go to the Vaults and do a bit of study. Maybe we can get you back on your way home before Master Sagari decides you've had enough of my lessons and sends you off to Mistress Joria. I'm not even sure your illusions hiding your identity would hold up under her scrutiny."

As sure as he was that even Joria would never be able to sift through the complex sphere of reflections he had woven to disguise himself, Jamus would rather not confront the Mistress of Illusion in her classroom. A casual meeting to satisfy his curiosity of what she was like in this time and place was one thing, but he had never had much luck confusing her with his uncanny talent for her class assignments and he didn't intend to start now.

The Vaults were exactly as they should be as well except much less cluttered than they were at home with Senital as the Master. Once he took charge, there were always scrolls and open books lying all over as he pursues some project or another. Now the tall study tabes were bare and the shelves neat and organized.

Still, it didn't take long for the room to take on its more familiar appearance once Senital started pulling texts. "Here's something," he said, pulling out a parchment page. "It's in the Eldentongue, but one of the mages has translated it. '*The Hand weaves the tapestries of time. Threads broken, threads mended by those who pass the weaves. Only one in the Circle can mend them, only one can mend the path of Turan's Way, only one can mend the past, mend the present, mend the future, make the image whole to fulfill the promise made,* '" he read aloud. "If this is accurate, you certainly are right about there being no time in these tapestries of yours. I hope that offers some reassurance."

"Not much new there, but, as you say, reassuring." Jamus rubbed his eyes wearily. "Be it within a tapestry or not, it must be getting late. I'm feeling very tired all of a sudden."

"I never see the sun or feel the winds change when I'm down here. Come on, Lad, if Evenmeal is done perhaps we can convince the cooks to serve us a Lastmeal snack. My stomach's grumbling and Mistress Ferna is a good hand with baking."

"Mistress Ferna," Jamus said as they climbed the stairs and headed out into the last breaths of Weswin. "She is in my Keep as well."

"My goodness. Her baking skills would have doubled by then. I can hardly imagine how wonderful that would be."

The darkness hid Jamus' grin. He was going to take special care to make sure nothing he did in this tapestry was ever going to affect Senital's future with the baker. If anyone deserved some happiness, it was the little mage of the Vaults.

*****

"March," Dax ordered to the nineteenth recruit of the day. He was wasting his time, ordering his potential soldiers to cross the floor in the palace Hall while the Prince watched and counted. While they were not turning down any of the young men who came to join the new royal army, Gareth had decided he needed an elite squadron to surround him when they went off to battle. The march was to find the likely candidates. It was absurd, but even Dax knew better than to cross the Prince when he had decided on something.

The elite squadron was not exactly Gareth's idea. It was one Edra had put into his head. Using the Cauge as a model, the Arculan had suggested a special guard for the Prince as well as a cavalry unit similar to the Riders. "You need men sworn to protect you alone, My Lord," he said, "and horsemen to ride at your behest. You decide the test for your guard—something to prove their worth. Then we'll need some fine horses to suit your mounted unit so the people will stand in awe of them. In my world a man rider's worth was measured by his horse. The beasts are far more common here in Turan, but the common people still appreciate a good mount and the man astride it."

"Something like the animal Juris Kala's companion rode in on," Gareth said. "Beautiful black creature. We'll have to ask him where he bought him. Perhaps there are more like him. We might not accomplish it at first, but can you picture a whole troop of cavalry mounted on identical horses riding into battle?"

"It would be a thing of beauty, My Lord." Seeing the opportunity to further secure his own position in the palace, Edra took up the challenge. "You know, My Lord, I was accounted a good judge of horseflesh in my homeland. I would be pleased to find ones worthy to represent the Royal seat if you wish."

Gareth clapped his hands in delight. "Wonderful, Edra. You have such marvelous ideas. Oh, and do find a good mount for me. I am by all accounts a good rider, but I had a bad turn with a brute of a beast months past in the last circle and it took me forever to recover. I'd want a docile animal now—something elegant and kind. I'm a bit more cautious about what I straddle of late."

Edra coughed, checking himself before he made a crude joke about that, considering the Prince's physical lack. There were rare times when Gareth might have appreciated it, but he was not drunk now, so Edra snapped his mouth shut and nodded.

"Could you find me a gray, perhaps? Dappled, I think. I would like to stand out, you see. While it would make me more conspicuous to the enemy, I'd have my guards. If you think it's wise, a gray would be pretty."

"Indeed, My Lord. I'll start asking around the city now. There may be some dealers at the Course who know of good breeders in Turan." He spun on his heel after a quick bow and hurried from the room before he was consumed with laughter.

Matters only became more absurd when Gareth decided that marching across the Hall would be a good test for selecting his guardsmen. Part of the absurdity was that word spread quickly of both the requirements of the test and its purpose as soon as the first nine men were examined.

"If you want to wear the royal livery and bow to the Prince's every whim," one man told another, do your march in twenty-eight paces, no more, no less. "Watch the far wall as you walk and count carefully, adjusting your stride to make the right number. If you don't want the job, well, then walk as you will."

Dull as he was to any details beyond his obsessive counting, Gareth hardly noticed how many of the men who passed his test were nearly staggering through their final steps to the last wall. Instead, he was delighted that, by the end of the day, they had managed to find forty perfectly-strided soldiers to march at his side, filling every twenty-eight spans of march with exactly twenty-eight steps. Whether they had either the strength or talent to fight for him with any skill mattered little as long as they could keep their strides exact.

Dax snorted with disgust at the whole display and headed for the local tavern to meet Melthus as soon as the testing day was done, his head pounding with one too many twenty-eights and a growing hatred for the Prince.

"He's a fool," he snarled, downing a pint of ale in one gulp. "If this is what Fleshers consider a good King, then it's a wonder the Shadow Lord hasn't conquered them a hundred times over—sorry, I should have said twenty-eight times over already," he spat. He waved his hand to order another pint, tossing a gold on the table to pay for both his and Melthus's drinks. "Have as much as you want, my friend. I have plenty of money. The Prince may be an idiot but he does pay me well."

"I can see that," Melthus said eyeing Dax's heavy purse. "Do you think his twenty-eight stride soldiers will fight for the Dark Lord as well if we need them? I'm finding recruits for the Tamor's cause in the streets, but I cannot promise their skills. Trained warriors would do us some good."

"Well, the beauty of it is that apparently, the Prince's enemy and our Lord's enemy are one and the same."

"The Rivermaster and his kind?"

Dax nodded and finished off another pint. "He harbors a grudge against them. I haven't quite gotten the whole story yet, but I've heard some of the women in the palace giggling about some kind of curse the Sorcerer put on the Prince. I'm sure Grell...Arista will have find out the details soon enough. The Prince was pretty cozy with his Aunt about some kind of secrets. She's no fool herself, our shadowmate. She'll find out what it's all about."

"If Gareth plans on making war on Magiskeep, you will train them honestly then, I take it. I had thought our time in Aberdeen would have been spent hunting together instead of actually pursuing our duty to the Dark Lord."

"I'll still have time to hunt," Dax replied. "After dealing with that buffoon, I'll need some recreation. You know he has a Sorcerer as an advisor?"

"No."

"One of the Arculans, one I know well. Edra once of the Cauge. He's missing a hand. When I was The Searcher he made a pact with Tamor. I suspect he had to give the ring back." He grinned and slapped his hand down on the table. "One more drink and we'll go hunting together. There are many dark alleys near the docks."

X

Tamor and Sorra made it back to the cabin in a quarter of the spans it had taken them to reach the Dragon's Lair. Once the Dark Lord knew the roads, he was able to lift the horse's strides to take to the clouds. The animals had been too weary to protest or exalt in the new mode of travel, their spirits completely broken by the journey. Tamor's Healing skills had kept them somewhat sound of body, but his chanting had drained what little heart they had ever had.

But it was the Way of Shadows to drain life and will from everything it touched. It was the very reason for drinking blood to seek True Life once a Shadow wore Flesher skin. Otherwise, the shell would start to dry up, or rot, tainted by the poisoning of darkness. "You will need to eat soon," Tamor told her as he led her into the house. I spied a farm just down in the valley. Tonight, we will find you a feast to restore you."

"I am tired," Sorra said. "And thirsty. Amberwine would do for now."

"A toast then," the Dark Lord told her, conjuring a carafe and two goblets of amberwine. "We need to honor your success."

"Shall I offer a poem?" Sorra teased.

"Not if it keeps us out of our bed, Dear One," Tamor said, hardly thinking how strange it was for him to say such a thing. True Life was taking over more than just his body--it was also taking over his mind.

They toasted and spent the spans before Norwin lying together.

Darkness fell with windchange, and Tamor gently shook Sorra awake. "Come, get up. We need to find you something to eat."

Together, they made their way out into the moonlight. "It's bright...and beautiful," she said.

"I'll cast a cloud when we reach the farm so no one will see us. If we're lucky and you are hungry enough, perhaps we can find you more than one Flesher to feast on."

She smiled, her white teeth glittering.

The left the horses in the barn, choosing instead to make their way down the foot trail to the little farm. Natale's neighbors were but a half span's walk down a shallow hill by daylight. By night, it took the Shadow couple a quarter span more.

As he promised, Tamor cloaked the moon in clouds and pushed open the farmhouse door. The house had one large room, combining kitchen, sitting room and bedroom, all in one. There, on a cot near the back wall lay a woman with a toddler in her arms, both sound asleep. A baby lay in the cradle at her side. "The babe is mine," Tamor whispered. "You will have the mother and child."

"What shall I do?"

Tamor smiled and pointed at the baby. "Strangle that one. It should be easy—a first lesson in the hunt. I will take care of the other two and prepare your meal."

He cast another spell of darkness on them both and they approached their victims.

The baby let out a little squeak as Sorra's hands closed around its throat, and the mother's eyes flew open, "Romy? What's wrong?"

Tamor pounced, pinioning her and rolling her body over to crush the toddler underneath. The child began to scream and flail, but he held firm Magic and muscle binding her as the mother struggled to get away. "You are mine now, you and your little brat. Will you welcome the darkness?"

"My babies—Baren, you're crushin' 'im! Let me up afore he cain't breathe no more."

"That is exactly what I want," Tamor hissed, pushing down even harder as the child's cries became desperate whimpers.

"He's dyin', lemme off 'im. I'd do whate'er ya wants, jest let me babe alone."

"You'll do what I want whether he lives or dies," Tamor said, drawing his dagger. He rolled her again to face him tying her her body into coils of dark enchantment so she could not move. With practiced skill, he slit open the front of her nightgown and traced a line between her breasts down to her bellybutton.

She whimpered now as the blood began to flow. "Please, me babes, please."

Tamor bent his face to her breast and licked the blood. "Good," he said, "Warm. It should please my mistress. I do this for her, you know. It is her first feast."

The child was silent now and still. Tamor reached under the mother and dragged the little body out, dangling the child by one leg in her face. Tears streamed down her face. "Baren, my sweet little boy."

"Weep, mourn, Flesher. The grief and terror make the blood more sweet." He pinned her with his knee as he freed a hand to slit the child's belly so his guts spewed out, into his mother's face.

She gagged, screaming now, "No, no, no!"

Tamor beckoned to Sorra and slung the child's body to her. "An appetizer before the main meal," he said.

Greedily, Sorra put her mouth to the child's belly and began to drink.

Tamor grabbed the mother's chin, wiped some of the child's offal from her eyes, and twisted her head so she could see Sorra. "See? My Lady's joy is your sorrow."

"Baren, Baren," the mother cried helplessly.

"Now, to you." Tamor used his blade again, carving into her stomach. He knew just how far to go to keep her alive. Her screams were Shadowmusic to his ears, for each one seasoned the dish so much better. He slid his hand into her, feeling for organs, taking pleasure in the warmth of her entrails. At last it was time. Sorra was done with the boy. "Come, my dear one. The feast is ready. You must finish what I have begun. Do as you will." He handed her his dagger as she drew near the gasping woman.

Sorra studied the woman, whose face was already growing pale as the blood drained from her body. Then she bent and kissed her mouth. "I thank you for your kindness," she whispered.

Then, she plunged the dagger into the woman's heart, fell on her still-twitching body and began to feed.

Tamor threw back his head and laughed. Then he picked up the baby, retrieved his dagger, slit the little body nearly in half, and began to drink.

Their first hunt together had been nearly perfect.

*****

Jamus woke after another good night's sleep in the tapestry. At least he was getting some good rest and was feeling stronger each day. He got up, dressed in the gray tunic of Prenticeship, and headed out into the common dining room. His mind flooded with memories as he surveyed the tables full of laughing students eating and enjoying themselves before heading off to the rigors of the classroom. Out of old habits, he chose an empty table set apart from the rest and sat down. It only took a minute for one of the servingmen to place a platter of eggs, ham, and cheese in front of him. Feeling hungry for the first time in days, he began to eat.

"So, Farmer, we heard you didn't get a proper welcome to the Keep yet. At least not to the Scape."

Jamus looked up to see three older Prentices looking down at him. The tallest of the group, a lanky blond headed fellow, had his arms folded in front of him and was grinning. Jamus smiled back and stood. "It is a pleasure to meet you all. My name is Jarius."

"We know your name outworlder. We see the dirt under your nails too, from digging in your father's pretty little gardens. We just thought you'd like some extra water to clean up a bit." As soon as the Prentice finished, one of his companions poured a mug of water over Jamus' head while the other two doubled over with glee. "So much better," the first one sputtered.

Jamus clenched his fists, willing his reaction to utter calm. The Silver River bucked, yearning to respond. He needed to keep control of both the situation and his Magic. One mistake here in front of nearly a hundred Prentices would ruin his chances of repairing the weave and solving the riddle. "That wasn't a very generous welcome, I'm afraid," he said evenly. "I didn't get your names."

"I'm Sark, and me and my friends run the Scape the way we want to. Thought it was about time you knew that."

"I see," Jamus replied. "And just what does this running the Scape entail, exactly?"

"Oh, a smart one, eh? Let's just say you do whatever I tell you to do when I tell you. Won't make your stay here any easier if we decide to have a little fun with you, but it won't make it any worse either."

Bad enough, Jamus thought. Too much like the first time he'd ever come to Magiskeep as an outsider from the Rim. Bullies like Sark and his friends had tormented him then, making his life a misery. He didn't stand up to them then because he couldn't. Now, as Rivermaster, he was more than capable of teaching these boys a lesson they would never forget, and he didn't dare to raise his hand. At least not a hand of Magic. But he was no longer the skinny little boy he had been then. Though not much older in circle than Sark, he had been tempered by life and experience well beyond those circles. Time in the Arculan fields, at the bellows in FarIsle's forges, and more than one time in battle. He had seen Taren and his men face the enemy in hand to hand combat to protect him, their battle wizard, and though he'd never done it himself, he had memorized their techniques. Muscles could serve where Magic could not.

"Got nothing to say?" Sark mocked. "Look, boys, the Farmer's struck speechless. I think I'll give him a little taste of Prentice Art. What do you think?' He raised his hand.

Jamus mind raced. He leapt to his feet. In the few seconds of Sark's hesitation at casting his spell, Jamus adjusted his own balance and grabbed Sark's wrist with his right hand, twisting and wrenching back. He kicked back with is left leg and spun, pulling Sark along with him as he struck one of the other boys behind the knees with his foot, sending him and his friend sprawling the floor, where they lay, gasping for air. He yanked hard, pulling and twisting Sark's arm up behind his back as he pulled the boy against his chest. He put his mouth close to Sark's ear and spoke in a low, calm voice. "Never overestimate yourself, or underestimate your opponent, Sark. And never, ever, hesitate once you raise your hand. The wise Mage knows all before he casts his spell. Every detail is clear as Crystal Vision in his mind before his fingers dance the chant. If I had raised mine to you, you'd be dead by now." He caught a glimpse of movement from the floor and hissed, "Tell them to lie still. I am too angry right now to control the River. I may be no more skilled than the least of these Prentices, but I have downed a charging cavelbull with a spell I learned back home," he paused then emphasized the last words, "back home on the farm."

"Stay down, boys," Sark ordered hoarsely. He was starting to tremble.

Nearly satisfied, Jamus softened his grip just a little. "Now, I can't quite be sure, but considering the audience we've had for this little discussion, I suspect a few of the more observant Prentices may have picked up a pointer or two about how to handle a bully like you. If they work on it a bit, the basics really won't take too much strength or even size. Why, I've seen a lass of five circles down a billy goat twice her size just by using the right leverage. Most farmers never have to handle people the way they do their animals, but when a man acts like an animal, sometimes it's necessary." He let Sark loose and the shivering Prentice fell to his knees.

There was a stunned silence in the dining hall until one student began to clap his hands together. A moment more and the whole room erupted into applause.

Jamus glanced around at all the now smiling faces and offered an awkward little bow. He wiped a drip of water off his nose and was about to sit down again when he felt a tug on the sleeve his tunic. He looked down into the face of a little curly-headed girl staring intensely up at him with her beautiful green eyes.

"I can make a dryin' spell for ye, Sur. I just learned how yesterday in me pratical arts class. I done it better'n anybody in the whole class so they sent me over to do one to dry you off, iffen ye'd like."

Jamus smiled, and bent down to her. "Why, thank you, Mistress. I would very much appreciate that."

She screwed up her face in concentration, then lifted her hand. Jamus felt the River's feeble response, enough, perhaps to dry the annoying drip, but no more. He called the Power gently, seeking just enough to help her with the spell, but no more. The waters flowed to her hand, ever so carefully. He saw her eyes widen in astonishment, but she bravely held her hand steady.

His hair, his face, and his clothes dried completely, and he knelt in front of her, his eyes level with hers. "Thank you, My Lady. You are indeed skilled. I feel much better now. Tell me, who taught you such a wonderful spell?"

She pointed toward the far side of the hall to a tall woman in a gray robe. "Mistress Joria, Sur. She teaches us the...the pratical arts. She says it's 'portant we learn how to take care of ourselfs with our Magic."

Joria had long been the Master of Illusion in the Keep. What was she doing teaching the "pratical" arts to little ones. Was this the riddle?

"I thought I'd heard the Mistress taught the Second Art here."

"Oh, yes, she does, she does!" the little girl exclaimed. "But Master Sagari wants to be sure us little'uns who be too young to unnerstan the bigger Magic knows how do some good stuff first. His son, Sagin's in my class. I done the dryin' spell even better'n him. We're gonna learn how to Magic cook a egg today. Do you know how to cook a egg just right?"

Jamus, who had chanted many a meal, shook his head. "Not just right."

"You should come. Mistress Joria is the kindest lady ever. She'd be happy to have you come to our class. Please? I want her to see how dry you are."

Seeing Joria was far from something Jamus wanted to to, but the little girl's earnest plea was too hard to ignore. "I will," he said. "You did not tell me your name, though. I am Jarius."

"I knowed that already. Everybody in the Keep talks about strangers when they come." She looked over at Sark, who was slinking out into the hall followed by his two limping compatriots. "Some people talk mean, but not my class. Mistress Joria says we be the nicest students she's ever had." She drew herself up proudly, "My name is Jenda an' I am going to be a Master here one day."

"Considering how well you dried me off I am sure you will," Jamus agreed. "I would like to finish my meal before I come to your class. Can you tell me which door I need to find?"

"Up the stairs at the end of the hall, that way," Jenda said pointing to the right. "Then count three doors on the right and you'll be there. I'll tell the Mistress you are coming soon's you finish your eggs. But you could have a egg in class if ye still be hungry." Giggling, she trotted happily off to her classmates, who gave her hugs and congratulations for being the brave one with the stranger.

Joria glided over to her little group of PrePrentices and herded them from the Hall, offering a quick smile to Jamus just before she stepped out into the hallway.

He ate slowly, trying to sort it all out. For the first time in his entire life, the demons of his childhood were losing their grip. He had faced the bullies here and won. Of course, he was a man now, with a man's muscle and a man's confidence, but it made little difference. The terror he'd felt tumbling headlong down the stairs with Sarn and his friends laughing behind him was gone, and this time not because of his Magic.

Joria's class was waiting for him and if part of the riddle was solved, facing her might well be another part of it all. He got up, and headed down the hall, again testing the weaves of his disguise and going over and over the story of this life he had created in his head. This Mistress was not easily deceived.

Jenda bounced off her stool and ran over to Jamus as soon as he came into the classroom. She grabbed his sleeve and pulled him up to the front of the room. "Mistress Joria, this is me new friend, Jarius. Do ye see how dry he is?"

"Why, yes I do see how dry he is, Jenda. You did a fine job of casting your spell for him. I am quite proud of you. Prentice Jarius, I am glad to finally meet you. I am Joria, Master of Illusion in Magiskeep, and it is indeed an honor to meet such a dry man."

Jamus coughed, working hard to keep a straight face. He was nearly ready accept the hand Joria offered in greeting, to touch her fingers as was the custom of the Keep and thought better of it. He knew too well how potent his touch could be. The Mistresses in Magiskeep had fallen too many times to the strange allure his command of the River had on them. He wasn't altogether sure that attraction would hold here in the past of Magiskeep, but he wasn't going to risk it. He pretended he was not aware of the custom, and bowed slightly instead. "I am just a farmer's son, Mistress, and a dry one at that, but I have heard you are teaching your class how to cook eggs today and I could well benefit in a lesson on that myself. My father has a good flock of layers. It would be a good skill for a farmer's son to master."

"Master Senital has told me you have a good facility for basic Comprehension, so I'll do my best to explain the lesson in more Prentice terms for you. My little ones here need to learn in other ways until they are ready to comprehend Master's Art. Come, sit down here by my study tabe while I teach. Feel free to ask questions."

Jamus nodded and sat. His fingers idly traced the edge of the tall, slanted desk. Again, it was so familiar, for he had often stood behind it offering recitations in this very classroom—or at least he would stand there some thirty circles to come.

"Now," Joria said, "to cook the perfect egg, we must remember how to call the flame. Can anyone tell me how?"

A little boy in the back row waved his hand in the air. "We gotta get mad."

"No we don't," Sagin, Sagari's son objected. "We gotta think warm things like the sunshine on our face. If we get mad, the Spellfire comes and that would burn the egg to a ash pile."

"Sagin is right. Eggs are fragile things, inside and out." She cracked the egg's shell and let the insides slide into a pan she had set on the countertop in front of her. "We must think about a small fireplace, a table torch, perhaps, or, as Sagin has suggested, the sun. We need to think how it feels. Does it make us smile? Do we laugh?"

Jamus caught his breath. Joria was teaching the Silver Magic, not the Gold. Jarien, his son, touched the Silver River. It was the very reason they had needed to bring Rath to Magiskeep to help control his power. These were children, still to young to comprehend the logical, reasoned use of the Golden Water. And here was Joria, teaching them to channel and control the Magic of emotion. He was fascinated.

"Now," she said, "you must picture the egg cooked exactly the way you like it. And once you have that picture in your mind, taste the egg in your head and feel how delicious it is and how happy you are eating it. Then, and only then, let all those feelings out through your fingers and cook your egg." She extended her hand over the egg in the pan and it sizzled to a perfect fry with creamy white framing a perfectly centered yellow yolk.

For a half span or so she supervised her young charges, making some of them giggle to set their chantings free while others had to frown and get a little frustrated in order for their Magic to work.

"Now, practice on your own while I explain the lesson to our guest." She sat down next to Jamus. "They are so young their minds do not yet have the discipline to call the River as Masters do. Their hearts, though, have no trouble working and the River indulges them in their innocence. When they grow older, we'll teach them to be true Magicians. For now, we let them play."

Jamus hardly knew how to answer her. All this time, and the Masters of Magiskeep had held the secret of the Silver River in their hands and never even known. Certainly, they had Spellfire, but to them it was the evil embodiment of Magic Unrestrained. Yet here, that same Magic was considered simply a children's toy. Joria had no idea of how important it was. The image of Jarien flashed into his head again. If these children could learn to control their impulses and find ways to guide the Silver Waters carefully, so could his son. A world of possibilities opened up before him. How many other children with the Gift lived in his world? And why, in the name of all Magic, had the Keep forgotten how to train them?

"I have been taught Magic is not a game," Jamus said.

"Precisely why I would not teach you to cook an egg the same way." Then she smiled, "But somehow, my young friend, I have a feeling I really don't have to teach you much, now do I."

"I am here to learn, Mistress."

"The question is, Jarius, just what is it you are trying to learn? I saw you in the Hall. You took those bullies down without raising your hand, so at first, I thought you were exactly what you claimed to be, an ignorant farm boy with talent and not a clue as to how to use it. But then, when Jenda tried to dry your clothes, I felt the River surging to your hand. You pushed it back, channeled it into a trickle, just enough to fill her tiny hand and no more. Unless I am mistaken, there was so much more, and yet you held it easily. So tell me, stranger, just what you want from Magiskeep?"

The only consolation Jamus had was that she had not mentioned his sphere. Either she could not sift it, as he hoped, or she had not tried to sift it, which was the problem. If she saw his real face now, she was not the kind of person to forget it. What would the future bring then, when they met in his Magiskeep? So far, nothing he had done would have such impact on the future. He had to avoid that, at all costs. "I'm not sure, Mistress." He stole a quick glance at the class. All the children were too engrossed in their cooking experiments to be listening. "I am a Seeker, of sorts. I have a riddle to solve and the answers I find here will affect the path of Turan's Way."

She nodded. "We have had such visitors before. I have learned not to ask too many questions of them. Cook an egg as simply as you can, Master Jarius, so the Mistress Jenda will feel her invitation to class has changed your life for the better and then go leave us. I will try my best to forget I ever met you."

Jamus let out a puff of air. He didn't even realize he'd been holding his breath. He turned his attention to the egg she'd handed him and held it for a moment. He cast an easy spell of heat and then handed it back to her, the shell still hot and steaming. "Hardboiled," he said, and then, as she asked, he left the room.

*****

Now that the mystery of how Edra's Magic worked had been revealed to him, Jyp began to study his companion even more closely. It didn't take him long to see how much effort it would take for Edra to channel his power to get a simple casting done if it needed an exact result. He was fine with general spells. Starting a fire in the hearth, brewing a pot of keldherb, and even conjuring all kinds of wonders for Gareth was hardly a problem. After all, if the Prince wanted a fresh surlep, any surlep would do. He never demanded one with no seeds or no hint of yellow in its skin.

Now it all made sense. He remembered one day when the leg of a chair in their room had broken and Edra mended it with one of his casual, easy spells. It seemed to be fine. Then, Jyp sat down and the chair collapsed under him. This time, he took a good look at the broken leg. For some curious reason, the grain of the wood ran crosswise instead of lengthwise. He studied the wood for a time, and once he comprehended its unusual nature, he cast a spell of Recreation, letting the Magic flow sideways into the break. The leg mended solidly and had not broken again.

Fortunately for Edra, most Magic in the Royal palace did not demand specifics of him and when they did, he would turn to Jyp for help, relying on the Keep trained Sorcerer to take care of the details. Jyp hadn't quite figured out how that might benefit his own cause, so he made a mental note of it and simply watched.

Meanwhile, Edra was in his glory doing his best to recreate his beloved Cauge with all its splendor here in Aberdeen. First, of course, had been Gareth's elite guard. Then came the Riders, whom Gareth had dubbed his "Scarletteers" because he had decided on red tunics emblazoned with a gold flying horse. Edra would have preferred different colors and a different, name, but he let the Prince have his way.

"Letting the Prince have his way," was becoming the new truth in Edra's mind, for Gareth was far too eager and ready to follow every suggestion the Sorcerer made, almost to the point of blind obedience. When Edra suggested stelin swords forged from the smithy on Farreaches, Gareth sent messangers at once. When Edra wanted the foot soldiers wearing tall boots, every leathermaker in Aberdeen was recruited to start cutting and sewing. When Edra wanted a mock battlefield with high and low ground, mounds and battlements, barricades and obstacles for the army's training ground, Gareth had squads of groundskeepers, carpenters, and masons hired before Sowin's turn. The field to the west of the palace, under King Gailvarg's window, was a mass of construction within a span. The royal treasury diminished, but the workers were happy and the Prince was gaining the favor of the common people. Taverns near the palace filled tables every Midmeal and barstools at Weswin. The streets near the royal seat flourished.

Edra remembered fondly how much esteem the Cauge in Arcula had earned by all its efforts to establish an empire. He had poured money into the crafts villages, tailoring uniforms for his guard, contracting furniture for the Cauge Hall, and building the Hall itself. By the time the work was completed, the people of Arcula had prospered enough to keep them happy for at least three full circles before the truth of what they had done struck home. And then, it was too late. The Cauge had become so powerful, so infused into every aspect of Arculan society, there was no way to escape its oppression.

Edra had learned the lessons well. The only flaw had been the Sorcerer from beyond the Wall. Now, with Gareth's thirst for vengeance against that very enemy, the former Cauge First Hand was growing more and more confident that any empire he built in Aberdeen would stand forever. The Prince was proving a worthy puppet, and all was going quite smoothly.

He had no idea that unlike Arcula, there were eyes watching in Aberdeen, ears listening, and long memories who knew the stories of Wizardchase when rebellion had driven the Magic from Turan for fear of exactly the same kind of empire building Edra was pursuing now. The irony of it all was that the eyes and ears belonged to those who touched the rivers themselves—Seers and Sorcerers who had more than enough power to challenge his plans.

For now, though, they just waited.

XI

Salene wrapped the blanket back around Jarien after she fed him and tucked him into the cradle. After leaving Jamus in their rooms, she had finally settled back in the suite she had lived in throughout her childhood in the Keep. The cradle was the very one her mother, Salecia, had rocked her to sleep in, and the bed she was sleeping in still had the comfortable dents in the mattress she had made herself in all the circles she stayed here. The familiarity of it all granted some solace, but it could not make up for the ache in her heart from missing Jamus.

"I want to see him," she said when Sarena came to report that Jamus still had his fever.

"No, Salene. Becca is with him, and she says his symptoms match those of an illness that struck the Keep nearly fifty circles ago. It's not safe to be near him if it is, for you would get sick too."

"But you said he was going to recover. So would I."

"And Jarien? Becca tells me when that illness struck, hundreds of children died--only children. Her babies, and at least ten more in her little village alone. Your father lost his first son, you know."

Salene nodded. "He told me over and over. I don't think he was capable of loving again after Sagin's death. He married my mother more out of lust than love. Oh, I suppose he felt something for her, but neither she nor I could ever satisfy him completely. I learned to ride and hunt. I wore breeches instead of gowns and when I was little, I even cut my hair really short, thinking it would please him if I acted more like a son than a daughter. None of it worked. Even when he brought Jamus here, he didn't change. I think he got even worse, as if Jamus' very presence and his talent for the Magic was mocking his loss."

"He was a hard man."

"He was cruel and ambitious. I don't even think grief can excuse that, or what he did to me. No matter what had happened to him in the past, there was no excuse for that."

"You didn't let him ruin you, Salene. Look how beautiful a life you have now."

"By all accounts, neither Jamus nor I should ever have been able to find happiness, and yet we have. It hasn't been easy. It breaks my heart to know how Jamus has suffered. So many times, Sarena, so many times. He should have broken by now, but all it's done is made him stronger. That's why he's going to get better, isn't it?"

Sarena put her hand on Salene's shoulder to comfort her. "He is Jamus, the Rivermaster. It is not written in Turan's Way that we will lose him now."

"Turan's Way," Salene said angrily. "Damn Turan's Way for what it's done to him. Now it's taken him from me again. It's not fair."

"I'm meeting Master Senital in Jamus' room in a span," Sarena said, moving away to look at herself in the mirror by the window. Absently, she smoothed the skirt of her gown and pulled her hair back, tying at the nape of her neck with her scarf. "He and I have been doing some research to try to find a way to cure Jamus. I still find only darkness when I Touch him, but it's much quieter and not as threatening as it felt before. There's a dairy in the Vaults we've been trying to read and the tapestry in your rooms that might offer some clues.'

Salene caught her breath. "Tapestry? What tapestry?"

"There was one behind the curtains on the wall across from the bed. You didn't know it was there?"

"By the Blood, if I had I never would have kept Jarien in that room. Those tapestries are like mirrors, doorways into other worlds. They open into Turan's Way--past, present, perhaps even the future. I was with Jamus in one from circles far in the past. We lived a life there where everything we did was important, I think." She shivered, and hugged herself, rubbing her hands on her arms trying to get warm again from the chill of her memory. "There was a great battle. Jamus had fought it many times before I went with him into the weave. There was something he had to do to mend the threads to assure the path of Turan's Way. It wasn't until I was there to Heal him that the riddle, as Jamus called it, was solved. Then we were able to come back home."

"Jamus was injured in the tapestry? It's that real?"

Salene nodded. "It is, Sarena. Anything can happen. Jamus has traveled in many tapestries, from what he's told me. Some in his dreams of a single night and others for circles. Just like the Way of Mirrors, time has no meaning in them. The war we fought lasted for months, or at least it seemed to."

"What happens when Jamus solves the riddle?"

"It seems to depend on the answer. Sometimes the future changes. But it's always for the good of Turan's Way, part of destiny. Sometimes, the riddle leads Jamus to another River, and another Dragon. Again, his destiny as Rivermaster." She sat down on the edge of the bed, still shivering. "Always, though, always it takes him away from me, somehow. If there is a tapestry in that room and he gets lost in it...." Her voice trailed off. "You say he is in the bed?"

Now Sarena did not know how to answer. All that darkness when she Touched Jamus might be more than she had first thought. And where was that consuming magnetism his Magic always had on her? She had felt no attraction. What if the Jamus in the bed were not Jamus at all but a mere reflection? "I don't know, Salene. It looks like he's in the bed, but you and I know well your husband is a master of illusions, weaves, spheres and reflections none of our poor heads can even begin to understand."

"Then how can we know where he is? And if we don't know, does he?"

"Becca is with him," Sarena repeated. "She is his anchor."

"I pray to the Hand it may be so," Salene said, reaching out to rock the cradle. "It's all I can do."

Senital was waiting for Sarena at the door to Jamus' chambers. "I hope you haven't been waiting too long, Master. I was talking with Salene."

"Poor girl," Senital said. "Being married to a man like Jamus is hard enough, but when something like this happens…"

"She knows about the tapestries, more than you, I, and all your chronicles do. She traveled one with Jamus."

"Ah, this is most interesting. Did she offer anything that might help us figure this all out?"

"Let's just say she confirmed most of what we suspected. The tapestries somehow create a passage into other times and other worlds. Once inside, Jamus needs to do something that will correct the course of Turan's Destiny that has somehow been disrupted. Once he does, the tapestry is mended and the world is set right."

"So, if this tapestry has a broken weave, there is something wrong in our world?"

"Or the world of tomorrow. It's not all clear to me yet. Maybe it never will be. Salene said sometimes the journey is just to teach Jamus something he needs to know."

Senital considered this, as he leaned his hand on the door handle. "Almost as if the tapestry is a part of his mind? His knowledge and learning? Interesting, interesting indeed. A hole in the tapestry might be a gap in his Mastery of the Rivers. No wonder he needs to mend it. Let's go in and look at this picture and see if we can make anything out of it. Maybe it's really a simple wall hanging after all and we are just trying to chase a sparret's tail."

Rath was in the room with Becca when the two masters entered. She did not acknowledge them since she was absorbed in studying the mirror instead. Becca rose from her spot beside Jamus bed, and bowed, "'Tis an honor ta have two Masters here for the Lord. Did ya come ta Touch 'im agin, Mistress Sarena? Fever ain't much better, but he's a mite quieter sleepin'."

"No, Mistress Becca. I'm afraid I've done all the Healing I can."

"Waste of time calling the Gold," Rath said, turning away from the mirror to look at the visitors. "Best One be in Shadow."

"What do you mean, Rath?" Sarena asked.

"Only part here, part there," Rath tilted her head towards the tapestry. "So hard to tell. Speak of it as Dragon, not twoleg." She shook her head, her eyes stopped whirling as if she had taken some kind of control over herself. "When I speak as a woman it is clear to you. But Lord Jamus is in the world of Dragons, and I can only tell you of it in Dragon ways. For you, it will be hard to understand because it is all riddles of a kind."

"But you do know where he is and you know of the tapestry."

Rath nodded. "It is far from here."

"What did you mean when you said Lord Jamus was in shadow?"

Rath's eyes began to whirl again, her hair shimmering as if it were made of silver scales, "Way of Dragon, Way of Weave, Way of Mirror, Way of River all be same. Walk in shadow, walk in sun, time mean nothing anywhere the Dragon fly. Must choose fly or no fly. Kiselor have Dragon wing, so fly. Fly now, fly then, time mean nothing."

"Dragonspeak," Senital said, shaking his head in confusion. "It makes no sense."

"To Dragon it does," Rath replied. She glanced at the mirror again, nodded in satisfaction and headed to the window. "Hunt now. Sometime good in sun." She climbed up onto the stone sill, spread her arms, and leapt out shape-shifting into her Dragon form as she swooped up into the clouds.

Senital clapped his hands in delight, "Oh my, Oh my! I've heard the story, but I never thought I would see it for myself. You know Dragons are the embodiment of the River itself, the Eldest of the Elden Magic. She can shape-shift into most anything she wants." He stopped, put his hand to his mouth, looked over at Jamus lying on the bed, and then muttered to himself. "They are the River. The River can do anything. The Dragon, the Way, the River. Oh my, oh my."

"What is it, Senital, what are you thinking?" Sarena asked.

"Lord Jamus is the Rivermaster, might he have the Dragon power too?" He stayed Sarena's protest with a waggle of his finger. "Think of it. Rath said Jamus was in Shadow. Now I see her change her skin at will, almost as if she wears whatever shape she chooses, not at all locked in one body or another. Legends say the Shadows are reflections of ourselves, and wear the Flesh if they so choose, just like that Dragon. But what if they decide to discard their skins and fly instead? A human body would be a burden then."

"'Must choose to fly or no,' Rath said," Sarena replied thoughtfully. "You're suggesting Jamus left that body behind so he could go into that weave?" She pointed to the tapestry.

"I've looked at the fabric, and indeed there is a flaw in the weave, but even as I was studying it, several of the looser threads started to bind themselves back together. The colors and images were becoming more distinct too. Look," he pointed to an image in the tapestry. "Here, see that child smiling?"

Sarena peered at the little face. "She looks happy."

"When I first saw her, she was crying," Senital said. "I am sure of it."

*****

What had Kashar, his Golden Mother, told him of the tapestries?

Small occurrences, even small lives, make little difference in the Circle, for the Hand will always guide small matters back to Turan's Way in the end. The great events will refuse your interference, despite your great efforts. If indeed, one should change, it is because you have unraveled a secret. Be wary, then, My Son, for the Magic is often jealous of its mysteries. It is not often easy to perceive their truths.

He had been cautious so far, trying not to change the past recklessly. He had fought the bullies in the Hall, but how much could that matter? While it had perhaps made life easier for the younger Prentices, he himself had benefited the most by coming to terms with the trials of his own childhood. Observing Joria's class and learning of how children touched the Silver River so naturally was enlightening but not a world altering revelation. His own son, Jarien, had taught him that before he had stepped into the tapestry. So what was the secret he had yet to unravel? Where was the big riddle, the one he needed to mend the weave?

Something to do with Sagari, he decided. He was the only thing out of place in the whole of this Magiskeep. Or was he?

Becca. She would still be a young woman. He needed to find her.

He left the palace and headed for the stables. Josep, his stable master, was Becca's brother-in-law, Jeamel's brother. If he remembered, Becca and Jeamel had married when they were both barely twenty. If Josep was here, he could tell him about her.

The stables were smaller than he knew but just as neat and well kept as Magiskeep tradition demanded. He heard a challenging snort and stepped into the well-swept aisleway to come face to face with Sagari's magnificent white stallion, Coranth, in the end stall. "Well, I see you are still the king here, eh?" he said. The horse eyed him curiously but did not charge the door as he had so often when Jamus had approached him in the Magiskeep of his time.

"E's a beauty, ain't 'e?" the stablehand said.

Jamus turned to see a younger Josep leaning on a pitchfork by the feedroom. "Thought I heard somebody come in."

Jamus smiled, "I am Jarius, a visiting student here in the Keep. I heard you had some beautiful horses here and just had to see them."

"An' right ya are," Josep agreed, grinning as he hung the fork up on the wall. "I be Josep, stable lad here. Gonna be master someday, iffen I keeps ma nose clean." He laughed. "Ya ride?"

"I do," Jamus replied.

"We gots some fine guest horses iffen ya got the mind ta saddle up whilst yer here. Lemme show ya. That great beast is Master Sagari's love, Coranth. 'E's got spirit and 'e takes after the Master, tough, but kind in 'is own way. Over here, though we gots Shadowmist an' Goldiegirl." He rubbed the palomino mare's head affectionately over the stall door. "She's a sweetie. Gonna make a line o' fine foals, methinks. Master Sagari's gonna breed her next circle."

Jamus nodded. The mare's beautiful head reminded him of Salene's Flax. He would have to look up the breeding records when he got back home, almost certain this was the foundation mare in her line. The gray in the stall next to her nickered, shoved his head over the stall door, and nuzzled Jamus' tunic. Jamus secretly conjured a few surlep candies. "I have a treat for them, if it's all right with you, Josep," he said, showing him the candies.

"O, sure, that'd be fine. They gits them all the time, the beggars. Give Shaddie a sweetlin' an' he'll be yer friend fer life. Ya looks like ya'd fit him real good."

Jamus stroked the horse's dappled neck and then scratched him under his chin, between his jowls. Still chewing the candy, the horse closed his eyes and let out a puff of air through his nostrils. "What a good boy you are," Jamus said. The gelding's color reminded him of Whim, and he felt an ache of longing to be back where he belonged. "Tell me, Josep, do you have family here in Magiskeep, or are you alone like I am?"

"I got's family, off in Tallridge, north o' here. Me brother Jeamel an' is wife, Becca. I think Jeamel wants ta git a job in the palace soon, but he ain't got here yet. Be nice iffen he does. Becca's like the best cook in the whole kingdom, an' I miss 'er stew."

"Having your family nearby would be wonderful," Jamus agreed. "I plan on going home as soon as I can myself. This Magiskeep is really a grand place, but I too miss my family. The horses here reminded me how much."

"So ya gots horses at home?"

"Oh, yes. We breed some fine ones. Drays and riding horses. We're trying to make a cross that would take the best of both. There are people who want elegant carriage horses with the strength and stamina of coarser drafts, you see."

"Inneresting," Josep said. "Might be somewhat ta think about when I gits ta be master here. I bin thinkin' the Keepbreds would sell real good in more'n jest Magiskeep iffen we could git 'em cross the Rim. It ain't so much the money, but it'd be right nice ta up tha quality of the stock of all Turan. A good horse kin make a good man, iffen ya knows what I mean."

"That's true," Jamus agreed. "In some places, I'd even imagine a man's worth might even be measured by the quality of the horses he keeps."

*****

Edra needed cavalry mounts for Gareth's Scarletteers. The stables of Aberdeen offered meager stock. There were a few teams of exceptionally fine carriage horses he knew about and he did intend to find out who had bred them, but pure riding mounts were another issue altogether.

He decided the only logical step was to go to the center of Aberdeen's horse world, the Course, to see if any of the racing stables had horses for sale or knew of breeders who did. While the racing season was still on break, most of the trainers were still in residence, and there were plenty of wise heads to consult.

Master Drew was one of the trainers with a full barn. "I've three or four for sale, My Lord," he said when Edra approached him. "Only two would have the bone and temperament for calvary, though, if that's what you want. The others are a mite flighty and light. None of them has the speed to make good on the Course, so the owners put them up for sale. Bless them for wanting them to get good homes though, so I'm charged to keep them here until I find the right buyer. I think the royal palace would be acceptable."

Edra examined the two horses Drew showed him. Well bred, and a bit stockier than most of the runners in the barn, the bay and chestnut would make a good start for Gareth's stables. He struck a bargain, made arrangements to have the horses delivered, and then asked, "Where else can I find some horses? I need at least twenty for the Prince's riders. More, if I can find them."

Drew rubbed his chin thoughtfully. "There are maybe three more horses here at the Course. Let's see…Mistress Talia's got her stock up at the farm, northeast of here. She will be back sometime later today to check on two fillies I've been watching for her. I can send word when she gets in so you can talk to her. Otherwise, there's a Lord Delran out in Telma who's got quite a reputation for breeding fine stock. You might want to take the time to go see him if you've got a heavy purse. You're not going to buy cheap, but you are going to buy quality."

"Is there a good tavern nearby where I can wait after I look at those other horses for sale?"

"Aye, there's the Forgetful Friend just over at Cuver Street. Serves a find Midmeal during the season, but I'm sure they're open now. They do a good business most days."

Once Edra had selected and paid for two more retired racers, he headed for the tavern, ready to enjoy a good meal and some strong ale. The royal palace had a good kitchen, but good tavern fare was something altogether different.

He was not disappointed. The ale was dark and foamy and the food, heavy and flavorful. The cavel roast, the special of the day, was so tender he didn't even need his knife to cut it. With only one hand, he had to tear off the bread from the crusty loaf with his teeth, but when the food was this good, table manners be damned. He was enjoying himself too much.

"Ye want a refill for thy ale, Milord?" the serving girl asked. She was young, shapely and very blonde, something Edra valued in women. The Cauge had always cherished the fair-headed, and she was a beauty.

"I would, Mistress. I thank you." He pushed the mug over to her with the stump of his left arm.

"Oh," she said, staring at his arm. "I'm sorry, Milord, I don't mean to be rude. I just didn't realize…."

"This?" Edra said, waving his stump in the air. "Had a bit of bad luck a while back. I'm nearly used to it now. I didn't mean to offend you. Usually, I keep it my lap so it doesn't bother people."

"It's just that with so many Healers in the city, I would have thought," she checked herself. "Oh, I guess a Healer wouldn't be able to do much, now would she? It's all mended now as best as it can be."

He sighed. "Magic might do something for me, but I understand sorcery is frowned on in Aberdeen." Something in her reaction had piqued his interest and he decided to question her further. "Do you know of a good Healer around here?"

"Mistress Jada of the Whispering Gardens has a wonderful collection of herbs. If anyone ever could heal, she could. Then there's Master Jyp. He's gone to the palace, though."

'Jyp? H-m-m, what do you know of him? His name sounds familiar."

"Oh, not much," she replied a little too nervously. "He has a good reputation here in Cuver Street."

"You said he was a Healer."

"Herbs too, I think," she said, "like Jada. Oh, I see the cook is beckoning to me. I need to go. Do ye need anything else, Milord?"

"Unless you're willing to offer your bed, I think not," Edra said winking at her.

She blushed and hurried off to the kitchen.

The Caugeman made a note to follow up on the suggestion when he had a chance. Surely royal prerogative would count for something if he did decide to have his way with the girl. Seeing her roused feelings he had nearly forgotten in the austere atmosphere of Gareth's castle. Since the Prince could do little with women himself, he discouraged Edra's appetite whenever he had the chance and until now it had not mattered. The Power and prestige had been distracting enough. She was pretty, though.

"My Lord?" the messenger from the Course disturbed his fantasy. "Master Drew sent me to tell you Mistress Talia is in the stables. He says she will be glad to talk you if you can come now."

Edra pushed away from the table and got up, leaving a large tip of two gold for the girl and followed the stableboy back to the barns.

Talia was rubbing down one of the fillies who insisted on dancing in the crossties instead of standing politely. "You are a silly girl, Tandy," Talia said, "Every other horse would love the attention and you? You'd rather just go out and run."

"She does look full of energy," Edra said. "How old is she?"

"Just past three circles," Talia replied. "She's run just one race and won so she's quite proud of herself. Every time I take her out of the stall she thinks it's time to run again. I appreciate her spirit, but she does need to learn some manners."

Edra laughed, "Like a lot of children I've known."

Talia smiled. "You are looking to buy some horses for the Royal cavalry?"

"Indeed I am, Mistress Talia. Master Drew tells me you might have some good prospects for me?

"I do, at my farm. It's not far from the city. You're welcome to come and have a look. Not every horse is meant for the Course like this little lady. I have a good number who'd be better off not setting foot on the track."

"When can I come?'

"My husband and I are heading back before Weswin. Until the Course reopens we'll be staying at the farm, so any day after tomorrow would be fine."

Edra was about to set a date when Erlik emerged from the tack room to his right. His mouth snapped shut in surprise.

Erlik strode over to Talia and put his arm protectively around her shoulder. "So, Edra, I never expected to see you again."

"Erlik," Edra said, keeping his voice even searching his brain for the best way to handle this potentially dangerous situation. Erlik had been one of five rebels he and the rest of the Cauge had banished to the sea. Despite the fact that he himself had landed on Aberdeen's shores after his own banishment, it never occurred to him the same fate might have befallen another. "I am surprised to see you here."

"Why? Because you wish I had drowned?" Erlik felt Talia cringe. "He's Cauge, Talia. First Hand, last I knew. He and his cronies set me adrift in the ocean hoping the SeaDragon would rid them of me."

"That was a long time ago," Edra said. "The Cauge is no more and I am now like you, an outcast from Arcula. My sea voyage taught me a lesson in humility, I am a changed man."

"The rimsnake may shed its skin, but the new one it wears is always the same color."

"You wound me, Erlik. You always had a shaenis tongue. That was why we had to send you away. The people wanted to follow you against us. Surely you can understand that."

Erlik shook his head, holding Talia even closer. "Your cruelty, debauchery, and tyranny against the people of Arcula earned my rebellion, and I'd have been proud to lead the people to stop you. I bless the man who finally defeated you and the judge who set you to the sea."

Edra held up his left arm, missing his hand. "Have I not paid enough for my mistakes? You know how hard it was crossing the sea. The utter loneliness, the fear, the thirst when the water ran out, and the dreadful loss of Magic in the deeper waters. I suffered the same misery you did and lost my hand in the futility of battle to preserve my precious Cauge. I have been molded anew by that forge of suffering. I am a changed man."

"He's working for the Crown," Talia said.

"Gareth?" Erilk said. "Is that so much better?"

"Sh-h-h, my love." Talia protested. "We agreed you would not engage in political debate anymore. Besides, it would be good for my stables to have some of my horses in the Royal Calvalry. Could you set aside your differences for the sake of my reputation as a breeder and trainer?"

"Business, strictly business," Edra insisted. "And I won't complain about your prices."

"Why would you?" Erlik spit. "It's not your money, it's the King's and most of it's from taxes on the common people."

"Fairly shot, Erlik. But young men from the city and Provinces are eager to serve the Royal Seat and some are even bringing pensions with them. We've already doubled the treasury set aside for the army with funds from wealthy families who want their sons to learn to be men. It will be their money I spend on the horses."

"See, Erlik? If the rich are paying, how can it be any harm? You know I want to earn my way."

"For your sake, I'll try to stay out of it," Erlik said, "But I don't trust him, and if I even suspect he's up to his old ways, I will not stand silent."

"Fair enough," Edra agreed. "I too will do my best to forget old grievances. Two days from now, Mistress? How long a ride is it to your farm?"

"A day on a good horse," Talia said. "Head east out of the city. Ask for the Mother's Love. It's a tavern on the way. The innkeeper there will set you on the trail to my farm. You can spend your night's there."

Erlik breathed out in relief, glad to hear that Talia was not inviting Edra to stay with them at the farm.

"A good plan," Edra replied. "I am looking forward to seeing those horses of yours. And, I think I should also make sure I come back when the Course reopens. I think I'd place a gold or two on this little lady of yours. What is her race name?"

"Tandella's Pride," Talia, said. "She's named after my mother."

"Two days, then," Edra said and he turned on his heel and left.

"I've never seen you like this," Talia said sliding out of Erlik's embrace to lead the filly back to her stall.

"You never saw the Cauge," he replied. "They were vicious, Talia. Monsters. He's lying through his teeth to claim he's reformed. I meant what I said about a rimsnake. Only he's worse. At least a rimsnake attacks only when it's provoked. Edra would just for the sheer pleasure of it."

"Well, he is working for the King now."

"The King, or the Prince? He and Gareth are too much alike for my mind."

"I'll tell you what, Erlik. If it eases your mind any, we'll put the best horses in the high pasture when he comes and just show him the lesser ones. They're still finer than anything he's going to find within the borders of Aberdal so we can save the good ones for our rebels, eh?"

"Rebels? Are you planning a war, My Love?"

Talia laughed. "Let's just say that after meeting Lord Jamus and knowing you, I have learned the company of Sorcerers demands a woman be ready for almost anything."

Meanwhile, Edra had headed back to the palace just a span ahead of the five horses he'd bought at the Course. He'd managed to strike a deal to buy one of the elegant harness horses on the way, assured the animal was quiet and sane under saddle. It was a big gray gelding, with a flowing mane and tail, good bone, and perfect manners. Hopefully, it would suit the Prince and keep him occupied while he was acquiring the rest of the horses they needed. Gareth was short on patience and expected instant results from every command. If Edra could occupy him with teaching the horse to cross the battlefield in twenty-eight strides, he figured he'd have at least a good month to buy the rest of the beasts.

*****

The Forgetful Friend had closed for the night, but behind its shuttered doors and windows, it was bustling with activity. Jada had called the Counsel in emergency session and dozens of residents of Cuver Street had come in witness. Such gatherings were always well-attended, but this one had more importance than usual.

"Ye be right, Mistress Jada," Seymor said shaking his head in disgust at what he had seen just blocks from the tavern. "Two bodies. Prostitutes, slaughtered. Drained of whatever blood wasn't spread all over the room. Near turned my stomach inside out."

"Shadow," Jors replied, gulping down to keep his own stomach in place. "Two rooms no one will ever want to use again from the looks of them."

"Two rooms," Jada said. "That means Shadows. Men, most likely. Most women around here won't take coin from naught but men."

"Ya said ya whiffed somewhat afore. Didja ere figger where it come from?"

Jada shook her head. "The odor was too faint. It was when the Knight and Lady came in, but I took a good sniff of them, and there was nothing. Besides, we're going to have to find two men, and that Dax is quartered in the palace now."

"So how do we find the killers, then? It's said they each need to drink the blood of a dozen to be satisfied," one of the residents asked.

Jada was not the only one in the room with Magiskeep training. There were at least ten other Keep Sorcerers in the street, and probably more in other parts of the city. "We send out word, and warning. For now, it's the women we need to worry about as they are easier prey. But no one is safe. They'll keep to obscure places seeking out victims they don't think anyone will miss. They hunt at night, the darker the better. Set the Watchers's Eyes and tell them to look for strangers. The Course isn't open now so we won't have as many random travelers about, but when the races start up again, it's not going to be as easy."

"There be a way ta tell Shadow from man?" Sim asked.

"There's the smell, like rotting flesh. Otherwise? It depends. If they don't have much knowledge of men's habits, sometimes they act, well, a bit peculiar. They can't always answer questions about things they should know. It might be something ordinary, like what kind of boots are good for riding. Or, if they look like somebody who's lived in the city a while, they might not know where a street is or how to find the shoemaker's shop. They wear the skin of someone they've killed and to keep it fresh they need to drink the blood of the living or someone who's just died."

Seymor pounded his fist on the bar and dropped his head. "Those women…those women, the dead ones. Their eyes were wide open and they looked as if they'd been screaming. The blade cuts on their bodies weren't deep enough to be fatal. Just enough to draw blood."

"This isn't their first kill, then," Jada said, working her jaw to keep her voice calm. There was no point in panic yet. The Watch needed to be rational in their search and able to warn residents with some sense of order and control. "They knew what they were doing. Are we sure these are the first murders in the city?"

"Hard to say, Mistress. Aberdeen's not always the safest place around, especially around the docks. Sailors come and go, and there are rumors of pirates and impressers about. Man goes missing now and then, who's to know?"

"That's exactly why they're hunting here. Ask around the docks if you can." Jada said. "The folks there can be pretty tight-lipped, but you might find out something useful. What about the rooms where they found the bodies. Was it a House?"

"No, just a rundown tavern. The girls rented rooms for the month. Tavernkeeper was already drunk abed when they came in. Said they had different men most every night. He knew what they were up to but the coin was good, and he said they were sweet to him."

"Poor lasses," Jelda said from her table by the door. One of the Keepbred herself, she had nearly fallen into prostitution before finding her own Magic when she was only fifteen. "To think of earning a living that way."

"As long as there be men willin' ta pay an' women willin' ta lay, whoren'll be the way," Sim said, quoting and old rhyme. "It's a sad thing but part o' life, I spect. 'Tain't right, 'tain't right fer sure."

"We can't change that, I'm afraid, much as I'd like to. There be only so many jobs a woman can hold to earn a living. It's not fair, but it's the way of the world. It's up to us to help them when we can, and right now, warn them. We'll send some of our women out. They'll listen better if they hear it from another woman. In the meantime, I'll consult the Seers. We might be able to get a scrying."

"Too bad we ain't got a Seer amongst us now, ta look over them rooms. Might be able to See somewhat."

"Didn't Jyp say there was a Seer in the palace?" someone asked.

"Aye, that he did," Jada replied. "Prime Juris of the whole of Turan. Jyp said she's a friend of the Rivermaster. Could be she'd come out if we asked. Have those rooms been locked up?"

"Yes, Mistress," Seymor told her. "After we got what was left of the bodies out for burial, the landlord locked the doors and said he wasn't ever going in those rooms again. I have a feeling his purse is going to change his mind in a Sevenstin or so, but he's sure for the time being."

"Jors, go to the palace and tell Jyp what we need. See if he can get the Juris out here. If she knows Lord Jamus, she'll understand how important this is. The rest of you, jump to it. I'll send a bird to Grandisite to find out if there's a Seer with a Swirlypot here in Aberdeen we can consult. We need a True Seer, not one of those charlatans down by the docks who prey on tourists and race bettors. All they do is take people's money."

Sim shrugged, "I knows what ya mean. I talked ta one down by the Course an' every nag she tole me ta bet on finished dead last. When I askt fer ma money back, she tole me somebody musta turned her Swirly back ta front on 'er an she was seein' the race backward." He laughed, "Cost me twenty denerets, ta larn ma lesson. Ten fer her, an' ten on the racers."

"Well, we'll be sure to avoid her, then," Jada said. "Shadows are already reflections. The Hand only knows what we'd be seeing if her pot showed us reflections of reflections."

The band of Sorcerers broke up slowly, those assigned tasks leaving the tavern at irregular intervals so as not to arouse suspicion. Despite the fact that most of Cuver Street's residents were part of the

Counsel meetings, there were a few neighbors who had no idea what
went on behind the inn's shuttered doors.

Jelda moved over to take Jada's arm to help the older woman
to her feet. "I'm going to be at your side, Mistress. The Shadows
may think a woman you age would be an easy mark. I know you can
take care of yourself, but I'll feel better watching out for you." Keep
trained, and talented in several Arts, Jelda had served as a bodyguard
to more than one lady visiting the Course. Now she fully intended to
use those skills to protect Cuver Street's matron.

"I'll take the offer," Jada answered. "Most times, I'd send
you packing your bags, but I'll admit, these murders have unnerved
me more than I'd like. Shadows in Aberdeen would be bad in the
best of times, but with all that's going on in the palace, these are not
the best of times."

"I take it Master Jyp has been ferreting out some disturbing
information."

"Most I've already shared with the Counsel. Jyp's had to
keep his eye on the other Sorcerer, that Edra along with the Prince.
He's sure Gareth has been poisoning the King, but now there are
moves to build an army. All of it bears watching."

The two women glanced nervously around them as they
walked along the cobbled street heading for Jada's cottage. The
moon was full, casting shadows in the alley, but none of them
moved.

"Did you ever actually encounter a Shadow, Jada?" Jelda
asked.

"I did. Back in Magiskeep, a long time ago. I was still a
young, bold Apprentice then, studying the Sixth Art with Master
Jarenda. There was a strange fever that struck the Keep and I was
sent to one of the far villages up north, a little place called Tallridge.
The fever was bad there and a lot of folks were sick. I tended them as
best I could, but Healing was not the fine Art it's become now. All
we could do was treat the symptoms. One of the younger mages, a
brash fellow named Sark, tried to go into the Way of Mirrors
thinking he could find a door into another time where there might be
a cure. Somehow, when he was there, he unleashed two reflections,
Shadows of himself—at least that's what they looked like when you

could make out their faces." Jada brushed her hair away from her forehead as if her hands just needed something to keep them busy as she continued her story. "At night, those monsters could have been anywhere the way they blended into the darkness, but by day, you could see vague outlines and features almost like misty images in a mirror. After the second day, one of the little children died from the sickness. The family lay her body in the sitting room for a day of mourning and burial after. That night, someone broke in and carved it to pieces, and it looked as if all the blood had been lapped up by dogs."

"Did you know what Shadows did then?"

"Senital, in the Keep, knew the Eldenlore. When word got back to the Main Keep, he sent messages back warning us of the dangers. By then we'd lost another little one and the same horrible thing had happened. From then on, we were on guard and as the children died—they were the only ones the fever killed, you see— we'd bury them right away, unless they were of the Magic, of course. Those little babes just faded to ash on their own as all children of the River do."

Jelda frowned. "But you said you faced the Shadows? How?"

"Well, there was a wee little lad so near death, I couldn't leave his bedside. I was trying everything I could dream of to save him. It was late in Norwin when a gust of wind pushed clouds over the sky and it got so dark even the maglit lantern in the room couldn't light up more than a pitiful circle around itself. That's when I smelled them. The stink of rotted carrion filled the room and nearly took my breath away. I cast another spell of light just as a long, sinewy black tendril started to reach for the boy. It looked like a terrible snake, but instead of a head, it had a sharp claw. I nearly screamed and in my panic unleashed a bolt of Spellfire at the damned thing. The room lit up and I saw the Shadow like a tall, thin man with those snakes for arms and behind him another Shadow just as terrifying. My first blast of Spellfire struck the front monster in the chest and the second hit his companion in the head. If I hadn't still been screaming myself, I think my head might have burst with their bellows of agony. They writhed and spun and then collapsed in upon themselves into a pile of black ash. The winds gusted again and swept them up and away out the window."

"And the boy?"

"He breathed his last less than a half span later. I hadn't been able to save his life, but I spared his body."

"It must have been horrible for you."

"It taught me, Jelda. That night I learned the power of Spellfire against the darkness and I learned how helpless I really was in the face of death. It's what drove me to study the Herblore and become a Master of Compassion."

"Could you cure that fever now, with all your knowledge?"

"I don't know about killing the fever, but I do know I could kill a Shadow."

XII

Shadowmist was no match for Whim, but he was a good, solid well-trained animal and it only took Jamus one turn around the paddock to evaluate him. He was the kind of horse who wanted to stay four square under his rider, moving easily to Jamus' shifting weight. He was light to the bridle, yet eager to go. "Are you sure it's all right if I take him out to the far villages, Josep? I might be gone for a few days."

"Master Sam tole me it were up ta me ta decide iffen ya was a good enow horseman ta ride out. From what I seen, yer better'n Lord Sagari hisself in th' saddle. Shaddie's a good boy, but kinda lazy. I never seen him work so good for nobody. Did ya have some kinda spell in that candy ya gived him?"

Jamus laughed. "He just wanted someone to understand him. He thinks he's quite a special fellow, you see. When I told him that and gave him the candy, he decided he let me ride him, that's all."

Like Riverman. Good hand.

Jamus kept a straight face, pretending he'd not heard the horse. Instead, he asked Josep to open the gate and simply rode quietly out to the western trail. Once he was far enough away from the stables, he acknowledged the conversation. "So, you decided you wanted to talk to me after all. I wasn't sure I could hear you in this world."

River be yours, here, there, everywhere. You like Mist?

"Mist, so that's what you like to be called?

Shaddie for littlefoot. I big.

"You are a fine, big horse, indeed," Jamus replied, "Handsome too. I have a horse of my own who looks a lot like you."

Whim.

Jamus started. This Magiskeep was some forty circles before Whim had even been a thought in his head. He had created the stallion from the River's Magic and his own desire. How could this horse even know he existed so far in the future. "How do you know Whim?"

Silvermane be in your heart always. Time not matter to heart. See me now, remember, make Whim.

The idea was intriguing. He had the image of a great silver horse when he had chanted Whim. Perhaps Shadowmist had been in his mind—a memory he didn't even realize he was going to have. Circles, mirrors, reflections, tapestries and time itself twisted in the warp and weave. If he had not walked the Way of Mirrors as many times as he had, he would be totally confused by it all. Now, it seemed perfectly normal. "You are a fine inspiration, Mist." And indeed, he had used the mist of Crystal Lake to conjure his stallion. One more part of the riddle?

We windstep?

"Do your want to fly?"

Make stony path easy on feet. Make long way short. Get oats soon.

Jamus had never quite thought of it that way. His horses had always seemed to enjoy the thrill of lifted strides. It appeared Mist had a much more practical approach. "We can be there for Midmeal if the trails are as I remember. Have you ever been to Tallridge before?"

Not know. What see?

"The mountains," Jamus replied. "Big tall hills with white tops to the north and west, where the sun comes up."

Twoleg barns. Hay on top. Mist eat, get hit. Good oats in fourwall make up for mean.

Most of the cottages in Tallridge had thatch roofs. No wonder someone hit Mist if he had tried to nibble on them. Somewhere, there was a good stable, though, even in the tapestry. "What's the road like going there from here? Do you remember any places along the way?"

Wide to place of big tree. Walk careful for long time. Watercross then path of many carts.

A wide trail to the forest. As Jamus recalled, the trees stretched for perhaps three spans of riding at the walk. Then there was Stonybrook to cross. From there, the road was well traveled.

He'd ridden to his Tallridge in his own Magiskeep enough to know
these trails were nearly the same. "We'll windstep, Mist. I know the
way."

They reached the main road to Tallridge in three lifted
strides. From there, Jamus kept them grounded rather than risk
landing on a farmer's cart. It took another span to reach the village
gate, just as he predicted, in time for Midmeal.

Set in the northwest corner of Magiskeep, Tallridge was
framed on the north by the foothills of the Norreaches and on the
west by the foothills of the Rim. There were perhaps two hundred
families living there in this circle, with a small number of farms on
its outskirts. Many of the villagers were miners who combed the
mountains for flamegems and amyris which they traded for good
carried across one of the few safe passes through the Rim in and out
of Turan proper. During the chillmonths, trade and mining were
impossible when the mountains filled with snow, but now, during the
warmseason, the village was busy with travelers going to and fro.

Tallridge's two little inns did a thriving business during
those months but only the Bread and Butter stayed open all circle.
Set in the south of town, it had a reputation for some of the best food
in all of the Keep and was already in this time gaining popularity as a
vacation getaway for visitors from the whole of the kingdom. Becca,
and her husband Jeamel, never put a tavern in their little inn, relying
instead on good food, comfortable beds, and several acres of gardens
and grounds where guests could just relax and enjoy a stay in the
fresh mountain air.

Jamus settled Shadowmist in the inn's neat stone barn, and
made his way up the graveled path to the inn's door where he was
greeted by a young maid who ushered him in. To his delight, Jeamel
was behind the counter, smiling and pleased to welcome him. "Come
in, Sur, come in. I seen ya ride trough the village gate. I knowed yer
horse right off. Me brother grooms for the Keephall an' that be one
o' his charges. I take it ya be a Magician?"

"My name is Jarius, Innkeeper," Jamus replied as he signed
the guestbook. "I am staying at Magiskeep for some study. My father
has a farm far south of here and I've never seen the northern
mountains."

"Well, iffen it's mountains ya wants ta see, ya come ta the right place. We gots lots ta look at. There's a pretty little waterfall up a ways an' a colored canyon ya kin tour if ya's a mind ta do some more ridin' on the morrow. Toby's a fine guide and if ma Becca packs ya a lunch the trip'll cost ya jest a deneret on yer bill. We don't' serve no likker here in the Butter, jest sos ya know but there be a tavern just down the way that'd be glad ta take yer coin. Sometimes the Follymen comes here, though. Tells an' sings more kinda family tales, though so if ya wants the bawdy, go ta the Merrymaker over yon. Lemme see, what else I needs ta tell ya?" Jeamel pulled out a little notebook from his pocket and was about to consult it, when two little toddlers dashed out of the back room chasing each other. The little girl was screaming with delight and the boy tried hard to keep up as she dashed behind the counter and wrapped her arms around Jeamel's leg.

"Papa, Papa, save me. That mean ol' tark's tryin' ta eat me!"

The little boy stopped in his tracks let out a little roar and waved his hands in the air with his fingers curled up like claws as he waited to pounce.

"Oh, he is, is he, Sira? Well, Papa will protect you." Jeamel squared off against the snarling "tark" and held up his quill for defense. "Back off ya evil beast. I gots ma sword ready ta spit ya iffen ya dares ta try ta eat ma little lady."

The little boy snarled again, and leapt, right into his father's arms. Jeamel began tickling him for all he was worth and the boy burst into giggles as the two of them sank to the floor in a wrestling match while Sira jumped on top.

Soon, it was clear the two children had gained the advantage and Jeamel was forced to plead for mercy. "Lemme up, lemme up," he cried in mock panic. "I surrender, ya gots me Lady o' the Cat an' Tark o'the Mount. Ya done tricked me agin."

"Oh, Papa," Sira laughed, "ya be so dumb ta git caught agin."

"You shoulda knowed," the little boy gasped, rolling off his father's stomach.

"Never, Jeb, ya surprised me agin. Guess yer Papa's jest not sharp enow ta be a Mountman, eh? Think he'll earn a livin' keepin' ta the indoors."

"Silly Papa," Sira said.

"Sira, Jeb!" Becca called as she came out of the kitchen. "What are ya two li'l pupkits up to now, ya leave yer father alone. 'E's tryin' ta welcome a guest."

Jeb got to his feet and eyed Jamus carefully. "Whatcha hidin' fer?"

Jamus started. What did the boy mean? "I'm standing right here, Jeb."

"Yer hidin', but I won't tell." He got up and trotted over to his mother. "Kin I have some snappies?"

"Not now, Jeb, it's too near Midmeal. If you eats all yer soup like a good li'l tarklet, then ya can have two snappies. Now go on, ya too, Sira, an' git washed up." As the two children ran off, Becca turned to Jamus. "Welcome ta The Bread an' Butter, Sur. I gots a good veggie soup fer Midmeal an' some fresh baked brown bed wid creamy cheese. Ya kin have keldherb or calidew ta drink, but iffen ya want somethin' hard ya ain't gonna find it here. I don't hold wid servin' likker when I gots little'uns in the house."

"Soup would be fine," Jamus replied, wishing he could say more. Becca, at twenty circles was a lovely young woman, by any standards and already he could feel her warmth. Of all the people in the world aside from Salene and his son, he loved Becca the most. She had been his solace when he was an unhappy little boy in the Prentiscape, his support and comfort when he suffered under Sagari's hand, his safe haven from his nightmares, his advisor in love, and by all accounts his mother. To see her happy, thriving, and doting on her own children made his heart ache to take her in his arms to tell her how much he loved and appreciated all she had given him.

But this Becca hadn't given him anything—yet. She didn't know who he was and hard as it was for him, he had to keep up the pretense. He made his way over to a table by the window and sat down, staring out to the Rim beyond. What had little Jeb meant by saying that Jamus was hiding? Could the little boy have seen through his disguise? Children and the Silver River, could it be? Again, the riddle. Was this another piece of it? He hoped he could talk to the boy alone before he left the village.

Then as the maid placed a steaming bowl of soup in front of him, he shuddered. Jeb and Sira were Becca's twins. In his Magiskeep, they were dead. His stomach turned and he pushed the soup aside, taking a sip of keldherb instead.

"Whatsa matter?" Becca asked. "Ya don't like ma soup?"

Jamus started again, this time from his reverie. He hadn't noticed her come from the kitchen with a plate of bread and cheese. The other tables in the inn were filling fast and the young maid was hurrying about trying to take care of all the guests. "Oh," he said lamely, "it's a little too hot. I'm going to let it cool."

"I takes pride in servin' ma food fresh off the fire," Becca laughed. "Never think o' whether ya burns yer tongue on it er not."

"My name is Jarius," Jamus said smiling back at her. "I told your man there I came to see the mountains. From the smell of this wonderful soup, I think perhaps I should have come for the food."

Becca laughed again and the music of it was beautiful. He'd never heard her laugh like that. "Most folks say they gains a belly here. Ma name's Becca an' ma man there be ma husband, Jeamel. Them two li'l wildcats are ours, iffen ya dint figger that out on yer own. We bin here jest past two circles now runnin' the inn."

"You're doing quite well," Jamus said, nodding towards the nearly full tables. "Is it this busy all the time?"

"Most days," Becca replied. "Ain't got all the rooms full, but the tables do good. They likes ma food."

"I can see that," Jamus said. "How about the Chillseason? You can't have too many travelers then."

"The villagers still likes ma stew," she said, "An' there's more folks'n ya'd think what likes the snows. Come here fer the Givin' Days an' such. Anyone in the Keep what jest want's ta get away from their life an' take a rest gits 'ere sooner or later. Ya'd be surprised. Ain't a long trip fer a Magician what know how ta get 'is horse's feet off the ground iffen ya knows what I mean."

"I do," Jamus replied, pleased to know she knew about lifted strides. But, Josep was her brother-in-law and working in the Keep's stables, he would know of the Magic's unique mode of travel. "I lifted a few strides myself on the way here."

"Figgered. Ya dint look too worn when ya first come in. Had an easy ride, did ya?"

"Yes. Shadowmist is a good horse."

"He oughta be. Me husband's brother tends 'im an' all the other good horses in the Keep. Josep says they be some o' the finest mounts in all o' Turan."

"They may well be," Jamus agreed, "although I haven't been through all of Turan to see."

"We gits lots o' traders from acrost the Rim, an' ain't a one e'er come in on a horse half so good," Becca said. She glanced over at the maid who was scurrying back into the kitchen. "Well, Master Jarius, ya gots ta excuse me. Looks like Merriam's gots her hand full wid the other guests. I better go help the poor girl afore she falls ta a faint."

Jamus nodded and watched her go. She was so happy, so content, reveling in her life. It broke his heart to think how hard it must have been for her to lose so much of it.

The soup, cooled now, was just as delicious as he'd expected.

*****

Gareth was up early with Easwin's change. He used to stay in bed till well after Firstmeal, but the excitement of creating a military empire had made him into a new man. Soldiers rose at dawn and so did he.

But today was different. The Elite guard could drill on their own, for he had another mission. His father, even after giving his support of the army, was in the way of Gareth's larger ambitions. Still caught in his pursuit of a lasting peace in Turan, the old man would never let his son use the army in anything except defense. And attacking Magiskeep was not a defensive action.

Gareth had considered creating a mock invasion using Edra's and Jyp's skills in sorcery. While they were somewhat limited in talent, he knew they could create some effective Magical flames to level some villages and blame it on the Sorcerers. It was still a good plan, but one to keep in reserve in favor of dealing with the primary problem first by getting rid of his father.

He dressed and hurried out of his rooms, heading upstairs to the Queen's Closet and bedchamber where his Aunt Arista was staying. Pushing aside the handmaid who tried to tell him his Aunt was still abed, he barged through the closest and into the room beyond. "Auntie, wake up at once! We need to talk now."

He pulled open the bed curtain. Arista lay sprawled on the bed, naked under a single sheet. She was more lovely than he'd thought, and despite his lack of manhood, he felt an ache in his groin and an urge he had to force himself to resist. Right now he needed her help more than her body. That could come later.

He reached out and shook her shoulder, "Aunt Arista. I need your help."

She rolled over on her side, exposing her buttocks and opened her heavy-lidded eyes, "Nephew, what could you ever want from your dear Auntie at this hour and here, of all places?" She did not try to cover herself.

"Your herbs," Gareth said backing away despite himself. "You brought your herbs as I asked?"

Grella's heart lurched. She sat up in the bed, pulling the sheet around herself as if she had just remembered her modesty. "Herbs? Oh, yes, my pouch." She had Arista's leather bag, but the flasks and pouches inside were just a jumble to her.

"My father, your brother-in-law, is proving a hindrance to me. You recall the letter I sent explaining everything, of course."

"Letter. Oh, yes, the letter," Grella lied. She would have to find a way for him to explain further. "You weren't too explicit."

"Of course I wasn't. If anyone had intercepted it, they would have accused us both of treason, and even a Prince is not immune to the headsman's ax. I simply told you my father needed tending and your special herbs would do wonders to end his pain."

"Ah, yes." Apparently the Prince had more in mind than simply curing the King's illness.

"So you brought the herbs?"

"Yes, Gareth I did, but I haven't used my special mixture in quite some time. And, as you may know, the blend does take several days to cure before it becomes most effective. Would you be needing it right away?"

Gareth stole a glance around the room to make sure no one was hiding in the corner, listening before he replied, his voice nearly a whisper. "As much as I want to be rid of the old snake there is no rush. My army is training well and I am occupied with other tasks. Prepare your brew and make it potent. I don't want those damned Healers of his to be able to cure him this time."

"It will take some time, then," Grella improvised. She was on her own this time and without The Searcher or Melthus to help her, the task ahead was imposing. She had absolutely no knowledge of herblore let along the concoction Gareth needed to murder the King.

"Take all the time you dare, as long as it's ready when I want it," Gareth said. "Once it's done, then you and I can perhaps discuss more intimate matters." He ran his eyes up and down the lines of her body behind the sheet, smiled, and left.

Even in Shadow, Grella would have normally delighted in his suggestion, but now it chilled the flesh she wore. She shivered. She was enjoying the skin and didn't want to part with it. Clearly crossing the Prince was not in her best interest. His plan to kill his father was proof of that. He was not the sort of man to be kind to those who failed him.

"Zeta," she called to her handmaid.

"Mistress?" the girl hurried in from the outer closet. "You wish to dress?"

"Yes, I do, but I also want some information. Are there herbers in the city? Good ones, who know the plants and their uses."

"Why, yes, Mistress. The Whispering Gardens out near the Course grow nearly every herb known in Turan. Madam Jada is the Tender there and she is well spoken of as an expert in the herblore."

"Oh, good," Grella put her hand to her head. "I have been plagued by headaches since I came to Aberdeen and would dearly love a cure."

"The Palace has two Healers, My Lady. Surely one of them could help you."

"Dear me, no. They are men, and, well, I do think my pain stems from some more feminine issues, if you understand what I mean. I would much prefer to consult a fellow woman."

"Of course, of course, I understand completely, My Lady. If you'd like to go today, I can send down to the stables to prepare a carriage."

"That would be fine, Zeta. I'll have a quick bath, light fare for Firstmeal, and then be off."

"Shall I come with you?"

"No, no, my dear. Take the day off if you wish. I'll have no need of a maid." Nor would I want one, Grella thought. The less anyone else knew of the true purpose of her trip, the better. The headache excuse was a stroke of genius and she was quite proud of it. Who needed companions when she was quite capable on her own? Besides, Gambel had said the streets near the Course were good hunting grounds, and she was hungry.

Porridge and a cup of keldherb with cavel milk satisfied her body, enough to give her the energy to make it through the day. For now she could wait for nightfall and take care of matters in Westportal.

The carriage drive to the Whispering Gardens carried Grella from the elegance of the palace grounds into the streets of Aberdeen, where it didn't take long for the wealth and luxury of royalty to fade in favor of the bustling middle-income surroundings of merchant shops, and then into the poorer sections of the city where men stood around with their hands out, hoping for a coin from a passerby to feed their families. It was here Dax had recruited many of Gareth's foot soldiers, eager to serve the royal army with its promise of a fair wage. As she looked out the window at the poverty around her, Grella wondered if Melthus too had mined these same streets for Tamor's forces, promising them gold and immortality for joining his shadow forces. And of the two, who would garner more loyalty, the crown, or the Black Dragon?

Closer to the Course, things improved again, with neat little houses and well-tended streets leading to the tourist inns and taverns. There, the driver headed east, then north again to finally stop at the gates of the Whispering Gardens. The footman helped Arista down.

"Come back in three spans to pick me up," she ordered the driver. Then she handed each man a gold sovern, "Enjoy yourselves at one of those lovely taverns I saw on the way here and see the horses are tended." Then she stepped through the gate.

The fragrance of herbs and flowers overpowered her senses, stopping her in her tracks. Nothing else in the time she had worn this skin had ever affected her so. How wonderful to be so full, so captured by such an amazing feeling. Her eyes widened as beds of flowers blossoming in all kinds of vibrant colors stretched before her. There were winding paths to wander, green hedges separating sections lined with waving brellums, shimmering oaks, and other leafy trees she couldn't name. She could see fountains scattered about and several little foot bridges crossing streams. Her breathing steadied as all her thoughts seemed to float away on the warm gentle breezes caressing her face. Such beauty was almost too much to bear and for one brief moment, her Shadowself lost its darkness and she smiled.

So this, she thought, was what it felt like to have True Life. For the first time, she understood the longing so many of her kind had for it. And with that thought the bloodlust rushed back. She would need to hunt, and hunt again until she had drunk from her twelve and earned the right to experience the intoxicating sensations of living for whatever eternity she chose. Recovering her purpose, she headed down what looked to be the main path in search of the herbwoman. As long as the sun was shining, her feast would have to wait.

It was not long before she saw a little building nestled in a grove of willows. Outside, a woman was picking herbs for her basket. "Mistress Jada?" Arista called to her.

The woman straightened. "I be Jada. We met afore when ya first come ta Aberdeen. Ya was with a fine lookin' lord. Grella, was it? "

Grella hesitated, then covered quickly, "My maiden name. I am actually Lady Arista, of the royal seat, Madam. I've come for your assistance."

"An' what kin a poor herber like me do fer the crown, eh?

"Oh, it's not the crown, it's a more personal nature." She took the strap from around her neck and held out the bag of herbs. "My mother's circle closed not long past and part of my inheritance was this pouch of herbs. I never mastered her art, I fear, so I have no idea what to do with them."

"Come in, come in, then, Jada's always pleased ta teach the lore. We'll see whatcha gots an' I kin advise ya what to do wid it."

The inside of Jada's cottage was filled with even more heady aromas and Grella felt her resolve drifting again, as if the herbs were trying to heal her dark thoughts, but she waited a moment and the sensations passed as they had before. She opened the bag and spread the array of vials and pouches out on the wide table.

Muttering to herself, Jada quickly sorted the herbs into four groups, her hands quick and sure. The first group she pushed to the side, leaving three on the table. "This be a fine collection. Yer mother were a true Master, I kin tell. Now here's what Jada's done. Them what's put over there," she pointed to the fourth pile, "ain't fer no novice, and lessen ya force me I cain't let ya leave wid them on yer person. They can be deadly in the wrong hands an' I don't want no fine lady like yerself killin' somewhat accidental like."

Grella suppressed a frown as she looked at the vials. Those were likely the very herbs she needed. Then she nodded, for darkness could be her ally here too. "That's wise, Madam. And the rest?"

"Well, ya got's yer healers and soothers. I'll make ya a list. There's some nice selfweed and tellison here fer pain an' healing. Gots some varleyroot ta give ya energy when yer all tired out, or after a sickness. Oriote here makes a fine sleeping potion too." Then she held up a packet she'd set to the side. "Now this, this is a good'un fer ya ta learn. Palion. 'Tis a strange herb, loving and dangerous all in one. Ya takes the seeds and stems an' boil 'em real good an' ya gots one o' the best soothin' and sleepin' medicines in the whole o' Turan. An' that's the only reason I be leavin' it in yer bag. Elsewise, it'd be over there with the malroot, 'cause you err in brewing the palion, or ya use the flower by issolf, an' ya gots one o' the deadliest poisons in the whole o' Turan. Mind ya, it's easy ta do it right an' jest as easy ta do it wrong."

"I hope then," Arista said, "that you will teach me to do it right."

Jada nodded again, pulled out an array of utensils and began the lessons.

They worked together for some two spans, mixing and remixing tonics and healing potions, covering all the basics a novice should know including the proper use of palion, the curious purple flower with two faces. Finally, Jada straightened up rubbed her back and sighed. "There ya be lass, all ol' Jada can teach ya for one sittin'. Ya be welcome ta come back iffen ya's a mind, and iffen not, yas know enow ta keep ya out o' trouble with that bag o' your'n. I took out most o' the danger. I'll keep them dangers here for ya in yer mother's honor. That way she be remembered. What were her name?"

Grella's mind raced. What had Gareth said? He said she was the King's sister-in-law. She could afford the risk of making up a name, "Ariana," she said. "We were from one of the Far Isles."

"Ah, sea folk then. Ya said ya come from the crown?"

The lie's weave was becoming complex. Grella had to be careful. "I am related through marriage, not blood. My family had not often been to Aberdeen."

"I see, I see," Jada said. "Well, I be honored ta have ya come anyways, an honored more iffen ya lets me show ya the gardens."

"My carriage will be back in a span, so we have time. I'd love to have a tour."

"Come on then. Ma surleps be the sweetest in the world. We kin have us a treat an' a nice chat whilst I show ya the most beautiful gardens yer ever like ta see."

For the next span, the two women wanders along the meandering paths of Whispering Gardens, enjoying the sunshine and sampling the sweet fruits of the trees. Delicious though they were, surleps and popples did little to satisfy Grella's growing hunger. There was only one food for that, and after Norwin's change, she intended to fill her belly.

XIII

"Twenty-eight," Gareth repeated. "Twenty-eight elite guard for me, and twenty-eight Scarleteers to ride in the crown's name. And look here," he rolled out a parchment scroll filled with all kinds of diagrams and arrows. "I've arranged some of the marching patterns for the foot soldiers. See? We put them in squads of twenty-eight. Seven in each rank, four deep. Then they march, twenty-eight paces for each span of the field—we'll mark it off at first."

Dax studied the diagram for a while, trying to make sense of the direction of march. The images formed a kaliadoscopic rotation over the field, creating lines and circles with no practical use in battle at all. From afar, it would look as if some artist were painting the grass with men, weaving in and out of their ranks to create spiraling images instead of maneuvers of war. "Very interesting, My Liege. I suppose this is to confuse the enemy?"

"Of course, of course. See here? This rank counts twenty-eight paces and then turns right. The next does the same and soon they meet and cross each other in a most beautiful display of precision marching. What enemy would not be dazzled by this? And even the seven. Why most armies march in lines of even numbers. Will our opponents not be confounded by our ranks? They'll be prepared to defend against six, eight at most, but not seven. How can they cope with seven? Why, it's sheer genius."

Even Gambel, who had only worn Dax's skin for a handful of Sevenstins, could see the foolishness of the whole mess. His own experience with battle was limited, and he would never proclaim himself a master tactician, but this was ridiculous. Yet prudence checked his reaction and he said, "Very original, Your Highness. Something no one has ever considered before, I am sure. I will drill the men in march if this is your command. I doubt the common men of foot can master the twenty-eight paces, however. If you recall, we tested so many for the Elite and they failed. Perhaps we could be a bit more lenient with the main of the army—teach them more common maneuvers instead? Then we can save your masterful plans for your own guard. Four ranks of seven each would more than suffice to create these wonderful patterns you have drawn."

"H-m-m-m." Gareth mumbled. "It would not be so grand with only one unit. I had pictured so much more, but perhaps you are right. The dolts we have in the regular troops cannot even count to twenty-eight, much less march it. We will train the Elite, and later the Scarleteers if you can find horses with matching even gaits."

"That might take a while, My Lord. Horses are even bigger dolts than men. There too we may have to compromise."

"I hadn't thought of that," Gareth said. "That fine gray Edra brought me marches quite well. I was able to rein him to twenty-eight strides across the hall just yesterday."

"You rode him in here? In the hall?"

"Of course, it is the testing field, is it not? Until we finish our battleground and mark off the correct distances, then where else could I test my mount? He will need to practice, but he was a fine choice for a King, a fine choice."

Thankfully, Gareth was not King yet, Gambel thought, and the Dax in him readily agreed. More and more his Flesher body was taking over his Shadow being, but until he had drunk more blood the two were often at odds. This time, they agreed. The Prince was either a raving lunatic or a total idiot. "That was a good way to see if he was the proper horse for you, Sire. I'm glad he passed your most brilliant test. There are not many fine greys around with his presence and elegance."

"He is a beauty, Gareth agreed. Now you must not let Edra buy anymore greys, you know. Dark horses for my calvary. I want to be seen when I ride out admist them."

Good target for the enemy, Dax thought. *I'd be pleased to take a shot at him myself,* Gambel replied. "I understand completely," they said aloud. "I will certainly inform Master Edra of your orders. "

"Good. Now how is the practice field progressing?"

"Another two Sevenstins, from what the foreman tells me, My Lord. Until then we can use the north gardens to practice. We were lucky to have recruited two former Knights of the Hand to help with weapons training. While Lord Edra and I are certainly capable, there are now nearly three hundred men to train. Some have a bit of skill with the blade, but many do not."

"Bowmen, bowmen? Do we have bowmen?"

"We do, My Lord, at least twenty-five…er, twenty-eight. It is just a beginning as an army needs many more to conduct a proper war, but it's a good start. As our reputation grows and word spreads throughout Turan, I know there will be many more to sign up."

"I am not short of patience," Gareth replied, "as long as there is progress. We shall have a grand parade some two Sevenstins hence when my battlefield is ready. Then I shall decide if you are worthy to stay on as my general."

"My Lord," Dax said, bowing. He had not considered that Gareth might think of replacing him. The stakes were higher than he'd thought. His priorities had to change. He could not afford to play at training his men to march and fight any longer. And he needed to seek True Life with greater intensity. Both efforts had been half-hearted so far. But if he wanted to survive beyond the next Sevenstins, he either needed to please the Prince or become immortal. He snapped to attention, saluted, and turned on his heel, marching out the door.

He made it to the exit in exactly twenty-eight strides.

Once in the hall, he jogged out to the stables to find Edra, who was preparing to leave the city on another horse buying trip. "Master Edra, a word, if you will."

"General Dax, I am always ready to listen to you."

"The Prince bid me tell you he wants only dark horses for his Scarleteers. No more greys. He likes the one you found for him and doesn't want anyone else to stand out when he rides with his men."

"I'll be careful to follow his instructions, Sur. Prince Gareth is not a man to be crossed."

"That I know," Dax agreed. "He says he only wants twenty-eight riders in his cavalry, so you need to think of that when you buy."

"Twenty-eight. I should have known. We will need reserve mounts, but I will try to only show the Prince the number he wants. I can easily stable the others at the Course if need be. We do have thirty stalls set aside here in the Royal Stables."

"Don't fill them all, then," Dax warned. "The Prince was very clear about twenty-eight."

Edra tried hard to measure Dax's attitude. The man was either a useful ally or the Prince's Follyman. He decided to risk finding out. "Twenty-eight, no more, no less. If I never hear that number again, I would be most content."

Dax took the bait. "You'd be content?" he spat. "You could mark me so happy I'd look a fool."

"No more than the Prince," Edra said. "He does have some peculiar ideas."

"You should have been up there with us just now," Dax sighed. "Twenty-eight horses is only the half of it. He has a whole set of march plans demanding every soldier count his steps."

"Bory, does he expect men to count in the middle of a battle too?"

Dax laughed bitterly, "Hah, if he had his way they'd count footfalls and sword swings and if the enemy took twenty-nine of either, they'd just have to surrender."

"He's a fool, then," Edra stated, glad to know Dax was a friend.

"Either that or a madman. I don't know which is worse. All I can say is we'd both best watch our backs. Neither sorcery nor the sword can guarantee safety against someone like him."

"Thank you for the warning, General. I'll keep all this in mind when I select the horses. Do you have a mount yet?"

"No. I am not the keenest of horsemen," Gambel replied, taking over Dax in this case. He remembered far too well how the horses had behaved in the stable near the Course when Edra had come to get them. "The damned beasts don't seem to like me much."

"A good warhorse will ride for any man who masters him. All I need to do is find the right animal for you. One that's obedient to a fault. A general needs an impressive mount. Maybe I can find one with size and a kind heart for you."

Gambel sighed and Dax nodded. "That would be good, I suppose. It would be easier to command from the saddle."

"Then leave it my hands." Edra bowed with mock formality. "And so I take my leave of you, General Dax. Do be sure to seek twenty-eight at every turning. I myself will be so glad to be free of the city I will not even bother to count the coins in my purse." He threw his saddlebags over his back and headed into the stables.

Dax shook his head and walked back to the palace, trying hard not to think of how many steps he was taking along the way.

Edra wasted no time in saddling up the chestnut he'd bought from Master Drew down at the course. Solid and sensible for a runner, the horse proved to be smooth-strided and bold as he walked through the city streets. He was a little green to the aids, having known only the life of a racer and not how to respond to the legs and hand of casual rider, but he was a quick learner ready to please the man on his back. "I shall name you Fireheart," Edra said, patting the gelding on the neck with the stump of his left hand. He had always admired the bond his Riders in Arcula had with their Striders and thought perhaps he might find such a match in this animal. He cast a small spell of affection and when Fireheart snorted, he was sure the horse was agreeing with him. He smiled for the first time in months. "You will have to learn to answer only one hand, my boy," he said sadly. "I could tell you the story of how I lost my other one, but it grieves me too much to remember. I would give anything to have it back."

He did not notice the black cloud passing overhead as he spoke. It followed him at some distance along the streets, and when he finally left the east gate of the city, it hovered closer.

Edra pulled up the collar of his traveling cape, as a chill of cold air brushed his neck. Fireheart began to jog nervously and the Caugeman was having trouble controlling him. Finally, in desperation he cast a calming spell by thinking of the placid waters of a nearby lake and the horse settled to a rocky walk. "You're not used to the open road, eh?" Edra said. "You'll learn, my boy. Until then I'll use my Art to keep you under men. Magic had its benefits."

"Does it, Sorcerer?" a voice asked from behind.

Edra spun Fireheart around to find himself facing a black form blotting out the roadway with inky, wavering tendrils. The Sorcerer raised his hand but before he could cast his spellfire, the form dissolved, then reshaped itself into a burly man dressed in a leather apron over breeches and a homespun shirt. "I just want to talk," the man said.

Edra kept his hand ready before him. "Then talk. I have no love of Shadows."

The man's gaze dropped to Edra's left stump. "Even if the Shadow has your ring, and the thing attached to it?"

Edra started. "My hand? You have my hand?"

"Not here, not now. First the bargain must be struck. Lord Tamor can forgive when it serves his purpose."

"We lost the battle. I paid with this," Edra held up his butchered arm.

"The battle, as they say, is not the war. Tamor is not done with the Rivermaster. You are forging a new alliance against him in the world of mortals. There is work being done to add to your numbers. The Black Dragon will rise and the Circle will close. Would you rather be counted among the victims or the victors?"

"That question needs no answer," Edra said. "What do I need to do?"

"Swear allegiance."

"I tried that before."

The man laughed, it was a hollow, dreadful sound. "Indeed you did. I can speak with The Dark Lord's authority and, if he tells me so, act with it as well. He sent us to Aberdeen to find his army and you have become an important part of its birth. Agree to join with Lord Tamor when the time comes, enlist your Prince in our cause, and you will have your hand."

"How do I do all this? The Prince has a general. Must I enlist him too?"

"The General is already enlisted, Sorcerer. He and I are close acquaintances. It is the Prince who needs turning."

"I can agree, but how will you know the Prince has agreed?"

"The General will know. He says you are the greater influence on Gareth, though. It will be up to you. How and when you do it matters little as long as it is done. The Dark Lord needs time to put his own plans in motion. All you need to do is be ready for his command."

"And you? What will you be doing while I do all this?"

"I will be anywhere I choose, finding my own soldiers, as I have been since I left Lord Tamor's keep. There are many unhappy souls in Turan who need the relief Shadows can offer. And much blood I can take when I thirst. I pity Dax that, for he is locked within the confines of the city. I can hunt the whole of the Provinces."

Edra shivered, remembering too well the desecration of the corpses on Arcula's battleground by Tamor and his minions. Rumors of bloody murders in the streets of Aberdeen had reached the ears of some of the palace servants and he had overheard. Now he understood. "How many Shadows are in Aberdeen?"

The man smiled, "Dax and I are not alone. Let that be all you need to know. Now, be on your way, and think on what I have said. Prove yourself worthy and you shall have all you want. Defy the Darkness and you will pay with more than just a hand." With that, the man's image faded into Sowin's already reddening sun.

Without thinking further on it, Edra spurred Fireheart into a long-strided gallop, hoping to reach The Mother's Love before Weswin's change brought back the night.

*****

Without any clues to the riddle, Jamus decided to enjoy his stay in Tallridge, letting the tapestry' story play out as it would. Of course, the best part of it all was staying at Becca's inn, eating her food, and sharing company with her family. The twins were adorable mischievous toddlers and watching them with their parents was a good learning experience for him. He had worried about raising Jarien, wanting to be sure his son never lacked for the love and direction he had lost at such a young age. Becca and Jeamel were role models he wanted to emulate more than anything he'd ever wished for.

They were fair and firm with the children. Always certain of
the behavior they expected but never ruining the fun of play. Sira and
Jeb had the freedom to run, explore, and touch everyone and
everything in the inn, creating all kinds of wonderful games and
learning how to hold interesting conversations with any guest who
would indulge them. All it took was hard stare and a wag of her
finger from Becca and they would stop in their tracks, close their
mouths, and scurry off to the back rooms if they went to far with any
of their adventures. He never heard Becca raise her voice, but if she
pulled one of the children aside to chastise him, she would kneel
down, meet his eyes with hers and speak in a low voice, making it
clear she disapproved of whatever he had done. Invariably, the
intimate conversation ended with a big hug, and more often than not,
a cookie from her never-empty cookie tin.

"Just what do you say to them, Mistress?" Jamus asked after
one such episode.

"I tells them plain and clear in words they knows, just what
they done wrong, why it was wrong, especially iffen it was hurtin'
someone. Then I ask 'em ta tell me back why it was wrong and say
they's sorry. Iffen they hurts someone they gotta say they be sorry to
them too or they know they are gonna haf ta sit in their room until
they does. Then I tells 'em how proud their Mam is 'cause they
unnerstan' and promise not do to wrong agin. Then I tells 'em how
much I love 'em and iffen they give me a big hug, I'll giv'em a
snappie. Not sure they remember fer the next time the itch gits to
'em but they sure remember the snappie."

"Does it work every time?"

"Most times. Sometimes, though, they are bad 'cause they
feel bad about somethin'. Then I askt'em ta tell me about the sad
they feel. Ya, gotta know when ta tell an' when ta lissen. The
lissening can be even more important ta the li'l ones. Iffen ya don'
lissen when they little, they ain't gonna tell ya nothin' when they
grows big enow ta do bad that matters. Ya want 'em ta always know
yer gonna lissen, ya know?"

Jamus nodded. Becca had always listened to him, never
judging or expressing her opinion until she had let him tell her all his
troubles. Now that he looked back on all those times he'd gone to

her, he realized she had already taught him all he needed to know about raising his own son. "You are a good mother."

"I tries ta be. I don' know what I'd do if anythin' happened ta those li'l ones o' mine. They be my whole heart, aside from ma Jeamel, that is. He's a good Pap to 'em and a good husband ta me. We gots the perfect family and the perfect place ta rais'em."

"The inn is truly a special place," Jamus agreed, "and this part of Magiskeep is beautiful. I can see why you like it here. But, is there a school nearby where the children can learn to read or write? And they both have a touch of Magic, if I'm not mistaken. Did you ever think of taking them to the Keep itself?"

"Mistress Brinda down the way can teach'em their numbers and letters. More than enow for'em ta run the inn if they've a mind or any business they be fit for. As fer the Magic, sure, they be touched, but Jeamel an' me don' hold that so important. Man's an' woman's hands was made ta work. I want ma babes ta know how good it feels ta git somethin' cause o' what they done ta git it, not 'cause they wiggled they's li'l finger an' it jest come ta 'em."

How many times had Jamus heard that? He'd learned himself when Magic deserted him that hard work had its rewards. But Magic had its place too. "Mistress Joria had a class at the Keep for young children teaching them Practical Magic—things that might save their lives. The class I attended was learning how to cook an egg and how to dry off if they got wet. A child lost in the mountains here could protect himself from cold and starvation with skills like that. They learn to make a fire or weave a simple blanket. From what I know of the Magic they use, it will fade as they grow older and lose much of its power, but while they are little and vulnerable, it can be well used. You could take your twins there when they get just a circle older to study." He stopped, took a gulp of calidew from his cup, and simply stared into it. Becca's twins were destined to die within the circle. They would never be old enough to join Joria's class.

"Might be good," Becca said. "I'll talk it o'er wid Jamie. 'E keeps talkin' about goin' ta the Keep proper ta see iffen they needs a good steward in the Hall. This'll give 'em a good excuse ta see what's doin' there."

"He wants a job in the Keep? What about the inn?"

"We ain't talked it all over yet. Inn's doin' good as I said, but he thinks I works too hard. Much as I likes it, there be times I'd be happier jest bein' with the babes. An' me an Jeamel wants a big family so I'm gonna need alls the time I can git ta raise ma wee ones."

Becca's twins died in Tallridge. Perhaps, if he could get them to move to the main Keep, he could change that destiny. Was it one of the small things on Turan's Way or something the tapestry would deny?

"You could come before the season changes, while I'm still there. I could speak for you, and certainly for Jeamel if you wished."

"We gots lots o' business comin' through till season end, lad. Much as I 'preciate the offer, as long as the tourists be lookin' at them mountains, and the traders be crossin' the Rim while the weather holds, I cain't afford ta leave. An' if I ain't going, Jeamel and the babes ain't goin' neither."

"I'll have to head back to my father's farm for harvest come Fullmonth," Jamus lied. "I won't be at the Keep any later. Surely you can give up a Sevenstin here."

"Kind o' ya ta offer yer help, but ma inn be too important. I can't leave till Chillmonths at the earliest. Mebbe ya kin get back yerself when the harvest is in? We could meet then."

It was hopeless. Once Becca made up her mind, Jamus knew there was no way to change it. She was one of the most determined women he had ever known. Turan's Way, no matter how cruel, would not be denied. "That sounds like a good idea," he agreed lamely. "Let's plan on it."

"So," Becca said, "now that's settled, whatcha gonna do today ta keep yerself busy? Ya ain't been ta the waterfall yet, have ya? I kin pack a nice meal fer ya and the trail's plain marked. 'Tain't the kinda day ta spend indoors."

"That sounds nice," Jamus replied. Right now he really did want to get away to think things through, someplace where his brain was clear and he didn't have to see Sira and Jeb bounding about so full of life.

With Becca's sack in hand, he headed out to the stables to saddle Shadowmist and ride out. The twins were there ahead of him, jumping off bales into a pile of straw on the stable floor. Apparently they had opened one of the bales to make their landing pad and were making a grand game of scattering it all over the floor with their dramatic leaps. "Look Sira, I kin fly," Jeb cried as he flapped his arms and landed in the center of the pile on his belly.

Not to be outdone by her brother, Sira climbed up on an even higher bale and leapt after him. "I kin fly too, e'en more!"

Jeb pointed up to the loft, "Iffen we goes up there we can really fly, Sira, com'on."

"Stop!" Jamus shouted, freezing the children in place. Then, remembering Becca, he lowered his voice. "All right you two, I think it's time you started thinking about what you're doing."

Two pairs of wide frightened eyes stared up at him. He knelt down in front of the twins. "Are we bein' bad, Master Jarius?" Sira asked.

"I know you're having fun," Jamus replied, his own gray eyes meeting theirs. "But you need to think a little harder. First, you have made a mess of this beautiful stable by putting that straw all over the place. That will make some very hard work for the stableboy because he will have to clean it up. Second, I know all the jumping is a lot of fun but the loft is very high. If one of you jumped from there you would get hurt. That would make your Mam and Pap very sad and you would cry. I know you don't like to cry, now do you?"

"No," the two whispered almost together.

"Now I want to know you understand what I just told you."

"We made a mess," Jeb said, "an' that were mean ta Master Tomas."

"An' jumpin' outta the loft was a bad thing ta think on 'cause we was gonna break a leg or somethin'" Sira said, being the wiser of the two.

"I'm sorry," Jeb said.

"I'm sorry too," Sira replied. "Are we gonna have ta tell Master Tomas we sorry too?"

Master Tomas is not here to see the mess you made, so if you clean it up for him, I think that will be apology enough. There is a hay fork over there and a broom. I'll help if you want me to."

"No," Jeb said firmly. "Me an' Sira made the mess. We gotta clean it up. That's what Mam says."

The two set to work as Jamus tacked up his horse keeping his eye on the two. Every now and then he gestured slightly with his hand setting flakes of straw back in place in a bale by the side.

Soon most of the loose straw was either in his new bale or in a neat little pile the children had struggled to collect. Both the broom and fork were too big for their little hands and short legs, but they never complained and would have kept at the task for a span, if Jamus had not stopped them. "Now, sweep that pile of yours into that empty stall. It has some bedding already so a little more won't matter."

Diligently, Sira manned the broom and pushed most of the loose straw through the door. Again, when they weren't watching, Jamus whisked all the stray pieces into his bale, leaving the aisle as spotless as it had been before the game had begun.

He reached into the sack Becca had given him and called the twins over. He knelt again. "You've done a fine job. I am so proud to know the two of you. Thank you for being so good."

Sira reached over and gave him a kiss on the cheek while Jeb hugged Jamus' arm. Before he even thought about it, he swept the two children into his embrace, hugging them as he tried to stop his tears. How could Turan's Way be so cruel to such sweet little ones.

"Wassa matter, Jarius?" Sira asked from the folds of his tunic. "Yer heart be beatin' real hard."

Jamus released them and rocked back on his heels holding out two snappies he had found in the meal sack. "I am just very happy to know you," he said. "My heart is bouncing with joy."

Grabbing the cookie, Jeb grinned, "These be from Mam's kitchen. We not s'posed ta take stuff from strangers, but these be Mam's so they's all right."

"Anyhows, Jarius ain't no stranger. He an' Mam talk all the time," Sira said, taking her cookie gently and putting in her pocket. "I'll ask Mam afore I eat mine."

Jeb was about to take a bit of his snappie and then he too put his in his pocket. "Me too. We always gotta ask Mam."

Jamus smiled as he got up. "Be sure and tell you Mam exactly how you got those snappies, please. Tell her the barn is all cleaned up, so she can keep our secret too. She'll be even happier than I am to hear it."

As the twins raced back up to the inn, Jamus felt the tears roll down his cheeks. "At least they didn't see me cry," he muttered.

Make good sire.

"What?"

Make good sire. Treat foals with good care. Mist like.

"I didn't know horses had opinions about raising children."

Fourleg have feeling about many thing men not know. Young need learn many thing. Mare teach, sire teach, other horse teach. Way of fourleg, way of twoleg. No different.

"I never really thought about it that way," Jamus said.

Twoleg think too much. Better just do. We windstep?

"Perhaps a little," Jamus said. "If this waterfall is where I think it is, I may know the trails after all."

Sure enough, the Silver Falls were exactly where he expected them to be. He and his parents, seasoned Mountmen, had brought him here dozens of time when he was a child. It was one of the few things he remembered well from the days before his mother and father died in the rockslide in Cowltop. It seemed that everywhere he went in this tapestry, he as facing a part of his life he needed to recall for some reason or another. Here, though, all he felt was the love his parents had had for him and for each other. Jorel and Shanda had always watched out for him, always listened, always cared, just like Becca. Just like the father he was going to be to Jarien.

As the water rushed over the rocks, he heard the River whisper. "Another thread mended. Yet the riddle goes on."

"Kashar?" Jamus knew her voice.

"Now the circle of love closes around you. The past is forgotten. You may live anew in your own son. Be content. For now the River is at peace."

Jamus dismounted, climbed up on a flat rock near the falls, and let the water's music fill his ears. The rushing soothed his mind, and he found himself at peace as she had suggested. Becca's food tasted better than ever and his senses filled with the sheer beauty of the place. Silver water cascaded from the rocky ledge above, sparkling in rainbows made by the sun. The foamy rapids below swirled into a deep whirlpool as bottomless as the River itself. He wanted to sit here forever, drinking in the wonder and that blessed peace.

"Hey, ho there!!"

Jamus turned to see a lone man hiking out of the mountain pass, leading a pack horse behind him. He got up and held Shadomist's reins to keep the horse from trotting over to meet the packer. "Hello," he called back. "Where are you bound?"

The man led his animal to the edge for the water to let it drink. "I'm taking the south trail right down to the Keep proper. I've some trinkets from Turan I promised to deliver to the village craftsmen." He soaked his scarf in the water, and mopped his brow. "It's a bit hot today, isn't it?"

"It is," Jamus replied. "I've been staying at the inn in Tallridge. Lots of cool mountain breezes, I think."

"Ah, the Bread and Butter. Fine place. Best food in all of Turan let me tell you and I've eaten everywhere. I always make it my last stop on the way back home. My name's Ferg, and I've been trading with the Keep for the last ten circles." He soaked his scarf again and wrapped it, still wringing wet, around his neck.

"Jarius," Jamus said. "I'll be back at the Keep soon myself."

"Say, ye be a fine young man, do ye have a lady?"

"I do."

"Well then." Ferg walked over to his horse and pulled out a beautiful colored woven scarf and handed it to Jamus. "Only ten denerets and a bargain at that. There's a wonderful cloth maker in Aberdal who make all kinds of wonders. Any lady'd love to have this."

"Not today," Jamus said, but had he not been in the tapestry, he might well have bargained to give it to Salene. Regretfully, he handed it back. "It really is beautiful. My wife appreciates gifts made by craft artists. But I can't buy it now."

"Bargain today, gone tomorrow," Ferg said as he put the scarf back in his pack. "Ye going to the Keep?"

"In a day or so."

"Be glad to share a mug with you if we happen to meet up again. Well, I'd best be off. I know where I want to camp for the night and if I don't make feet soon, it'll be dark before we get there. There's a nice patch of grass for Whiteface here to nibble on, and a soft bed of sand for me to spread my blanket. It's home on the trail for the both of us." He pulled the horse back to the trail and waved farewell. "Take care of yourself, Jarius. It's been good talking, but someone's gotta make the denerets to pay the bills, eh? Come on Whitey, let's go." And off he went, taking the south fork at the first turning in the trail.

Jamus finished his meal, smiling again as he nibbled on the last snappie, thinking of Becca's twins. Here, by the waterfall, he felt a surge of hope that maybe there yet be a way to save them. But he also knew that in his world, fifty circles beyond this moment, they were dead, lost forever to their grieving mother. What was Turan's Way for them? How could such beauty exist while such tragedy waited? Was there anything he could do?

Small occurrences, even small lives, make little difference in the Circle, for the Hand will always guide small matters back to Turan's Way in the end.

*****

"The child is the key," Tamor said. He and Sorra were back at Natale's cottage after their successful hunt. She had been nourished, and he satisfied. Now it was time to discuss his plans for her. "The Rivermaster has a son. If I have him, then I have his father."

"How will you do this?"

"You will do it for me," Tamor said. He walked over to the mirror and peered in, willing his vision into the Way, searching until he found Jamus chamber. He hissed when he saw the empty cradle and Jamus lying alone in the bed with an old woman at his side. "The baby should be there."

"I see him," Sorra whispered, "can't I kill him as he sleeps?"

"He is warded, Mistress, and a master of reflections. Only Blackwing himself can kill him. We must bring him to the Master."

"So, I will never taste his blood?"

"You can have the babe when I am done with him. By then you will have earned the right to drink. For now, you must control your thirst and walk the world as this Natale whose skin you wear."

"She limits me."

"You can always leave the body behind to hunt if you need to, but you must be careful. You will be in Magiskeep, the lair of the River itself. Many eyes will see you, many minds may sift you. You must use all the knowledge the Dragon gave you, all the wiles he granted to keep your true identity a secret.You will watch and listen for any word of the babe, and then you will find a way to steal him and bring him to me."

"They will watch him. It won't be easy."

"Hide in the shadows so they never see you, or gain their trust, whichever you decide. Blackwing's will is never easy, but it must be done. Find your own way. I will be there if you need me, but I did not choose a fool."

She smiled and took his hand in hers, kissing it gently. "I will miss you."

Tamor stroked her cheek with his other hand. "I have never felt this way before. Is this why Fleshers cherish their skins so much?"

"You have True Life, My Lord. What is it like? It is worth the seeking?"

"I don't know, dear one. When I was still Shadow, I felt no pain except for the longing to live. Now I ache at the thought of losing you. It is a most curious sensation. How can I know if it is worth it if I have never felt it before?"

"This skin I wear yearns for you," Sorra said. "Before the Dragon touched me, all I knew was my lust for revenge. Now I lust for you inside me. If this is what you feel, then I too want True Life so we can share it together."

Tamor took her into his arms and carried her to the bed.

*****

Arista sent the carriage back to the palace after it left her off at a little inn not far from the gardens. She told the driver to return the next day near Sowin to pick her up. After he had left she walked several streets south to another inn she had seen when she, Gambel and Melthus had first flown into the city.

The Rudder and Wheel was dingy and unkempt, tucked away at the end of a neglected alley, generally ignored by all but the lowest citizens of Aberdeen. There, a deneret paid for three nights and no questions asked. It was the perfect lair for a hunting tark or a Shadow. The innkeeper didn't even look up when Grella laid her coin on the counter. He simply handed her a key and nodded to the stairs.

Her room was in the back and the end of the hall. To her satisfaction, she found a narrow staircase leading to the alley in back, giving her even more privacy. She unlocked the door, put her bag of herbs under the bed, and locked the room back up, chanting a small spell on the lock to assure no one broke in while she was gone. Then she headed out to hunt.

To her disappointment, the streets were empty. It was too quiet for a Warmmonth night when at the very least prostitutes usually hung out on the corners to wait for drunken workmen or lonely sailors coming from the docks. The shadows were deep with the moon on the wane, giving her perfect cover, but for what? Where was everyone?

She had been walking for a nearly a span, crisscrossing the blocks before she finally heard someone calling to her, "Mistress, Mistress, over here!"

She headed toward the voice to find herself face to face with a young boy of perhaps twelve circles.

"Why are you out walking the streets alone, Mistress? Ain't you been warned? Most every house in the quarter had a messenger. It ain't safe to be out and about in the dark what with the killers on the loose."

Grella paused, and Arista pretended to shudder in fear. "Oh, dear, oh dear, I'm afraid I've gotten lost. I heard no word about the danger so I left my room at the Rudder and Wheel to get some fresh air—the place is rather dreadful, I'm afraid, but all that a poor widow like me can afford. I walked a bit and found myself all turned around. Now I can't seem to find my way back."

"The Rudder?" the boy asked. "That's no place for a fine lady like yourself, but if you've paid your board already, then the Rudder it is. It's three streets down and two over, out near Dustbin Alley. But you shouldn't be walking out alone. Suppose I escort you. My names Sorty and I have a bit of the Magic so I can protect you."

"Magic?" Grella's mouth began to water. Sorcerer's blood could be worth six mortals' depending how much Magic they possessed. It was said a Shadow would know at the first taste by how sweet it was. The boy was young, but age mattered little to the River. "Oh, my, I didn't think there were any Sorcerers in Aberdeen. It's a bit frightening to meet one."

Sorty pulled himself up to his full height and threw his shoulders back. "I would be Magic enough to Prentice at the Keep, Mistress, and I follow Rule and Vow even here in Aberdeen. My Mam's going to send me across the Rim when she has money enough."

"Well then, if you can get me safely back to my room at the inn, I shall give you a silver for your education. I saved enough from my purse by renting that room to have some to spare, and I would know it was going to a worthy cause."

"There's no need to pay me for the service, Mistress," Sorty said. "I was out here to keep watch for trouble and the Rudder's in my duty walk. Taking you safely home is exactly what I am expected to do."

Grella smiled. His nobility would make him all the sweeter, just for the sake of it. Better to feast on a good man than a street ruffian or whore. Arista shook her finger at the boy. "Now, now I wouldn't hear of it. My son would be about your age if he'd lived and I'd consider it an honor to play a part in seeing that you have the education I could not give him."

"I won't tell you to take my hand," Sorty said. "'Cause I may need to raise it to cast if we do run into danger. So stick close behind me. The Rudder's not far, but some of the alleys are a little twisty."

Together they made their way to the inn. When they got there, Grella took showed him the back staircase. 'The innkeep said this is an easier way to get to my room. The stairs are a little steep though. Could you take my arm?"

Sorty extended his hand to her and as he did, Grella snared it with the first dark binding coil, loosely set so he would not feel it. Once up the stairs she unlocked the door and asked him in.

Sorty hesitated. "It ain't proper for a man to enter a lady's room," he said.

"Oh, don't be silly, Sorty. After all, I am just an old widow and I need to get my purse." She started to bend over to look under the bed and cried out. "Oh, my back. Oh dear and my purse is under the bed in by satchel. Be a dear, would you and pull it out for me?"

Reluctantly, Sorty walked over to the bed, and as he did, Grelle snapped the first coil tight around his wrist, lashed out with the second snare to his other hand before he could react and, with more strength than a woman could ever have, flung him to the mattress and lashed him to the bed posts. He flailed against the restraints and kicked out at her, but already dark tendrils were snaring his ankle and soon he lay helpless, bound hand and foot.

Grella leaned over him letting her Shadow face slither in and out of her Flesher skin as she leered at him. "Such a kind boy. Such a gentleman to a poor old widow. Has a woman ever touched you, Sorty? Have you ever touched a woman?" She lowered her face to his and put her mouth on his tight lips, her tongue flicking out like a rimsnake's.

When she backed a little away, he whimpered, "Lemme go! I did right by you. Lemme go!"

"Now why would I ever do that?" Grella asked, unlacing her bodice to let bear her bosom. "Have you ever seen a real woman, Sorty?" She plumped her breasts with her hands. "See? Men yearn for these. I don't quite know why they find them so fascinating. Do

you? Here, now, get a closer look." She leaned tone, her chest close
to his chin. "You can suckle if you want, little babe. I won't mind."

Sorty twisted his head away as her soft flesh pressed into his
cheek. "Lemme alone!"

"Oh, no, my little one, that is not why I brought you here.
We must be together." Her fingers worked their way into the laces of
his breeches. She pulled them away and stroked him gently. "There,
there, lad. You are a man after all, I see. And look, already waiting
for me."

Sorty struggled against the hot flame beating in his groin, but
fear and her chantings were having a strange effect on him. He could
not control himself. "Stop it. Lemme be!" His heart was pounding,
his eyes wide as he saw her take off the rest of her clothes and climb
on top of him. "First, my pleasure, then my feast," said as she
straddled him and pushed herself down.

Sorty screamed and squeezed his eyes shut but not seeing
did nothing to quell the terrible sensations ripping through his body
as they joined. He arched and twisted trying to get away, but Grella
was his master and there was no escape. She groaned in ecstasy and
it all seemed to go on forever until she finally pulled away, and sat,
panting on the edge of the bed while he moaned in utter misery.

She let him lie there, thinking it was over while she dragged
her bag out from under the bed and pulled out a thin dagger. When
he was quiet again, she moved back over to him, grabbed his chin
and turned his head to meet her gaze. "There, there little one, now
that you are a man, I have another treat for you." She held the blade
where he could see it, shushing him with her finger to his lips.
"Another kind of fear now, eh?" she said, stroking his neck with the
flat of the knife. "It would be so easy to kill you, and normally, I
would. But you are of the Magic, and a dead Sorcerer fall to dust. I
do not need a pile of dust. I need your blood."

"No, no," Sorty gasped, an even worse terror gripping him.
She was Shadow. Bad enough to be raped by a woman, but the
Darkness itself?

"Go ahead, scream if you want to. I have cast a silencing
spell on the chamber, but even if I'd not, it would not matter. With
coin in his hand, the innkeeper is blind and deaf and the other guests,

if there even are any, have too many secrets of their own. Now do tell me when it hurts. I'm a novice at some of my carving and want to make sure I'm doing it right."

Sorty whimpered as she cut a line along his chest. Then she plunged the dagger into his belly, slitting a gash just deep enough to open him up without touching any vital organs. He began to scream and cry, gagging on his own tears a she lowered her face and began to drink.

Sweet, sweet, sweeter than calidew. River blessed, life most precious, flowing into her own belly, seeping into her veins, filling her heart with hope for True Life and filling her stomach with food. She must be careful. He must not die. His blood must flow fresh through his own veins lest it dry to the dust of Sorcerer's death and curdle inside her. When to stop? His heart was already fainter, his breathing shallow. The taste was exquisite. Nectar.

She forced herself to pull away. She looked down at his pale body, naked, bloody and spread-eagled on the bed. He had stopped whining, but his face was streaked with tears. She freed his hands and feet from her enchantment, wiped the blood from her face, washed herself in the laving bowl on the bedstand, and dressed. Then, she picked up her bag of herbs, took one more look at him to assure herself he was still breathing and left the room.

There was still enough darkness to make it back to the little inn near the gardens where the carriage would pick her up to take her back to the palace.

It had been a most refreshing Norwin.

XIII

Simen was completely fascinated by the work going on in Gareth's battlefield. Every imaginable sort of obstacle an army on the march might face was being simulated by over a hundred workmen. There were hills and valleys, stone walls and fences to climb, ditches to leap, some filled with water, others with sharpened spikes set at angles. There were palisades of iron and wood, a rocky slope with a cliff on the other side. There was a muddy morass, fallen logs, a castle wall, and a stretch of rock-strewn roadway with holes and boulders scattered about to be leapt or avoided by a running warrior. Some of the workmen tested their mettle against the challenges even before they were finished building them as if they were too tempting to ignore.

Around the outside of the huge field, there was a training track for the cavalry set with jumps, ditches and even a stream of water diverted from the lake beyond. The stream fed into a pond with more jumps and banks where a horse's courage and surefootedness could be tested and trained. There were targets for mounted bowman, practice dummies for jousts and sword strikes. The whole of it was an amazing construction designed to prepare an army for nearly any kind of battle on horse or on foot.

But there was more to intrigue Simen than the massive effort itself, for along with it came nearly an equal lack of effort. The workmen, being paid by the span, were finding all kinds of ways to waste time while still appearing to be working full force. First, one might play the role of foreman, supervising, and stopping his workers to inspect their efforts. Then his team would gather, spend a long time in consultation before going back to reset a post or stone, sometimes dismantling what they had already built to build it again, in the same way, measuring and fussing over each placement as if it all were being adjusted to some new and more exact specifications. Some groups took spans to mark, measure and pace out their jobs over and over before even turning over a shovelful of earth. The carpenters carving some tall climbing poles used up three huge logs, nearly getting them ready to be set in their foundations before deciding they were too short or too crooked to be of any use. The useless logs were carted away by slow oxen, unusually stubborn and difficult to drive.

Engineers spread parchments of plans on every flat surface and called their foremen over for consults between hammer blows. Those consults sent the foremen back to their crews for more consults and even more time spent talking instead of building. Shovelers dug and refilled holes, masons mortared rocks and sledgehammered them apart before the mortar dried only to set them again at such a slightly different angle it was nearly impossible to see any change. Halfway through Easwin and again, after their Midmeal break, halfway past Sowin, everyone stopped for a half span's rest with waterboys running to and fro, never quite getting to every crew until nearly another half span had passed.

It was all becoming quite entertaining and from the second-floor library window in the castle, Simen watched and laughed at how clever the workers were. The best part was when the Prince himself visited. Then all the men bustled about looking busier than they had all Sevenstin. They must have had good spies posted to warn them of a royal visit, for he could always predict Gareth's arrival by the sudden changes in the work habits.

It was entertainment worthy of the theater and fodder for enough Follyman's tales to keep his audience laughing for nights on end. He certainly wasn't bored in the palace, with the sights outside the window and all the books on the library shelves. All this kept him quite content while he waited for Kala to complete whatever duties the King demanded of her. Then, when she was finished, the two of them would ride out into the city to explore and discover whatever wonders Aberdeen's many streets had to offer.

This day, they were heading south to the famous Whispering Gardens. Since the Course was not yet open for racing, Kala had convinced Simen the gardens would be as good a choice, claiming they were renowned throughout all of Turan for their beauty and unique collection of plants and herbs. It was said anything that ever grew in the world, grew in whispers behind the Gardens' walls.

"Plants," Simen moaned. "They just sit there doing nothing. At least horses move off the spot."

"Well, the horses aren't moving anywhere right now, so you might as well just forget about that. If you decide to stay on for the next Sevenstin, I promise we'll go to the Course together and I'll even let you bet on some winners."

"You'd use your Sight for me?" Simen asked with feigned innocence. "Wouldn't that be cheating?"

"I was thinking perhaps you'd use your own common sense and put your wagers down on some of Talia's runners. She has one of the best records at the Course, you know."

"I saw her horses at the farm and I can see why," Simen agreed. "Erlik had no end of praise for both trainer and beast."

"They seem to be very much in love," Kala agreed.

"Much like you and Dale?"

Kala sighed. "More conveniently so, I fear. At least the two of them have both common purpose and a common place to live. Dale and I have neither at the moment."

"You could find a way to settle down if one or the both of you decided to compromise."

"I worked all my life to become Prime Juris," Kala said, "and Dale worked all his life for the good of Tulene. There isn't much room to compromise something so dear to each one of us. You, of all people, Jamus' brother, should understand that. You may be free, but Jamus is not, and his marriage suffers for it. Salene is, thankfully, a strong independent woman herself, so somehow, she manages to cope. But it can't be easy for her, especially with the baby."

"You loved Jamus once, yourself."

"I did, from the first moment I saw him. It may have been that peculiar attraction of his Magic, at first, but once I got to know him, the Magic mattered far less than the man. If he'd asked me, I would have married him on the spot."

"And given up everything you've worked so hard for here in Turan?"

Kala paused and frowned. "I never even thought of it when I was with Jamus."

"But you do when you are with Dale?"

"Not when I'm with him. When I'm with him, all I ever want to do is stay. Then I forget everything except how much I love him." Kala paused, then she laughed. "I'm a bit of a fool then aren't I? You may be a Follyman, Simen, but you make more sense than most anyone I know."

"A Follyman must be a keen observer of his fellow men," Simen told her. "It's where we get our best material. Now, before you settle your head back on the affairs of State that so easily keep you from following your heart, let's go see these famous Gardens. I am starting to crave a nice fresh salad."

When they reached the garden's gates, instead quiet plants, they met a crowd of shouting people. "Get Jada! There's a boy hurt bad! He's gonna die."

Simen called to one of the men, "What's happened?"

"Lad's been nearly killed over at the Rudder and Wheel. Bertem came to get Jada, she's the Healer. Says the boy's really bad. That's his mother over there." He pointed to a woman, crying hysterically while several others tried to comfort her. He looked up at Simen. "We could use some horses. The inn's a long walk and Jada's too old to run."

"Kala, get the boy's mother up on Silk with you. Where's this Jada?"

A man escorting an old woman carrying a satchel emerged from the crowd. "Bring her here," Simen ordered. He reached out his hand and when the woman took it, pulled her up onto the saddle in front of him. "Where is the Rudder?"

"Seven streets over to the west and two north, kind of in an alley."

"Good street in front, nearby?"

"Aye, sir, there be a little square right where the streets meet."

"Hold on, Mistress," Simen told his passenger. "Put your arms around his mother's waist Kala. Don't worry about the reins. Silk knows what to do." He wrapped one arm tightly around Jada and raised his hand. "Now, Magwin!"

The black stallion leapt forward with Silk close behind and lifted into the air, vanishing from the astonished crowd's eyes in and instant.

"Sorcerer," someone whispered.

"The Hand be blessed," said another.

They landed lightly in the square in front of the Rudder and Wheel Inn. Simen dismounted, and pulled Jada down from Magwin's back before she could catch her breath. Kala and the boy's mother slid to the ground beside them, Kala holding on to the other woman's arm to keep her from collapsing.

"Sorry," Simen muttered as he took Jada's satchel and drew her along with him to the inn's door. "I had to get us here as fast as I could. I should have warned you."

"Magic," Jada gasped. "You're a Sorcerer."

"I am," Simen replied. Then he saw the innkeeper. "Where's the boy?"

"Upstairs, last door on the end, the maid's with him."

They hurried up the stairs and pushed open the door.

Sorty lay on a bloody bed, curled up in a ball, barely breathing. The maid, at his side, scooted out of the way. "I found him in the hall when I come in ta sweep. Looks like he crawled out there ta call fer help. Poor little mite. He's hurt bad, all cut up in the belly."

"Cut," Simen asked as the boy's mother rushed over and knelt beside her son. "Kala, can you See anything?"

Kala hardly needed her Vision to know what had happened. She had seen the results of Shadow's attacks before. But all those victims had been dead. Why was this so different? She opened her mind to the Sight, but all she found was darkness. "Shadow," she said as Simen nodded. "But why didn't it kill him?"

Jada had rolled the boy over on his back and was gently prying his hands away from the terrible gash in his belly. "Lost a lot of blood. He's barely alive."

Sorty's mother fell on her son, caressing him in desperation. "My baby, my poor baby."

"Get her out of here," Jada ordered. "She can't help him now. I have to Touch him and she's in the way."

Kala took the sobbing woman by the shoulders and dragged her away. "Come, Mistress. There's nothing for you to do until the Healing's done. Trust me. I cannot lie to you."

"My babe, will he be all right?"

"It's up to the River now," Kala said. "I can see no further than the darkness."

Jada bent down and listened to Sorty's chest. "His heart's fluttering. Sorcerer, take my hand. We'll go in the River together."

"I'm not a Healer, Mistress."

"No matter, I need a strong swimmer. Take my hand."

Simen did as she bid.

The world shattered around him in a paroxysm of pain, wrenching into his gut, consuming his body. He cried out, but already they were diving into the River, the golden waters closing around them silencing his scream.

Down they went, the currents battering against them. He struggled against them for a moment, then surrendered, holding hard to Jada's hand as they plunged deeper into calmer waters where he could swim for her.

"Why are you here?"

He looked up to see a Golden Woman radiant and glowing on a rock beside him.

"Who are you?" Simen asked.

"Youre true mother," the woman said. "You are the Rivermaster's brother."

"Jamus…I am." Then his mind cleared and he remember what Jamus had told him. "Kashar."

She smiled. "You know my name. Why are you here?"

Jada, her voice trembling. "The boy is dying. I need to Heal him."

"Swim deep," Kashar replied. "The Dragon will answer. The boy is close enough to death to need his touch. Take her, Simen."

"I don't know where to go. I've never done this before."

"You are born of the Rivermaster. Follow your heart."

Simen let his mind empty of everything except the desire to Heal Sorty. He swam with the currents, letting them pull him downward in what seemed a neverending spiral. Then, his feet struck sand. He hugged Jada close and saw Sorty lying at their feet.

Suddenly a huge head poked out of the nearby cave and a huge rainbow colored Dragon glided out to face them. "Ask."

Simen worked hard to keep his voice from trembling as every one of Jamus' stories about his journeys into the River raced through his head. "Kisel," he whispered hoarsely.

The Dragon lowered its head to fix him with its whirling rainbow eyes. "Not be Kiselor. How know name?"

"I am his brother," Simen replied.

"Reflection," the Dragon hissed.

"Jamus—Kiselor gave me life."

"Why bring little one? Not much offering to Kisel."

Jada pulled away from Simen and stepped protectively in front of Sorty's body. "He's not an offering. I won't let you eat him. He's here to be Healed."

The Dragon focused its gaze on her, and though she shuddered, she stood firm. "Old meat too tough. You brave."

"I have lived my life. The boy is young, he deserves to live his."

"Move. I look," Kisel commanded. Jada stepped aside. The Dragon lowered its head and sniffed Sorty's body. "Smell of Shadow. Be so?"

"We think a Shadow tried to kill him," Simen said.

"Not dead."

"No. If we're right, the Shadow needs him alive, at least long enough for his blood to be useful."

"Want True Life to serve my brother. Fools," the Dragon hissed. "One day Blackwing will eat them all." He looked back at Jada. "You Heal," he said.

"I am not strong enough," Jada replied. "That's why we came to you."

"Brother strong enough," Kisel said, turning his head towards Simen.

" I don't know how to Heal," Simen replied.

"Never study," the Dragon said, pointing his claw at Simen in what looked to be an admonition.

Suddenly, Simen felt like a truant schoolboy, caught by the teacher. "No, I never bothered."

"You study." It was another command.

Simen gulped and nodded.

"Make vow. Dragon have memory forever."

"I promise," Simen replied, his heart growing lighter as he did. He knew now that Kisel was going to help them and Sorty would be fine. And a new hope flickered in him with his mission. If indeed he could become a Healer, it would be a treasure. "I promise," he repeated.

"First lesson," Kisel said. "See kitling well. Belly together, heart strong. Believe."

Simen concentrated. Believe. How many times had he heard that? It was the core of Magic. Without belief, there was no Magic. He stared down at Sorty, his thoughts focusing on how the boy would look, healthy and well again.

"See blood flow inside, not out. Little tunnels, all strong, Heart like pump draw to and fro. Lungs bring air, strong, deep."

Simen listened to the Dragon's words, hypnotized by their rhythm. His own heart beat powerfully, his own lungs filled with great breaths of air.

"Woman, too," Kisel said, but there was no need, for Jada had joined in the Healing already, her expertise adding to the effort Simen was making. She knew the secrets of the Sixth Art and drew on them now, letting all her skill flow into the boy's body.

Sorty gasped, took a deep breath. The gash on his stomach and the cut on his chest sealed, his skin, though still pale, took on a pinker hue. His heart stopped fluttering and settled into a stronger, even beat. He moved from the sleep of death to the sleep of healing.

"Is done." The Dragon said. "Kisel no need Touch. Brother do. Good lady do. Very good in River, Jada."

She started from her trance when he said her name. "How do you know me?"

"Always know best of River. Always." Then without another word he retreated back into his cave.

The waters surged in from above, surrounding them and finally carrying them upward on an exultant wave.

They knelt, side by side, their hands locked, their heads on the bed, exhausted. Sorty stirred, and though he would not wake up for some time, he would live.

The door opened. "Simen, are you all right?" Kala asked. "I thought I heard you cry out just now."

It seemed spans had passed since he had cried out. But there was no time in the River and to the world, it was only a moment. "It is done," he said. "Bring Sorty's mother. She can help him now." As Kala hurried off, he looked over at Jada, still asleep. Then he surveyed the mean little room. With a casual wave of his hand he transformed it, cleaning up the blood first, then adding another bed, soft coverlets, a table with chairs, a carpet on the floor, and a comfortable armchair by Sorty's bed. He lifted Jada and placed her gently on the second bed. She stirred. "Don't worry, Jada. It's all right. The boy is Healed. You need to rest."

"Dragon," she mumbled.

"We'll talk about it later," Simen told her.

Sorty's mother rushed into the room and over to her stricken son. "Is he going to live?" she asked, enfolding him in her embrace.

"He'll need time to recover. The Healing has done all it can. He will live and grow strong again. Care for him as if he's getting over a sickness. We'll see to it you have food and drink and anything else you need. He can't be moved yet, so you'll have to stay here with him for a while. I will make sure the innkeeper does right by you."

"You Healed him?"

"Jada Healed him," Simen replied. "I just helped a little. She needs to rest a while too. Is there some friend you can have come sit with you for a bit?"

The woman nodded. "Jelda. She's a good friend to Jada too, so she can help take care of her."

"Mistress Jada will be fine after a good rest. It's going to take longer for Sorty."

"I don't know how to thank you, My Lord. This has been such a terrible day. Jur Kala tells me you name is Simen. I am Celia."

"Sorty has been gifted with the Magic," Simen said. "Your husband?"

"Aye, his father, Seth, was a Sorcerer. He wasn't too strong in the Magic himself, but he always said Sorty had more talent. He wanted him to go to Magiskeep to study. Then, we lost him in a dreadful fire. It's been hard ever since. I've been trying to save the money to send Sorty to the Keep, but it's not easy for a single mother with a growing son who needs to eat."

"Has Sorty had any study at all?"

"Oh, there are teachers in Cuver Street—that's where we live—but nothing like he'd get at the Keep. He's learned a lot of good skills, and certainly how to protect himself. That's why I wasn't worried when they sent him out on the Watch last night. He's perfectly capable, you see. I don't know how this could have happened. He's a smart boy."

"Why was the Watch set in the first place?" Simen asked.

"Shadows," Celia said. "There were two murders not far from here that bore the mark of Shadowkill, or so they say. The Counsel met and decided to warn everyone, particularly the women, of the dangers of being out after dark. They say that's when the Shadows hunt. The Watch is made up of Sorcerers who can defend us against such attacks. Sorty can cast spellfire, you see. I hear it's a good weapon against the darkness."

"The only weapon," Simen agreed. "It is the only way to destroy a Shadow. Your Counsel was wise."

"So be it. They've been good to Sorty and me, that's for sure. Messages went out all through the south of Aberdeen and word may be spreading to the rest of the city, warning everyone to keep on the lookout for two men trying to lure women into places like this."

"Men."

"The dead were two women. They'd been raped and slaughtered. Who else but men? No woman could overpower anyone like that."

"But a woman could overpower a boy, " Simen replied. "Especially if she pretended to be vulnerable, frightened, or in some way in need of his help. Sorty wouldn't come here with a man unless he were already bound and gagged. But a woman? "

"He'd lend a hand to a woman," Celis said, taking Sorty's hand in hers. "He's a gentleman, he is. And the Watch was told to get any women off the streets and inside to safety. Do you think that's what happened?"

"It would explain a lot. When Sorty wakes, we'll have to ask him. There's no point now. When Jur Kala tried to sift him she could only see the darkness. But as he continues to heal, his eyes and his mind will open up again. He'll tell us what happened, and hopefully, identify his attacker."

"What if she comes back?"

"Not likely," Simen answered. "The last thing she'd want is to get caught when there are Magicians around. But I will set a ward of protection around this room to keep you all safe inside. It will only admit those you allow to come in. Be warned, though. Don't trust anyone you don't know, no matter what they say. I need to go with Kala back to the palace. We'll be back in a few days to see how Sorty is and how he's doing. If he's awake and feeling up to it, Jur Kala can question him then."

"I will be careful, My Lord. I almost lost my son once, I'm not going to let it happen again."

"Remember, only those you know."

Weaving the solid silvrin threads of a Sphere of Protection around the room, Simen left and met Kala downstairs.

"We need to get back to the palace," she said. "The King is expecting me to sit a trial this Sowin and we'll need to hurry so I'm not late."

"We can't lift strides now. The streets will be busy with too many people to see us. Bad enough I used my Power to bring Jada and Celia here."

"That was Cuver Street, Simen. From what I've been told by the last messenger who scurried through here most of those people at Jada's gate were Sorcerers themselves. They've been sent out on Watch throughout the quarter now and are sending delegations into other parts of the city to warn of murderers on the loose. I wouldn't be surprised if the palace will be roused by the time we get back there."

They left the inn mounted up and headed out to the street, just as the royal coach passed by. Inside, Arista called to the coachman to stop.

"Jur Kala, Master Simen, what are the two of you doing down here in such a rough part of town? Nothing wrong, I hope."

"A boy was nearly killed last night, My Lady," Kala replied. "We came to investigate."

"Dear me, I hope the lad is going to be all right."

"He will survive," Kala said.

"Bless the Hand for that," Arista said. And bless the Dragon I succeeded, Grella thought. The young Sorcerer's blood had infused her with an unexpected vitality and the news promised it would continue. "To think, I was out here in the city myself last night. I might have been a victim. I visited the Gardens yesterday and stayed on until Easwin, thinking to spend another day enjoying their beauty, but the gates are locked. I'm going back to the palace, but I would have liked to see Mistress Jada again before I left."

"The mistress is here," Simen told her. "She Healed the boy. She's going to spend a day or two resting from the ordeal and watching over him, so I don't think the Gardens will be open until the end of the Sevenstin."

"She is a fine Herbalist," Arista replied. And a Sorceress for sure, Grella thought. The boy's injuries were far beyond what any herbs could cure. She should have suspected. Jada was far too learned in the herbal lore to be simple country woman. She licked her lips as a risky plan formed in her head. "Then I'll come back another day. She is a lovely woman. Do wish her well for me. Coachman, on." She waved farewell as the team of horses picked up a brisk trot.

"So, I guess we can't tour the Gardens either," Kala said, pretending a heavy sigh of regret.

"I thought we had to get back to the palace for a trial."

"Have you lost your sense of humor already, my dear Follyman? I was just teasing." When Simen didn't smile, she too grew serious. "What's wrong? I thought the Healing went well."

"Too well," Simen said. "We faced the Dragon."

"Which one?"

"The Lord of all Dragons, Kisel. The boy was nearly dead, we had to go deep into the Magic to save him and whether I meant to or not, I took us to the very bottom of the River."

"I thought only Jamus could command him."

"Oh, he tolerates the Rivermaster's brother, apparently. I can't say he thinks too much of me. He thinks I'm not living up to my potential."

"Bory, Simen, you are the best Follyman I've ever seen. You're talented, smart, funny, and you have a beautiful voice. What more can he expect of you?"

"He told me I needed to study to be a Healer. And worse, he made me Vow that I would. Only then did he help me find the way to save Sorty."

"I thought Jada...."

"The Dragon charged me to Heal the boy. Jada lent her skill, of course, but it was my Magic, not hers."

"Does she know what happened?" Kala asked.

Simen shrugged. "I don't know. When we came back out of the Chanting, she had collapsed. I hadn't the heart to wake the poor woman considering how exhausted I felt. We haven't spoken since."

"All the more reason to come back here in a few days. I'll talk to Sorty and you can talk to Jada. I'm not sure either one of us will be too happy with what we find out, though."

They turned their horses north and picked up and easy jog, heading for the royal palace.

*****

Jamus spent four more days enjoying the company and scenery of Tallridge before heading back to Magiskeep. On his way back to his room in Prentiscape, he noticed a cluster of children talking excitedly in the hall. As soon as she saw him, little Jenda broke from the group and ran over, holding up a stuffed toy for him to see. "Look Master Jarius, I gots me a stuffy dog. It come all the way from Aberdal, or so Master Ferg says. He gived every one of Mistress Joria's class one. Sagin's got a stuffy horse, an' Jil's got a stuffy cat. Wanna see 'em."

Jamus smiled. Normally he would have been delighted to share the children's joy in their new treasures, but he was too tired now. For some reason, the journey home had exhausted him and all he really wanted to do was go to bed. "Tomorrow, Jenda. I need some rest now. I just got back from a long trip and I'm very tired."

"I could sing you a sleepy song if you want," Jenda offered.

"Thank you, sweet one, but I will fall asleep just fine by myself this time. Now go back and have some more fun with your friends."

She grinned and bounced away back to the giggling classmates.

True to his word, Jamus went to his room, took off his boots and traveling cape and dropped on top of his bed. He was fast asleep within a matter of minutes.

A dream came. He was wandering in the Southreaches, far from the Keep, far from even the most remote villages. It was hot, the sun blazing down on him. He'd never felt so hot.

His eyes were dazzled by the sun reflecting off the desert sand. His body ached with exhaustion, every step an effort, every movement painful.

Why? Why was he here? Which way? Which way should he go?

He sought Vision, calling the White Dragon, but the call went unanswered. He called to Rath, but she did not hear. He sought the River, but the Gold Waters dried up and blew away in gusts of sand. Sand instead of water.

Up ahead, he saw a shining shore. Waves rolling in and out in endless repetition. He tried to run, but his feet sank in the unforgiving sand, slowing him to a crawl. The shore beckoned.

Then rising from the horizon, he saw the Great Sea Dragon, tentacles dripping with strands of water weeds.

He cried out, and the Dragon bellowed, beckoning to him.

Come, Kiselor. My water waits. Come.

Come.

He woke to the soothing feel of a cool towel on his forehead.

"So, you wake at last. Bless the Hand you are a strong man, Jarius. The fever has killed three children already. Yours has broken." It was Joble, one of the tapestry's Keep's Healers. "How are you feeling?"

"How long?" Jamus asked hoarsely.

Joble offered him a cup of water and Jamus drank greedily. "Nine winds have changed since we found you here. When you didn't come out for Firstmeal, one of the maids came to see if you were all right and found you fevered. Since, there have been four women in the Keep with the same symptoms and," his voice choked. "...the children."

"Who?"

"Little Jenda, Jarry, Sitha. Now all the rest of Joria's class of young ones are sick, even Sagin."

"Sagari's son?"

Joble nodded. "The Master is beside himself. Even the Masters of Healing haven't been able to do anything."

"But I'm better."

"Not for anything I've done," Joble said. "My Touch didn't even ease your delirium. You were calling out for Dragons, from what I could tell."

"I was dreaming," Jamus replied taking another cup of water and sipping from it. "I was in the desert."

"I should think. You were burning up. But it's over now. If the women's recovery is any indication, you should be fine by Sowin's change. Weak, but over it. I'll send for some soup if you want it. You'll need to eat to regain your strength."

"The children. What about the children?"

"There's nothing we can do. We've tried everything and they just seem to slip away. "

"Jenda was such a sweet little girl."

"She was a charmer, that's for sure. The Keep will be much darker without her light heart shining. But I don't know what will happen if the Master loses Sagin."

Jamus pushed up from the pillows. "I have some skill in the Sixth Art."

"Lad, as much as you might wish it, you cannot be a match to the Masters here."

"I can try."

"You need to rest."

"I need to try to save Sagin, and the others if the Hand wills it. Sometimes, sometimes the River answers me when it refuses others. I can't explain it, but it does. Help me up." Jamus grabbed Joble's arm.

Joble shrugged. "If you can make it to Sagari's chambers, I'll be surprised. But I'll help you if you're so determined. There's naught anyone else can do. If Lord Sagari accepts your offer to help, so be it."

Joble was right. Jamus was hardly strong enough to walk, but with the Healer's help, he managed to stagger up the stairs to Sagari's chamber. The door was open and Healers of all kinds were hurrying in and out, carrying bundles of herbs, bowls of water, vials and even books. When Jamus finally entered Sagin's room, no one even noticed.

Sagari was kneeling by his son's bed, his head in his hands. His shoulders were shaking and he looked like a broken man.

"My Lord," Joble said. "Master Jarius has just recovered from the fever himself. He has some skill in Healing. Perhaps his personal experience with the illness will give him insight."

"It's too late," Sagari sobbed. "My son is dying. He's hardly breathing anymore."

"Please, My Lord," Jamus said. "Let me try. Sometimes the River sings to me."

Sagari moved a little aside. "Touch him. Heal him. Bring my son back to me."

Jamus leaned over and put his hand on Sagin's chest.

A blast of fire pummeled him, but he held on, taking the boy in his arms, running into the desert. The sand was deep, pulling at his feet. He struggled but forced himself to go on.

Ahead, the shimmering shore, and the Sea Dragon, waiting. Why come now? Left me.

"I didn't need you then, now I do. Where is the River? Your brother, Kisel?"

"Why?"

"Damn you, I am the Rivermaster. Three Rivers are mine, enough to command you to do at least this. Show me the River."

The Dragon slithered aside to reveal a pool of golden water.

Jamus plunged in. Man and boy, they sank into the depths, past Kashar who beckoned, past the Time Lord sitting silently on the rocks, down, down to the sandy floor in front of the Rainbow Dragon's lair.

"Kisel. Your Rider calls. I need your Touch."

The Dragon peered out of his cave. "Rivermaster hurt?"

"Not I, this boy." He laid Sagin's body down.

"You Heal."

"I cannot. No one can. Only the Dragon. Please."

The Dragon studied the child, poking him with his claw. For a moment, Sagin's breathing steadied, his pulse grew stronger. Kisel twisted his great head to get a better look. "Wrong kitling."

"What do you mean? He's just a little boy. He's dying. You have to help him. I command it."

"Kiselor command, Kisel obey. Not Turan's Way. Cannot turn the Way. Wrong kitling."

"He's dying, what do I have to do to make you save him."

"Kiselor command. Turan's Way command. Kisel obey one, not other. Cannot do for Rivermaster. Way be bigger even."

Jamus choked back a sob--his own body, still weak from his illness, betraying him as he fell to his knees beside the child. "Sagin," he whispered. "I am so sorry. I tried, I tried,"

"I tried. I am so sorry."

Sagin heaved a huge sigh and then stopped breathing altogether.

Sagari threw himself on his son's body, kissing him, and throwing his arms around him as if trying to hold on to him, but already the child was fading into dust and ash, as all Magicians do when they die. Tears streaking his cheeks, the Golden Sorcerer raised his head and screamed once. Then he looked down at the dust sifting through his fingers. He stared at his hands for a long time in a frightening and utter silence.

Jamus, collapsed at his side, felt two strong hands on his shoulders pulling him away. "Come, Sur, you'd best get out of here. There's nothing more you can do. Nothing anyone can do. You need to be gone when the Master comes to his senses."

Jamus let Joble half carry him from the room.

"We'll go to Mistress Joria's chambers," Joble said. "She'll know what to do."

But Joria was deep in grief herself, sitting alone in her room with a pile of stuffed animals on the table in front of her. She picked up the little stuffed horse and brushed its mane with her fingers. "All of them, now," she said. "All of my little ones. Sagin was the last. He was a strong boy, you see. I thought if anyone would make it, he would. Nine children dead. They were so happy just a Sevenstin ago when Ferg gave them these toys. 'All the way from Aberdal,' he told them, and they were all so excited. We had a lesson that day, with his story of the cloth merchant who made these, I taught them all about how to sew a seam. You should have seen all the crooked little hems they put on the scarves they made."

"Scarves," Jamus said, sinking into a chair before his legs gave out.

"Jenda made this one for me," Joria said, pulling out a little crooked blue scarf from her belt. "She said it was pretty like I was, so she wanted me to have it."

"Scarves," Jamus said again, something nagging in the back of his brain. But he was too exhausted to think it through. Something about scarves.

"I caught a bit of the fever myself," Joria said. "But I recovered quicker than most."

"Three other women have been ill, and one's husband. Bless the Hand they had no children yet. They've all recovered too."

"But not the children," Joria said, looking up at the two men. "All nine, dead."

"Master Jarius tried to Heal Sagin. For a little while, his Touch was working. The boy started to rally, I'd swear to it. His breathing eased and his fever cooled. Sagari was ecstatic. He could feel Sagin's heart grow stronger."

Jamus nodded tiredly. "I almost won. Almost."

"Then the air grew still and heavy, dropping down on all of his, making it hard even for us to breathe. It was horrible. All I remember is hearing your voice, Jarius. You kept saying, 'I tried, I tried.' And then, poor little Sagin breathed his last."

"I couldn't change it," Jamus said. "Turan's Way....I couldn't change it."

"Destiny?" Joria asked, throwing the little horse angrily back on the pile. "This is destiny? Nine lives as payment for a pile of stuffed toys?"

"Scarves," Jamus repeated for a third time, but this time he remembered."Ferg."

"Ferg, the Merchant. What about him?"

"Was he sick?"

"He said he didn't feel well, and he kept mopping his brow. But he never had a fever like this," she said.

"He gave the children the toys," Jamus said. "And the women who were ill. Did they buy scarves from him? He had some beautiful ones. He showed one to me when I met him on his way to the Keep."

"Mina's back to work here in the Keep," Joble said. "I think I saw her in the hall. I can go ask her."

Jamus raked his hand through his hair and leaned back in the chair. "Ferg told me he had a cloth merchant who made all kinds of wonderful things. Who else bought things from him?"

Joria shook her head. "I don't know. He generally sells through all the villages."

Suddenly, Jamus sat up, "Is he still here in the Keep?"

"He left several days ago heading back to Aberdal."

Jamus head reeled as he remembered meeting Ferg at the waterfall. What had he said? "Ah, the Bread and Butter. Fine place. Best food in all of Turan let me tell you and I've eaten everywhere. I make it my last stop on the way back home." By the Blood, Becca! He struggled to his feet, battling his fatigue with every ounce of strength he could muster. "I have to get to Tallridge, now."

Joble, back at the door, shook his head. "You can't even get down the hall without falling down, Sur. Whatever business you have in Tallridge can wait." He took Jamus' arm to steady him. "You were right about the scarf. Mina has one."

"Burn it," Jamus said. "Burn all of them," he pointed to the stuffed animals. "Burn anything Ferg sold to anyone when he was here. Go to the villages, find everything. You'll find people with the fever there too. Pray to the Hand none of them are children."

Joble put his hand on Jamus' brow, "Is your delirium back, Jarius?"

"The cloth, the cloth from Aberdal. Everyone who's been sick has touched it. All the children, Joria, the women, and me. Now he's gone to Tallridge. I have to get there."

"Look at yourself, Jarius," Joria said. "You're too weak to go anywhere."

Jamus sank back onto the edge of the chair. "Varleyroot. Is there some in the Keep?"

"We Healers have it," Joble said. "But it's risky to use."

"Get me some. I've used it before when I needed to recover quickly. Just a drop or two. That's all I need."

"Varley's not good for body or mind. You'll pay for using it."

"Get it," Jamus ordered.

Joble looked over at Joria. "Get him the herb," she said. "Someone needs to go to Tallridge to warn them, and Jarius knows the people there. They'll listen to him."

Joble hurried out of the room. Joria pushed the pile of animals off the table and into the fireplace. With a flick of her wrist, she sent a bolt of Spellfire to burn them to ashes. "I thought I could keep them as mementos."

"Curses, more like," Jamus said, leaning heavily on the armrest. "It's too late for the children here, but maybe I can save them in Tallridge."

"Are there many children in the village?"

"One child more is too many," he replied, his voice breaking with weariness. "Yes, there are children. I don't know how many, but there are two I love nearly as much as my own."

"You have children?" Joria asked.

"A wife and a son," he said. "Too far from here, I'm afraid. I can't get back to them until I solve the riddle."

"You spoke of that before and said something about Turan's Way. Does that mean these children's deaths were part of an unalterable destiny?"

"Unless I have been lied to, yes, I'm afraid so. There was nothing anyone could do to save them."

"And the children of Tallridge? Are they also to be victims of the Way?"

"I don't know, Mistress. I really don't know. But if there's anything at all I can do I intend to do it, no matter what the consequences."

When Joble returned with the vial, Jamus put two drops of the potion in a cup of water and drank it. Then he slipped the vial into the pouch and tied it to his belt. Already feeling stronger, he nodded to Joria and hurried from the room and out to the stables.

He didn't bother waiting for Josep. He saddled Shadowmist without even brushing him and was mounted up before he left the aisle of the barn, nudging the horse into a trot that broke to a gallop once they passed the gate. A moment more and they soared into lifted strides taking them to Tallridge in less than a span.

But Jamus knew it was already too late.

XIV

Impatiently, King Gailvarg tapped the arm of his throne with his finger as Juris Kala lay her hand on a cart that had been pulled into the Great Hall. Two farmers stood on either side, each making claim on the vehicle.

"I don't understand it, Sire," Kala said as she broke from the near trance of her Seeing. "The cart has an equal touch of both men. This is, indeed most unusual. Neither man is lying about owning it."

"You are supposed to have my answers, Madame Juris. Why are you here in Aberdeen if you cannot supply them, eh? These two farmers have fought in our streets over this pitiful little cart nearly causing a riot."

"That may be so, My Lord, but each has a rightful claim. I need to ask more questions of them to help you decide who should take it home."

"More questions? We've already spent a span asking questions. My patience is wearing thin." His eyes darted towards the western door of the Hall. "The workmen are building a new wall on the battlefield. Did you see how carefully they lay the stone?"

"The farmers, My King," Kala said.

Gailvarg rose from his seat and wandered to the door, peering out into the next room. "The put each stone down so carefully. It is quite wonderful to see."

"Indeed it is wonderful," Kala agreed. "So is a farm cart when it's all full of taroots. Why a clever farmer who knows how to stack his produce can carry twice as much as a farmer who stacks carelessly."

Gailvarg turned. "Do taroots stack like stone?"

"They might," Kala said, pleased to have returned the King's attention to the problem of the cart. "I would think this cart might carry a good load if the right farmer owned it."

"A farmer who could stack?" The King asked. "Which one of you can stack?" he asked, looking first at one claimant and then the other. "Shall we bring some taroots in to test you?"

"I do not grow taroots," the farmer on the left said.

"Then you cannot stack," Gailvarg said.

The second farmer, to Kala's surprise then answered, "I grow taroots, My King, but when I fill the cart, I do not stack them. It takes too long to pile them carefully."

"So you do not stack."

"I do not, My King."

"I will not grant the cart to someone who does not stack. The wall will not be strong if it is not stacked. You cannot mortar if the stones are not stacked."

"We are talking about taroots, not stones," Kala reminded him.

"Why would you build a wall with taroots?" Gailvarg asked, clearly confused. "Taroots do not make a good wall. What happens when they rot or the cavel eat them? The wall would fall."

Patiently, Kala tried again. "My Liege, the wall is of stone, the cart is full of taroots. We need to think about the cart and which farmer has the right to fill it."

"Which cart?" he asked.

"The cart here, in the Hall," Kala pointed.

"Why is there a cart in my Hall?" the King asked. "Take it away! I do not allow carts in my Hall."

"You asked us to bring it here," one of the farmers said. "My King, we were obeying your command."

"I would not command a cart in my Hall. I would like a wall to see how the stones are stacked, but not a wall of taroot. Why do you talk of such things? Take the cart and go. I am done with taroots." One of the farmers stepped forward to protest, but Kala stayed him with a wave of her hand. Gailvarg turned back towards the door. "I said go. I want to see the wall."

The farmers, one pulling the other pushing, managed to get the cart out into the corridor, where they waited, in complete confusion.

"Your Majesty," Kala said. "I did not hear you render a decision about the cart. Which farmer should have it?"

"Give one the wheels and one the bowl and make sure they learn to stack taroots so the mortar sticks. Why do you bother me with all these questions when the stones do not even fit in the cart?"

"It is a market cart, My Lord. It is not strong enough to carry stones for a wall."

"Then why would anyone want it? Burn it. If it cannot make a wall, it is useless."

Kala shook her head. It was hopeless. "If you grant me Right of the Crown, My Lord, I will decide which farmer should have the cart. You are far too busy to be worrying about carts when there is a wall to watch."

"You choose the cartman or burn the cart," Gailvarg replied, staring out the door. "I am going to count the stones they use. If they have already started, I will command them to take the stones away and start again so I can count." He walked out the door to his window.

Kala took a deep breath to steady herself and went out to the farmers. "The King has granted me Right of the Crown. That means I can choose who should have the cart."

"It's all right, Madam Juris. We can share the cart for now, as our families did for the last three circles. The only reason we each made claim is because our farms have grown and prospered so much we each need a cart every day. We can make do until we earn enough money between us to buy another cart."

"Madam Juris," Micah asked nervously, "is something wrong with the King? He wasn't making much sense to me."

"The King has been ill," Kala said. "It is difficult for him to make decisions right now. That's why he gave me the Right." She smiled. "I am pleased you found your own way to settle the dispute. I would be honored to help you both by giving you the tribute for finding a way to assure the peace of Aberdeen." She pulled two gold soverns out of her purse. "As Juris, I have this purse to use as I wish in times of judgment. Take the money and find another cart. If your farms continue to prosper, you will each need a cart of your own. In return for tribute, you must share a tenth of your crops each month of the Greenseason with the poor of our city. The alleys near the Course have many who need food for their tables."

"Ned," Micah said, "if we buy a bigger cart together, we can set up a stand where people can come for our vegetables. You know we always have some left after market day, and we've often talked about how sad it is when it goes to waste. Would that suit your judgment, Jur Kala?"

"Do other farmers have leftover produce as well?"

"Almost everyone does," Micah replied. "Sometimes we throw it to the pigs. But I would much rather feed people with it. I think the other farmers might agree. We don't know the city, though. I've never even been to the Course myself."

"Nor have I," Ned said. "I wouldn't know where to put a stand."

"Mistress Jada cares for the Whispering Gardens. She would be able to help you," Kala said. "I'm going to see her in a few days and I will speak to her on your behalf."

The two men left, dragging the cart out of the palace, all the while busily discussing their new project.

Simen, had been quietly observing the scene from a bench by the window where he had been waiting for Kala. "Well done, Madam Juris. To think you have kept the peace and fed the poor all in one day."

"I wish it had been the King and not me. Gailvarg was useless. He's lost his mind, Simen."

"S-h-h-h, not here. Someone might hear you."

"I don't care. How can I? If the room had been full of witnesses, they all would have seen what a fool he was. All he was worried about was some wall they're building on the battlefield."

Simen smiled. "Well, it is rather interesting. It's another one of those 'spanwage' projects of theirs."

"Spanwage? What do you mean by that?"

"Come over and see," he said, beckoning her to the window. "The Prince is paying the workmen by each span. The longer a job takes to complete, the more money each man makes." He pointed to a crew of masons building a stone wall on the right side of the field. "It's just about time now. They have three tiers nearly done. The mortar's not even dry yet. This is the third or fourth time they've started to build."

"I don't understand what's so interesting. It's just a wall. Why is Gailvarg so fixated on it?"

"Well, I don't know why the King's watching but I do know why I am. Just wait a moment. Oh, there he comes. That's the foreman, from what I can tell. At least the foreman for the day. They take turns."

"So?" Kala looked out at the scene below. What could possibly be worth watching for spans on end?

"All right now, keep your eye on him. He's taken out his measuring rope."

The foreman pulled a long piece of rope out of his bag. It had knots in it at regular intervals. With the help of one of the workmen, he stretched it out across the base of the wall. Then they measured the distance of the wall from another obstacle. Then the stopped and counted the stones in the first tier. Then, they discussed something and measured again. Soon, the foreman's arms were waving about is if he were yelling at the men. While Kala couldn't hear anything, it was clear he was getting angry. He pointed at the wall. Soon the men had picked up sledgehammers and were knocking the stones apart. "But they just built that," Kala said. "Why are they taking it down? I looked strong and straight to me."

"Oh, it was," Simen told her. "It was, most probably as nearly perfect as a wall could be."

"I don't understand."

"That's because you've never had to struggle to feed your family. You've always had coins in your purse, enough to give two gold soverns of your own to two farmers telling them it was money from the royal treasury."

"You knew," Kala said biting her lip. "I had to do something. The King was useless and those poor men didn't deserve to suffer any more because of his incompetence."

"Those men, down there, don't deserve to suffer either. Many of them have needed jobs for a long time. They've struggled to feed their families. Now they're earning a living and working hard for it. But their clever enough to find ways to make even more money. Remember, they get paid for each span they work."

"Spanwages," Kala said, smiling. "It's a good thing the Prince's pockets are deep."

"It's money from the Royal Treasury, but those men have paid their taxes, and from what I've heard, higher ones than they should be paying. Since Gailvarg has taken ill, Gareth has tripled the taxes on his citizens. The money just sits in the vaults. He hasn't used a deneret to repair the roads. Those men, down there, should be building walkways and fixing holes in the streets, not building walls for soldiers to climb over going nowhere. I can't begrudge them trying to earn as much as they can."

"I don't often hold with cheating, but I do appreciate their ingenuity. How many times did you say they built that wall?"

"I've seen at least three over the last two days. It's a pity we have to go back to the Rudder and Wheel come Fourday, I might miss seeing the wall finally finished."

"You mean you'd stay and watch? You're as bad as the King."

"I doubt he sees the same thing I do, Kala. If he's as honest a man as you say he is, he'd never let such nonsense go on, especially since it's public money."

"In that you're right, Simen. But that man in there," she nodded towards the Hall, "is not the Gailvarg I once knew. He's lost, confused. He's lost his mind. I thought he'd get better after Jyp Healed him, but he's gotten worse."

"Gareth is still his heir. As long as Gailvarg is King, no matter how mad he is, the Prince is held in check. I shudder to think what will happen when he takes the crown."

*****

"I have the potion you wanted, Your Highness," Arista said when she met Gareth in his private chambers. "Palion, blended and unboiled. I tended it so it has no color. It should be tasteless in amberwine."

Gareth took the vial from her hand and held it up to the light. "Is this enough?"

"Enough to kill ten men, My Lord. My impression was that you wanted something particularly potent."

"There is no cure?"

"Unless the Healer is right there at the moment the victim drinks, no. The potion works quickly. It only takes a moment or two."

Gareth smiled. "When I am King I would be pleased to have a sister Queen at my side. Do you know anyone who would be interested? It's purely a ceremonial title, but there are many benefits to make up for the lack of power." He stepped closer to her, and played with the laces of her bodice with his fingers.

"I do know someone, someone close who would like to sit beside you. She would like you to sit very close as well."

He leaned in, his mouth almost touching hers. "I have learned to pleasure women in most unique ways. Someday, someday soon I will again be able to pleasure them as a man should, but trust me, I am not without skill even now."

"I am sure you are not, My Lord," she replie,d pressing closer.

Gareth put the vial on the table, and pulled her into his embrace, kissing her hard and long. She let her body go limp in his arms, offering surrender if he wanted it. His hands groped her breasts, squeezing hard through the thin fabric of her gown. She whimpered and he clutched her buttocks, pulling her tightly against him as he rubbed his own hips against her, over and over.

Then, without a word, he pushed her away. "Just a taste, Auntie. When I am done with my father, we will finish the meal. I have much to serve you. I think you will be pleased."

Arista leaned against the edge of the table, panting. Her skin was hot and she was trembling.

And she was hungry. How long till Norwin? Grella wondered. I need the darkness, and only one more, only one more.

Gareth picked up the vial and left the room, smiling.

He found Gailvarg in the room west of the Hall, staring blankly out the window. "Father?"

Gailvarg did not turn. "They are building a wall. Did you see?"

"Yes, Father, I know. I ordered it. It's going to be a fine wall when it's finished. It's taking a long time. I don't know why, but I've never tried to build a wall myself, so I don't know how long it should take."

"Building a wall would be nice," Gailvarg replied. "The stones are smooth and cool. Who are you?"

Gareth started. "I am your son, Gareth."

"Oh, I thought you were the Healer. Did you bring me a potion?"

It was too perfect. Gareth held out the vial. "I have one here, Sire. I'll put it in some wine for you. If you drink it you will feel much better." He poured a goblet of amberwine, added the palion and carried it over to his father.

"I like the wall," Gailvarg said. He took the goblet, drank it down, and turned back to the window. His eyes widened in surprise. He spun back around, took one step, reached out his hand to Gareth as if pleading, and then collapsed on the floor.

Gareth bent, put his head to the King's chest and when he heard nothing, pried the goblet from his hand, wiping it clean with his handkerchief. He got up, placed the goblet on the top shelf of the bookcase, checked one more time to make sure Gailvarg was not breathing, took a gulp of air, and began to shout. "Help! Someone, help! The King! Something's wrong with the King!"

Jyp and Corm, the Prince's manservant, were first in the room answering the Prince's cry. Jyp squatted down by the old man and put his hand on his chest, seeking a Healing. Simen and Kala rushed in from the hall.

Jyp's expression was all Simen needed and he ran over to the fallen King and knelt by his side, placing his hand next to Jyp's.

Darkness. No breath, no heartbeat, nothing. Oblivion.

He looked at his fellow Sorcerer and shook his head as tears began to stream down Jyp's face. "He's dead," he said as Jyp nodded. "We are too late."

"The King is dead," Corm whispered. Then he squared his shoulders and repeated it again, aloud, "The King is dead. Long live the King." He knelt on one knee before Gareth who stood, his hands covering his mouth, his body shaking. For all the world he looked consumed with grief. But looks were deceiving, for behind his hand, he was laughing instead.

It took Gareth a while to compose himself, but when he did, his voice was steady. "In the Name of the Hand, I take the name of King of all Turan. In our sorrow we seek comfort. In our loss, we find gain. In our time of trial, we find strength. Blessed be the Hand. May it take the King into its keeping and protect us, his successor."

"And so the crown shall be passed," Corm said. He walked solemnly to the outer hall and called out, "Ring the message bell. Call the people to the palace square. Throw open the shutters to the balcony. The King is dead. Long live the king."

The palace exploded in a flurry of activity. Soon, in the north tower, the great bell began to toll. The people in the streets below, the worker on the battlefield, the merchant in the shops around the palace, and anyone within hearing started running to the square their gazes focusing on the balcony above.

While the royal servants carried Gailvarg's body to his bed to lay him gently down until the time came to prepare it for burial, Jyp, Simen and Kala waited in the side room with Gareth.

"Your highness," Kala said, "I am so sorry. Your father was a good man."

"He was the King," Gareth replied, "and now I take his place. It will be good for Turan to start anew. Gailvarg's day is over, now mine begins."

"You must take time to mourn," Kala told him "The people need it from you. You will not inspire their loyalty if you do not give your father due respect and honor."

"Mine will be a new world, Madam Juris. I have waited long enough for this day. I will not waste it on foolish ceremony. We will lay him to rest in a fine tomb if that's what the people want, but to do more in his name is not necessary. He is dead. He is no longer King. I am, and I will make the choice."

"Then, you will have to excuse me. It is time I left the palace."

"You are here at the order of Grandisite, My Lady, and you will do your duty. Tomorrow I well celebrate my coronation, and you will officiate."

"Ask a Priest of the Hand to crown you, Sur. I do not choose to."

"The Priests forsook the royal seat long ago, Mistress, and even the Knights are scattered. You are still Prime Juris until the Five or Kolea herself release you from your Vow, you must do as I command. It falls to your office to preside at the coronation if there is no Priest to stand."

Kala bowed, ever so slightly.

"My Liege," Corm said as he opened the door. "It is time. There is a crowd gathered in the square. We must proclaim now before they get restless." He bowed and extended his arm, directing Gareth out into the hall that led to the balcony.

Kala sat heavily in the chair by the window where Gailvarg had spent his last spans watching the workmen at his precious wall. Simen stood silently at her side looking down on the empty battlefield, still only half constructed. "I wonder if the men will come back to work today."

"It will be up to the Prince. Tradition holds that the Kingdom should have at least one day of mourning with no work to be done."

"Gareth seems short on tradition," Simen said, leaning on the windowsill.

"Hush, Simen. If we listen,we should be able to hear Corm's announcement and anything Gareth says."

They sat quietly. Then they heard Corm's voice echoing from afar. "The King is dead. Long live the King."

Only silence followed. Where were the cheers for the new monarch?

Then they heard Gareth. "People of Aberdeen, my father the King wanted his Kingdom's rule to be assured at his death. I am his legitimate heir and to honor according to his wishes, I have made claim to the crown. It is mine by right of birth and mine by right of my Father's declaration." He waved a parchment in the air. "My

Father's will with the royal seal proclaims me King. I take the honor willingly ready to do good for the people of Aberdeen and the betterment of all Turan. Will you stand with me?"

Again silence. Then, Corm began to applaud, gesturing to the crowd to join in. There was a modest response. But too many people were weeping, grieving for the King they had loved, the man Gailvarg was before he had lost his mind.

"The people don't seem too enthusiastic," Jyp said from the corner where he had crouched down, head in hands from while Gailvarg's body was removed from the room. "If only I had come in sooner. Corm insisted on talking to me and I couldn't get away. I swore I'd never let Gareth be alone with his father."

Simen moved away from the window and looked around the room. Then, he spied an empty vial lying behind a book on the desk where Gareth had forgotten it. He walked over and picked it up to sniff it. "Kala, can you use your Sight on this?" He held out the vial for her to see. "I can't smell anything, but there's a drop of clear liquid left in it."

She took the Vial and examined it carefully, letting Vision sift its Truth. "It's not clear, Simen. It's a shining purple."

"Palion," Jyp said. "The most potent poison in all Turan. By the Blood, I was right. Gareth poisoned him."

"And how do we prove it?" Kala asked. "We can show the vial, but what evidence is there that Gareth gave it to his father?"

"Proof enough for me," Jyp said. "The vial, Gareth and the King were all in the room together."

"Even I would not find in your favor in the Challenge of the Law, Master Jyp. Coincidence is never confirmation of a crime. While I agree with your theory, in a Truthseeking, it would be just that, a theory, not fact."

"So we do nothing?"

"There's not much we can do, for now. Gareth will become King according to the law. We just have to watch and wait."

"The Hand save us all," Jyp said, dropping back down into the corner as if he could hide from the truth facing them all.

Simen knelt beside him, "You can't give up, Jyp. We have the vial. Where does Gareth keep his potions? Have you seen them? Have you seen this?"

"He had no palion, and I managed to dispose of whatever dangerous herbs he had. He never noticed. He wasn't an expert, that's why Gailvarg lived as long as he did."

"So, someone had to help him. Who else in the palace, or in Aberdeen, for that matter, does know herblore?"

"Jada, of course," Jyp replied, "and a handful of local Healers. Everyone I know is loyal to the Counsel and then means loyal to Gailvarg. He was a good King."

"After the coronation, we're going back to the inn to see Jada and Sorty. Maybe she can help us," Simen said.

"The coronation," Kala sighed. "I'm not looking forward to it. Just the thought of putting the crown on Gareth's head makes my blood run cold."

*****

Darkness, Gailvarg dead, promise of a seat beside the new King, all perfect gifts after circles of waiting. Grella, born of the mirrors, a reflection trapped and doomed to an eternity of in the Way needed only one more drink of Sorcerer's blood to gain True Life. It had all been so simple as if the destiny of Turan had been written just for her.

The plan had formed when she had met Kala and Simen at the inn where the boy was. But it wasn't him she wanted, it was Jada. If the woman had healed the boy's injuries, then she had used Magic. A Sorceress's blood would be the perfect feast to celebrate all her successes and assure her immortality.

The genius of it all was that the Fleshers would never expect a Shadow to be so bold or foolish to strike in the same place twice and so soon after a previous attack. Gambel and Melthus had warned her to seek remote places and victims no one would notice. Gambel, having nearly Lived himself as The Searcher, had expertise in the hunt and well knew the way of Shadows. But habit taught the Shadow hunters too. They had sent their messengers out to just the kinds of places her companions used as hunting grounds. She, on the other hand, would do the unexpected and strike swiftly with surprise.

Now, this body she had learned to covet was a burden. Cumbersome and slow, as much as the young Sorcerer's blood had revitalized it, she needed shed it for the night's work. Struggling against its new hold on her, she slipped out of the skin, leaving it to lie as if asleep on her bed and drifted through the window. Out in the street, she walked on the clouds, relishing the nearly forgotten freedom, and headed towards the Rudder and Wheel.

The window to the rear hall was open.She climbed in and moved silently to the door of the room where her prey waited. She unlatched the pitiful lock with a spell and peered in. There was a small smear of blood on the doorframe. Sniffing it, she smelled the boy. He must have gotten out of the room after the attack, explaining why he had been found so soon. All the more reason for her to act quickly. She could see the mother, asleep in a chair by the boy's bed, and Jada, the Sorceress, asleep on a bed to the left. She would glide in, chant the boy and his mother to keep them quiet and then pinion the old woman to have her feast.

She slipped through the opening and into a web of silver threads, snarling her arms, whipping around her legs, pulling her into a Sphere of enchantment. Grella struggled in vain to pull away, but each effort only drew her deeper into the complex trap until she found herself surrounded by bars in which she could see her own reflection, Shadow with grotesque features vaguely resembling a face with a huge mouth full of sharp teeth. It was if she had been plunged into the Way of Mirrors, the worst of all worlds for one who had escaped it not long before.

She stilled herself, trying not to panic. If it was the Way, there had to be an exit. She was Shadow, born in this prison. She knew its secrets intimately. But so had the Sorcerer who had woven the spell. Carefully, so as not to disturb the threads to set them spinning, she turned around estimating the direction she had come in. Soon, behind each of her reflections she could see the open door, her way out. But which reflection? Any one could be a passage into the endless corridors of the Way or even another world where all her efforts would be lost along with her Flesher body. So close to Life and now, so far away. She uttered a curse and fought the impulse to batter at the images. The last thing she wanted to do was shatter the wrong one in a fit of rage.

Rage, hunger, and intense desire were true Shadows' only emotions, but Grella had learned in the skin to think beyond the moment, and now she drew on all her new wisdom. She calmed herself and began to study the reflections. There had to be a way to find the right door. One image revealed a glimmer of water where the hall should have been. In another, the door itself had one extra panel of wood. In another, she could just see the bedpost of Jada's bed, too close to the door itself. And in another a slight smear of blood in the shape of a small boy's hand.

Grella smiled, her terrible mouth curling up at the corners in an ugly grimace. Then she carefully pushed aside the slender threads in front of it, and stepped into that reflection. One step more and she found herself back in the dark hall of the Rudder and Wheel. She took one more glance into the room, saw the two beds, mother, child, and the Sorceress, all as they should be.

She was going to have to feed, somewhere, for the ordeal had weakened her. Remembering well Gambel's advice, she headed out to the streets and the comfort of the clouds, heading north where she would strike in a little street far from the Rudder.

*****

Gareth decided to celebrate his coming coronation by proving to Arista that his prowess as a satisfying lover was not diminished by his physical lack. He had often experimented with Corm, testing how hands and mouth could satisfy a man's desire, and since taken one or two prostitutes from the streets to see if he could please a woman's as well. But for the soverns he gave them, they might well have lied. Yet their moans of pleasure convinced him he had developed some skills and he longed to see if a real woman, one who wanted him, would find him worthy.

It was well past Norwin when he made his way to her room. The palace halls were empty and no would ever see him as he slipped inside. She was sprawled on the bed, deep in sleep. She wore only a flimsy nightgown, pulled up so her legs were bared. Her skin looked pale and creamy white in the moonlight. He moved over to the bed and put his hand on her leg, stroking her gently.

"Auntie, dear Auntie. I've come to seal our bond. I promised you power, now you must promise me satisfaction." His hand traced the inner side of her thigh. "Auntie, wake up."

She did not move. He slid his hand up higher and leaned over to kiss her, his tongue seeking into her slack mouth. Her skin was cold, her lips soft and cool. His hand moved higher, touching her between her legs his fingers playing, teasing. "Auntie, Auntie," he repeated in a singsong voice. She still would not wake. "Have you taken a sleeping-draught, my dear one? Wake up."

Was she breathing? It was hard to tell. Gareth pulled his hand out and pressed it against her breast, trying to feel her heartbeat. When he felt nothing, he lay his head on her chest to listen. There was a sound, faint, distant, as if coming from spans away. "What have you done? One of your potions gone wrong? Am I going to lose you before we have our fun? How can you do this to me?" He kneaded her breast with his fingers, relishing the feel of her softness, getting at least a little comfort from her. He ached to do more, to seek inside her to find her place of ecstasy and touch it, hearing her cry out with delight and squirm under his body. But this limp and unresponsive body could not please him tonight.

"Tomorrow then," he whispered in her ear. "When I am King, we can play together with my crown."

At that, he got up, left her room and headed for Corm's chambers. At least he would not spend the rest of the night alone.

*****

Just before sunrise at Easwin's change, Grella returned to the room in the palace. She had found a drunken man in an alley. The catch had been easy, a good thing since her encounter with the Sphere had drained much of her strength. She had killed him quickly more out of necessity than compassion for his fear. Because of that, his blood had been no more than enough to fill her Shadow belly sustaining her but not satisfying her larger need. But there was more to this one because he had downed half the tavern before she had found him and his blood was tainted with the brew.

Fortunately, the worst of the alcohol's effect didn't hit her until she made it all the way back to the palace and had taken on her skin again. For good or bad, it was a woozy Arista who woke up to the windchange. She rolled out of bed. A bleary-eyed search of the room found her gown. She stuffed herself into it, fumbling to tie the laces in the bodice, tucked her feet into two mismatched slippers, and tottered to the hall in search of someone to share Firstmeal with her. For some reason, she was feeling quite sociable and wanted to chat.

On the first floor landing, Kala was discussing the coronation with Corm. "I hope the Prince knows that his hasty decision to accept the crown today will deny the Lords of the far Provinces the chance to attend."

Corm nodded. "We have sent heralds through the city and messengers to the closer holds in Aberdal. We will have a small audience I suspect. All the Prince cares about are enough landed witnesses to legitimize his title."

"That would be twelve then," Kala said. "I will keep count as the guests arrive. Only if we have the required number will I entertain the ceremony."

"They will be here."

"There wasn't much enthusiasm in the square when you announced the King's death and Gareth's ascension."

"The people of Aberdeen are not rowdy, Madame Juris, particularly in this quarter of the city. The are genteel and refined. I would not expect a dramatic outpouring from them." Corm smiled and bowed to her. "Trust me, the Lords will come. I will now take my leave of you. There are preparations I must attend to."

Kala nodded and started for the stairs when Arista stopped her. "Madam J'ris," she said, her voice slurring. "I like ta share Frismeal wid ya if ya haven't yet. I mean if you not eat yet."

Kala shook off her surprise at the woman's condition. "I have not yet eaten, My Lady. I would be pleased to keep you company. One of the maids was bringing me my meal in the study. I'm happy to share. They always bring me enough food for two."

"Ish good," Arista nodded. "Study'd be fine. Need ta sit anyhow. Stairt look a li'l wobbly this morning."

Kala took the other woman's arm to steady her as they made their way to the study. There, Arista settled herself in a chair by the big research table as Salene poured her a cup of water from the pitcher on the desk. "So, My Lady, we've not talked much before. You come from the Far Islands?"

"Do," Arista said. Grella, only slightly less drunk, remembered some of what she had managed to find out about her skin while she was staying in the palace. By asking questions of the servants, and listening carefully to Gareth and Gailvarg whenever she was around them, she had developed a reasonable knowledge of Arista's life. Enough, she hoped to carry on this conversation without making a mistake. But the fuzziness in her head was making it hard to remember. "Worl'sEnd," she said finally. "Sell stuff. Los' ma husband, ya see."

"Ah, yes, the King's brother, Galen. I am sorry, but you seem to have made a good life for yourself on your own."

"Like I said. I sell stuff. Trade with the sailors an' merchant schips."

"It must be very interesting meeting people from all over the world," Kala said. The maid had brought in a large platter of cheese and fruit along with a loaf of fresh bread. She set a pot of keldherb down. "Mira, please see if you can find Master Simen. I would like him to join us."

Mira curtsied, "Certainly, My Lady."I'll send one of the other maids up with some extra plates and cups and another platter of food." She hurried out.

"See what I mean?" Kala said, pouring a cup of keldherb for Arista. "We already have enough food for four, and she's going so send up more."

"So the ladies are having an early start," Gareth said from the door.

Kala rose and offered a slight bow. Arista leaned forward on the table and awkwardly pushed herself up, holding on for balance when the world threatened to spin sideways. "Yer Highnesh," she said.

"Well, Auntie, you seem to have started the festivities a little early, eh?" He sauntered over to the platter and took a big chunk of white cheese. "That explains why I could not rouse you when I came to your room last night. I had a question to ask and you would not wake."

"Room?" An alarm sounded fuzzily in Grella's head. "When was?" Arista managed to ask.

"Past Norwin. I was so excited about the ceremony I simply could not sleep. I kept thinking about which tunic to wear and wanted your expert opinion on my clothes."

"Closhe....Whadja want ta know?"

"I could not decide between the burgundy tunic and the red, but I finally went to Corm and we settled the matter together." He took a bite of cheese and licked his fingers as he chewed. "We chose the burgundy. It was more subtle, he said. And I do have to agree. Corm has an excellent sense of what a man should wear."

"I s'pose," Arista agreed.

"My dear Arista, if you are not in any better condition than this for the ceremony, I cannot allow you to sit beside me. I wish Master Edra were here. He surely would have the skill to sober you up."

"There are herbs, My Lord," Kala said. "My traveling companion, Simen, is a Follyman and has, I fear, much acquaintance with the spirits. I think he may well have something in his bags to help. I've sent for him."

"Fine, fine, as long as she's sober. I will not have my day ruined by a drunken whore at my side." He dropped the remaining cheese back on the platter, spun and strode from the room.

Arista sank back into her chair and took a long drink of keldherb. The brew did wonders to help sobriety, but her head was starting to throb. "I don't feel so good," she said.

"The liquor's wearing off, My Lady. As soon as Simen gets here you'll feel better."

A new maid brought in another platter of food and some extra empty dishes and cups. "Mistress Mira said Master Simen should be here in a moment, Madam Juris. Is there anything else you need."

"I don't think so, thank you," Kala replied.

As predicted, Simen arrived as soon as the maid left. He was carrying his leather saddlebag. "I heard you needed a Healer," he said.

"Lady Arista indulged a bit too much," Kala said. "I'm afraid she's suffering from the effects."

Simen smiled sympathetically. "Well, then, you've brought the right person to make things right, Jur Kala." He reached into his bag and pulled out a parchment packet. "Here, mix this in a cup of keldherb. Now, My Lady, if I may put my hands on your head, I think I can help soothe that headache."

Arista nodded, and this time Grella was of one mind. Simen placed his palms against her temples and called to the River.

Darkness.

Grella started. Sorcery! She felt the Magic, realized he would recognize her, and fled. Leaving the Flesher's body behind the night before had taught her how to separate her Shadow from the skin just enough to leave its life behind.

A sudden flash, and then the pain of the woman's headache hit Simen. It was all too familiar. The queasy stomach, the dull ache every moment threatening and then pulsing to a throb, the hangover filled him with its misery. Kisel's lesson learned, he knew the symptoms and knew the cure well having suffered both more often than he wanted to remember. He reached for the waters and the cool, soothing gold poured over them both.

He felt Arista shudder, an unexpected reaction and he had to hold her up. She was near collapse. But, he had never Healed a woman before and did not know what to expect. Perhaps she had fainted. Carefully, he took one hand away from her head and used it to brace her in the chair, letting the Healing finish.

Grella, invisible in the light of Easwin, waited a little off to the side until she saw Simen's Touch lighten and then, when she was certain he was done, she slipped back into the skin and sighed.

"My Lady?" he asked. "Are you feeling better? Here," he gave her the cup of keldherb laced with his packet of herbs.

"Oh my, yes. Why thank you so much," Arista said, taking a sip. "Your hands are quite skilled, Sur. I've never had so much to drink before. I don't think I ever shall again. This tastes good."

"A proprietary mix," Simen told her. "Gleaned from experience and far too many long nights in taverns, I'm afraid. As a Follyman, I tend to spend many an evening drinking too much myself."

"Well, don't expect me to join you," she said smiling weakly. "I certainly don't want to feel that way again." Then she threw her hand to her mouth. "Oh my, oh my, what have I done? The Prince, he was here, wasn't he? He saw me…he knew I was drunk, didn't he. Did I say anything foolish? He's been so kind to me. I hope I didn't offend him."

"The Prince is easy to offend, My Lady," Kala said, "but you didn't say anything wrong. He was concerned for your health and wished you better in time for his coronation. Apparently you are to sit beside him?"

"Yes, yes," Arista replied. "He has honored me as sister Queen. He must have truly loved his father to be so generous."

"I'm sure he did," Kala said breaking her Seer's Oath with another lie. "I am happy for you."

"When will the ceremony be?"

"I am waiting for news from Master Corm. As soon as we have word that enough Lords are gathered, we will begin. The preparations should be complete by Sowin's change so I would expect to hear half before Weswin."

"Oh good, good. Then I shall have time for a little nap to finish Master Simen's cure and then a lovely bath. Did the Prince say he was wearing burgundy? I seem to remember something about that. I have a gown of dark rose that should complement him well. Yes, yes, the rose gown." She got up and headed out of the room, muttering to herself about how pretty rose would look alongside the Prince.

Once outside in the hall Grella dropped the pretense. The Sorcerers may have laid a trap for her at the Rudder and Wheel, but here in the palace? They would never anticipate an attack. Besides, all she needed was one more good drink of Magic's blood and she would have True Life. Then no one could touch her. One more Sorcerer, and nothing to fear ever again.

And the Follyman was a Sorcerer.

XV

Jamus burst through the door of the Bread and Butter Inn to a scene of disarray. There were dishes on most of the tables, the floor had not been swept, and the lone serving girl was sitting listlessly by the dark hearth, her head in her hands.

"Where's Becca?" he demanded.

"In the childrens' room upstairs, " the girl said. "Oh, My Lord, it's terrible, it's terrible. The wee ones are so sick."

Jamus' heart sank. Without a word, he raced up the stairs to the room above to find Becca weeping by her twins' bed. Jeamel was standing, slumped against the window, staring blankly out.

"Becca?" Jamus said softly, trying not to startle her.

She looked up, her eye red, her face haggard. "Master Jarien. I'm afraid I cain't welcome ya proper. Ma babes, ya see….they," her voice choked on another sob.

"I know, Becca, I know. That's why I came. I have some skill in Healing. I want to try to help."

She shook her head. "The Healer done tried already, lad. She said there's naught ta be done. I'm gonna lose'em, like every other Mam in the village."

"Let me try, Becca, please? I can't bear it not to try."

She nodded and moved a little away from the bed to let him near. Sira and Jeb were lying side by side, each with a little stuffed animal in their hand. With a curse under his breath, Jamus pulled the toys away and tossed them across the room. Then he placed one hand one each of the children's chests. Their heartbeats were faint, their breathing shallow, their skin hot. He closed his eyes and called to the River.

The waters rose around them, cool, refreshing, promising, but no more. It was not here that the Healing would come. He drew a

*deep breath and dived down, into the deeper currents, drawing up
the ancient waters, seeking the sand below.*

Seeking the Dragon.

*They hit bottom. "Kisel," he called. "Your master
commands."*

*As before, the great Rainbow Dragon pushed himself out of
his cave. "What bring?"*

"Two kitlings," Jamus said. "They need to live."

*"Dead meat again? Bring better next time. Brother say he
come."*

"Brother. Your brother?"

"Kesel say you bring. He want."

*From behind the cave, one long black tendril swirled out,
licking Sira's face. Jamus leaped in front her, shielding her with his
body. "No. You must Heal her."*

*"Everendings ever be, sacrifice there is to me. Life for life is
my command. Thus my Darkness does demand."*

"You will not have her."

"One will satisfy you see, choose between most carefully."

"What is he saying, Kisel?"

*"One or the other," the Rainbow Dragon replied. "Life for
life. It be Turan's Way.*

*More black tentacles appeared from the left side of the cave
and finally the Black Dragon's grotesque form appeared, his jaws
agape, his ebony tongue licking the air.*

*"They're just children," Jamus pleaded. "What good are
they to you? If saving one will not alter Turan's Way, why not
both?"*

"One or other," the Dragon repeated.

*'There has to be a way," Jamus said, looking down at the
two children. He couldn't tell if they were even breathing anymore.
"By the blood, there has to be a way!"*

"Everendings, ever be, sacrifice there is to me."

*Jamus straightened. "Take me then, you greedy rimsnake.
Take me and be done with it, but let these children live."*

For some strange reason, Kisel smiled and nodded. "Light heart now, Rivermaster. Light heart." Then he turned his great head to his brother. "Take him."

Jamus turned and opened his arms, welcoming the end of it all. Sacrifice for Becca's babes, fair payment for all she had done for him. She would never know and he would never learn her love for that day would never come. Salene? Lost too and Jarien. But that was tomorrow.

Was this the solution to the riddle after all? Sacrifice? The final tapestry had woven his death.

Blackwing's dark coils wrapped around Jamus, tightening around his chest. He gasped for air, and as his lungs deflated the constriction increased. He couldn't breathe.

This was death, the complete oblivion. The end of everything.

Light heart, light heart.

Suddenly, his mind flashed in desperation. Light. Spellfire. The blazing force of Magic Unrestrained seared through his body. Heat beyond imagining.

Blackwing screeched.

Jamus lungs filled with a huge gasp of air and he opened his eyes to see the twins in the bed beneath his hands, each breathing deeply, their fevers broken.

In his head, he heard Kisel's voice. "The riddle be answered."

"The Hand be Blessed!" Becca cried. "Jeamel, our babes! Come see, my love. Our little ones. The fever's gone."

Jamus lay his head in his arms, exhausted and too weak to move. His mind raced, but none of it made any sense. He shouldn't be alive. That was not part of the bargain. One or the other. He looked up. Sira and Jeb were sleeping peacefully, still pale, but he knew they would recover.

But why was he alive? Spellfire? It should have killed him. And he knew Blackwing was not dead because even Magic Unrestrained could not kill a Dragon. What had he learned? He was too tired to think about it. Besides, Becca was more important. The

twins were alive, and their path on Turan's Way had been changed
for all time. What was that going to do to the rest of his own life?

"My Lord," Becca said, gently placing her hand on his
shoulder. "Be ya all right? Ya done a fine thing, a fine thing."

"I'm all right, Becca. I'm just tired, that's all. Healing takes
a lot out of me."

"I kin see that, an' bless ya fer it. Five wee ones in the
village done died. Ma babes be the only ones left."

"Are there more children left alive?"

"Aye, a few families from the edge o'town. Some o' the
poor folk."

"Anyone who bought goods from Trader Ferg?"

"Don' think so. 'e din't stay long this time. Jest gived the
little'uns the toys an' left. Said 'e smelt a storm comin' an' wanted ta
git cross the pass afore it hit."

Jamus pointed to the stuffed animals on the floor. "Burn
them, Jeamel, and tell everyone in the village who bought anything
from Ferg to burn it too."

"They just li'l trinkets, lad."

"They're the cause of the sickness," Jamus replied. "The
fever struck in the Keep too, but only where those damned little
trinkets were. Nine children are dead, Sagari's own son. There was
nothing I could do there. The River be blessed I had at least some
luck here."

"Healer's Art ain't luck. Ya oughta know that."

Jamus sighed heavily. "It was this time, Jeamel."

"Well, whate'er it was ya saved ma babes," Becca said.
"What kin I do ta repay ya?"

Jamus smiled. Although Becca did not know it yet, she had
repaid him already, a thousand times over. Then a thought struck
him. "You can move to the Keep. You told me Jeamel wanted a job
in the palace there. Go, and make a new life for yourself there. You
said you wanted to spend more time with your children. If you give
up the inn here, you can. They deserve you, Becca, all of you for as
much as you can give them."

"Josep's there," Becca said, "an' ya always said ya'd like ta
be close ta him. We ain't got no ties ta Tallridge an' wid the money

we'd git fer the inn we could git us a real nice house. Mebbe it's time ya foller yer dream, eh, mi love?"

"S'pose I don't git the job?"

"You will, Josep," Jamus replied. "When you get to the Keep, find Master Senital. Tell him Master Jarien sent you. Tell him I said it was important for you to get a job there and it was part of the tapestry of things. He'll understand."

"The tapestry?"

"Yes, don't forget. I won't be there. I don't think Lord Sagari wants to see me again, so I'm going back home...to my father's farm."

"Will we e're see ya agin?" Becca asked.

"I hope so, Becca, I hope so." Then without another word, he left the inn, mounted Shadowmist, and lifted strides back to the stables in Magiskeep. There, he unsaddled the horse and put him in his stall.

Stay.

"I can't Mist. I need to go home."

Like.

"I like you too, but I don't belong here."

Be sad.

"I will always remember you, I promise." He looked at the gelding and saw in him his own Whim, the silver stallion born in the mist of Crystal Lake and somehow knew it was no coincidence.

Then he headed out to the streets, looking for the path out of the tapestry. Once he left the palace grounds, it was really quite easy for there, in a little alley to the east, he could see the air shimmering. He turned, took one look back at the Magiskeep of yesterday, and stepped through.

Cool air washed over him.

"Jami, Jami, ma boy? Ya wakin' up now? Yer fever's broke at last. Come on, lad. Becca's here fer ya."

Jamus reached out his hand and Becca caught it in hers squeezing hard. "Becca?"

"Come on, Jami. Yer back wid me, is ya?"

"I've been trying to find you," he said. "You are in Magiskeep?"

"'Course I is. Made me a promise circles ago ta come here and here I bin every since. Yer the one keeps leavin'."

"Your twins. What about yer twins?"

"Sira an' Jeb? Why ya askin' after them? Sira's all the way 'crost the Rim in Aberdal runnin' her own little inn, The Mother's Love. I done tole ya that. An' Jeb? He's got a forge down south o' the Keep."

"I had a dream about them."

"Ya did? Mebbe it was the stories I was tellin' ya bouts how I almos' lost'em when they was babes. Fine young Healer, name o' Jarien cured 'em fer me. He's the one I promised I'd come ta live here at the Keep. Ne'er forget the lad. Looked a bit like ya in some ways. Warm heart like ya too. Wisht I coulda met him agin. Said his Pap had a farm out Farreaches way. Akst around the Keep about it, but no one knows fer sure. Ain't thought about 'im much o' late, but evry times I hugs ma boy or ma girl I thank the Hand fer' im. There now, ya gots me prattlin' on agin. Ya up ta some food?"

"I am hungry. Something easy on the stomach, though."

"I'll gets some broth fer a start. Bit o' water here." She helped him drink. "Ya ain't et fer near four days."

Four days? Was that all? It was a lifetime in the tapestry. "It seems a lot longer."

"Dreams kin be that way sometime," Becca said. "Jest hold on while I goes ta the hall ta git someone ta fetch the broth." She got up and went to the door. One of the maids who was waiting on call came over. "Tell Mistress Sarena the Lord's awake. An' send ta the kitchen fer some keldherb, a nice bowl of good broth an' some fresh bread. Tell the cook ta start a light meal fer later." The maid smiled and scurried off. She had good news for everyone she passed on the way to the kitchen.

Sarena was in the room soon after. She hurried over to the bed, and put her hand on Jamus' head. "How are you feeling?"

"Tired, weak, as if I've been away forever."

"You were very sick and there was nothing I could do to Heal you. All I could find was darkness when I Touched you."

"I've been on a journey, Sarena." His eyes strayed over to the tapestry hanging on the wall. Its colors were vibrant, the weave intact. The picture was clear now. There were still people in mourning and a golden sun dimmed by dark clouds. But now, the central figure, a woman dressed in homespun was smiling as her two babies played on the ground at her feet.

Sarena's gaze followed his. She too saw the tapestry. "It's mended," she said. Just then a maid came in with a tray of food. Sarena stopped her to check the dishes. "Good, broth, bread, and keldherb. A good choice for an easy meal." She looked at the maid. "You're new to the Keep. I don't recognize you."

"Natale," the maid replied. "I've been living alone far north of here, but I thought it was time I returned to the world."

Becca stood up to take the tray, "Good to see you again, Natale. It's time you put aside your grief."

"Mistress?"

"It's Becca, from Tallridge. Ah, I'm not surprised ya don't remember me. Ya had only about five circles or so when I finally sold the Bread 'n Butter an' left the Tallridge fer good."

"I don't remember you, but I do remember something about the inn."

"Ya oughta. Yer Pap wanted ta buy it ta git hisself outta the mines. I waited long's I could fer him ta git up the money. Rented it out ta Mistress Tarry fer nigh on ten circles afore I finally sold it fer good. Yer Pap t'weren't the only one what wanted that inn. Keep tellin' Jeamel we gotta go back ta visit some day."

"I haven't been back either. I think it would be most strange."

"S'pose it would. I heard about yer loss an' how ya went off by yerself ta live. Woman's gotta grieve, but it cain't go on forever."

Sorra tried hard to remember all the details she'd read in Natale's diary. There was no mention of Becca and just a passing comment about the inn. So far, so good. She wouldn't need to talk too much about that. But the "loss" as Becca called it was a different matter. Avalanche in the mountains, ah, yes. That was it. "It was a sad day when my husband and little son died in that avalanche. Some would say I was lucky to escape, but how can a wife and mother count herself lucky when she loses everything she's ever loved? I've spent nearly thirty circles remembering them. But now it's time to make new memories. I can never get them back, but I can learn to live again for them." With that she curtsied, "Is there aught I can do for the Lord? I'll be needed back in the kitchen."

"No, thank you," Sarena said, dismissing her. "We'll be fine."

"Later, come Weswin. I akst fer a heartier meal be made up for Jami," Becca said. "He'll be hungry then."

Jami, Sorra thought. What a cute nickname for the Master. Little Jami, eh? Were it her choice, she would lace his food with poison and be done with him. But Tamor had commanded him alive before his Black Master, and so it must be. Yet there would be pleasure for her in the end to see Becca's dear Jami on his knees begging for the life of his child. Where was the babe anyhow? She could wait. Serving in the palace was not so bad. She had a tiny private room way off to the back of the kitchen where she could shed her skin without anyone finding it. And though the job gave her plenty to do there was still time to wander about the village and surrounding farms at night walking in Shadow, hunting.

After Jamus had eaten, the woman drew him a warm bath in the tub they had brought into the room days before to cool him. "I'll help ya," Becca offered as he started to get up from the bed.

"I think I can do it myself," he said, grinning. "I still have a shred of modesty, though the Hand can only imagine how much of me the two of you have seen over these last few days." He had noted that he had on no nightclothes.

"Then let me send for Salene if you're suddenly so modest. I would hope she's seen you naked."

He laughed and sat up, keeping the sheet wrapped around him. "Indeed she has, but if I see her now, a bath would be the last thing on either one of our minds. Really, I'll be fine. Go on, come back in a span. I am the Rivermaster. I won't drown."

"Come, Becca," Sarena said. "Leave the poor fool to his folly. Once he's in the tub we can peek in now and again to be sure he's all right."

After the two women had left, Jamus tottered unsteadily over to the tub and climbed in. The water was warm and soothing. He resisted the urge to let it take him to the River for he'd had enough of

Dragons and dreams. All he wanted now was to feel clean and to soothe the dull ache in his bones.

The wind rushed at the window as Rath flew into the room and alighted on the floor. As had become her habit, she peered into the mirror for a long time as her shape finished shifting to woman. Then, without a word to Jamus, she walked over and started stripping the bed to put on fresh sheets.

Sinking a little deeper into the water, Jamus scrubbed himself with the fragrant lather.

"Why twolegs use white foam to clean self?"

"What?"

"White foam. Sand be so much better."

"Sand would scratch our skin," Jamus replied. "We do not wear coats of Dragonscales."

"When fight do." She turned to look at him and although her body was fully woman, her eyes were still whirling Dragon.

"True. Then armor protects us."

"Strange to need protect body." She stroked her hands down hers. "Weak skin to wear. Why Shadow want so much?"

At the mention of Shadow, Jamus sat upright. "What Shadow, Rath? Where?"

"Rath watch for Shadow in mirror. Shadow watch Keep. Must keep watch from both sides Rath think. Blackwing brag Shadow in world of Flesher cross Rim."

"You've spoken to Blackwing?"

"All Dragon speak." She looked over at the tapestry. "Best One solve riddle so Brother say. Blackwing wait for night of coming. Must keep watch."

"Can you speak plain? My head's still reeling from the fever and I don't understand all of what you're saying."

"No need. Rath watch for now." Then, her eyes stopped spinning as she completed her transformation. "The Shadows will not strike here, not yet. Blackwing wants his army first. Lord Tamor will raise one for him here and his servants are already raising one across the Rim."

"Across the Rim. That's where Simen is. I need to go to him."

"No, Rivermaster. Your place is here. It is here Blackwing himself will strike and you are the only one worthy to stand against him. Simen is not your brother by your Will but by Turan's. He has allies, more than you can know. Here it is just the Magic." Then she paused. "Unless we can break the Wall."

"The Wall between the Keep and Arcula?"

"It would bring an army to your side."

Jamus spelled the water in the tub to rinse himself off. "It never ends, does it."

"The Circle's End is not what you seek."

"No, it's not." Without thinking any more of modesty, he pushed up from the tub, grabbed a towel, and started to dry himself off. Little Jenda's earnest face appeared in his mind, her tiny fingers pulling at his arm. *I can make a dryin' spell for ye, Sur.* Jamus chanted his body dry with a simple wave of his hand. The only thing still wet were the tears running down his face.

*****

Simen dressed in his formal tunic of royal blue, but did not expect to be present at the coronation ceremony. The Law dictated that only the Lords of Turan would be welcome witnesses, with a later presentation of the new King to a more common audience in the Grand Hall afterwards. The main ceremony was to be held in the North Hall, a room of decided elegance with seats for over a hundred. But so far, only about fifty lords were in attendance and it did not seem any more would be arriving.

Gareth, in the sitting room beyond was pacing nervously back and forth across the floor counting. But no matter how he adjusted his stride, he could not make an even twenty-eight steps. On his twentieth attempt, he stopped and called for Corm. "How many lords are in the Hall?" he asked.

"Fifty-four, My Liege."

"Fifty-four. Oh, no, Corm, that will never do, that will never do. Even if you seat them evenly on both sides, that's only twenty-seven. We must have twenty-eight. Surely there are two more coming?"

" I don't believe so, Your Highness. We have already waited an extra span."

"You must find two more lords."

"Where shall I look? There are no more holds close to the city."

Gareth thought for a moment. "Is it not the King's right to make men lords?"

"It is, Your Highness."

"Then bring two men to me…wait. Bring that Simen here. He carries himself well and, oh yes, bring Jyp. Perhaps it's time I rewarded him with a title for all he's done for me. If I add to his Power, he may finally find the strength to cure me. Go on, go on, hurry now. We need fifty-six."

Muttering under his breath that he had not been selected, Corm trotted off to obey his King's command. It didn't take long for him to return with Simen and Jyp.

"Sire?" Jyp said, offering a slightly less than formal bow.

Gareth ignored the insult. "You, Jyp and you, Simen. In the name of the King of all Turan, we name you Lords of the realm. All the honors of title are bestowed upon you by our hand. Now, go to the hall and seat yourselves with your peers. Corm, hurry now. Get them seated. Twenty-eight on each side. Remember now."

Before either man could protest, Corm ushered them to the Hall. "Sit," he said, pointing to two empty chairs, one on each side of the aisle. "And if you know what's good for you you'll not say a word about this. His Majesty does not tolerate criticism well." He spun on his heel and marched back down the aisle to join his Prince in the sitting room.

Simen looked at Jyp, smiled and shrugged. Apparently his formal tunic had been a good choice after all. Above in the balcony, the herald trumpets played a fanfare. Kala, robed in her Juris gown of green and gold, moved up to the platform set in front of the room. She was followed by a page bearing a red velvet pillow holding the royal crown. She raised her arms and all the Lords rose to their feet as another fanfare blared.

The two wide doors in the back of the room swung open, and Gareth, head held high, marched in with Arista's hand resting lightly on his upraised elbow. He glanced neither left nor right but kept his eyes ahead, fixed on the crown. His lifelong ambition was finally going to be fulfilled and he had no intention of losing his focus even for a moment.

When he reached the platform, he motioned to Arista to sit in the gilded chair to Kala's left. Then he stepped up to meet the Seer face to face.

"Who comes to the Hall to claim the crown?" Kala asked.

"I do," Gareth answered.

"Who art thou?"

"Gareth, Prince of Turan, royal heir, son of Gailvarg. I claim the crown by right of birth and the provenance granted by my father's words. His command is sealed and I accept the honor with a free heart."

"Is there anyone here present who disputes this claim?" Kala asked. She prayed there would be at least some objection, but the room was silent. "Gareth, Prince and heir, to you accept the Seer's Touch to judge your claim?"

"I do Madan Juris, as is the custom of the land." He knelt at her feet and bowed his head, the last time he would ever again subjugate himself to anyone. He smiled, it had all been so easy.

Kala placed her hands on his head, trying to limit her Vision to just the matter at hand—whether or not the Prince's claim was valid. But soon as she opened herself, she was assaulted by images she could not even begin to sort. Arista, swirls of shimmering purple, a maiden screaming, a shadow lurking in a corner, flashing swords, Gailvarg falling to the floor, darkness billowing like clouds over the sun, a woman pale and still in her bed, and an endless corridor of reflections stretching to eternity. It was all she could do to keep her composure. Only long practice in the skills of her Art kept her on her feet and, although she could not stop her trembling, she finally found the answer to the question she had asked. "I find this man speaks the truth of his right," she said at last and lifted her arms above her head, her mind awash with relief at having broken contact. "In the name of the Hand and Turan's Way, I declare Prince Gareth to be Turan's rightful king."

The page held out the pillow. Kala took the jewel encrusted crown in her hands and gently placed in on Gareth's head, making sure her own fingers did not touch him again. "Behold, King Gareth. Hail to the King," she said without enthusiasm.

Gareth rose and faced the Lords. There were no cheers. Instead, they applauded politely.

The new King reached behind himself, beckoning to Arista. He took her hand and pulled her to his side. "Behold my Aunt Queen. I so name her to sit by my side and grant her authority as is befitting a consort to the King. She requires your respect in all things and she lives under my protection." Slight applause followed this pronouncement, but Gareth did not react. Instead, he and Arista processed out, hand in hand.

"Now what?" Jyp whispered across the aisle to Simen.

"We wait until we are sure the King has returned to his private chambers, and then we get the blazes out of here," one of the other Lords responded. "I'm sure our new monarch will be throwing a big party to celebrate, but I seem to have lost my appetite."

"Do all of you feel the same?"

"I cannot speak for everyone here, but the Prince is not well liked. But he is the rightful King and we will do our best to be loyal to him."

There was a buzz of quiet conversation throughout the room and soon, the Lords began to leave until, at last, Simen and Jyp were alone together.

"That was a strange experience," Jyp said. "It felt more like a funeral than a celebration."

"No one has yet had the chance to mourn Gailvarg. That may have put a damper on things," Simen replied.

"I doubt it. From what that Lord next to me said, there's little love for Gareth, at least here in the city."

"I suppose we should go to the Grand Hall for the reception. I was hoping Kala would come back out here after the ceremony, but I guess not. She seemed a bit distracted during the coronation."

"No wonder," Jyp said. "With all she knows of Gareth's true nature, it must have been hard for her to crown him. I thought she showed remarkable restraint."

"Grandisite teaches its Seers well, and she did not become Prime Juris by accident. She is a strong, amazing woman who knows how to control her Power."

"Admiration? Or something more, Simen?"

Simen laughed. "I have my own love back in Magiskeep. As for Kala, she's madly in love with Lord Dale, whether she knows it or not. My brother Jamus and I have known here for a long time, and let me tell you, in times of trouble, a man can have no better ally."

"I hope we don't have to test that accolade, my friend."

By the time the two of them reached the Grand Hall, whatever ceremony had been offered was over and the festivities begun. Gareth and Arista were seated on the two thrones at the east end of the room, being waited on by several maids and pages who continually supplied them with food and drink. There were two long banquet tables set with platters of sliced cavel, roasted fowl, and several kinds of fish. Vegetables and fruits filled other trays, surrounded by plates of cheeses and bread of all sorts. The guests milled about, picking and choosing from the various delicacies, heaping their plates, eating and then going back for more. Off to the side was a long bar full of ales, wines, and other beverages.

Simen recognized most of the diners as workmen from the battlefield. Lean and well-muscled, many of the men carried two plates in their hands and dangled a mug of ale from their fingers. There were a few villagers scattered about, and, of course, one or two Lords who had decided the food was worth their time.

At the far end of the bar, he saw Kala. She was putting down an empty mug and was about to pick up another. Simen pushed past several of the men near her and reached out to stay her hand. "How many have you downed so far, Madam Juris?"

"This will be my third," Kala replied. "I toasted him with amberwine and now I'm trying to wash the taste of it away with ale."

"You'll be needing one of my packets if you keep it up, Kala. Perhaps some calidew would be better?"

"Calidew won't wipe out the memory of what I Saw," she said pushing his hand away and taking a long draft of the ale. "I washed my hands three times after the ceremony. Now I need to wash my mouth."

"It never works, Kala. You always remember in the morning and the price you pay for one night of oblivion just isn't worth it. Trust me, I know."

Reluctantly, she put down the mug. "I'm feeling a bit dizzy anyhow. I suppose it wouldn't really do for the Prime Juris to fall down in the drunken stupor in front of everyone. Can you help me to my room? I'd like to get out of this damned robe. It's not very comfortable."

Simen took her arm and escorted her out and up the stairs. He hesitated at her chamber door. "Are you sure you want me to come in?"

"Bory, Simen, we've spent many a night sleeping out on the trail or in a Host House and you've never even tried to kiss me. As much as I might like it, especially tonight, I seriously doubt you are going to take advantage of me. Besides, we need to talk in private."

They went in together. Kala unfastened her robe, pulled it off and threw it on the bed. To Simen's relief she was wearing a simple green shift under it. "What is it you want to tell me?"

"It's all a confused jumble and not because I had too much to drink," she said, sinking down on the bench at the foot of the bed. "Gareth's head is full of all kinds of things I might interpret as evil. But three images stand out. I saw a shadow hiding in a corner, dark clouds covering the sun, and a hall full of endless reflections."

"Shadows and the Way of Mirrors are never good, Kala. As for the clouds? Hard to say. But it worries me. I wish Jamus were here. He understands these things better than I ever could."

"Some might say you are the better part of him Simen, and you of all people should understand the Way of Mirrors. So tell me, what would Gareth know of it?"

"This Seeing of yours, was it the present?"

"Sight can be fickle when it comes unbidden like that. I was trying to keep it under control, simply to verify he was telling the truth about his claim to the throne. The Vision overwhelmed me without my doing. Time--the past, the present, the future--have no meaning in such a Sifting."

"So it could mean Gareth is allied with Shadows from the Way, or he is going to form such an alliance?"

Kala shrugged, "I don't know, Simen. We already know there are Shadows in Aberdeen. I think we need to go back to the Rudder and talk to our young witness."

"Tomorrow," Simen said. "For today, let's at least pretend all is well in Turan. I have a feeling it may be our last chance."

XVI

Edra had found only seven horses at Talia's farm, quite disappointed to see how few good animals she had. He would have expected a successful trainer at the Course to have fine stable at home, but it was not so. A few of the young horses, not yet ready to be ridden, showed some promise, but the bulk of her stock seemed to be failed runners too fine-boned and lean to be worth anything as cavalry mounts. That left him no option but to continue on to Telma Province to meet with Lord Delran, supposedly one of the finest breeders in the entire Kingdom.

Because Talia's farm was to the north, he was taking the less traveled northern route through Lovental. There was some rough going and a broad stretch of thick forest with narrow trails hemmed in on both sides by scrub pines and tall sofferns. As he rode deeper into the shady woods, it grew darker even though it was full day as the leafy brellums and long needled pines filtered out the sunlight. It grew cooler, but the air was still, the wind unable to penetrate the thick foliage. The atmosphere was claustrophobic.

Suddenly, the light seemed to blot out completely and Edra reined his nervous horse to a complete stop, unable to see the trail any longer. The animal snorted and pawed, its body tense and trembling. Edra wished the animal to settle for fear of being unseated and the chant held the creature's hoofs in place, but it did not stop its shivering.

"Seeketh thee the power of night? Come to join the master's rite."

"Who are you? What do you want?" Edra asked, shifting in the saddle, trying to peer through the inky darkness.

"I want nothing. You are the seeker. The Master has something you want. Make the bargain and find your journey's end."

"The Master? Tamor?"

"Tamor is but one servant to Blackwing. It is Blackwing's will to grant your desire. I am Melthus, sent to gather the Master's army. I put the question to you. Do you wish to ride with us?"

"I tried that before," Edra said, holding up the stump of his left hand, "and this was my reward."

"All shall be restored if the vow is renewed. The Master forgives the fool."

"How can I trust you?"

"How can you not? Six loyals await you in the grove beyond. Join them, or die. The choice is yours."

Edra straightened in the saddle. "You forget. I am a Sorcerer. Whitefire burns from my hand. Now that you have warned me, there can be no ambush. I am not afraid of your ruffians."

"Allies or enemies? As for me, I am but one drink away from True Life. Go, face them. Ask them whatever you will. Choose. One of them is a traitor, the others sworn to the Dark Lord. Prove your own fealty and give me my feast. In return you will have your hand."

The air lightened, his horse relaxed and once again the dim sunlight lit the trail. His eyes darting to left and right, his hand ready to cast, Edra nudged his mount along. Up ahead, he saw a small clearing, with a campfire burning. Around it, six men were seated, cross-legged, their hands locked behind their necks as if they were being held hostage.

Edra dismounted, and warily approached the circle.

"I was told to come here," he said.

"We were waiting for you," one of the men said. "Do as you will. We have given our lives already."

"Sworn to the Darkness," another said.

"Giving all to be given all," a third one continued.

"Join us," the fourth said. "We ride in the name of Tamor."

"I wear the ring to honor Blackwing," the fifth said.

"We are one in the darkness," the sixth said.

"Choose my feast," Melthus said from the trees beyond. "One betrays. Take his sword and prepare him for me."

"And if I do not?" Edra asked, pushing his sleeve up his good arm to bare it.

"Then you shall be my feast. Choose."

The six men sat perfectly still, waiting in silence as Edra walked the circle behind them, considering what each one had said.

Finally, he bent and chose one of the swords. With one practiced stroke, he swung the blade to slice through the fifth man's neck, nearly severing his head. As the body started to fall, Melthus emerged from the shadow of the trees, cried out in triumph, and began to drink the blood.

Suddenly, the clearing was filled with billowing black clouds borne on a biting whirlwind, knocking Edra to his knees. The other men fell on their faces, covering their heads with their arms, wailing with the voice of the wind itself. Edra's eyes watered, leaves and debris slammed into his body, and he had to throw up his hands to protect his face.

His hands.

Two hands, the left one wearing an ebony ring.

He cried out now, not with the voice of the wind but with joy.

The whirlwind spun up, sucking the campfire with it and, when Melthus finally backed away, the slack remains of the fifth man's body.

"Now we both have what we want," Melthus said. He flexed his arms as if testing his muscles, smiling with bloody lips. "How did you know he lied?"

"He was the only one who spoke of himself and not all," Edra said, opening and closing the fingers of his restored hand, testing them as well.

"It is good you know we are one in the name of the Dragon. You are sworn now, as you were before, but this time, the price of betrayal will not be just your hand, it will be your life. The Shadows crave the blood of Sorcerers. Your Vow is the only protection you have. Honor it as you honor your life, for they are one in the same."

"I understand," Edra said.

"The five Loyals are yours. Do with them as you wish. They too are Darkness sworn. When the time comes, be ready. Until then, Blackwing's will be thine."

Melthus raised his hand. Again, the whirlwind of darkness swept down, but this time it enveloped him, lifting his new body into the sky. With a True Body, he could no long walk the clouds-- instead, the clouds carried him.

Edra turned to the five men still prostrate on the ground around the remains of the fire. "Get up," he ordered. "Get up and name yourselves."

One by one, the man rose. They were a scruffy lot, hard-eyed and muscular. Three wore common cloth shirts with leather vests marking them as laborers or farmers. One was dressed in a shabby tunic made of faded wool and the fifth wore a tunic of blue decorated with a ripped crest and shield.

"Ruddick," the first said, "used ta work the metal till me master accused me o' stealing. So I took up stealin' as a profession and done well fer meself e'er since. Full purse from Melthus convinced me joinin' the Shadowlord were a better way."

"Palen," the second said. "Lost ma farm ta the taxman. Ain't had two denererts ta rub together till now."

"Beryl," the third said. "Just lookin' fer adventure when Melthus met me on the road. Full purse an' promise of glory's all I need."

The fourth shook his head sadly. "Wish I had a better story. Jain, pitiful Sorcerer that I am. Not enough Magic to do more than feed myself. I can spell a campfire and cook a duskit though. Like the others, full purse bought my promise."

"I was a Knight of the Hand," the fifth Loyal said. "But I was stripped of the title for refusing a command. T'weren't easy to turn to the Darkness, yet here I am. Donner, sworn to a new Lord and ready to wield my sword in his name."

A motley group, but each with his own talent and, apparently, some sense of obligation to Tamor. Edra knew better than to trust them, just as he had known better than to fully trust any of his Guard or Riders when he ruled the Cauge. Money and fear inspired the kind of obedience he needed from these men. He could always conjure the money if he needed it, but the fear was another matter. "I am Edra, First of the Cauge in Arcula, now right hand man to Gareth, Prince of all Turan, and if I am not mistaken, soon to be King. I am also a Sorcerer. Be warned of that, for it you cross me, your pay will not be silver." He raised his hand and sent a bolt of Whitefire searing across the clearing where it felled a large pine with that single stroke. "By stelin blade or flame from my fingers, I promise you will forfeit your life."

Wide-eyed at the power of his display, the four turned and bowed. Only Jain stood for a moment more, studying the smoking tree before he to turned to Edra and nodded. "Spellfire is most convincing," he said. "I do admire your power of persuasion."

"Do you have horses?" Edra asked.

"Mountain ponies," Donner replied. "Tethered off behind those bushes, if they haven't broken free after that display."

"Fetch them and mount up," Edra ordered. "We need to get out of the forest to a host house at the border of Telma. We'll spend the night and then, at Easwin, go to Lord Delran's and get you some proper mounts. When we ride back to Aberdeen, I want a proper escort, not a bunch of poorly clad, ill-mounted ruffians. Only proper warriors will do."

"Ain't got but the clothes I'm wearin" Ruddick said.

"Never mind that," Edra said. "When the time comes, I will dress you properly. I can do far more than just cast Whitefire."

They rode until just past Weswin's turn when they finally reached the Host House. There, with the horses well cared for in the barn, they settled themselves in for the night.

*****

Gambel heard the cry to the clouds and knew that Melthus had finished his last bloodfeast. His own heart ached, knowing his former companion had gained True Life before he had, separating them in more than just the distance between them. Hunting was better outside the city confines and his role a Gareth's general had pinned him within Aberdeen's walls for too long.

The biggest problem was that since his and Melthus's kill, and later Grella's, the entire city was on alert. He had managed five more feasts on his own since, but even with the granting of favor Tamor had given him to take all the time he needed, he was still a half dozen feasts short of his need. What he needed was the blood of a Sorcerer or perhaps a Seer or two to satisfy him. Grella had found good hunting near the Course, but had been thwarted by Magic on her last visit.

"Some Shadowspawned Sorcerer cast a net of reflections around the inn," she told Gambel when they finally found some private time together. "I was almost trapped in the Way. Whoever it was has a keen Touch on the Magic, I can assure you. He is not to be trifled with."

"So there is a Waymaster in Aberdeen?" Gambel asked.

"It would seem so," she replied. "It may have been that Jada herself, for all I know. I couldn't get close enough to sniff her."

"She is of the River?"

"Indeed, as is the boy. That means there are more Sorcerers in the city. If I could find one, all I need is one more taste and I will win True Life."

"We are of the same mind, then Grella, for one Sorcerer is all I need as well. Melthus has been Gifted, you know."

Grella sighed. "Of us all, I thought he was the least adept, but the freedom he earned from taking an insignificant skin served him well. Here we are, trapped in noble identities, forced to decide whether to keep up the pretense to honor Blackwing's greater needs or to risk them for the sake of our own desires."

Gambel laughed bitterly, "Who could ever possibly imagine being in the good graces of the King could be such a detriment?"

"Does the King have any good graces?" Grella asked, smiling. "Were he not of use to us, I would drink his blood and be done with him. I'm not sure even the Shadowlord would want to share the rule with him."

"That may be so, but he does have power in Turan and already he's recruited a sizable army. Mortal warriors have their purpose in Blackwing's conquests. When the Great Circle closes, we can feast on the King. For now we need him alive to inspire his troops."

"There must be more Sorcerers in Aberdeen," Grella said. "The boy would not have been alone, and Jada is an old woman. Like grainsnatchers, where one lives more gather."

"So what do you propose?"

"We need to hunt together and by our calculations, it will only take one more drink of the River's blood to satisfy us both."

"It would need to be a Sorcerer of power, not a boy."

"Indeed. We're both obligated to the palace for the next eight winds until the celebrations are done. Here must our bodies abide. In the dark we can Shadowwalk to Cuver Street, all ears to listen for talk of Magic. Then, when we find our prey we can go together in the Flesh to hunt."

"A pact then?"

"A pact," Grella agreed.

Both of them knew the promise of a Shadow was scant, with no more truth than a reflection.

*****

Jamus' reunion with Salene and Jarien gave them three days together in the peace they both had discovered before his illness. They took walks in the gardens and spent spans relaxing under the brellums, sharing the story of the tapestry from without and within.

"Senital has a diary from a Sorceress named Jada. Apparently, she left the Keep soon after the fever struck. Pages were blotted out by time, or so we thought. Now I wonder if they have been restored along with the tapestry's weave," Salene said, as she leaned back into her husband's arms, her hand absently stroking Clouder's head as the dog lay with his head on Jamus' knee.

He was sitting with his back propped up against a tree trunk in the east gardens, enjoying the Sowin sun on his face. "You said she wrote about Sagari. I tried so hard to save his son, but the Dragon denied me. Sagin had to die to assure Turan's Way."

"It broke my father's heart," Salene said. "He never recovered. All my life he compared me to the son he'd lost and nothing I did could ever satisfy him. He became spiteful, as you well know."

"I suppose he adopted me trying to replace the boy, but it just wasn't the same. Now that I understand what drove him to such cruelty, I could almost forgive him, at least for what he did to me."

"Nothing can excuse what he did to you. By the Hand, Jamus, he tried to kill you—and not just once—and as for me...." She shivered and he wrapped his arms around her, pulling her close against his chest. "Nothing can ever forgive that."

"By then, his grief had twisted into hate. And he blamed Turan for bringing the fever to the Keep." He sighed and kissed Salene on the head. "So much misery and nothing I could do to stop it."

"If you had, would we be here? Would we have Jarien? How strange to even think what might have happened if you had changed things in the tapestry."

"But I did change things, Salene. I saved Becca's children. Before the tapestry was mended, the twins died too."

Salene sat up and turned to face him. "I always thought they were alive. I don't understand."

"How could you? As soon as I changed the past, the future changed with it, as did all that you ever knew. I can't quite explain what that all means myself. As far as I know, I'm the only person in all Turan who knows what might have been and what was before I solved the riddle."

"The twins were the riddle?"

"No. The riddle has something to do with the Black Dragon, but the twins were a part of it." He shook his head. "It will all have to make sense eventually, I suppose. The only blessing is that it is the final riddle."

"So it's over then."

"It may be just beginning. Rath has been watching for Shadows in the mirror. She told me Tamor is raising an army. We must be ready."

Salene gripped his hands, tears welling in her eyes. "So, it comes to that, does it? Just when we found some peace and happiness? What do you need me to do?"

"Nothing, now, My Love, except to watch out for our son. The rest is up to me."

He got to his feet and pulled Salene up with him. Hand in hand they walked back to their chambers, Clouder trotting along behind.

Becca was waiting for them, Jarien on her lap. "'E's a clever li'l one, e is, she said. Already e's bin grabbin' fer 'is rattle."

"It's been nearly four months since he was born," Salene said. "He's grown so much."

"That long?" Jamus asked. "Time has a way of flying by, even here." In the tapestries, in the River, and in the Way, time meant nothing. Here, every moment was precious. As he looked at his son, he remembered again the children in Joria's class. "You know, it won't be long before we need to think about his education."

"Jamus, he's still a baby."

"A baby with some extraordinary power, Salene. Rath may have put a chanting on him now, but how long will it last once he discovers his own Will? We need to think about that now."

"The lad's bin a good li'l one," Becca said. "Ya shouldn't be frettin' so. Yer lady's right. 'E's still jest a babe."

"Nothing's ever really that simple where Magic is concerned, Becca." He knelt beside her and reached out his hand to Jarien, who grabbed his finger in his little fist and held on. "Well, little one, you are strong, aren't you." The baby cooed. "You don't have to try to steal my heart that way, you know. You already own it." Jarien let go and wriggled in Becca's arms as Jamus got back to his feet. "I need to go see Joria," he said at last. "I'll leave the four of you to whatever mischief you're up to." He gave Salene a quick kiss, patted Clouder on the head, and left the room.

"Always thinkin' that man o' yourn," Becca said, lifting Jarien into his mother's arms. "Be better sometime 'e foller 'is heart steada 'is head."

Outside, Jamus leaned against the doorframe for a moment to collect himself. When he'd touched Jarien, he'd felt the pulse of the Silver River struggling to be free. His child was more powerful already than he ever would have expected. Rath's chanting was strong, controlling the waters for now, but for how long? And when could a child be trained?

"Not until he's talking and walking," Joria said when he found her in her study. "Circles ago, we had a group of precocious little one in the Keep. None quite as powerful as you're telling me Jarien is. We finally started a class to teach them Practical Magic so they could learn to channel their skills without damaging anything."

Jamus nodded. "Why don't we have such classes anymore?"

"Sagari banned them. His son, Sagin was in the last group I taught. When he died of the fever, Sagari tried to wipe away anything that reminded him of the boy. We lost nine little ones here in the Keep, all my class. I don't think anyone of us ever really

recovered, but Sagari was the worst. Sagin's death changed him into
a bitter, vengeful man. Drove many a good Magician from the Keep.
My dear friend, Jada, left after Sagari tried to rape her. She was
mistress of the youngest Prentices, an expert in their childish Magic.
Everything I know, I learned from her."

"It's Silver Magic," Jamus said. "Magic Unrestrained as we
call it."

"We realized that," she said, "and discovered the children
could get some control of it by using their emotions instead of their
logic. It wasn't easy but Jada had success with some of the littlest
ones. I didn't start teaching them until they were about four circles
old. I wouldn't know what to do with a child much younger."

"I met Jada when I was in Aberdeen," Jamus said,
remembering all too well his disastrous visit to the city. "Do you
keep in contact with her?"

"I do, but even on the wing, messages take a long time to
pass between here and Aberdeen. It's a long distance."

"No so through the Way," Jamus said.

"Not for me," Joria replied. "As good a friend as Jada may
be, I'd never travel the Mirrors to see her."

"I would," Jamus said. "There's time enough, though. We
still have some months before I really need to see her. In the
meantime, I was thinking you might want to teach the Practical Arts
again. Sarn may be Master of the Keep for now, but that doesn't
mean I've surrendered all my rights to him."

"It's about time you didn't surrender any at all," Joria said.
"When you were sick, he was strutting around like a hebird all sure
you were going to die. Asked about you every day but never once
dropped in to see you himself."

"Well, I do have to admit, once you get past his arrogance,
he does a fair job. A Lord doesn't have to be liked, you know. And
he's smart enough to stay out of my way. So would you teach the
class again?"

Joria laughed, "I thought I'd diverted your attention from the
subject. Let me think about it."

Jamus took his leave and went in search of Sarn. He wanted
to be sure his rival knew he'd recovered and he needed to warn him
again about Shadows. Rath's obsessive vigilance at the mirror was
more unnerving than he had realized. While an attack from inside the
Way was not impossible, it would take a Waymaster to succeed and
the only one he knew to be capable was Tamor himself. The thought
of his presence in Magiskeep was chilling.

He found Sarn in the Great Library, reading. "Well, I never saw you as a scholar, Sarn. When did you take up learning?"

Sarn glanced up hiding his surprise at seeing Jamus back on his feet. "I'd be lying if I said I was pleased to see you," he said. "None of us thought you were going to recover."

"My death would not have assured you Mastery, you know. That would have been up to the Gathering to decide."

"I've worked hard to make friends while you've gone off on your adventures, My Lord. Be that as it may, I doubt you came to gloat about your health. Is it time for me to hand over the Keep?"

"No. I still need you," Jamus replied. "I have another journey to take and the threat of Shadows does not relent. Rath insists she's seen something lurking in the Way of Mirrors and I have reason to believe Tamor is raising an army to march against us."

"More from your Dragon Lady?"

"Don't scoff, Sarn. Dragons cannot lie."

"They can be mistaken."

"I trust her."

Sarn closed his book and sighed. "I suppose I must too, then. According to the texts three Dragons work for the good of mankind, and it's the fourth we have to watch for. Rath is Silver, there is a White, and then the Rainbow. The Black Dragon is the enemy. Have you met them all?"

"I have," Jamus replied. "There's the SeaDragon too, but not many know of him. He's really a rather curious fellow. I much prefer Rath's company to any of the others."

"By the Blood, Jamus, you speak of them as if they were nothing." He tapped his finger on the book's cover. "Do you know how much power they have and how important they are to Turan's Way?"

"I do, Sarn."

"And all that power is in your hands, isn't it," Sarn said as the reality of it all finally hit him. "Rivermaster isn't just a title bestowed for no reason. To think, all this time I've underestimated you."

"I'm still a man, Sarn."

"What do you need me to do?"

"Consult with Rath while I'm gone. When she is fully human she is quite easy to understand, but if her eyes start whirling, she'll start using Dragonspeak and you'll have to decipher her riddles. I think it's hard for her to always express things in our language, so that may well be another warning sign. If she does confuse you, it's probably something really important."

Sarn frowned, "That's not good. What if I can't figure it out myself?"

"Go to Senital in the Vaults. Never underestimate him. Sometimes I think he knows more than all the Masters in the Keep, including me. If he doesn't have the answer, usually he can find it in those scrolls of his."

"Is that all?"

Jamus shrugged. "That's what I would do."

"Then it's enough," Sarn agreed. "I'll watch out for Salene and Jarien too," he said. "I know you worry about them, even if you don't admit it. I may have failed my own son, but I won't fail yours."

"Thank you, Sarn. We may never be friends, but can be allies."

By Sowin's Turn, Jamus was already riding East, heading north of Crystal Lake towards the Wall of Tears.

Once past the Lake, where the trees began to thin, Jamus was able to lift Whim's stride to bring them close to the invisible barrier between Arcula and Magiskeep. Then, he had to be cautious, lest they hit the Wall in a lifted stride.

As he neared the place in the desert where he thought the Wall might be, he began casting simple flashes of greenfire in front of him waiting to see where it hit. Finally, the bolt splattered out a short distance ahead. He dismounted and led Whim to the spot and reached out with his hand. It met solid rock in front of him.

Now came the time to puzzle. From this side, he still could see nothing. But since his last visit, he had been Gifted with the Sight and now he used it. He let his mind open to all, every sound, every smell, every sight, every sensation assaulted him as he focused on the Wall. Vision took him and he Saw, for the first time, the silver threads holding the stones together, binding them with the pain of incredible grief, lashing them solid with a lover's determination to keep the world at bay. There was more, for when Estor had lost his wife, he'd lost a son as well. The lore never seemed to speak of that. Jamus' his own soul ached with an agony only another father could comprehend and as it did, the pattern of the weave became clear. It was chaos. Emotion so potent had cast an almost incomprehensible knot of threads nearly impossible to unravel.

Yet, every knot had a beginning, and Vision sought to find it—the first thread. Betrayal. The moment Estor's wife had decided to leave him, breaking the Vow of their marriage. Jamus let his own heart open to that torment, reversing it with his own potent loyalty to Salene, an overwhelming sense of devotion. The thread snapped.

Anger flowed in the weave of the second thread, knotted by Estor's rage. Jamus sought the Silver Waters with his own abundant joy in living. His life was full of people who cherished goodness in the world and sought it at every turning. The second thread broke.

Despair sealed the third thread, and in response, Jamus filled himself with hope. With three Rivers in his hand, and the Rainbow Dragon ready to fly, what could a man do but hope? The third thread frayed and separated.

One by one, he countered each negative emotion mortaring the stones of the Wall with the blessings he found in his own life. As he did, the Silver River's currents grew stronger and stronger, undermining the Wall's foundation, eroding the bonds holding the barrier in place.

One thread remained—hate. The most powerful force of all, a weave of stelin threads, stronger than all the rest. To Jamus, it was the easiest to conquer. Forgiveness first to silence its protest and then the all-consuming love for Jarien and his mother. His heart nearly burst with the intensity of it as he fell to his knees, overcome by its strength.

The Wall collapsed as the last thread vanished opening the desert into the green meadows of Arcula beyond. Whim trotted forward and then dropped his head to graze on the lush grass. For the first time in hundreds of circles, the two worlds were joined.

He mounted up and lifting strides, headed along the familiar road toward Arcuse.

As he neared the city, the impact of the new government was obvious. The road was neatly graveled and realigned to go directly to the gates instead of meandering around the countryside. The fields around were lush, the lake sparkling with clear water, and a small, bustling village had sprung up around the city walls. As before the huge gates stood open, but the guards were smiling instead of stern and when they saw Jamus, they bowed as one ran off to spread the news of his arrival.

Whim had hardly set a hoof on the cobbles of the street when a rider on a huge bay came galloping towards them. Whim snorted and danced to the side as the other horse slid to a stop beside him.

"Jamus! Why didn't you tell us you were coming?" Covane asked as he held up his hand in greeting. "How did you get here? The Watchers from the north had no report of anyone crossing the falls."

"I came through the Wall," Jamus said. "Well, let me put it this way. I came through where the Wall used to be."

"The Wall? What's happened?"

"I broke the weave, Covane. The Wall is gone. Arcula and Magiskeep are one again as they were hundreds of circles ago."

"No. Impossible." The Rider studied Jamus for a moment and then went on. "You shouldn't have done that without consulting the Order. The people have a right to vote for such a thing. It's not our way to simply do such a thing without consult."

"I had no choice. Both our worlds are in grave danger and it's my duty to defend them. I can't protect Arcula if there is a wall between us."

"Come with me, My Lord. You will need to explain all this in the Hall."

On the way to the palace, they shared stories of the new lives both of them had lived since their last meeting. "How long has it been, Covane?"

"Nearly eight seasons now," the Rider answered. "As you can see, much has happened in Arcuse since the Cauge fell. The New Order have used the Cauge's wealth to improve the lives of nearly everyone in Arcula. Even Veriset has been reformed. There's a nice little inn there now where no traveler needs to fear poisoning." He grinned. "I don't suppose you stopped there on the way."

"I learn my lessons well," Jamus replied.

"Well, if you have a chance on the way back, stop in. The surlep pie is the best in all Arcula."

They reached the Hall, handed the horses over to two young stablegirls and headed into the palace. Still elegantly furnished, but with far less ornamentation than when the Cauge had sat, the Hall seemed far more welcoming than it had when Jamus had first come to Arcula. Then, he had been a prisoner, and soon named an enemy by Edra and his colleagues. Now, as the door opened, he was greeted as a hero, the Dragonrider who had conquered Tamor's army.

"Welcome, Lord Jamus," Gaila said. Once only a tavern singer, she had led the city against the Cauge and since had been elevated to First Seat of the New Order. Her golden hair was neatly braided and wound around her head and she wore a pale green gown complementing her intense green eyes. Her smile, though, lit up the room as she got up from her seat on the formal platform and dropped to her knees to Jamus. "We are honored to have the savior of Arcula here."

One by one, the other four followed suit. Corel, on Gaila's right, old Master Densil on her left, and two other women Jamus did not recognize all knelt to honor him.

"I thank you for your respect," Jamus said. "I am here on a matter of importance, though, so it would be easier to talk face to face rather than to the tops of your heads. Please, get up and dispense with any more formality. We know each other too well."

Gaila rose and smiled again. "Are you still singing, My Lord? Even a voice as good as yours still needs constant tuning."

"Mostly to myself," Jamus replied. "I'm still too shy to perform before an audience."

"It's a shame, then. But sometimes the duty of office keeps us from the finer moments in our lives. I haven't sung much myself lately. Ruling Arcula with honesty and justice is not an easy task. I can almost understand why Edra and his Cauge took the easy route and simply did whatever they chose to do."

"Tyranny does have some benefit—for the tyrant, at least," Jamus agreed. "That may well be why I am here."

"The people rule Arcula now. We have no tyrants," Corel said.

"I have come with a warning from the Silver Dragon. Tamor and the forces of darkness are planning an attack against the Magicians. I think their intent is to close the Great Circle."

"Why did you come here, then? You have your own kingdom to defend. Arcula can take care of itself."

"Not anymore," Jamus replied. "Blackwing intends to take all of Turan and that includes Arcula. Unless we all join forces against him, he will conquer us, one at a time."

"How do you know this?" one of the other seats asked.

"Lord Jamus is the Rivermaster, Celsia. He speaks to the Dragons. He is sworn by their Vows to tell the truth of things."

"Arcula can be of no use to him," Celsia countered. "The Wall divides us from the rest of the world."

"No more," Covane said. "The Rivermaster has taken down the Wall of Tears."

"By whose authority?"

"Mine," Jamus replied, straightening his shoulders. "I am the Rivermaster, Dragonrider, and Keeper of Turan's Way. The last riddle has been solved, the tapestries mended and now the time comes when we must fight to defend this Circle. This side of the Rim is the world of Magic, and here the Black Dragon will make his stand. Either we unite against him or fall by ourselves. There is no other choice."

"Your Magiskeep holds the greater Power," Densil said. "Magic here in Arcula is but a babe compared to it. What can you want from us?"

"You have firemasters already hardened in battle. And warriors who have faced the sword. My people have lived in peace too long to know how to wage war. I can rouse my Magicians, but the people? We have no army, no means of defense. Farmers and craftsman are not Riders or soldiers. And if I'm right we don't have time to make them any more than they are."

"Jamus is right," Gaila said. "If indeed the Wall is broken, we are more than honor bound to join forces. He defended Arcula— it is now our turn to repay the debt."

"Do we vote?" Corel asked.

"So be it," the last Seat agreed. She rose. "I, Riesa, support Lord Jamus in his quest. We will form an alliance and pledge ourselves to defend both Arcula and Magiskeep."

"I agree," Gaila said.

"I too," Corel added.

"There is no question," Densil said. "I support the Lord."

Celsia hesitated. "I am impressed by the loyalty you inspire among my associates," she said. "But I do not know you well enough to decide so quickly. I have the right to demand a Searching, do I not?"

"The outvoted always does," Gaila agreed. "Whom do you request?"

"Wolla," Celsia said. "She is wisest of the scryers."

"She knows me," Jamus said, remembering how Wolla had helped him discover the secret of the Silver Magic when he had been trapped in Arcula. "I don't want to jeopardize your decision if you think that's unfair."

"No matter," Celsia replied. "Wolla is sworn the truth and I trust her Vow implicitly. She would not betray either Arcula or the Order for your sake, My Lord."

"It will be good to see her again," Jamus said. "Where do we meet?"

"We will go to her," Celsia said. "She has a small cottage here in Arcuse and is staying there for the Warmmonths. I will go as witness with one other. Master Densil?"

"I would gladly go along, but Mistress Wolla...."

Celsia laughed. "It will do you good to see the lady," she said. "She's had her eye on you and yours on her for far too long. I've wanted an opportunity to get the two of you together."

"So, an ulterior motive in calling for a Searching?" Gaila said. "This is serious, Celsia, not some experiment in matchmaking."

"You know me better than that, Gaila. Sometimes making light of a serious matter eases the fear. Lord Jamus speaks of things I would rather not face. Leave me to my matchmaking so I can make the right decision instead of one motivated solely by my terror."

"Very well, as long as you understand. I take it we have some time to think this over, My Lord?"

Jamus nodded. "Lady Rath would warn me if the danger were imminent. So far, all she has seen are Shadows in the Way of Mirrors. But she has heard murmurings from her brother Dragons. They do not keep their secrets well."

"Then come and share Midmeal with us. Meantime we will send messages to Wolla so she will expect your visit later in the day," Gaila said. "Rider Covane, you will be in charge of the army, as is you duty. Alert your troops and call the Firemasters to the Hall. They need to hear directly from Lord Jamus what must be done. And, we must not forget the Watch. They too need warning to increase their vigilance along the northern borders. If the Black Dragon stirs they will be the first to know."

"You are well prepared, Mistress Gaila," Jamus said. "It would seem you've anticipated something like this."

"Once we were invaded by the Shadows, and we vowed never to be so again. The New Order is sworn to protect the people and we've made it an important part of our rule. We expanded both the Riders and the army and set up watchposts throughout the kingdom. I'm sure it won't be long before we get word that the Wall has fallen."

"I may have only broken a part of it, My Lady. Once I sifted its weave it was a small matter to undo it where I crossed."

"If part has collapsed, the rest will too," Densil said. "The OldLore says Estor created the Wall with one Heart, no more. Each stone set upon another, sealed with the whole of his sorrow. If you broke that seal, the stones will all fall, one tumbling the next and the next until all is gone."

As they walked to the dining hall, Corel continued. "I, for one, am glad of it. Arcula has been shut off from the rest of the world for far too long. We've grown stale in our learning. When Jamus first came, my eyes were opened to all kinds of possibilities I never even imagined."

"Ah, you Riders always did have wandering feet," Riesa said. "I would think, though, that our Magicusers could benefit from the training of Magiskeep."

"It would be interesting on both counts," Jamus replied. "Your Magicians and mine draw on different waters. Neither really understands how the other's power works. I do know now that Magiskeep's Sorcerers can draw on the Silver Waters, but I have yet to see an Arculan draw on the Gold. Still...." He paused, remembering his own trial learning how to use the Silver River. Serenec had taken him into the desert and forced him to use Spellfire until he became immune to its effects on his energy. The Magicians of Magiskeep would have to be trained the way he had. Who better than the Magicians of Arcula to be their teachers? "I think," he said at last, "that Magicians on both sides of the Wall could benefit from some training."

XVII

Simen and Kala arrived at the Rudder and Wheel Inn just before Sowin's turn. Celia, smiling for the first time since they'd met her, opened the door to their room. "Sorty is feeling so much better. He'll need a Sevestin more in bed, I suspect, but he's getting stronger every day."

"Has he talked about what happened?"

"Not much," she replied, forcing the smile now. "He says he doesn't want to tell me."

"Perhaps he'll talk to me," Simen said. "Sometimes it's easier for a man to talk to another man."

"Sorty's just a lad," Celia said.

Simen shrugged. "He's been through a lot these last few days. Things like that can age a boy more than you may think. Kala, suppose you take Celia downstairs for some refreshments. I'd like to talk to Sorty privately. I see Jada's not here."

"She left yesternight. She said all she needed was a good rest. Slept right through near eight winds."

"No trouble, then?" Kala asked.

"Second Easwin on the door to our room was left open. I could've sworn I'd locked it tight the eve before. But I've been so worried about my son, I can't swear to it. Other than that, it's been really quiet. Once the innkeeper saw what you'd done to the room, he started treating us like royalty. He hasn't bothered us a whit except to keep us well fed and the room clean."

"Good," Kala said. "Come on then, let's go sample some of that food downstairs."

After the two women had left, Simen pulled a chair up beside Sorty's bed. The boy was fast asleep, but when Simen took his hand, he roused. "Lemme go....I... Oh, I thought...I saw you somewhere before," he said as his eyes cleared from sleep.

"I'm Simen. I was here when you were injured. I helped Jada Heal you."

"Jada's a fine lady."

"Yes, she is. Sorty, I know it's hard for you to think about, but can you tell me what happened?"

"She wasn't a lady. I thought she was. That's why I tried to help her. But she wasn't like Jada," Sorty said, shaking his head. "I told my Mam I was only trying to do my duty."

"I understand you were on watch in the streets, keeping an eye out for Shadows. But you were looking for men, weren't you?"

"They said it was men what killed the ladies. So they told us to look for strangers. I wouldn't have talked to her if I thought she was one of them. I have Spellfire, you know. Not much, but I could have used it."

"I know you'd never go out unarmed, Sorty. But she tricked you, didn't she?"

"She said she was lost and needed to get back here to the Rudder. She was really nice. Said she was a widow. She was going to give me a silver when we got here."

"A silver would have been good payment. I bet you wanted to give it to your mother, eh?"

Sorty nodded. "My Mam works hard. Takes her a whole day to earn a silver. All I needed to do was bring the lady here."

"So you did."

"She had us come up the back stairs. Said it was shorter. Then, she took my hand to thank me and," he shivered, "it was all cold, like an ice cold rope grabbed my wrist and before I knew it, I was tied to the bed. I should've used my Spellfire. I should've."

"You couldn't, Sorty. Once the Shadow had you snared there was no way for you to use your Magic. Hers had already taken control of you. Even a Master would not have been able to escape."

"True?"

"True," Simen assured him. "Shadow Magic is very strong. When it catches you buy surprise you have no choice but to do whatever the Shadow wants."

Sorty cringed back into his pillow. "I didn't want to do it. I didn't."

"Of course not. Whatever happened, the Shadow was in control, not you."

"I saw her naked," Shorty said hoarsely. His hands gripped the hem of the blanket, his knuckles white. "She took off her clothes. I never saw a naked woman before, not even my Mam."

"Was she beautiful?" Simen asked.

Shorty gulped. "I closed my eyes. My Mam says I'm too young to see a naked lady. But she kept getting closer and closer. I did a bad thing, a real bad thing."

"She did the bad thing, lad, not you. Whatever happened, remember, you had no choice. You were chanted."

"I had sex with her, Simen. My Mam said it's only for a man and woman what's in love, but I didn't love her. I was scared of her. I tried not to do it, I tried."

"I know you did. She used powerful Magic to force you to do what she wanted. It wasn't your fault."

"My fault I came into the room."

"It was already too late by then. You didn't do anything wrong except to trust a lady who was no lady. She must have been quite lovely to trick you so easily."

Shorty shrugged. "She looked like my Mam, but she was dressed better. A fine gown, and traveling cape. I thought she was a real lady."

"Then she hurt you. She cut you with her knife."

"I was scared. Real scared. And it hurt so much. She said she wasn't going to kill me. She said she wanted my blood. Then she sliced my stomach and I passed out, I guess. I don't remember much after that, not until Jada woke me up."

"Her gown, Sorty. Do you remember what color it was?"

"Kinda a dark red."

"Now that you've told me all this, do you think you would let Lady Kala touch you? She is a Seer and she might be able to recognize the woman when you picture her in your head."

"I don't wanna think about her."

"We need to find out who she is, Sorty. You would be doing a fine thing to help us. She will hurt more people if we don't stop her."

"You sure she was Shadow?"

"No one else would want your blood. All the more sure because she did let you live. You have Magic and that's important to the Shadows. Your blood gave her special power. If you weren't a Sorcerer, you'd be dead."

"Be easier than telling my Mam what I did."

"Your mother loves you, Sorty. She loves you more than anything. She'll understand. Jur Kala will explain everything to her so she'll have to understand. You need to trust us."

"I trusted the lady."

"Indeed you did. She was very clever." Simen tried another tactic. "Do you know of the Seers?"

"They live in Grandisite."

"Jur Kala is one of the most famous Seers in all Turan She has sworn to never lie." He pulled a gold medal from the pocket of his tunic. "This is the King's medallion. I got it from him when he named me a Lord. If she swears before you, on this medallion, will you trust her?" He placed the disk in Sorty's hand.

The boy studied it carefully. "I want my Mam to see this. She knows everything about Aberdeen."

"That's fair," Simen agreed. "I'll go downstairs and bring your Mam and Lady Kala up."

He hurried down the stairs, interrupting the two women who were deep in conversation.

"Shorty needs to see both of you," he said. "He'll agree to a Seeing if we can prove you are honest, Madam Juris."

"Since when does someone dare question the integrity of the Prime Juris of all Turan?"

"Since a young boy has grown too wise to the wiles of women to trust one without proof," Simen replied, beckoning to her. "He wants you too, Mistress Celia. He says you are an expert in all matters of Aberdeen."

Back in the room, Sorty handed the medallion to his mother.

"This is the King's medallion. Where did you get it?"

"Master Simen had it. He says Lady Kala will swear on it for me."

"Sorty, you can't ask her to do that. She is a Lady of high esteem."

"It's all right," Kala said. "I understand. Sorty is a very wise young man to be so careful. Here, give me the medallion." She took it in her right hand, then placed it against her forehead. "By all that is sacred in Turan's Way, in the name of the King, in the name of all Grandisite, I Kala, sworn to the Light, do reaffirm my Vow to stand only for truth. The Light be all, the Light be blessed, the Light will bless." She kissed the medallion once and then handed it back to the boy. "It is done. I cannot lie to you, Sorty."

"Mam?"

"You can trust her, son. She wants to use her Vision to see if she can find out who attacked you. I would like you to let her do it."

"There's bad stuff to know, Mam."

"It's all right. Whatever bad things happened, we all need to face them head on," Celia said. "I trust you too, Sorty. You have always tried to do the right thing, no matter what. Let Lady Kala see if she can help us all."

Sorty nodded. "Go ahead, Lady. I'll do as you ask."

Kala approached the boy and put her hand on his shoulder. "I want you to think of the attack, Sorty. Try to see the face of the person who hurt you. Don't worry if I act strangely when you do.

Sometimes my Vision is very powerful and I have to work hard to control it."

The boy lay back on the bed, his body taut as he began to think of the dreadful night.

Kala let Vision come. At first, it was darkness, an overwhelming absence of light, as if the powers of Shadow were consuming her Sight, denying her Light. She opened her mind, accepting the darkness, welcoming it as part of the Seeing, letting it have its way as black coils pinioned her wrists and ankles, holding her to the bed.

Then a faint gray ray of moonlight filtered through, pushing the darkness aside as if it were merely a cloud in the sky. She saw a woman's form, vague, with fingers slowly unlacing the bodice of a burgundy gown. The rich fabric slid away, revealing the woman's breasts, her hands lifting under them as if to show them off. Then she slipped out of her skirt, her naked body dancing sinuously forward. Her long brown hair fell free of its pins, strands obscuring her face as she lowered herself down, down. Then her lips opened, offering a searching, demanding kiss.

Still, Kala could not make out her features in the dim light beneath the hair. The woman muttered something, and forced herself down. Kala's own groin tightened, her pulse quickened, and she struggled to pull away, but the dark coils trapped her.

The woman moaned in ecstasy, her body pulsing up and down, her hips pressing into Kala's flesh. Then, with a cry of satisfaction, the attacker threw her head back, her face illuminated in the moonbeams as she reached her climax.

Kala cried out with her, and in one powerful wrench, tore her hand away from Sorty's body and fell back, shaking uncontrollably. "By the Blood," she gasped. "Arista!"

Simen dropped to his knees and took her in his arms, rubbing her shoulders, trying to steady her, "Kala, are you sure?"

She nodded numbly, struggling to control her trembling body. "It was Arista, Simen. There is no doubt. She raped him first. I broke before the worst of it. But I Saw her clearly."

"Shetark," Simen cursed. "She will pay for this."

"She is Shadow. The only thing that will stop her is Spellfire. And we'd best do it quickly. If she feeds too many more times, even that will not be able to touch her."

"Who is this Arista?" Celia demanded, going to the bed to comfort Sorty who was sobbing softly. "You said she raped my son? Show me where she is and I will kill her myself."

"No, Celia. Jur Kala and I will deal with her. My word is a
Vow as strong as the Seer's. This woman is Shadow, and I am the
only one who can kill her."

"How will you find her? The Watch has yet to even catch a
glimpse of the murderers to killed before. What makes you think you
can track this one down."

"Oh, it will be a small matter," Simen assured her. "Even
now she sits at the right hand of the new King. She is his Aunt."

As soon as Kala recovered, she and Simen rode quickly back
to the palace, forming plans even as they trotted through the streets.

"As much as you may want to, you can't just kill her," Kala
said. "If you do, you'll risk the King's wrath, something neither one
of us can afford right now."

"Then we need to catch her in the act, with witnesses of her
debauchery."

"How?"

"She wants the blood of another Sorcerer. Suppose we offer
her some-mine."

"A trap? Simen that's dangerous."

"Only as dangerous as I let it be. The Shadow's skill is
surprise, coming on her victim unaware. If I'm expecting her, then
she'll never be able to snare me."

"So, how do we bait it?" Kala said. "She doesn't know you
are a Sorcerer."

"That is something we'll just have to remedy. We'll also
need a way to convince her I'm easy enough prey for her to risk
taking me here in the palace," Simen replied as they entered the
greeting hall and headed for the stairs up to their quarters. "We'll
need Jyp too. I may have to depend upon his Spellfire and not my
own."

"Surely you won't allow yourself to be defenseless."

"I'm not quite that big a fool," Simen said. "I do think,
though, that it would look a lot better if I appeared to be a victim
being rescued than rescuing myself."

Just before Weswin's Turn, they found Jyp in his study.
"Two things, then," Jyp said. We need the King as witness, and my
heroics?"

"Can you do it?"

"The timing is critical," Jyp said.

"Unless I'm wrong, Arista won't waste any time with me.
Outside, in the streets, she can afford to play with her prey, but here,
in the castle? If we can lure her in, she's not likely to take many
chances. All she wants is a drink of my blood and she'll have her

True Life. Now, come on, the coronation festivities tonight will provide the perfect opportunity. Let's set the plan in motion."

Simen and Kala found Arista in the garden, selecting flowers for the dinner tables. Two servants at her elbow carried cutters and baskets as she pointed to the blooms she wanted and let them to the picking.

Arm in arm, the couple casually wandered over. "So many lovely flowers to choose from," Kala said, "I don't know how you know which ones to cut."

"It's really quite easy, my dear," Arista replied. "I have my color scheme all planned out in advance. This time, I'm choosing only red and pink blooms. But not just ordinary red. It has to have just a hint of purple. See that caliblossom over there?" She pointed. "It has too much orange in it to match. Now this one is perfect." She indicated another blossom and the servant cut it for her.

"It would be so much easier if you had a bed of flowers all the same color, wouldn't it?" Kala asked.

"Alas," Arista replied, "the gardener did not think to plant that way, so I must spend my time searching. I'm already behind schedule as I still need to supervise the arranging of the blooms and see to the table settings."

Simen, meanwhile, had plucked one of the flowers from the basket and was studying it. "I could help," he said.

"You have a taste for flowers, Sur?" Arista asked.

"No, but I do have a taste for Sorcery," he said. "This is the color you need?" he asked, holding up a calibloom.

"That one is perfect," she replied.

He reached into the basket and pulled out one of the pink flowers. "And this is the pink?"

"Indeed."

"Then, I can simplify things." He raised his hand and made a few elaborate gestures to be sure Arista noticed his weaving. Then, he called the River. Two full beds of flowers transformed their colors to perfectly match the two blossoms in his hand.

Arista's eyes widened in surprise, but that was soon replaced by an unnerving glitter Kala noticed at once. The Queensister licked her lips nervously, covering quickly with a twisted smile. "Another Sorcerer in the palace. Does the King know?"

Kala put her fingers to her lips, "Sh-h-h, our secret." She put her arm back on Simen and the two walked back along the garden path.

Arista smiled again. Her suspicions about Simen were confirmed. He was more than just a Healer, he was a Sorcerer of merit, one well worth a feast. All she needed was the right opportunity to find him alone. Here in the palace? Why not? The halls were abuzz with activity during the coronation celebrations. Even if he screamed, no one would notice. How often was he alone? Then she reconsidered. The right herbs could send even the strongest man to bed early. Jada had left her with several packets of most effective sleeping potions. All she needed to do was slip some into one of Simen's drinks at the party and then follow him to his bed. As long as she could divert the Juris, it stood a good chance of working. The party was only two spans away and she needed to hurry to prepare the potion.

What she did not know was that Jyp was keeping a close eye on her. When she left the dining hall to go to her rooms, he cloaking himself with an illusion so he looked like a mere servant, followed close behind. He was able to peer through a crack in the door, to watch her pull her leather bag out from under the bed, pull out a packet of herbs and start to mix them into small vial filled with amberwine.

"So, she plans to drug me, does she?" Simen said when Jyp told him what he'd seen. "Then I will need to take some extra precautions. Don't tell Kala," he added. "The less she knows, the better. She is far too honest to carry on the pretense all the way through to the end. Just make sure you get the King to my rooms in time to see Arista attack me. As for the rest, we'll just leave that to the River."

"You're sure it will all work?"

"Not at all," Simen laughed. "But anything is worth a try."

*****

Gareth was having a hard time being sociable during the endless schedule of celebrations of his ascension. It didn't help that attendance was sparser than expected and that many of the guests were not particularly enthusiastic. Most of the people at this party were petty lords who had benefited by various tax laws Gareth had initiated in his father's behalf. He insisted the rich needed to pay lower taxes in order to have extra money to hire more workers. None of it had worked because the lords had put the surplus money into their already bulging treasure stores, leaving the poor unemployed. A few other guests included some of the overseer contractors who were still working on his battlefield. Their focus of conversation included suggestions as to how to expand the field, adding enough new projects to keep them funded until at least the start of Chillmonths.

Most of the women in attendance were already married, and far too shy to talk with him about much more than their husband's successes or the sights of the city. Totally bored with them, Gareth sought out Kala, who at least had a mind of her own and was not afraid to speak it.

"Jur Kala," he said as he approached her. "I understand you will be staying on for a time to help with the transition to the new court."

"I have been so ordered by Grandisite," Kala replied as she sipped a goblet of amberwine.

"I would have thought it would be your own decision, for the sake of Turan, of course."

"I would just as soon be off in the Lesser Provinces, My Lord, where the rulers care about what happens to the common people."

"That smacks of an insult, Madam," Gareth said, taking a pastry from a passing tray and stuffing it into his mouth. When he continued, a few crumbs spit out of his mouth. "I plan on being at least as good a King as my father."

"Large shoes to fill, Sur. Your father was a fine man."

"I thought, unless I am mistaken, that it was your opinion he was mad."

"Where did you hear such a thing?"

"My servants have trained ears, My Lady. Those wise enough to be loyal to me listen well."

Kala shrugged. "Your father was very sick this last circle. He had forgotten many things and was often confused. Your Healers were helping him a great deal, but in the end, healing his mind was proving harder than healing his body." She took a piece of fruit and nibbled on it.

"My Healers have limited skill," Gareth said. "If I had some of more talent here, perhaps my father would still be alive and I would be a happy man."

"Because of your father?" Kala asked, taking another bite of the fruit. Her green eyes studied him carefully as he answered. Even without her Sight, she was able to read the truth behind his reply.

"Let me just say a good Healer, one worth his skill, would make me a happy man."

"My Simen has some talent in the Art," Kala said.

"Does he, indeed?" The King asked, clearly intrigued. "Where is he, I'd like to speak to him."

Kala glanced around the room and saw Jyp, pointing towards the hall. She followed his gaze to see Arista heading for the doors.

"Excuse me a moment, Sire. I need to ask Master Jyp if he's seen Lord Simen. I don't see him in the room anywhere." She hurried over to Jyp. "What's wrong?"

"She put some kind of potion in Simen's drink. He said he needed to go lie down and now Arista's headed upstairs after him. It's time. Can you get the King?"

"Potion?" When Jyp nodded, Kala's heart lurched. If Arista had used some kind of herb on Simen, there was no telling what effect it might have on his reason. Drugged, he was in serious danger. She rushed back over to Gareth. "Your majesty, Lord Jyp says Simen has gone to his rooms and would be pleased to speak with you now if you have the time. Something about needing privacy to offer you some service or other. He said it was a good time to honor your coronation."

Gareth smiled. "This gathering will not miss me. Take me to this Healer of yours."

*****

Once she had put the potion in Simen's wine, all Arista had to do was wait. When she saw him start to sway a little on his feet, she moved to his side. "My Lord, are you all right? Too much wine, perhaps?"

Simen put his hand to his brow, "Tired all of a sudden. I can hardly keep my eyes open. Too many parties in too many days."

"It can be a bit wearing," Arista agreed. "Perhaps you should go upstairs to your room to lie down. I'll make excuses for you if anyone asks."

He nodded numbly and left the room, his gait unsteady.

Arista waited until he'd reached the stairs, counted the twenty steps in her head, gave him another forty to reach his bedroom and then followed. She took her time, hoping to find him already asleep when she reached the room. At the door, she paused for a moment, looked up and down the hall to make sure no one was watching and then slipped inside.

Simen was lying sprawled on the bed, his boot still on, his blue tunic partially unlaced as if he'd started to undress, then just given up. His left arm was thrown up over his head.

Convenient, Grella thought. Arista hesitated, wanting to stare at him for a moment. Grella indulged her. Even asleep, he was a handsome man, his features well cut, his body lean but muscled. She threw three dark coils out, one for his left hand, one for each booted foot, lashing him to the bed. Then as silently as she could, she moved to the bed and lifted his right hand to the bedpost, lashing it with the final coil. Her hand trembled slightly when she touched him as if there were some kind of strange connection to his flesh. Her heart quickened.

No. This was not the plan. She needed to do it all quickly. Yet he was too beautiful, too alluring. She pulled the laces of his tunic away, her hands caressing his muscled chest, stroking him gently. "So pretty," she whispered. "Now mine, all mine."

Simen's eyes flew open at her touch and he started to cry out, but she stilled him with a quick chanting. His mouth opened and closed helplessly as he struggled against the black bonds.

"Now, now, don't worry. Are all Sorcerers so beautiful? The boy was lovely too, but you are a man. I do wish I could spend more time with you now, but I shall save you for later. When I have True Life, I will find you again and satisfy myself with your manhood. Now, I must move quickly. You are all I need." She pulled out a dagger from the bodice of her burgundy gown and traced its edge with her finger. "Sharp," she said. "Always better when it's sharp."

She raised her hand and plunged down, slicing into his stomach.

The door flew open. Gareth stood there, his eyes wide with shock as Jyp pushed past and raised his hand.

"No!" Grella screamed, raising the dagger for another blow.

Spellfire flew from Jyp's fingers, striking her a moment before the blade hit home. She screamed again, in agony this time as the Magic flame seared into her. Arista's body crumpled to the floor as a whirlwind of inky blackness spewed out of it, twisting in grotesque battle against sparks of silver and white. Then with a horrible cry, the Shadow dissolved into a pile of dark ash on the floor, mixing with the crimson puddle of Simen's blood, spilling out from the gash in his stomach.

Kala cried out, "Jyp, do something! He's bleeding."

The young Sorcerer rushed over to the bed, sidestepping the withered, wrinkled body lying at his feet. "He's dying," he said as soon as he touched Simen. "I can't do anything."

"No!" Kala sobbed. "It's wrong, it's all wrong."

Gareth stood passively at the door. Then he shrugged and turned away. "I suppose this means I won't be Healed after all." Then he walked away.

Beneath Jyp's hands, Simen's body started to waver, its outline becoming indistinct. A moment more, and it too crumbled into ash, in the way of all Magicians' deaths.

Kala fell to her knees.

"By the Hand, somebody close the door before anyone else comes in," a voice said from the other side of the bed curtains.

"Simen?" Kala said, looking up, her eyes red with tears. The door swung shut behind her and she heard its lock snap in place. She saw Simen emerge from the corner, his hand raised to towards the door.

"There," he said. "now we won't be disturbed."

"Well done, my friend," Jyp said. "Even I could not tell the difference between reality and that reflection. You will have to teach me how to create such an effective illusion."

Simen walked over to Kala and offered her his hand. "My brother is not the only Magician who can create a Follyman out of thin air," he said, pulling her to her feet. "I doubt, though that my Magic is quite the match to his, but it did the job. Although, I must say, it was a bit harder than I expected."

"It wasn't you…on the bed," Kala said, her voice faltering. Feeling suddenly weak she leaned into him to stay upright.

He put his arm around her waist and helped her to a chair to sit down. "I'm sorry. We didn't want to tell you. It had to look real all the way through and you are too honest a woman to hide your true feelings. If you'd known you might have given us away."

She smoothed the skirt of her pale green gown with trembling hands. "I hope I am not such a fool as that."

"Not a fool, just too honor-bound to the truth."

"You'll have to leave the palace, you know," she said. "Gareth thinks you're dead."

"Just as well," Simen replied. "After your telling him about my skill as a Healer, I'm better off somewhere else. Otherwise I'd be the focus of his attention and lose all the advantage we have of my spying on him."

"How can you spy if you're not here?"

"I can be here anytime I want," Simen assured her. "My skills from the Way are not limited to creating a reflection of myself. Those same illusions can easily disguise me so I can't be recognized. For now, though, I'll be going to Cuver Street to stay with Jada. The Counsel has some good Inns for wayward Sorcerers and I intend to take advantage of their hospitality."

"Jada is wise to the workings of the Palace," Jyp said. "She's the one who sent me here. She worked as a servant for years, keeping Gailvarg honest in whatever ways she could conjure. When she left, all was well, and the King had become the good Master the city admired. It was only when he began to falter that she sent me. We knew Gareth was the one to target, so I became his confidant."

"Jyp pretended to help Gareth when Jamus and Salene were here. You've heard those stories, I know."

"Ah, the Prince and the Bocart," Kala said, her nerves steadier now as the explanation started to make some sense.

"Exactly," Simen said. "We know Gareth was poisoning his father. We know can also surmise that Arista's arrival in Aberdeen was part of his plan to finish what he'd started."

"Arista….the Shadow, whoever she was…had a bag full of herbs with her. I found out a few days ago that she had gone to Jada to learn how to use them. It made me suspicious, but it wasn't until your Vision with Sorty confirmed it."

"So that's why she was in the South Quarter?"

"Jada said she had a most unusual collection of rare herbs, many of them quite dangerous. She said the woman has absolutely no idea what to do with them. She took the worst of them away but left the palion because it is unique in the herblore, both a restorative and a poison."

"She had no idea what Arista was planning," Simen told her. "I don't suppose it would have made any difference in the end, anyway. Jyp tells me the King was fading despite everything he was doing."

"It might actually have been a blessing in its own way," Jyp said. "It would have taken months for Gailvarg to die otherwise. The madness you saw in him was just the least of what he'd have to go through before his circle closed."

Kala shook her head. "To think Gareth's murdering him was a merciful end."

Simen walked to the dresser and pulled out a pile of belongings. He packed them in his saddle bag. "I'll leave the rest here. It won't look so suspicious if you have to get rid of my things."

"What about Arista's body?" Kala asked. "Now that the Shadow's done with it, it's aged beyond recognition."

"A quick funeral for a murderess won't evoke much suspicion," Jyp said. "Besides, I used Spellfire. We can just char her a bit more and no one will notice."

Kala gasped. "You can't mean that. It's horrible."

"Practical," Jyp replied. "You go on, see Simen off and I'll take care of things here. I'll use the bed sheets to wrap her up, that way no one will notice the lack of blood on them."

Kala and Simen sneaked out the west exit of the palace, their leaving unnoticed as the party seemed to have gotten boisterous since they'd left. Once Simen left, she went back inside to make her excuses to the guests. Considering the circumstances, she hoped no one would notice her absence.

Gareth had other ideas. As soon as she appeared at the door, he made a grand show of rushing over to take her in his arms, offering dramatic comfort for her loss. "You poor dear, losing a companion like that. I didn't expect you to come back down after that horrible ordeal. I've told everyone about it. They are all tears for your friend. I have no idea what my Auntie was doing. She was such a sensible soul. Do you think my father's madness was contagious?"

Kala wriggled out of his embrace, shaking off the touch of him, and shook her head. "Master Jyp thinks she was bewitched by Shadows. As you well know, there are reports of them in the city."

"You are quite calm after such a dreadful experience," one of the ladies said. "I would be too shaken to even be able to stand, much less come back to the party."

"I am Prime Juris," Kala said. "I have been trained by the Masters of Grandisite to retain my composure in all times of trial. I will save my weeping for my private rooms."

"Did you love him?" the Lady asked, twirling a lock of her dark hair with her finger, as she leaned into the arms of a well dressed Lord. "I would die myself if anything happened to my dear husband."

"Lord Simen and I were friends," Kala said.

"How horrible it must have been," another lady dressed in a gold shaenis gown perfectly cut for her thick body offered from the side. Already a little crowd was clustering around Kala. "The King said Lady Arista had a dagger. There must have been a lot of blood. However did you not faint at the sight of it?"

"I closed my eyes," Kala said, stepping back. But Gareth was behind her and she was caught in the center of a far too interested group. "I didn't see anything after that."

"Oh, but the King said you cried out and begged Lord Jyp to help your friend."

"You must tell us all about it. It is too shocking to even think about, but to witness such a thing, my goodness, my goodness," another well-dressed woman said.

"I don't want to talk about it," Kala insisted, her eyes darting about the room seeking some kind of escape.

"You must," the first lady said. "The King has told such a dramatic tale already. We do need to hear more."

"By the Blood!" Kala shouted. "Simen is dead, the King's Aunt is dead and all you want is the thrill of hearing how they died. All right! It was ugly, horrible, disgusting. Do you want to know where she cut him? How deep the wound was? What detail will satisfy your sordid lust? Two people are dead and you haven't offered a word of mourning for them. Damn you all for your hard hearts. You're as bad as Shadows themselves." With that she spun on her heel, shoved Gareth aside, and marched from the room, leaving behind a group of slack-jawed women, staring after her in shocked surprise.

"Quite a display, My Lady," Jyp said as he intercepted her in the Hall. "It is said a Seer cannot but speak the truth. You are certainly blunt about it."

Kala took a deep breath before answering. "I am not usually that outspoken. I think the night has taken its toll on me."

"They deserved every word from what I heard," he replied. "Why don't you go up to your room and get some rest. I've taken care of the rest and I'll do my best to take care of those bocarts you left behind at the party. I could always use a little chanting to make them see the errors of their ways."

"Leave them alone, Jyp. They're Gareth's minions. We can't expect any better of them than we ever can of him. The worst part of it all is that I'm the one who handed him the crown."

"It's not your fault. According to the law you had no choice."

"It's Aberdal and all of Turan that will have to pay," Kala said, sighing heavily.

*****

After he left the palace, Simen rode straight to the Forgetful Friend. As he expected the inn was shuttered, the doors locked but as soon as he rode up, a young boy appeared from out of the shadows to take his horse. "Jest knock four times on the door. Wait and then knock two more," the boy told him. "They be expectin' ya."

Simen did as he was told and the door opened. "Master Simen, welcome," Jada said from one of the tables. Come, sit. Share a brew and yer story. Word's already come down from the palace that you're dead and ya done took the Shadow with you. Surprised it took ya so long to git here."

"You already know what happened?"

"Little runners have fast feet," Jada said, sliding easily out of the common tongue. "We have a good network. So it was that Lady after all. I should have known something was akilter when she came to me with those herbs. I told Jyp to keep an eye on her. Never thought she was Shadow, though. Taught me a lesson I won't soon forget. Here now, have some of Mistress Bene's roast to fill that hole in your stomach." She laughed. "Now isn't that the strangest thing? There is no hole in your stomach."

"The Lady punctured my illusion," Simen told her. "I must admit it was quite effective."

"I dare say so. Was that Keep Magic you used to fool her? I don't remember even Master's lessons covering that."

"A trick or two I picked up in the Way," Simen explained. "Not for the faint of heart, but useful."

"Brave man uses any means," Jada said. "So, we're one Shadow less, are we? How many does that leave?"

"Still the two men you were looking for, and no idea where to look for them."

"Let's see, the Lady. She called herself Grella when we first met. She was here at the Friend with a companion. Strapping fellow, warrior. Knight of the Hand if I recall. Said his name was Dax."

"The King's General?"

"Aye, from what our runners say. Never thought much about it. Then again, I never thought the Lady was a Dark One either. I'd say we'd best keep an eye on him, then."

"Warn Jyp. He'll tell Jur Kala. Dax won't be an easy target either. We do need to know what he's doing here. As far as I know, Shadows don't usually settle down in one place."

"Leading the King's army, no less," Jada said. "Bit of a worry."

"When Kala used her Sight on the new King she saw some disturbing Visions. We were going to talk to you about a scrying."

"I'm not a Master Visioner, but I do know one in the city. Mistress Katrin. She's not far from here. Her sister, Kadrid lived in Magiskeep. You might have known her."

"My brother knew her well," Simen said. "If her sister has the same talent, we will be able to get all the answers we need. Can we visit her tomorrow?"

"You go upstairs and get some rest. When a man's been dead as long as you have, he needs a good night's sleep," Jada said, winking at him. "We'll go see Katrin in the morning. She'll be expecting us."

*****

Dax paced his quarters in frustration. Grella's destruction had hit him harder than he'd expected and while he did not actually feel any grief for her loss, he was upset. He had found pleasure in having an ally close at hand and they had planned on hunting together. Now, the fool woman had spoiled it all by trying to take prey here in the castle. He supposed there was some twisted logic to it for her, at least. One more Sorcerer would have been enough to satisfy her for all eternity.

Curse it, for one less Sorcerer in the palace meant one less opportunity for him. There were still Jyp and Edra, of course, but after what happened, Jyp would be on alert, and Edra was too much of an ally.

He was left with either finding sorcery somewhere else or seeking out six more mortals of his own. And, on his own. Melthus was already sated, having the freedom to roam all of Turan to hunt, while he was stuck within the city limits. The new King had developed the annoying habit of visiting him at all spans with some sort of nonsense or other. Dax suspected there was more to the visits than it appeared, especially when Gareth showed up wearing nothing but a loose nightrobe, but he couldn't quite figure it all out. Had the Prince been a woman, it might have made sense, but this?

Still, it made it more and more difficult for him to leave the palace at night to hunt. His position as General of the Royal Army had become too valuable to risk. Every day he was managing to turn at least one or two soldiers to the Darkness with promises of wealth or even immortality, neither of which he ever intended to bestow. The poor fools were so greedy they believed his promises and then, once they sealed the bargain and bore the mark of the dragon—his thumbprint on their palms—it was too late for them to change their minds. Once touched by his Magic, they belonged to Tamor, ready, willing and able to throw down their lives for Blackwing.

Shadows and their Magic were effective warriors in battle, but mortal fighters had their uses, particularly in fighting the common people. Putting down rebellions without killing all the enemy provided victory and the conquered so the victor would still have a populace to rule.

Thus, Dax taught his soldiers both the skills for the grand battlefield as well as effective methods for capturing farms and villages without slaughtering the entire population.

The royal army was not huge. It consisted of twenty-eight squadrons of twenty-eight foot soldiers each. Twenty-eight elite cavalrymen in the King's personal entourage—the Scarleteers-- added to the general number and the plan was, once Edra secured more horses, to mount at least another twenty-eight riders to join the main army as the start of a full complement of knights, twenty-eight to each squadron. Dax would have ordered the men differently, of course, and recruited many more, but Gareth's obsession with twenty-eight kept his ambition in check. The only saving grace was that the new King could not count the number of Shadows Tamor would send to bolster their numbers. For now, his forces would do.

There were certainly enough warriors to bring Aberdeen into submission and, as they marched across the provinces towards Magiskeep, he was convinced more and more recruits would join up. The red and gold uniforms, polished armor, and status of royal patronage was a powerful attraction to all the malcontents in the Kingdom. Thieves and beggars alike would readily join the brigade along its line of march.

Fortunately, it looked as if there would be no opposition to whatever Gareth decided to do in his desire to destroy the Sorcerers. The city had no local militia and had been at peace for so many circles, he doubted there were even weapons in most homes. By the time the citizens realized the King was marching to war, Aberdeen would be under military rule and no one would be able to protest.

The plan was flawless. Gareth could do whatever he wanted. And so could Gambel.

PART 2

XVIII

Edra and his gang had ridden hard, moving quickly through Lovental and into Telma in less than eight winds. Now they were near Delran's Keep where the horses he needed were stabled. Although his purse was heavy with coin, he had decided to spread the wealth among his new compatriots to guarantee their loyalty rather than spending it on honest purchases. Like most of Turan, a lasting peace had made the Lords soft and unprepared for combat. He was sure Delran was like all the rest. Getting the horses he wanted was going to be an easy task.

Yet, close to the foothills of the Rim, Delran was not a completely easy mark. Bandits had roamed the lands around his hold for enough circles that he did have some plan of defense.

When one of his watchers raced into the yard warning of Edra's approach, he took the first action to preserve the safety of his people. "Joss, take all the women into the house, to the safe room upstairs. Set whatever wards you can with your Magic to keep them safe. Get the younger lads up there too, Jebe and Nobby. Go now, and hurry."

Joss ordered the women upstairs then hurried out to the stables to get the boys.

"I ain't leaving Shimmy," Jebe insisted. "If there's gonna be a fight, I gotta be here wid 'im."

"You have to come with me, Jebe," Joss said. "You won't do Shimmer any good if you get yourself killed. He can take care of himself."

The boy shook his head and ran to the ladder where he climbed up into the loft to hide. Joss nearly followed, but when the shouts from the yard became louder, warning that the riders were in the lane, he raced back to the house to protect the women as Delran had ordered.

Meanwhile, Delran had armed four of his men with swords from the house while another five stood by his side with common axes and shovels. If he'd had more time, he would have called reinforcements from the fields, but this would have to do. If these were the usual kind of ruffians, his little defense would be more than enough to get rid of them.

Edra and his band trotted up the lane and stopped at the gate, facing Delran and his men. "We need horses," Edra said.

"I sell horses to honest men," Delran replied.

"We didn't come to buy," Edra said. "I am Edra, emissary of the King and I come in His name to procure animals for his cavalry. I want to assess your stock and go back to Aberdeen with those I consider fit for the royal stables."

"King Gailvarg has always been a good customer."

"Gailvarg is dead. Have you not heard? Word reached me along the way here that Prince Gareth now sits on the throne as Sovereign. His purse does not pay for what the royal seat needs. As his subject, it is your duty to give him what he wants."

"My horses are my livelihood, Sur. I surrender my wealth to no man. I proclaim my right to defend what is mine."

One of Delran's men stepped forward, his sword at the ready. Edra raised his hand and sent a bolt of spellfire at the defender. The man screamed as his body crumpled to ash at Delran's feet.

"Sorcerer..." Delran sputtered, backing away for the first time in his life.

"Are your lives, your household and all that you own worth the price of a few animals? I do not intend to fight you for what I want. I will simply take it as it pleases me, and leave the rest in ash if that is what you want. Now, whose want is greater, eh?"

"Put down your weapons," Delran ordered to his men. "We cannot fight the Magic. Not now. Perm, take the Sorcerer to the stables. Let him see the horses. He can take whichever ones he chooses."

"My Lord?" Perm asked, "Are you sure?"

"Quite sure," Delran replied through gritted teeth. "I cannot jeopardize the entire Keep for the sake of my horses. We can always breed more beasts. Men are another matter altogether."

Two of Edra's Loyals dismounted and headed for the barns, while Perm lead the others to the stables, leaving Jain behind to guard Delran's band. Pitiful Sorcerer as he was, he could still command the Spellfire enough to keep them at bay and when one of them tried to move against him, he set a blast at the man's feet to prove the point.

"Hey, lookie what we found in the barn," Donner said as he shoved one of Delran's serving girls into the aisle in front of him, "Hiding in the hay, she was."

"Let me go," Helia whimpered as he pushed her down on her knees. "The Lord'll make you pay if you hurt me."

Edra smiled. "One woman? Where are the rest? There must be more." He grabbed Perm's arm and spun the man to face him. "Where are the rest?"

"Where you will never find them, Sorcerer," Perm replied. "Lord Delran is not such a fool to leave his women unprotected."

"So, stashed away, eh? Ah, well, she will have to do. I don't have time to waste searching this dirty hold. Go on, have your fun with her while I conduct our business."

Ruddick pulled Helia to her feet and dragged her to one of the empty stalls. "Ya want us ta save some fer you, Milord?"

Edra waved him off, "Don't bother, Ruddick. There are plenty of inns on the way back to Aberdeen. I'm sure I'll have my fill then."

"How dare you!" Perm shouted trying to break free of Edra's grip. "Leave her alone. I swear...I'll...."

"You'll what, little man?" Edra snarled as he drew his dagger and pulled Perm towards him. "Did I thank you for showing us to the stables yet? No? Then accept my appreciation now." He yanked Perm hard into the blade, jamming it in and up until it reached the man's heart. The body dropped at his feet even as Helia began to scream in earnest as one by one Edra's gang had their way with her.

Edra casually strode along the aisle, looking over the horses. There were forty stalls in the stable, and forty beautiful animals, all better than any he had seen in all Aberdal. When he reached the end, he whistled in surprise. There stood a magnificent shining colt, gold and silver all in one. "Well, well, my pretty. At last I have found myself a suitable mount. You are going to be mine."

Suddenly a little boy dropped from the loft above into the stall where he spread his arms defiantly to protect the horse. "Ya leave 'im be! This is my Shimmer an' 'e ain't goin' nowheres."

"Well, well, well, a mini-warrior. So this is your horse, is it? No more, little man. He's been claimed in the name of the King."

Jebe's eyes darted wildly about, then he spun around to face Shimmer, "Run Shimmy. Get out of here." The colt looked at him uncertainly, then swirled into a whirlwind of gold and silver mist and disappeared only to reform at the far end of the aisle where he stood, waiting for another command from his master.

Edra grinned. "Chanted is he? All the better." He lunged
forward and pinned Jebe in his arms. "Tell him to obey me, or he'll
lose his master. I swear I'll kill you if you don't do as I say."

Helia's screams had faded to sobs and whimpers.

"Lemme go," Jebe said, trying to twist out of Edra's grip.

"Call the horse."

"Ya cain't have 'im. He's mine."

"Tell you what, little man. You're coming with us and your
colt will too. Otherwise, I will burn this stable down and the house as
well. Your friends will lose everything they have."

"Mam…," Jebe said softly.

"Your Mam too, wherever she is. I'll not even look for her if
you come along quietly and bring your horse with you. Understand?"

Jebe nodded numbly. "Come, Shimmy. It's all right. We's
gonna take a trip now. I'll be right wid ya, don't ya worry."

The colt pawed the ground nervously, but soon walked back
over to the stall to wait while Edra put a halter and lead on him.
"Lads, come on," the Arculan ordered, "It's time to go. Pull up your
pants and pick a horse to ride back. We'll leave the drays behind.
We're taking all the horses we can find here. Now let's get going.
It's a long ride back to Aberdeen."

The men emerged from the stall, Beryl still lacing his
breeches. Then they chose new mounts, saddled up and headed back
out into the yard. Edra tossed Jebe up behind Jain once the young
Sorcerer was mounted.

"Remember we have the boy," Edra said, pointing his sword
at Delran, "just in case you have any ideas about ambushing us on
the way. I am rather more skilled at carving than killing, just so you
know."

"I won't forget this," Delran swore, shaking his fist at the
Sorcerer. "This isn't the end of it."

"Surely not," Edra agreed. "It is a beginning of sorts. Come,
men, let's go. Keep the horses together. We don't want to lose any
on the way back." With that he kicked his own horse in the flank and
sent him cantering off as the others moved to catch up.

It was all Delran could do to contain his rage. One man dead
and he didn't even want to think about what had happened in the
stable. Helia's cries had been testimony enough. As soon as the band
left the yard, he and the rest of his men ran to the barns.

They found Helia lying in a pool of blood, barely alive. Her
dress lay in tatters, her naked body curled on the floor, her hands
over her face. "Go to the house, and get Lurela and Minda," Delran
ordered as Benji knelt beside the stricken woman. "Don't touch her,

lad," Delran ordered as he pulled off his long tunic and handed it down to the stablehand. "Cover her gently and just stay by her side until the other women get here. She won't abide a man's touch right now." Then he straightened as one of the other stablemen approached him, his eyes wet with tears.

"Perm's dead, My Lord. Blade to the heart. Looks like it was quick, at least. He was a good man, my friend."

"He was," Delran agreed. "We'll do the best we can to give him due honor, Dom, but you know as well as I do we have more important things to do right now."

Dom nodded. "Aye, My Lord. If these men were indeed emissaries of the King, then the time has come to take measures against them."

"Tell Joss to go out to the north field and bring in the herd. We'll need horses. Ride yourself to Tulene as fast as you can to tell Lord Dale to set the fires. He'll understand. We'll meet in the city square in two days' time. That should give those from Doral and Lovental West time to meet us. Someone must have word about what's happening in Aberdeen by now if Edra knew of Gailvarg's death. I was a fool for not keeping in touch with Tulene myself."

"We've been at peace a long time, My Lord. There was no need to worry."

"I've let my guard down, Dom and now three good people under my protection have paid dearly for it."

"Don't forget the boy." Benji said.

"How can I? Make sure someone is with his mother, would you? We don't want her doing anything foolish. Keep her calm and assure her we'll get him back safely."

"I'll do my best, My Lord," Benji said, "but it would help if you were there."

"I need to pack my bag to ride," Delran said. "I'll see her later. For now, just tell her the Knights of the Hand have never failed to fulfill a promise."

*****

Rumors of war spread quickly through the Riders in Arcula. Peace had always provided pleasant respite, but to hardened warriors, the promise of battle stirred their hearts. It took Covane less than half a Sevenstin to gather nearly forty Riders to their cause with the promise of many more, some who had left the Cauge circles before, disgusted with Edra's rule. Now, with Arcula's safety once again in danger, they were eager to return to action.

The regular army roused as quickly, ready to defend the homeland against the Shadowlord.

Magiskeep's defense was another matter.

When Gaila explained plans to send troops West along with Jamus, some of the Generals were hesitant. Then, when they heard of Celsia's demands for a Searching, they became adamant. "Why should we risk our lives on foreign soil? If the Shadows attack Arcula, this is where we make our stand."

"What if Wolla's Searching suggests otherwise," another General asked.

"Then we make our own decisions. Some here don't hold much with the Mard, no matter who calls it, be a Scryer or a Sorcerer. The freedom we won when we overthrew the Cauge is not taken lightly."

"Lord Jamus proved himself to us on the battlefield defending Arcula," Gaila said. "Do we not owe him something in return?"

"We owe him thanks, no more. Besides, it was the Dragon who defended us."

"Only because of his rider," Gaila said. "She did not fly alone."

"We hear what Wolla says, then we decide."

The Seer's cottage had been built since Jamus' last visit. It had a new roof and fresh coat of paint as well as carefully sculpted flower beds and neatly trimmed bushes lining the cobbled walkway to the front door.

"The New Order wanted to give Wolla something for all she's given the city with her Visions. She wouldn't accept any money, so the sent a crew of craftsmen out to give her a home in the city.

"It suits her," Jamus said. "As I recall she is ever ready with a smile."

"And a prank," Covane replied, "so watch yourself."

Celsia and Densil, along as witnesses to Wolla's Vision, had fallen a few paces behind. Whey they caught up, she stepped past and knocked on the cottage door. "Mistress Wolla, it's Car Celsia of the New Order. We're here for the Visioning."

A moment later, the door opened and Wolla peered out, "So ye be. Oh lookie, it's me first love back at last!" She opened the door wide and pulled Jamus in by the sleeve of his tunic. "Dragonlord come to see me again? I was wondering how long it would take ye to realize your life was rift without my loving."

Jamus grinned. He'd had enough of Wolla's "wrapping" as she called it, to know she was trying to play him for the fool. He decided to turn the tables on her. "I was indeed bereft, My Love. My wife is a wonderful woman, but not half the lass you are. I've had an ache in my loins for some proper bedding, so I thought I'd come back to Arcula for you."

Celisia, Densil, and Covane gasped, but Wolla started to laugh heartily. "You aren't going to wrap Old Wolla with your foolery, Kiselor, but you sure did shock your companions here. 'T'was a good one, I must admit. Seems you've lost a bit of your modesty since I last saw you."

"I've lived a bit more than I'd intended," Jamus replied. "This world has a way of changing a man."

"Even without my Swirlypot, I can tell that. Well, don't you all stand there with your mouths hanging open, I've set chairs by the scrying table for the lot of you and fresh sheets on the bed of whichever of you fine gentlemen decides to spend the waning spans naked with me."

Covane's Rider's instincts kicked in. "By your will, Mistress. If it's Rider you desire in payment, I honor the code."

Wolla grinned again, and sidled up to Densil. "I was thinking I'd like a more mature man. I've had my eye on Denni's backside for a long time. Always bending over his gardens he is. Now that I've seen the face that matches the bottom, don't find it any less appealing. A man so skilled with tending beds should be good in one himself, eh?"

Age had nothing to do with how much a man could blush. "I wouldn't know, Mistress. I am not a Rider."

"Well, anytime you want to trial yourself, I'm a fair judge of men," Wolla replied tugging a little at the low neckline of her simple cambric gown as leaned down to sit in her chair. "Bit hot for this time of the season," she said, patting at the seat of the chair next to her for Densil to sit as well. She undid one lace of her bodice. "Be a lot cooler after Weswin. Good night for sleeping, methinks."

Jamus sat to her right, trying hard to keep a straight face. Somehow, he suspected this was not Densil's first visit to Wolla's cottage. "We do need a scrying, My Lady."

"So be it," Wolla said, nodding to Celisia and Covane to sit across from her. "I ken the scrying be for the Dragonrider here? He never comes just to visit."

"I would, Wolla," Jamus protested, "but it never seems to work out that way."

"Life takes its own road in the Rivers, Kiselor. The waters run dark in times like these. Talked to the Swirly a Sevestin ago and saw just Shadows. Knew the time'd be someone would come to my cottage. Let's see what Swirly wants to tell us today."

She and Jamus stared into the slivrin pot as the waters inside it spun in a whirlpool down into its depths. Jamus felt the Vision pulling at him, drawing him into the currents, as if he too could see with Wolla's eyes. He let his mind open as he'd learned in Grandisite.

Three armies marched across a grassy plain below the foothills of snow-covered mountains. One marched east, horsemen and foot soldiers. The second marched west, riders, foot soldiers and silver-robed figures gliding as if on water. The third march north, golden robed images towering over a line of small silver figures ranked before them.

They were not marching toward each other for it seemed they traveled on separate planes, each going forward with the same focused intensity to meet the enemy.

Above, a dark cloud hovered, black and heavy blotting out the sun.

Wolla's voice began to murmur in his ear, soft, persistent, in the singsong rhythm of a prophecy,

"Three fronts on the battlefield
Three to save the light.
One with royal majesty
Twisted by the night.
Two with silver water's pow'r
Shall the battle be
Mortal soldier, on the front
Seeking to stay free.
Three the mighty Blackwing's goal
Silver, gold and all
Swallowing the purest light
Lest the Circle fall.
Victory cannot be won
Without sacrifice.
One whose love has no compare
He shall pay the price."

There was a great roar, and a clash of arms, blades and axes clanging against shields and armor. Horses screamed, men shouted battle cries falling away to cries of pain. Above the fields, the clouds themselves seemed to clash, the golden sun and silver moon slashing beams into the darkness, no longer passive masters of the sky, but chargers now, forces refusing to be ruled by the weather, but rather to rule it themselves, denying the storm.

Then, the Vision exploded into a blinding white light, consuming all, blotting out even the waters themselves.

Leaving both Seer and Sorcerer breathless, falling back against their chairs.

"So tired of riddles," Jamus said at last, scrubbing his face with his hands.

"Swirly never talks plain," Wollas said.

"What does it mean?" Celisia asked.

"Blackwing rises," Wolla said. "The Shadows are preparing to wage war. That much is certain."

"The battle will be waged on three fronts," Jamus continued. "If I understand well enough, one will be with the Silver River in Arcula, one with the Gold in Magiskeep. It's the third I don't quite follow. It seems as if the Royal army will be waging the third, but why? King Gailvarg is a peaceful monarch."

"Suppose the Shadows attack in the rest of Turan?" Densil asked. "Won't they have to defend the other side of the Rim?"

"It didn't seem they were the defenders, but rather the attackers."

"The King battling his own people?"

"My brother is in Aberdeen. He may know something. I have to contact him."

"Sending messages will take forever," Celisia said. "Do we have time?"

"There is no time in the Way," Jamus replied. When he saw her confused frown, he shrugged. "The Vision has no urgency, yet. There have been no signs of Shadows this side of the Rim yet, but we do need to take precautions. There are remote farms and villages in Magiskeep, and here in Arcula as well. If Tamor has sent spies or emissaries, he would start in places where they'd escape notice. We need to spread our defenses far and wide to keep watch."

"We still have to settle the matter of whether or not Arcula is going to join forces with Magiskeep and send you men at arms."

Jamus looked at Wolla. "Mistress, you Saw as well as I, perhaps better. Three fronts to the battlefield. Which was Magiskeep?"

"The Gold and Silver," Wolla said. "Or so it seemed. The army marching north. No warriors, just Sorcery."

"But Gold and Silver," Jamus said. "An alliance of the two Rivers?"

"Perhaps. If so, all you need from Arcula is Mard."

Jamus chewed his lip thoughtfully, his brow furrowed. Serenec? Did his Mages in the Keep need to learn from a Master how to control Spellfire? It had made sense when he'd thought of it before and now it made even more sense. "Arculan Magic holds the secrets to the Dragon's Tongue, what we call Spellfire. It's the only weapon that works against Shadows. I have more than enough Magicians in my Keep to hold off a battalion of Shadows. They just need to be trained."

"Then you do not need our army," Celisia said.

"No," Jamus replied. "It seems Arcula will need its soldiers. Your Firemasters are trained from the last great battle, but mine are not."

"I'm not sure the Order will want to lose any of them."

"We will consult," Densil countered. "This decision is not ours alone to make. The rest of the Order and the people have a right to speak."

"Very well," Celisia agreed.

After bidding Wolla farewell, Celisia and Covane headed out the door. The Seer tugged at Jamus' arm to hold him back even as she winked at Densil, who was lingering by the hearth. "Ye have friends in Arcula. Look to your warriors, Kiselor. They are sworn to you and will not desert you."

"Thank you, Mistress." He looked over at Densil. "Master Densil, I take it you have further business with the good lady. I see that your horse is bedded for the night, if you'd like."

Densil shrugged. "That's up to the lady."

"The lady," Wolla replied, "is pleased to have the company."

With that, Jamus headed out the door, smiling more than he might have expected considering the rest of the news. At least, as far as anyone could tell, Tamor and the Dragon were not yet on the move. What worried him was the prophecy regarding the rest of Turan. For a moment he regretted leaving Densil inside, but, as Wolla had said, he did have friends in Arcula, and it was time to seek them out.

"Covane, do you know where Garv is billeted?"

"Last I heard he was west of the city. Little place called Talltree, not far from Landhold. Some of his men work for Mardel Elyese. Four days ride from the city. I can take you there if you'd like."

"Tomorrow," Jamus said. "I think I need to talk to the Mardel too, so we can make a few days of it."

Covane smiled, "For me a few nights?"

"I take it you and the Mardel have been sharing time together since I've been gone?

"She is a fine woman, Jamus. Being with her, I can almost understand how a man can truly be satisfied with only one woman in his life. I've been a Rider too long to know if I can change, but Elyese, well, she does make me think I could."

"People do marry in Arcula, don't they?" Jamus asked.

"The common people do. The Riders, the Mard? They've lived too long in self-indulgence to give of the pleasures status affords. Marriage locks two souls together, each surrendering freedom to be with the other. Can a person of power be so selfless?"

Jamus considered his words carefully before answering. How many times had the River forced him to leave Salene alone? Even now, he was here in Arcula without her. Yet, his thoughts were never far from her and Jarien. It was fear for their safety driving him even now. Certainly, the fate of Turan was at stake, but if his wife or son were in danger, he would abandon Turan's Way to save them first. "I would give up the whole world for my wife and child," he said at last.

*****

"I be sorry, MiLady," Becca said as she nestled Jarien back into his cradle. "But ma son, Jeb's havin' 'is first born. His wife Terra's a wee thing wid no 'sperience wid babes. She's a fine lass, mind ya, but not the kinda cook I be. Due in a Sevenstin, we reckon, an' I oughta be there fer 'em, ya know."

"Of course, Becca," Salene replied, "your family needs you. It's been wonderful having you here for Jarien, but I have plenty of people here at the Keep to help me. You go to Jeb and Terra and don't think twice about it. As soon as you're ready we'll have a coach to take you. Do you want Jeamel to go with you?"

"Bory no! Man's go half a deneret o'sense when it come ta babes. Iffen I had my way I'd send Jeb back here 'til the wee one's done come. Ain't nothing worse than a Pap hangin' 'round when woman's work ta be done."

Salene laughed. "Bless me for saying it, but Jamus was my rock when Jarien was born."

"Yer husband ain't like mos' men. Course ya already knows that. 'E's a good'un, 'e is." Becca nodded and tucked the blanket around Jarien's body. "I was thinkin' mebbe ya could take on Natale fer a spell ta watch the li'l one whilst ya be tendin' the business o' the Keep, eh?"

"Do you think she'd want to?"

"Worth askin'. I knew her Mam good an' she were a fine woman. Like ta think her daughter larned from her. Asides, she's too bright a lass ta be scrubbin' floors and the like. Why, she kin read 'n write as good as any Mage. Bet she knows some good tales she kin tell yer lad ta help put 'im ta sleep."

"I could use a good sitter for him now and then. Lady Rath is here, for now, but she does tend to disappear from time to time."

"Not sayin' much agin her, but the lady ain't got the warmest heart in the Keep. I s'pose that Scalewing blood don't make her the cuddly type, iffen ya knows what I mean. Babes need hugging sometimes."

"Yes they do," Salene agreed. As much as she appreciated Rath's intense devotion to watchin out for her and Jarien, she was more a guard than a nursemaid. Jarien deserved tender hands when she could not be with him. "I'll talk to Natale first chance I get. Right now, let's get you off to Jeb's."

When Becca had left to get her things from the cottage, Salene called one of the maids from the hall. "Can you find Natale and send her up here?" She asked. "And if you would, I need someone to tell Josep to send a carriage to Becca's house to take her to Southgate."

The maid hurried out and Salene sat in the chair next to Jarien's cradle. She rocked him gently, reveling in the hint of a smile on his face. How could anything so beautiful be hers? He was already starting to look like Jamus. Was he going to grow up to be as powerful? And what if he were? Was there room in the world for two Rivermasters?

She shivered. It was almost too much to bear. Every time their world touched perfection, something found a way to interfere.

Suddenly, she heard a voice calling to her. Where? It was Simen, and he was in the mirror.

"Simen, what is it? Is something wrong?"

In his room in the palace of Aberdeen, Simen had used the Way to open a portal to Magiskeep. "Is Jamus there?"

"No, he's in Arcula. He's worried, Simen. Rath thinks there's danger from the Shadows."

"She's right, I'm afraid," Simen replied. "They've already attacked people here in Arcula. King Gailvarg is dead and Gareth has taken the throne. He's been building an army for some months and rumors are spreading that he wants to get revenge on the Magic."

"Because of what I've done to him," Salene stated flatly. Is this what would come of the chanting she'd cast on the Prince?

"The whole of Aberdeen knows he deserved it," Simen assured her. "I don't think there's a woman in the city who'd want it any different. Kala thinks he's half lost his mind, like his father."

"Gailvarg?"

"It's too long a story, but the King had gone mad at the end, and it could well be Gareth suffers from the same affliction. Your spell was just a part of it all. He's obsessed with power, and Magiskeep is a threat to him."

"How can he attack across the Rim?"

"I don't think he's even considered that, but the way things are going here, it may not matter. There's a rebellion in the wind. I don't know what it will take to set things off, but it's coming. I wish Jamus were here."

"We're keeping watch here as well, Simen. That's why Jamus went to Arcula. Rath has warned us that the Black Dragon and Tamor are preparing for battle."

"So, it begins," Simen said. "All the prophecies coming true at once. Are you safe?"

"Safe as I can be with a Dragon hovering over me. I thought we'd have more time."

"When Jamus gets back, tell him to check the mirror. I'll be here a span before Sowin, every day, watching for him. We need to talk."

Salene nodded. "Tell Kala I miss her. I wish she were here." As soon as she said, it, she realized how true it was. The Seer was a good friend and one of the strongest women she had ever known. Between the two of them, no Shadow would ever have a chance. As Simen's reflection faded from view, she turned away. She did not see the dark form lurking in the far corner of the mirror where he had been standing.

Natale came into the room soon after. Dressed in a simple brown dress, she looked much younger than Salene had remembered when she'd first seen her. "You wanted to see me, My Lady?"

"Becca suggested you might be able to take her place as Jarien's nursemaid. She needs to take care of her own family. It's an easy job. I'm here most of the time anyhow, but now and then I need to tend to affairs of the Keep."

"I haven't tended a babe in many a circle," Natale said. Sorra was gloating. It couldn't be more perfect. The Sorceress was practically handing the child over to her. "I don't think I've forgotten how, though."

"Becca said you had a son."

Natale nodded sadly. "Lost him and his father in an avalanche." Sorra was surprised to feel an ache in her heart. Wearing the Flesh had some unexpected consequences. "It took me circles to get over it."

"We never really recover from losses like that," Salene replied, thinking of her own lost baby. "We just learn how to live with the memory."

Natale curtsied, "Hopefully, then, memory will serve me well in caring for your son. I would be honored if you would accept me."

"Becca spoke highly of your mother."

Again Sorra felt a curious tug at her emotions, but she pushed it aside for Tamor's sake. "My mother was a special woman. I would like to think I have her gift with children."

"Becca was staying in the room across the hall. She's already taken her things so the room is free for you to move in. I'll ask some of the maids to help you."

"No need," Natale said. "I didn't bring much here to the Keep when I came. I've lived a simple life for a long time. When do you need me for your son?"

"Tomorrow will be soon enough," Salene said. "I've already attended to my duties today." She hesitated, "I did not tell you that you will not always be alone with my son. He has another caretaker who visits frequently. Lady Rath. Do you know of her?"

"I haven't been in the Keep for more than a Sevenstin, My Lady. Despite what many people think, gossip does not always travel here."

"Then I'd best warn you. The Lady is rather unusual. She is Dragon."

Sorra started along with Natale, one of the few times the two were truly one. "Dragon?"

"She transforms into a woman, thank the Hand. I don't know what we'd do if she tried to come in her true form. I'm so used to her Magic, I tend to forget about it myself. Just don't be surprised when she comes flying to the window."

Natale's wide eyes betrayed Sorra's shock. "Dragon," she repeated numbly.

Salene put her hand on Natale's arm, "It's truly all right, Natale. She cares for all of us here, especially Jamus. He is her rider and she is more loyal to him than even I can comprehend. She would never hurt anyone who was caring for his son. You'll get used to her quickly. Becca certainly did."

Natale took a deep breath as she glanced over to the window. Sorra's mind lurched. Dragons sensed Shadows keenly. One encounter with this Rath and her plan was doomed. She needed Tamor. "I'll do my best," she said at last. "I'd better settle myself in my room now. Please excuse me." She hurried out.

She pushed the door open into the room across the hall, relieved to see a tall dressing mirror in the corner much like the one in Salene's chamber. She stood before it, whispering over and over, "Tamor, My Lord, My Love, My All, hear me. Hear me. I am here. I need you. Find the Way. Listen to my call. I am here. I am here." It took several repetitions of the call before Tamor's image appeared in the looking glass before her.

"Why do you call now? Have you the babe?"

"Not yet, My Lord, but I have been given the duty as his nursemaid. The opportunity is near." She swallowed hard. "Yet I am afraid."

"You? Afraid? What need a Shadow fear from a child?"

"It's not the child I fear. It's the Dragon."

"Dragon? Blackwing?"

"No, one called Rath. She is here as caretaker. She has not yet seen me."

"And a good thing that," Tamor hissed. "She would see the darkness at once and all our plans could be unraveled. Must you see her?"

"I have no control over it, My Lord. She comes and goes as she pleases when she pleases. If I am with the babe when she does…"

"Then you need a ward," Tamor replied. "I can bind a chanting to obscure your Shadow, but be warned, it will only make the skin you wear stronger. Your will can weaken in the face of Flesher's emotions. You must resolve yourself to keep your Vow to me."

"I would never betray you, Tamor."

"Natale would," he said. "Her essence lingers in her skin. Lessen yourself, and she will grow more powerful. It would help if you could feed."

"It is difficult in the Keep. I am surrounded by Sorcerers."

"Leave the skin behind and go to the villages beyond. Find prey to refresh your strength. Leaving the skin will weaken it, even as you gain." He raised his hand to her and Sorra felt a stab in her heart as if someone had clutched it and squeezed. Gasping, she dropped to her knees as a dark weave enveloped her. "It is done," Tamor said. "The ward is set. The Dragon will not recognize you for

what you are. But remember, you must feed yourself so you will not
be lost."

"I will, My Lord," Sorra promised as she struggled back up
to her feet. When she looked back in the mirror, all she saw was
Natale's reflection.

It took two spans for her to settle into the room. Then she
headed to the dining hall for Evenmeal. Several of the maids she had
worked with congratulated her on her new status, rousing a strange
feeling of warmth. Sorra alerted, remembering Tamor's warning.
Friendships with mortals was a danger sign. She must not succumb.
She thanked her well-wishers, finished her meal quickly and went
back to her room to await nightfall. The sooner she feasted, the
better. This skin she wore was a potent mistress.

Norwin's turn brought a moonless night, perfect for hunting.
Sorra left the body on the bed, and slipped out into the darkness,
silently stalking the thick clouds. Freedom. Something she had not
experienced since taking on the skin. But Tamor's chanting had
given her to power to shed the Flesher's body at her will, not his.
Now she could hunt at will, unhampered by the weight of mortality.
She ran through the sky, relishing the liberty. Her eyes always
seeking for a place to land.

Then she bolted back, cowering against a bank of gray
wisps. There, off to the east, she saw a mighty scalewing, soaring
and diving. She watched in fascination as the Dragon swooped
down. There was a bleating cry and the creature rose up again, a fat
mountain goat in its talons. To her relief, the Dragon flew off again
well north, disappearing into the mountains.

"So the Dragon hunts as well tonight," she said. "We are
greater kin than I realized."

Inspired by the monster's display, she peered down and
spied a small farmhouse, set well away from the little village of
Tallridge. She stepped down and looked in the window. A man lay
on a wooden cot by the fire, with a little boy lying on a mat by his
side. Two. No more. Which first?

She opened the door and crept in. If the child cried out, the
father would waken. Better to silence him take the man by surprise
and finish the boy afterward. Quickly, she threw her coils about the
child, sealing his mouth shut with one wide tendril. His eyes flew
open, but he could not make a sound or move. Sorra put her finger to
her lips as her Shadow form resolved itself into a sinuous image of a
woman. Within a breath, she snaked out more dark lashes, binding
the man to the bed an instant before he woke trying to flail free. "No

point," Sorra whispered. "There is no escape. The question is whether I kill you first or your son."

"Take me," the man rasped. "Leave the boy."

Sorra shook her head. "I am most hungry. Grief adds season to the feast, I think. The child now, you as the main course." She grinned as she pulled the dark dagger from her belt. Pure conjuration of all the Shadow's thirst, the black blade plunged down, into the child's belly. He writhed once, then lay still as she dropped down beside him to feed.

The father howled as he strained uselessly against his bonds.

Sorra looked up, her mouth dripping with blood. "The young make fine appetizers. My hunger is greater than that. What will you give me for your life."

"Nothing, you shetark. You kilt ma son. I ain't got nothing left."

"So you wish to die?"

"No man wisht sech a thing, but when 'is life ain't worth a lick, 'e don't' wisht ta live."

"Plead, at least, a little," Sorra said, "I can make you do what I want."

"So be it," the farmer said. "T'ain't no matter."

"We shall see," Sorra said, tracing her blade around his nipples, slicing into his skin. When the farmer did not flinch, or cry out, she pressed harder into his breast. Again, he did not respond. "My, you are a brave one. Most men would cry for mercy."

"Dead men never do," he said. "Ya already took ma heart, ain't got no feelin's left."

"You aren't dead yet, dear one. The pain has just begun." As much as his restraints would allow, he shrugged and even smiled at her. Sorra's temper flared at his passivity. She carved into his stomach, her dagger ripping into his organs, and yet, he did not make a sound, except for one deep, relieved sigh. She screamed in rage and plunged her blade in again and again until his body lurched with one last gasping breath as he died. Furious, she fell on him in a savage feeding frenzy, gulping his blood as fast possible.

The taste was sour in her mouth--the first time a Shadow feast repulsed the diner.

XIX

His army marched back and forth across the field, between the obstacles for close order drill practice, each soldier matching stride for stride twenty-eight paces to each specific point. It had become a standing joke among the recruits who knew every street around the palace by the number of twenty-eight strides it took to navigate them.

"The TipTop Tavern's five twenty-eights from the palace," one man would say. "Not much of a hike for a quick brew if you've a mind."

"Take two twenty-eight more around the back and you'll find a good lass with a warm bed to share. TipTop ladies is fine ones bein' so close to the royal seat."

"Good thing they be at two twenty-eights and not a twenty-nine or they'd be awful short o' gittin' inta soldier's britches."

"Damn straight," another said. "Only trouble is, they got fourteen stairs up ta the beddin' floor."

"Good count," the other replied. "Fourteen ta go up, and fourteen ta go back down, long's yer still sober an' ya gots yer twenty-eight."

"All depends on how long ya take under the covers," the third said. "Take more'n twenty-eight plunges an yer all out fer another twenty-eight. Wears a man out, it does."

"N'e'er thought o' that," the first soldier said. "Guess I gotta build my stamina for the ladies, eh? Usually, wear myself out nigh on to twenty."

"Bit yer tongue, lad. Do twenty o' anythin' in the King's name an' yer gonna pull yer las' pay fer sure."

"Trader's Ark out by the docks gots twelve steps up to the whore loft," the first soldier said. "Far enough from the field to lose count, if you know what I mean."

"You go that far fer a lay?"

"Anywhere to get rid of the numbers," the first man replied. "They say the King's eyes don't see much past the TipTop. After that, they go blind. Good for the man who doesn't mind walking at his own pace now and then."

"Long as yer not wearin' the colors and yer off duty, don't see no harm. Ya goin' a night?"

"Span after Weswin turn," the first one replied. "Be glad of company."

"I'll meet ya in the square."

Before any of them would have a chance to enjoy the night, they still had to face a full Sowin on the Practice Field, and this time with the King in attendance. Hard enough to please General Dax, who was a determined taskmaster, but the King was another matter.

First, despite the fact that they would be crawling, climbing and running through a dirty and wet obstacle course, they were expected to wear their formal uniforms. For men of foot, this consisted of sleeveless gold colored tunics, emblazoned with the red royal crest. Under the tunic was a long sleeved cream colored shirt matched by cream britches and brown leather boots. While the clothes were moderately comfortable for the required exercise, cleanliness was another matter. Mud and grass stains were nearly impossible to remove. Each man had been given his first outfit when he'd joined the regiment, but if he needed a replacement, his pay was docked accordingly. By now, nearly every man had two sets of attire, one for formal march and the other for practice under the King's eye.

That led to the second problem. If Gareth were in the mood for ceremony, before the practice runs, might demand a march in review during which time he would examine the men's turnout to be sure their uniforms met his standards. Mud or grass stains would nearly always put a soldier on report, confining him to his quarters for a Sevenstin with at least a two deneret dock in pay. It was a vicious circle whether to risk punishment and a fine for dirt or to wear a pristine dress uniform only to ruin it on the field and risk the fine of having to buy a new one. Since new clothes cost eight denerets, most of the recruits chose to risk the dirty clothes in hopes the King was not inclined to a review rather than risk the clean ones, at least until they had been called to task four times.

This day, to everyone's relief, Gareth refused the formal review. He was in a more playful mood, choosing instead to operate the bully ram next to the mud pit. The ram was a particularly nasty swinging post hanging on a swivel over a narrow bridge that crossed the pit. The idea was for each soldier to run at speed across the bridge while the ram swung around over it, forcing him to either leap or duck under the post along the way. Failing the task meant a painful and miserable topple into the mud pit beneath where the victim would have to crawl out to dry land on his belly.

Most days, the ram operator swung the beam in a regular pattern, allowing his fellow soldiers a fair chance at getting across unscathed. But the King was another matter. He had learned to control the swing of the ram to make crossing nearly impossible. He took delight in timing the beam just right to knock man after man off into the swampy muck. Bruised ribs and knees mattered little to him as he laughed, watching his army claw their way to shore, their lips sealed from cursing aloud so their royal liege could not hear.

This day, of the one hundred twelve infantry required to cross the bridge, only two made it safely, one by sheer luck when Gareth was distracted by a runaway cavalry horse. That, of course, meant that he was two short of a proper count twenty-eight on the number24 of fallen men. "The two who crossed must meet the challenge again!" he ordered. "The number has not been met."

The two soldiers, still dry and nearly done with the rest of the course were brought back before their royal commander. The first one, a young recruit hardly bothered to run once the ram began to swing. Instead, just before the beam hit him, he slipped off the bridge on his own while the King laughed with delight. "Risk the beam and down he fell. One to go and all is well."

The second soldier, a seasoned warrior, proud of his skill, met the challenge with a strong leap and made it across a second time.

"Again, again," the King commanded. "Dare the ram at my hand."

The soldier was about to run again when one of his compatriots poked him in the ribs, "Blood, Davon, fall, will you? We'll be here til Norwin if you stay dry."

"Got my pride," Davon answered.

"So does he and if you meet his head on, there'll be the dark to pay for all of us. Swallow yours and let us get in to Evenmeal."

Davon stepped up to the bridge. He gritted his teeth, started to run. Just as he neared the range of the beam's swing, he leapt again, clearing the post as it swept under his feet. But this time, instead of landing square on the bridge, he angled to the side, teetered on the edge for just a moment, and then slipped into the muck below.

King Gareth cheered and clapped his hands. "Even those with pride fall down on their bellies to the Crown. Come, all a round of applause for your conquering monarch. It pleases us to hear you honor my battle skill."

"Pulling a lever ain't no battle prowess," one of the men in the back rank whispered. "Even the catapult takes a brain to aim."

"King'd claim knocking his men offen needs aim."

"Yeah, what he aims is ta make fools o' us all. I'd like ta see 'im test the bridge hisself. Nothin'd please me more than seein' him on 'is face in the muck."

The thought of it sent a stifled ripple of laughter through the back rank of men. Fortunately, Gareth did not notice. He was too focused on his speechmaking. "Soon you march against the enemy who, We can assure you, will use battle axes as their rams and swords to make their points. You train in safety here to learn the ways of war, but nothing will prepare you for the reality. Some of you will give your lives out of love for Us. Duty will cost others limbs and bloody wounds. Pain and sorrow fill the true field. Every breath you take in Our name honors the crest you wear. For Us you sacrifice. For Us you march. For Us you give all. Kneel now and repledge your Vows to Us as is fitting."

One by one, the army knelt, many muttering curses.

General Dax stepped forward. "We, the warriors of Turan, do revoke our selfish need for the sake and love of our Royal Liege, Monarch of the realm, King Gareth the Great. For his honor we pledge our very lives. We will obey his command, defend his name, and do his will. All say, 'Aye.'"

As one, the army said, "Aye," although, for some reason, it was not as loud as it might have been when over eight hundred voices spoke together. When a vow was made by all instead of individually, it was impossible to tell who joined in and who denied the swearing.

Davon, for one, had kept his teeth clenched, the grit of mud still on his tongue. While his companions on either side noticed, they had hardly mumbled their own consent, choosing to cover his silence with their less than enthusiastic voices. Once dismissed, they left the field together, waiting until they were alone to discuss what had happened.

"Hard time with the King," Slane said. "Don't think it's fair that a man has to fall just to please him."

"I would think he'd have been pleased to have one of his warriors succeed in such a difficult test," Derrin said.

Davon grunted, "All he wants is glory for himself. Did you once hear him say we were fighting for the good of Turan? We pledged to him, not the country."

"Some of us pledged," Slane said. "Though I myself, said 'oy,' not 'aye.' "

"Did you now," Derrin replied. "I think my own tongue slipped a little too. At least I said something."

"If you think I should have even pretended to swear to that bocart, you've another think coming. Man with honor of his own finds it hard to lie in matters of such importance."

"But you march in his name."

"I march for silver and a good billet. Been a long time without either."

"That's what the King counts on, Davon. He's built the main of his forces on ruffians, thieves, beggars, and young fools who think a uniform is promise of glory."

"After that speech about blood and death, could be a few of those young fools are thinking twice?"

"Pah," Slane scoffed. "You're seasoned warrior enough to know better. You should remember the days of your youth when you thought you were immortal. Speech like that goes right over your head."

"One real battle is all it takes to make a man grow old," Davon replied.

"I want to know who this enemy is we're going to fight."

"There are rumors of Shadows in the city."

"So I've heard, but not one word about that has ever escaped even the General's lips much less the King's. More like the other rumor I heard."

"The one about the Sorcerers?"

"That's the one that's taken wings," Slane said. "It's also the one I like the least. Marching on Magiskeep is a madman's mission. Do you have any idea of the power they have?"

"Witness the King without his clothes and you can see the best of it," Davon laughed. "But from what I've heard, that's what drives him."

"Revenge."

"Exactly," Davon said. "Nothing at all to do with the defense of Turan. All he wants is payback for his own inadequacies."

"And get us all killed in the process? How do we fight the Magic?"

"With our blood," Davon replied. "Unless the King has his own Sorcerers."

"There's Edra and Jyp," Slane said.

"Two against a Kingdom? Pitiful reliance, if you ask me. There must be more Sorcerers this side of the Rim. Would they bargain with him? To what end?"

"Some, I suppose, left Magiskeep for good reason. They might hold grudges themselves."

Derrin, glanced around quickly to make sure no one else was within hearing distance and then asked, "And what about you, Slane? Do you hold a grudge against the Keep?"

Slane started. "Why would you ask that?"

"Your name hints of the River."

"And yours of the Hand," Slane answered evenly. "Do you hold a grudge yourself?

"Only against fate," Derrin replied. "When the Tower disbanded, Davon and I fell on hard times. Not much call for a Knight's skill anymore. Oh, a few Lords in the outer reaches might need protection from bandits and rogues, but a world at peace has little need for warriors. I haven't any craftsman skills nor a head for learning. Bit of muscle for farm work or drudger chores make for lean times. I don't march for grudges. I march for money. But you? You didn't answer my question."

"No grudge worth my life. The Master of Magiskeep who drove me out, Sagari, is long gone. I hear his successor is a just man. Bad memories don't inspire me to play even an old fool on the field. If we do march against Magiskeep, I doubt I'll make it across the Rim with this army."

"You'll desert?"

"Let's just say I'll vanish."

"Then you'd better take twenty-seven others with you," Davon scoffed. "I'd hate to think what would happen if you left the King one short."

*****

Edra was finding the journey back to Aberdeen slower than he had planned. Driving a head of forty horses was the least of his concerns. Once he had figured out which of the mares was dominant, he'd put a rope on her and led her along beside Fireheart and the herd followed. A few of the bachelor stallions strayed now and then but they had been raised by men and much preferred the company to being left to fend for themselves in the wild.

Not that the lands they were traveling were particularly wild. For the route home, he'd chosen a more southerly route, just north of Tulene, taking him through the heart of the farmlands of Telma and into the settled areas of Lovental. He had no reason to worry about being seen with stolen animals. He was on the King's business, authorized to do as he needed to secure the horses and, he felt, to take care of his men.

The boy, Jebe, posed a minor inconvenience. The golden colt was constantly trying the walk at the side of whichever warrior was carrying him, and the boy had had a miserable habit of constantly talking. Finally, Edra silenced him with a spell. That problem solved, they had to find a way to secure him for the night. It was Palen who hit upon the solution--to keep Jebe out of the colt's sight by tying him inside a sack which they then could put almost anywhere it was convenient without having to worry he might escape. This freed the men to plan how to best serve the King's needs while better serving their own.

Unfortunately for the villagers and farmers along the way, that meant taking whatever supplies or pleasures he and his band wanted. Normally, his first rest stop at a small settlement in the east of Telma would have roused an instant militia against him, but his Magic effectively checked all resistance. The little Host House which served as an inn to the settlers provided the gang room and board for the night as well as some much needed companionship for Edra.

"Normally, I'd set you men free to find your own lays," he told his men, "but there are too many houses in the settlement for me to ward for you. Tonight, you stay here in the House and enjoy whatever benefit it can afford you. Otherwise, you might meet a dagger in the dark and my Magic won't be able to protect you."

"I could use me a beddin'," Ruddick sighed, looking over at the farmer's wife who was serving the food. The settlers took turns serving in the House and this night had fallen to her family. Her daughter, a lass of but fifteen circles, was in the kitchen while she served. Her husband and son were out in the barns tending the horses. Ruddick's gaze unnerved her, but she went about her work, her ears sharp to everything the men were saying. "The lass at the Lord's were fine, but I cain't say ma appetite's been sated."

"I, fer one jest want a soft bed fer the night," Palen said, yawning. "Never were too good at traveling."

"Thought I might have a bath," Jain said.

"What about you, My Lord?" Donner said, looking over at Edra, who was downing his third tankard of ale. "Sleeping alone?"

"I've a thirst for more tender flesh," Edra said. "Used to be, when I was in the Cauge, it was my duty to woman all the virgins in the city. I'm a bit out of practice, but I do remember the singular pleasure it afforded."

"Ah, the kitchen maid," Donner said. "Shall we go fetch her?"

"When I'm done with my meal. I always do better when my stomach's full." He laughed.

The mother's sharp ears did not miss a word and when the men weren't looking, she dashed from the common room into the kitchen. "Riga, get out of here, now."

"What's wrong, Mama?"

"Those men…just get out. Do as I say."

The girl dropped her bread dough on the table and ran to the door. It was locked tight. "Mama, the door…."

Her mother hurried over and tugged at the handle to no avail. She ran to the root cellar door and found it bound tight as well, along with all the windows, shuttered and sealed. "It can't be. These doors have no locks."

"Magic don't need no locks," a voice said from the door. "Our master be sorcer. 'E wants ya here in the House, and that's the end o' it. Now, ya both kin either come quiet with Beryl an' me or kickin' and screamin'," Ruddick said. "I like the second, but I don't know about ma master."

Ryala moved protectively in front of her daughter. "I'll go quietly if you just leave my daughter alone. She's only a child. Please."

"Please me, she'll do right fine ta please my Lord," Ruddick laughed. "'E said he liked 'em tender." He strode into the room, shoved Ryala aside and into Beryl's grip. He grabbed Riga by the arms and pulled her to him. She screamed.

Outside her father and brother were just coming in from the barns when they heard her cry. They started running to the inn door only to find it bolted shut. They raced around the building, facing shuttered windows and sealed doors at every turning. "Go get an ax, Gen, hurry."

The boy ran off as his father pounded on the door all the while his ears rang with the voice of his wife and daughter calling for help, then pleading to be left alone.

Gen brought two axes back, but at the first blow, both men knew it was useless. The blades struck air within a hairsbreadth of the door. "Socered," the father moaned. "No way to get in."

"No way to get out, either," Gen said, hefting his blade. "First man sticks his head out is going to lose it."

"Don't be a fool, lad," the father gasped as he sank to his knees before the door. "Whoever chanted the door's got enough power to protect the lot of them."

"What do we do?"

"I'm going to sit here and weep, son, and just hope your sister and her mother can make it through till morning. You go to the Herbist's cottage. Stay there until the sun hits the window and then bring her back here with you. Our women are going to need her."

"I want to stay. Maybe we can find a way in…."

"Go lad. Do as I say. Better your ears not hear any more. By the blood I'm not sure I can stand it myself, but I won't leave your mother, not now. Go on, get out of here."

Once Gen had gone, Tobin sat with his back to the sealed door, his arms over his head, a broken man.

"So, you are a pretty lass," Edra said when Ruddick shoved Riga down into the chair next to the Sorcerer. She was quiet now, tears streaming down her face, her jaw tight. "Here now, have a sip of ale. It'll warm you. You're shivering."

"Not with cold," Ryla said. "She's terrified. Can't you see? She's just a babe."

Edra reached out and curled his hand around one of Riga's breasts. "Plump little babe, in all the right places," he said. "Fourteen, fifteen circles? Never been with a man, I hope. Pretty little lass like you should still be fresh." He forced the rim of the cup against her lips, "Drink." When she shook her head, he smiled. "First lesson for a lass. When a man tells you to do something, you do it." His fingers squeezed hard on her breast and when she gasped, he poured the ale into mouth. She gagged and swallowed to keep from choking. "That's better," he said. "No finish the rest on your own."

"She's never had any liquor," Ryla protested. "Leave her be."

"Will you stop your prattling, woman? I know what I'm doing. I've laid many maids in my time, so count your daughter lucky she'll be made a woman under me. Blood, Ruddick take that mouth upstairs with you and put something in it to keep it quiet."

"What, My Lord?" Ruddick asked, grinning.

Edra made a crude gesture. "Whatever suits your fancy, lad. Whatever suits your fancy." Ruddick grabbed a hank of Ryla's hair to better control her and twisting her arm behind her back pushed her along in front of you.

"No, Riga. My baby. Leave her be. Please, don't hurt her."

"Shuddup," Ruddick ordered. "Ya'll be screaming soon enow when Beryl an' me have our way. Hah, Beryl, ya think we oughtta wake Palen so's he kin join the fun?"

"Nah," Beryl replied, grabbing a towel from the counter to knot around Ryla's mouth to stifle her cries. 'The three o' us kin

have our fun widdout him. Anything's left he kin have iffen he
wakes up afore we go. Serve 'im right fer sleepin' in."

The pulled Ryla into one of the bedrooms and threw her on
the bed. Then they began to undress, saving the pleasure of
undressing her when they were ready.

Downstairs, Edra forced Riga to finish another half tankard
of ale, all the while fondling her breasts and stroking her neck and
hair. He'd loosed her blond curls from the clip and played with the
strands with his fingers. "All the fine women in Arcula were fair," he
said. "Did I tell you I was First Hand there? It wasn't just my Magic
that put me there. Oh, no. I had a way with people, I still do. I'm the
King's man here in Turan. He depends on me, you see." He hooked
his fingers in the laces of her bodice and slowly worked them free,
his hands caressing the soft flesh of her breasts. "Women have paid
to give themselves to me, to feel my hands like this."

Groggy from the ale, Riga swayed under his touch, her brain
wanting to flee, her body too affected by the alcohol to respond. "I
don't want to…I don't."

"You are just a girl. How would you know? It is an honor to
have a man of my esteem take your maidenhood." He pulled the
sleeves of her blouse down, exposing her chest. "You are still so
fresh, so new. It is indeed a wonder to behold."

Riga bit her lip and whimpered as he rubbed her gently,
stroking down her belly. "Come, little one, there's a bed waiting. I
need to explore you more." He pulled her into him, lifting her onto
his lap, his mouth meeting hers in a hard, full kiss. She tried to turn
her head away, but he forced her mouth on his with his hand. Then
he got up, still holding her stifling her cries with that hand over her
mouth.

She was light to carry, still more a child than woman, but it
made it all the better for Edra. He was again the Cauge, Master of
Arcula, the one whose right to do as he willed was unquestioned. He
took her upstairs to his bed, lay her down and made sure she watched
as he stripped off his own clothes, preening and posing before her
wide eyes. "Let me prepare you," he said, sidling over to the bed,
dagger in hand. He slit her skirt at the waist, then pulled the fabric
away, finally cutting off her undergarments until she too was naked.
His chanting stilled the worst of her protests, leaving her to stifled
weeping and screams strangled in her throat. He hovered over her,
his hands groping between her clenched legs forcing them open.
"Gently, gently," he murmured. "Yield your treasure gently now.
The first time is always the hardest for a maid, the best for a man. I
will teach you to surrender, teach you to respond, teach you to know

pleasure." He kneaded her belly as her body began to shake and then, when he was ready, he had his way with her.

In the room beyond, Ryla cried out again, her own pain mingled with terror for her daughter.

Outside, Tobin slammed his hands over his ears and prayed to the Hand for Easwin's turn. By then, he hoped it would be over.

*****

When the sun finally rose, Edra and his men raided the kitchen, stocked up on whatever supplies they could carry on horseback and headed back out to the common room.

"Good night, eh, Milord?" Ruddick asked.

"More to come," Edra replied. "It will take us the better part of two Sevenstins to get the horses home. Farms and villages all along the way, although, I must admit, not many will quite match this one. It's not often a man can have a maiden like that. She was most refreshing."

"Din't hear much from her room. 'Course we had us a wildcat ta handle. Fought like a shetark, jest the way I likes it."

"A man of my caliber doesn't evoke much protest once I shed my breeches," Edra said, strolling to the counter to get a bottle of ale to take with them. "You should have seen her face. She was overwhelmed. Almost spoiled the pleasure to have her so willing. But she was a maiden, that's for certain and once you've had one, there is nothing quite so satisfying."

"Ain't ne'er done a virgin meself," Ruddick said. "Must be quite a time ta know that what yer doin' makes a woman."

"Oh, it is, Ruddick. Tell you what, next time we find a maid, I'll let you join me. It wouldn't suit to let you try the first time without some instruction, after all. I'll guide you in first, you see, let you feel it. I've done so many I can spare one for you. I am a master, after all."

"That'd be quite the treat, Milord," Ruddick agreed enthusiastically. "Ya'd honor me like that?"

"In the Shadow way, we are all comrades," Edra replied. Assuring Ruddick's loyalty to him and not just Tamor was important. "You others. If you've no experience with maids, I'll make the same offer. If we ride together, we must share the treasures we take."

They headed for the door. On the way, Beryl picked up the sack with Jebe inside and slung it over his shoulder, ignoring the feeble whimper from inside.

Just as Palen was about to lift the latch, Edra stayed him. "Wait. Never forget the husbands and brothers. I will cast a shield for each of us before we go out. No weapons can harm us then. But don't let the words enrage you. We will be cursed by fools who do not know the power of the King's blessing or my hand. Ignore them. What we choose to do is with Royal consent. I have his seal."

"We are the King's men," Jain said, lifting his chin proudly. "Carry yourselves as is fitting."

Palen opened the door.

Outside they faced a group of shouting settlers armed with rakes, shovels, axes and an odd sword or two. In front stood Tobin, his ax at the ready. "What have you done to my wife and daughter?"

"Made your daughter a woman and your wife sore between the legs," Edra answered easily. "I'm sure they both learned a great deal. You should be pleased to know they had such seasoned teachers. You, of all, should benefit next time you take your woman to bed. As for the other, she's primed and ready for a husband."

"Damn you!" Tobin cried, breaking from the grip of one of the other men who tried to hold him back. He swung his ax wildly at Edra only to have its handle shatter in his hand when the blade struck against an invisible wall around the Sorcerer.

"We do not march unprotected in this land," Edra said. "Waste your time consoling your family and sent your friends home to tend their gardens. We are done here." Then, with the other four men in close order behind him, Edra strutted off to the barns to collect their horses so they could be on their way.

Choking back his rage, Tobin raced into the inn and up the stairs with the Herbist. There was little either could do to mend the damage the raiders had done, but at least they could ease the women's pain.

There was nothing else to do.

*****

In two day's time, word finally reached Tulene as to what had happened in Delran's Keep. Still breathless and sweating from a long hard ride, Dom gave a quick bow of respect. Then he straightened and said, "Lord Delran sent me to tell you to light the fires. He says to meet in two days' time in the city square."

"What's happened?" Lord Dale asked.

"Raiders led by a Sorcerer sent by the King. He had the royal signet. They took horses for the cavalry, killed two and raped one of the women."

"Delran is all right?"

"Aye, My Lord. We didn't even try a defense in the face of Magic. The Lord's wiser than that."

"The woman?"

"She was alive when I left. One of the housemaids, sweet little thing. They took the stableboy too, Jebe."

Dale knew the name. "The lad who helped save Lord Jamus from the bandits a while back? He and his mother are living at Delran's hold. You say he's been kidnapped?"

"Yes, My Lord. Sorry to say we couldn't do anything to stop them. Edra wanted the boy's horse and the colt wouldn't go without the lad, so he took them both. The horse is chanted, you see."

"Ah, yes, I've heard of him. Whim's son. Sooner or later he's going to cause some trouble for those horse thieves."

"The fire, My Lord? Delran said you'd understand."

"I do." Dale beckoned to Dover, one of the Hall guards. "Go to the tower. You know what to do. It's time to ride again as one."

Dover nodded and hurried off.

"Does Delran need anything more from us? Tulene's resources are his."

"No, Lord Governor. Jern, the Healer is probably there by now to help anyone who was hurt and Delran still has two herds of fine mounts. He'll be bringing some with him when he comes for those who need them. I'm already well mounted myself."

"Your horse will be well cared for while you rest, Sur Dom. We'll share Midmeal while you tell me all about these men who ride with Edra. I need to hear every detail of what happened."

Together the two men went to the Governor's chambers where they sat to eat. When Dom had finished his story, Dale shook his head and sat silently for a long time. None of it made any sense. Even with Gareth on the throne there was no need for war. Was Edra acting alone on some insane mission he had created himself? The whole thing stank of Shadows, and that was exactly what Delran feared. He would have had no other reason to call for the fires.

By now, Dover had reached the tower, and the flame had been lit. Soon towers all over Turan with glow with the signal fires spreading the call all the way to the Sacred Citadel, the ancient hold of the Knights of the Hand. There, what the world thought were mere remnants of Turan's Elden warrior race still taught and practiced the Old Ways, waiting for the call. They had been expecting it, for the augurs had Seen Shadows rising in their scrying waters. Behind the ice-covered walls, those with knowledge of the Eldenlore knew the signs. The final batter was upon them and as Destiny required, they were ready to mount a defense as their kind had always done in the face of the Great Circle's closing.

High in the gilded tower a great fieron bell began to toll. Dust and cobwebs from long circles of silence drifted down from it with each slow swing. Ten times it tolled, then three more, calling those near to Tulene, while one lone final ring told the rest to make their way to Aberdeen. The bell paused for a full span and then repeated the pattern, sending the code back to the fires which flickered and pulsed to repeat the message. The flames flared and faded through Telma, Lovental, Doral, Nantel, Aberdal--Turan's five Provinces calling the Sworn to duty. All who were able, all who dared, all who still chose to wear the emblem and all it signified.

Lord Delran opened up a leather trunk in his chamber and pulled out a pale blue tunic emblazoned with the crest of a great white eagle carrying a lightning bolt in one talon and a rainbow in the other. Still lean and fit after many circles as a landholder, he slipped the tunic on. Then he pulled out a leather scabbard with a sword. He slid the weapon out, examined the shining stelin blade, tested its edge with his finger and, satisfied, strapped the belt around his waist and put the sword back in the scabbard. He pulled on a pair of tall leather boots, placed a light dress helmet on his head, and headed downstairs.

Lurela, Nobby, Joss, and all the rest of the servants were waiting for him. He stopped on the lowest step. "I made a Vow circles ago in the Citadel as a Knight of the Hand. My sacred duty is to defend Turan against the Shadows. I have every reason to believe that this Edra, who scavaged my hold, is an instrument of the Darkness."

"He came in the name of the King, My Lord."

"Aye, but on his hand he wore Blackwing's ring as did the men with him. It is not something more eyes would see, but mine a keen to the Shadow's ways. He may serve the King, but he has a great master. Where one Shadowsworn rides, more will follow. I am going to Tulene. I need one good man to go with me to help me herd the horses I am taking along. Some of my comrades will need good mounts."

Joss stepped forward. "I'll go, My Lord. I'm the best man with the horses."

"My son," Lurela asked, wringing her hands nervously. "You haven't said anything about Jebe."

"I will bring Jebe safely back to you, My Lady. I made that Vow when he was taken and I don't intend to break it. Edra is going to Aberdeen. As much as he covets Shimmer, he must be careful not to hurt your son, for he is the only thing keeping the horse where Edra wants him. We will find them soon enough." He stepped down from the staircase, walked over to her and knelt at her feet. "I swear this again to you. I will bring your son safely home."

She held out her hand. As he kissed it, she said, "I will pray to the Hand every day for you, My Lord, and for my son."

Delran rose. "Waiting will not be easy. Jern will come back in a day or so and stay here with you all. I am hoping he will bring another Magician with him as I asked to help secure this hold should any more Shadows come."

"What about our friends in Magiskeep?" Beryl asked.

"If this is indeed the Dawn of the Black Dragon's rise, our friends in Magiskeep will be too busy defending themselves to worry about us. By my reckoning, the Shadows will gravitate to Gareth and his army. They may have already infiltrated its ranks. Edra is only the surface of the peril we face, but it will be a long time before they bother with the far provinces like Telma."

"Yet Edra came here," Beryl said.

"Only for the horses," Delran replied. "He doesn't know I have any more than he already took. He won't be back."

"So we wait."

"As I said, it will not be easy."

With that, he and Joss left the house to go to the stables. "How much Magic do you have, Joss?" Delran asked when they were out of earshot of the porch.

"Enough to weave blankets for the horses, and enough to cast a blaze or two of Spellfire, if that's what you're asking."

"You've answered my question," Delran replied. "There are Knights as able, especially those who have been in recent training in the Norreaches."

"I thought the Knights were disbanded," Joss said.

"The Watchers are never still," Delran said. "And the Citadel was never abandoned despite the rumors we have chosen to circulate. We always knew the day would come when we would be needed again."

"How many of you are there?"

"Hard to say," Delran answered."We'll take thirty horses to Tulene. Many of the Knights already have mounts, but those who've taken on new lives will need them. Our men are all over the Provinces. Those in the West and South will muster there. The rest will meet in Aberdeen."

They collected a herd of thirty of Delran's best horses, ones that had been turned out in the fields when Edra had raided the Hold, and set out across the Province, taking the most direct route to the capital.

By the time they reached Tulene, they had been joined by seven others, all wearing the eagle crest, ready to fight in Turan's defense against the Shadowsworn.

*****

No less than twelve farms and villages suffered under Edra's men on the way back to Aberdeen. Five maidens had learned hard lessons under the Cauge lord's keen direction, and ten men had lost their lives in pitiful attempts to protect their women and homes from the raiders. The Sorcerer had grown bored with casting wards to protect his band against attacks and simply let his men cut down the opposition with their swords. He was beginning to enjoy the bloodshed again as he so often had when he had been First Hand, relishing the look on men's faces as they died, always wondering how it felt to clutch desperately at life as it left the body. Facing death was most often a Sorcerer's choice rather than his fate, and he planned on living a long time himself. And yet, death fascinated him. Watching men die by the blade was so much better than watching them burn by Spellfire.

They had gathered gold along with provisions, enough to keep his five companions happy and his own purse full. He himself had no need of money, but the men doted on it, counting out coins and a the few goblets and dishes they'd collected from the wealthier landholders as if they were the greatest treasure in the world.

Edra knew better. Power mattered more than wealth as he had proven by taking Delran's horses instead of buying them. With power, a man could have anything he wanted. Gold might have afforded lesser men influence, but Magic, his most precious gift, was worth far more than even the Royal treasury.

Yet, here in Turan, far from his home in Arcula, he could never quite be sure how strong any chanting would be. The Spring always answered his wishes, but it was fickle in spirit. Sometimes, it leapt to his fingers with merely a frown. At other times, he would need a full blown fit of temper to send a simple casting.

Jain, on the other hand, a Sorcerer with much less Skill, never seemed to lack when he raised his hand. He could always easily add ale to an empty tankard for a thirsty friend or spell a campfire in an instant. It took no effort for him to conjure a corral for the horses each night and it was he who had woven the sack to hold the boy captive whenever it was needed.

The boy. What to do with the boy? Keeping him bound was a simple matter since he was small and weak, and the sack was most useful when they needed him out of the way. But Edra always had to keep watch for the golden colt who seemed to dote on the boy. Had the horse not been so incredibly beautiful and so clearly Magic-blessed, he would have killed the lad and set the animal free long ago. But his ego and an overwhelming desire to claim the beast as his own denied him that solution. Over and over, his mind pictured himself astride the magnificent animal, leading the King's army into battle. Gareth would glare at him with jealous eyes, but the Royal liege was half the horseman he was and the colt would be a fiery war steed far too keen for his hand.

So Jebe lived, a tormented prisoner, bound and gagged by Magic until the day he was no longer needed.

The boy had other plans. He may not have been able to speak, but his eyes were open and each time Jain or Edra used their Sorcery, he watched, carefully memorizing each gesture, trying to learn the weaves. Edra's Magic was a puzzle. The little Keep training he'd had denied the kind of casting the Caugeman used—Magic Unrestrained, guided by emotion rather than logic. Yet it intrigued him, more for its imprecision and erratic success than anything. Still, it had its uses, for when it flowed freely, it offered mighty force and impressive results. Jain's more limited skills, though, taught him the most. Even without the discipline of a Keep taught Mage, he managed simple tasks with exact ease. Never once did his fires flare out of control as Edra's did, and he could bring the frenzied herd back to order with perfectly placed coils of chanted rope around the necks of the lead horses with a single flick of his wrist.

Jebe watched and learned from everything he saw, practicing with his own fingers whenever his hands were loose enough to move, struggling to find the touch of the River. Little by little, with each try, the waters offered him reply, sending small shocks of energy through his thin little body, teasing it with promise of so much more.

Jain had taken on the task of tending him, giving him food and drink and loosing his bonds whenever he needed to relieve himself. Those moments became the focal points of Jebe's life in captivity. The briefest times of freedom bore him up, giving him at least some hope of either escape or a finish to what seemed an endless journey. Nearly three Sevenstins of nights sealed in a sack was almost too much to bear, but each moment of sunlight during the day and Shimmer's constant devotion kept his spirits up more than one might have expected. The first Sevenstin had been the hardest when his terror had blocked out everything. But the horrific routine of being tied and bagged soon took its toll on his fear, changing it to a numb acceptance and opening his mind to inward thoughts and, at last, Shimmer's voice in his head.

Jebe be scared. Shim watch. No twoleg hurt.

Where have you been, Shim? I needed someone to talk to.

Scare make head deaf. Now better. We run?

I can't I'm all tied up.

Shim eat ropes.

They are Magic. Even you cannot break them. I need to find another way.

Magic eat Magic.

I know. I need to find the River. I am not strong.

River find Jebe if want enough.

The colt's reply troubled the boy. There was some meaning in it he could not quite understand. Beasttalking had its limits. The animal only comprehended the world through its own experiences, not its master's. Magic to the horse was second nature. Bred from Jamus' Magicked stallion, Whim, Shimmer had inherited his father's strange abilities and used them freely. He could fade into a cloud of mist and reappear at will, raid the feed bin and dissolve back into his own stall before anyone even suspected he'd been out. He was elusive as he chose to be and bonded completely to Jebe. And yet, he was incapable of explaining how he accomplished any of it. How easy it would be to slip his bonds, if Jebe had the colt's skill. Instead, he had to resign himself to suffering captivity, finding solace in learning little by little how he might use the River to his advantage.

XX

As Jamus rode through the well-tended arbors and fields of Landhold, he remembered well how hard working here had been. Danvar had been a fair but stern overseer, and while Jamus had certainly suffered for the first Sevenstins of labor in the fields, he had also grown muscle and even some skill at fighting from swinging his sickle during the harvest. As it had been with most of his trials, the experience had hardened both his body and Will. Now he was Master of three Rivers and preparing to inspire armies to war.

Arcula would be well defended by its veteran army and Spellcasters well used to Spellfire. While he still had no idea what was going on in Turan proper, he knew Simen was there and with allies like Kala, Dale, and the whole of Grandisite's Seers, he was relatively sure they too would be ready. Magiskeep, though, was another matter. There, where Magic abounded, so had peace for so many generations that his Mages had never learned how to defend themselves, much less the Kingdom.

It was for that reason that he'd left Arcuse and taken the four day ride south to Landhold. He needed to ask for help and collect on debts owed.

Talltree, a little cluster of forest a span off the main road, was fast becoming a prosperous village of its own. Capitalizing on the lack of skilled craftsmen needed by all the farms in Arcula's south, Garv, Jamus' former compatriot, encouraged men to bring their families here from Arcuse's bustling streets to start new lives in the countryside where soft breezes stirred the tree branches and their children would have room to run and play along the banks of rippling clear streams. He had succeeded in bringing in blacksmiths and wheelwrights, carpenters and harness makers, all manner of craftsmen whose talents were needed by farmers who were willing to pay well with crops and supplies. Everyone was prospering, and Talltree had just opened a tiny little inn of its own with an attached common room suited for public meetings and celebrations.

When Jamus and Covane rode up to the Water's Edge, the inn door opened and Garv, followed by a laughing group of villagers, rushed out to greet them. "My Lord," Garv called, "when we gots word it was indeed you on the road, we started right in preparin' a feast in yer honor. Come in and join us in celebrating your return. Dorge'll take good care o' yer horses as he always done. You jest git right down an' join the fun, eh?"

The two men dismounted and went into the Common Room, where, as Garv had predicted, a fine feast was laid out for the whole village to share. Cavel roasts, fowl of all sorts, taroot pies, vegetables piled high on platters, along with nearly every variety of fruit grown in Arcula's abundant farms, cheeses and pitchers of amberwine, ale, and calidew covered a dozen large tables where the diners could freely help themselves. Set all around along the walls were smaller tables set with dishes and knives, spoons, and some curious utensil Jamus had never seen before. When he walked over and picked one up to examine it, Garv grinned. "Hobar calls it a foodspear. Makes it easy ta pick up stuff ya wants ta eat widdout usin'yer fingers. He's a mighty good hand with the metal, he is. Always thinkin' o' newfangled things ta make. Gotta admit, this one ain't so bad. Keeps yer hands clean from the pork fat so's the lasses cain't slip outta yer grip so easy."

"Speaking of lasses," Jamus replied, "is Moka here with you?"

Garv puffed up proudly, "Pleased ta tell ya me an' Moka done pledged true ta each other. She's in the kitchen bakin' somethin' er other, but she tole me ta tell ya now that she's been spoke fer yer gonna have ta mind yer manners no matter how much ya lust after her."

Jamus grinned this time. Where Moka was concerned, he had always known she was in love with Garv no matter what had passed between them. Her only interest in him and been fueled by his Magic and since he had learned to weave a Sphere around that, Garv had nothing to worry about. "She is a beautiful woman, Garv, and as much as I might enjoy sharing time with her, I have always known she was yours and you the only man she could ever truly love."

"Think ya tole me that onct."

"I believe I did," Jamus laughed. "Took you long enough to listen."

"Me Lord!" Carby called from across the room and soon all of the nine Fire Casters Jamus had trained from the small group of Warriors of Garv's clan were back together, enjoying the food and drink as they swapped stories of their past adventures and new conquests. Covane found himself drawn into the group as a welcome

comrade whose support and loyalty to Jamus had earned him good
stead with the other men.

Weswin passed in celebration and pleasure, with Jamus
forced to join in the communal sing after Evenmeal. When they
heard his voice, he was pressed to sing alone. He whispered
something to the lute player and stood next to him as the musician
struck the first chord. He sang the only song he knew all the way
through:

> "*Blessed the land where fair Arcula lies,*
> *Kissed by the sun and the rain,*
> *Touching the hearts of her people who love*
> *The spirit of sweet freedom's reign.*
> *From the mountains she falls to the valleys below*
> *Where the grass green and gentle all grows,*
> *To farmland and city and canyon and wood,*
> *To her heart where the silver Spring flows,*
> *We will sing on the wind*
> *On the great dragon wings*
> *Of the land where the silver Spring flows.*
> *In the ancient of days, all her people were one*
> *In the hope of tomorrow's new day.*
> *Then the darkness took hold and cold sorrow was born*
> *Taking all of the promise away.*
> *And through all the long night, not a star could be seen*
> *Even though longing eyes vigil kept*
> *For the Shadows were master and covered the bed*
> *Where the great silver dragon still slept.*
> *We will sing on the wind*
> *On the great dragon wings*
> *Of the land where the Silver spring flows.*
> *The Seasons passed by in a river of tears*
> *Till the people forgot how to cry*
> *And empty hearts broke in a silent despair*
> *Of the Great Dragon's promise to fly.*
> *Then a bright golden sun rose its head in the west*
> *And the Dragon awoke and took flight*
> *Burning darkness away in one glorious span*
> *Blessing all with a wonderful light.*
> *We will sing on the wind*
> *On the great dragon wings*
> *Of the land where the Silver Spring flows.*
> *Of the land where the Silver Spring flows.*"

The lute player struck a final chord and the room burst into applause and shouts of praise as Jamus bowed.

"What other talents have you hidden from us?" Covane asked, clapping Jamus on the back.

"Gaila taught me that song when I was last here in Arcula. I've never forgotten it. I don't think my brother did either. He's supposed to be the Follyman in the family."

"Give'im some competition fer the denerets," Garv laughed. "Ain't heard singin' like that in a circle. Iffen ya ever wants a job in Moka's inn, ya gots my word fer it."

As if on cue, Moka, who had been missing for most of the evening, entered the room pushing a cart holding a three-tiered cake. It was decorated with blue and silver icing and on top, there was a man riding a silver dragon on the wing. "I figgered we ne'er got ta give the Dragonlord proper honor," she said.

Jamus stepped over and admired the creation, his eyes brimmed with tears. Moka's baking talent was clear but the honor itself mattered more than all her skill. These people were truly grateful for his presence. They wanted nothing more from him, accepting what he had given them when he had ridden Rath to battle deserving of their thanks and devotion. The little world they had created for themselves was an incredible accomplishment, and as he cut the first piece of cake, he vowed to protect it in the great battle ahead.

If the Great Circle closed, villages like Talltree would fall to ruin when all knowledge was swallowed by the Darkness. The craftsmen's tools would rust, the roofs and walls of their inn would fall to rack and ruin and they, so bright with hope for the future, would sink back into ignorance, seeing nothing of the future past surviving to the next day and the day after.

When the cake was reduced to crumbs, and most of the villagers had left, Garv, Moka, Covane and Jamus sat by the fireside, sharing one last drink before bed. Covane and Garv were enjoying tankards of dark ale, but Jamus, wise enough to know his own intolerance for alcohol, was sipping a cup of soothing keldherb.

"So, wid all the fun, we ne'er did ask ya why ya come back ta Arcula," Garv said.

"I wish it were to spend every day like this one has been," Jamus replied, "but Turan's Way has other plans, I'm afraid. The Black Dragon is stirring, and your own Silver Lady, Rath, has prophesied that Lord Tamor and his Shadows are preparing for war.

"Ya shoulda finished off that bocart when we beat his army the las' time," Garv said.

"If I'd been able to, I would have," Jamus said. "But his Master is a formidable foe and I was not ready then."

"Are ya ready now?"

"I'll have to be," Jamus answered. "That time will come when it comes, no matter what I do. It's the people of Turan I'm worried about now. I don't want people dying by Shadow hands if I can help it. Arcula is well prepared to defend itself and I've already warned the First Order of the danger. It's my own Kingdom that's vulnerable."

"Ain't ya gots Sorcerers?"

"I do. Magicians who have practiced peace for hundreds of circles. They know nothing of war."

"They be Firecasters, no? Ya gots the skill."

"Only by hard learning from Master Serenec here in Arcula. My Mages cannot use Spellfire the way I can, or the way you can. I learned that when I was here before. In my River, those who send it cannot sustain its power. I need help in teaching them how to use it and still survive its impact on their energy. Until I do, they are almost defenseless against the Darkness."

"So ye seek Mard Serenec."

Jamus nodded. "And Mardel Eleyse. She is a skilled Magicuser in Arcula. Her command of the Silver River—the Spring—is as strong as any. She would be able to teach my Masters well in its Touch."

"An' ye ne'er thought ta ask yer Warriors ta ride wid ya back ta yer home?" Garv said quietly. "The Nine gots Dragon Tongue enow ta defend the Wall itself if need be."

"The Wall is gone," Covane said, shrugging. "And since you won't need to defend it, I would think you and your men would be quite willing to go with us back to Magiskeep to help our Dragonlord."

"Us?" Garv asked. "Ya going ta the Keep, Rider?"

"If Lord Jamus will have me, I will. I don't know how much good a sword will do, but mine is his."

"Arcula needs all of you," Jamus protested.

"Not a whit,' Garv replied. "Ya said yerself Arcula is well defended. Lady Gaila ain't been no fool since she took the Seat. Me an' the others left Arcuse proper a circle gone 'cause there weren't no need fer us. The Riders what stayed after the war took ta training a good army and all the Caugesworn what holds the Spring took ta praticin' the whitefire. Knocked down ne'er twenty old buildings in the process, but they got good at it. Made a lot o' construction worker happy an' set up a fine corps of FireCasters."

"And so you left."

"Warriors be an ancient race. We gots our pride. Iffen the Mard don't need us, we don't need them."

"Magiskeep would need you," Covane said. "My sword, your fire? Do you think your Mages would welcome us, My Lord?"

"I would be grateful...."

"Ain't no call ta be thankin' us fer anythin'," Garv said quickly. "We bin sworn to ya since ya took to the Silverwings. We owe ya a debt we kin ne'er repay. Ya let us go ta this Magiskeep o' your'n an' we'll keep watch where ere ya needs us."

"The northern villages would be the first line of attack," Jamus said.

"Then we go ta the villages. We'll go where ya send us, MiLord, ain't no two ways about it."

"I'll come too," Moka said, pulling her hair back behind her neck into a bun. "I gots some Magic an' Healin' skills ta go along. 'Sides, I don't wanna let this man o' mine outta my sight now's I finally gots 'im."

"Then it's settled," Covane replied, raising his hand to silence any further protest from Jamus. "Tommorrow we ride to Landhold to talk to Elyese. We should find Serenec there, or at least be able to contact him. Once he left Laydrith before the war, he never went back."

"You still keepin' time with the Mardel, Rider?" Moka asked.

Covane shrugged, "The Lady and I do have an understanding of sorts. But I am still a free man."

"A fool, iffen ya ask me, which ya dint." Moka laughed. "It's the Rider blood in ya cain't keep yerself ta jest one bed. Ain't like a good Warrior." She patted Garv's thigh. "The Eld knew how ta treat a lady, all ya Riders know is how ta bed one. Ya could larn a lesson from the Lore."

"I've thought about settling down," Covane replied, raking his fingers through his blond hair. "I've been a Rider too long to change my ways easily."

"Have you talked to Elyese about it?" Jamus asked.

"Tried to. But every time I think about it I feel like I'm about to put my leg over an unbroken colt. Never know if you're going to stay in the saddle or hit the ground."

Jamus laughed. "I know the feeling. Typical when a man tries to talk to a woman."

"Don't ya go castin' 'sparagin' remarks about talkin' ta women," Moka said. "Man don't need ta talk when he knows how ta ride. Speakin' o' which, I gots me a hankering for a straddle. What say ya, Garv?" She started to unlace her bodice.

Jamus grabbed Covane's arm and got up from his chair. "I think it's time for us to go upstairs to our rooms, Rider. If we don't get some sleep we'll never make it to Landhold in the morning."

With Covane close behind the two man hurried up the stairs to their rooms, leaving the fur rug and the fireside to Garv and his wife.

Once in his room, Jamus slipped off his boots and lay down on the bed. He was tired and was nearly asleep when a clap of thunder startled him awake. A dark cloud covered the moon, sending everything into darkness.

Then, as lightning flashed outside, a wisp of blackness began to slither in from the window. Instinctively, he set his Sphere, and sat up, staring into the center of the room where a misshapen cloud had settled.

Everendings ever be, ye shall never fly with me.

Fools are all who dare to fight, surely they will lose the light.

Let despair and sorrow fill those who do not bide my will.

Everendings, ever be, pain shall be my gift to thee.

"Kesel, show yourself," Jamus demanded, using the Dragon's name to gain whatever advantage he could.

Dare speak my name? Value life so little?

"I do not fear you. Not when you are alone like this."

Blackwing has many.

"Many what? Fools who think you will keep your promises to them? You deceive men with your lies, curse Shadows with false dreams of life. You have vowed to kill me, but why should I believe a liar?"

Three River only. Four never.

"That's what you've come to tell me? Even if I cannot command the Black Waters, it will not matter in the end. All I really have to do is dam them."

Circle's close near. Then what Kiselor know? Nothing.

"So that's it, is it? Do you think I am not prepared? I too have many."

Fools all.

One black tentacle snapped out lashing at Jamus' face. It struck his Sphere and the Dragon screamed out in pain, pulling back against the wall.

Pay for pain. You pay.

"I pity you, Blackwing. You have nothing. You thrive on ignorance, gather minions from men you deceive, accept false loyalty, hold court with Shadows who have no substance, never know the joy of love. You are alone, empty, a spiteful hermit in a dark cave afraid to fly in the sun. Knowledge terrifies you, for with it men can see your true face, a vacant hollow in the fabric of the world."

Everendings ever be, spawn of Magic cursed be.
Drown thy virtue in thy tears, I am all the world fears.
Everendings ever be, suffer for this pain to me.

The black mist swirled again and flowed back out the window as the storm raged outside.

Jamus rose from his bed, his gait unsteady as he made his way to the window to close the shutters. The rain was pouring down. Why? Why had Blackwing come now? Had the Dragon wanted to kill him after all? His only hope was that his words had hurt the creature more than his Sphere. His Magic would never kill Kesel, but wounding him in body and spirit might at least buy them more time.

But what if it all was just another one of his dreams?

The storm denied him.

He was fully awake.

*****

Tamor heard Blackwing's call and knew he had to answer quickly. The Dragon tolerated no disobedience from his servants no matter how powerful they might be. He traced his footsteps on the billowing storm clouds as they raced across the sky, making his way north to his Master's cold lair.

Kesel was lying in his cave, his head resting on his front legs, his ebony eyes closed.

Tamor dropped to his knees, his head bowed, "You called me, My Lord."

The Dragon opened his eyes and fixed his icy gaze on Tamor. "You love me?"

Tamor's head snapped up. Love? It was a word that had no meaning to a Shadow. And yet, he had grown fond of Sorra. He felt nothing like that for the dreadful creature he now faced. A twisted loyalty, perhaps, fed by promises of ultimate power when the Great Circle closed. How to answer? What did the Dragon want from him? "I do not think I know how to love, Great One."

"Alone is not joy."

"We can find satisfaction in solitude," Tamor replied. "It brings peace."

"We make war."

"Only to gain our peace. When men are ignorant again, we can do anything we desire. They will fear us, and fear our power and we will thrive on their fear."

"You love me?" Blackwing repeated as if it was the only question that mattered.

"I do," Tamor lied, hoping it was the right answer.

Blackwing held out his injured tentacle, the black flesh still smoking where Jamus' Sphere had burned it. "Hurt."

"Poor Dear One," Tamor said, imitating as best he could the crooning of a mother for her injured child. The Dragon was pathetic to be whining about such a small thing. He reached out his hand and sent a Healing spell to the wound. As Blackwing sighed in relief, he patted him gently, "I will make him pay for hurting you."

"When?"

"Soon, but first there are things I must do. I need the Dragon's Blessing, though."

"I give." The great creature caressed Tamor's forehead with the healed tentacle.

The Dark Lord trembled at the first touch then fell back as power seared into his body, wracking it with incredible pain and ecstasy blended together in one terrible impact. As the Dragon pulled away, Tamor fell forward on his face, lying prostrate on the rocky ground, gasping for air.

"Hurt?"

Tamor waved the Dragon away. He could not abide its touch again. "No," he managed between breaths. "Overcome with the pleasure of it all. Such wonder. How can you live with such power inside you?"

"Alone," Blackwing said.

*****

Gareth was pacing the floor, too distracted to even bother counting steps. His army was nearly ready except for the horses. He had envisioned himself riding at the head of his Scarleteers, his own red tunic decorated with enough gold embroidery to outshine them and mark him as their superior. He had designed a standard with a red background and a gilded horse backed by a golden sword and a silver battleax.

He had already mastered the sword and was working on learning the ax. The feeling of the heavy bladed weapon in his hand was exhilarating. It was fine to pierce and slice with the sword, but the ax? One stroke could lop of an enemy's arm, his leg, or even better, his head. What pleasure to finish off a foe with one well-timed swing. And even better to do it astride a magnificent warhorse. His gray was a fine animal, easy to ride and strong, but perhaps Edra would bring back a better animal, one magnificent enough to match his ax.

He was about to head out to the field to practice when the wind picked up. A cloud blotted out the sun, sending the room into darkness as the torches on the wall blew out. A mist slithered in from the window, then settled into the shape of a man, standing in the center of the floor.

Gareth rubbed his eyes with his hand, but when he opened them, the man was still there.

"Son of Gailvarg," he said. "What do you seek?

Gareth found his voice, despite his fear, "I wish to be a man and a warrior."

"I am Tamor, Lord of Darkness, servant to Blackwing. Name thy desire."

Gareth glanced down at his crotch. "To be a man," he said.

"And how will you pay?

"I am the King. I can so command and offer no gold."

"It is not your gold I want. Your Vow will do."

"Vow? To whom? You are nothing to me. I live in the light, not in the shadows. How can I trust you?"

"You were already halfway to my heart when you murdered your mother and father. Is it so far to go the rest of the way to regain what you have lost?"

"Prove yourself. Let me test your Magic and then I will decide."

Tamor laughed. "A wise King indeed." He gestured once and grinned.

Gareth felt a bulge in his pants. He pulled them down and stared between his legs to see his manhood restored. His heart raced, "Corm!" he cried out to his manservant who was never far away.

Corm opened the door, his mouth gaping as he saw the King standing naked from the waist down, "Your Majesty?"

"Get me a woman, at once," Gareth commanded.

It took only a matter of moments before Corm dragged one of the palace maids into the room and shoved her into Gareth's waiting arms. The King flung her onto his bed, yanked up her skirt and straddled her without a word. Then, he thought better of it and whispered in her ear as he dropped down, "The King seeks pleasure

in you, Mistress." He kissed her full on her lips then bit them as he
had his way with her.

He made love violently for some time as Tamor stood to the
side watching, his own loins aching, pulsing with each thrust. He
longed for Sorra, yearning for her soft body as he never had for any
woman before. The maid's cries and sobs teased his ears, sending
shivers through him. His gaze was riveted on the bed. When Gareth
finally pulled away and threw the whimpering woman to the floor,
he realized he'd been holding his breath and let it out in a heavy sigh.

Gareth pointed to the maid who was crawling to the door,
clutching at her torn dress, trying to cover herself. "Get out," he said.
"Get out and be sure you tell the other whores in the palace the King
is whole again and intends to repay them for all their laughter at his
expense."

When she had managed to get out the door, Tamor emerged
from the shadowed corner, "Are you satisfied, Your Majesty?"

"Hardly," Gareth replied. "I have many days of abstinence to
make up for. But this," he waved his hand down over his crotch.
"This is worth my promise."

"You swear to the Dragon then?"

Gareth nodded as Tamor reached out and took hold of his
left hand. "So be it." He slid an ebony ring on the King's finger.

As the dark metal touched his skin, Gareth cried out in pain.
The ring seared his flesh, burning itself like a brand into his finger.
He tried to pull it off to no avail as it buried itself into the bone.

"Sworn," Tamor said. "Edra defied the Dragon once and lost
his hand. You will lose much more if you do so."

Gareth was on his knees, holding his hand up, struggling to
bear the pain. "I will not defy him. I have too much to gain and too
much to lose."

Tamor reached out again, the Dragon's Blessing waning
with one last bit of Magic as he eased Gareth's agony. "You will be
told what to do soon." Then he swirled back into a cloud of mist and
drifted back out the window.

Gareth rocked back on his buttocks and shouted, "Corm! Get
me another. I am still hungry!"

*****

When Jamus woke, the sun was shining, but the fallen trees
and soggy earth proved he had not been dreaming the night before.
Whatever the real reason for the Black Dragon's visit, it pressed the
urgency of his mission to find a way to defend the Keep.

Quickly, he packed his saddlebags and hurried downstairs to find Covane already up and nearly finished with Firstmeal. "You slept later than I expected," Covane said. "I would have wakened you, but I figured that storm might have kept you awake. We've only lost a span of travel time anyhow. Garv's gone to get the horses ready. Moka's in the kitchen packing some provisions. Have some food and by the time you're done we'll all be ready to ride."

Jamus sat down and half-heartedly took a slice of bread and some eggs from the platter. "I'm not very hungry. Too much food last night."

"It was a fine party. Had a bit too much ale myself. You can't be hungover, though. Never saw a man drink less."

Jamus grinned wearily, more tired than he expected, "I have to be careful. Liquor's gotten me into trouble too many times. Better not to take any chances."

"Too bad. It's a good way to forget things a man wants to forget."

"Like how to deal with the woman he loves?"

Covane stared into his cup of keldherb. "I thought about what you said last night. With all that's happening, it might not be the right time, but I am going to tell Elyese how I feel. She's a fine woman you, know. Despite being Cauge and all that, she really is a fine woman. A man couldn't go wrong taking a lady like that for his wife, now could he?"

Jamus shook his head. "Absolutely not, Covane. Marrying her would be about the best thing you could ever do for yourself."

" 'Bout time ya got yer head on straight, Rider," Moka said as she came out of the kitchen. "Ya been pining over that lady o' your'n fer months. Too bad it took threat o' Shadows ta set ya right."

Jamus snatched up another slice of bread and got up. "Come on, let's get going. We've a good ride ahead and we don't know how the roads will be after that storm."

"Washed out, I reckon," Moka said. "Too many streams out this way. Makes fer good crops, but pays the devil when it rains hard."

Together they headed out into to the square. There were more than the nine Firecasters Jamus expected. Two more Riders and five settlers were mounted up and waiting.

Covane nodded to the Riders, "Carlin and Ezra," he said. "Friends from the old days."

Garv waved to the settlers. "More Warriors of the Eld. We're leaving some behind ta watch the village. They be a few more at

Landhold, I reckon. We oughta have us a nice little brigade fer ya ta take home the time we're all done, eh?

Jamus swung up on Whim as the stallion pranced, eager to be off.

We windstep now?

No, my friend. We cannot, not now.

No fun.

Sometimes we have to be serious. These men are good friends. I need their help. We need to stay on the ground to keep them all safe.

Not safe when Black Scalewing fly.

You know he was here?

He come kill. Think surprise. Best One smarter.

So that was the plan. A clever attempt to end the battle before it even began. Did the Dragon think him such a fool to be such easy prey? He was mistaken.

Think he want see Best One only. Easier to fight when know.

We've met before.

Not as Three River and part Black already.

Part Black? Have I touched his Waters?

Solve last riddle.

I don't understand.

Kisel say you will.

"My Lord?" It was Covane. "Are you all right? You haven't said a word since we left the inn. I thought I heard you muttering something."

"Sorry, I was thinking. I'm not used to riding with so much company."

"It is quite a group," Covane agreed. "Firecasters, Warriors and Riders, the elite of Arcula. You should be honored."

"I am, Covane, truly, I am."

XXI

As soon as the horses were safe in the Royal stables, Edra went into the palace to see the King. He found Gareth in the Great Hall.

Gareth was wearing his scarlet tunic and a pair of tight-fitting breeches that hid little as he hung one leg over the arm of the throne his showing his new body to the world.

Edra knelt before, him his gaze diverted, for the most part, "Your Majesty, I have returned with the horses for your cavalry."

"Well done, Master Edra. As you can see, I too have had some success since you left."

"I am pleased for you, Sire."

"So, now I am ready to ride to war against my tormentors and to repay my debt to the Sorceress. Think you so?"

"I never doubted you, My Lord."

Gareth swaggered down from the platform and reached out his left hand to help Edra to his feet. When Edra saw the ebony ring embedded in the King's scarred finger, he raised his own new left hand to Gareth's.

Gareth face broke into a twisted grin of triumph when he saw Edra's restored hand and the black signet. "Come, my friend, get on your feet and show me theses horses you bought for me."

Edra pulled himself up, wincing as the metal of the two rings touched and sent a shock through his body. "Who said anything about buying?' he said. "The King needs no money in the land of loyal subjects. Your purse is still full."

Together, they made their way to the stableyard.

Gant, the King's stablemaster, had separated the herd into three pens, one for the mares, one for the geldings, and one for the stallions. The horses were milling nervously about, nickering for herdmates they had bonded with on the long journey from Telma. Edra's comrades waited silently off to the side, expectant of thanks from the royal liege and reward for their loyalty. The sack lay at Jain's feet.

Before Gareth could examine the animals, Shimmer trumpeted and dissolved out of his pen only to appear an instant later in front of the line of thieves.

The King took a step back, putting Edra between him and the golden colt. "What is that?"

"Ah, he's chanted," Edra explained. "He was too magnificent to leave behind."

The colt strode over to the line of men and began to nuzzle the sack which began to wriggle.

Shim, stop.

Jebe hurt?

No. Where are we?

Many men. New one with big power.

In the city?

Many wall.

"He is wonderful," Gareth said. "Have you ridden him yet?"

"No," Edra replied. "He only obeys the boy."

The King frowned. "What boy?"

Edra motioned to Jain who untied the sack and dragged Jebe out. Too weak to stand, Jebe collapsed into the young Sorcerer's grip. "We kept him in the sack so there wouldn't be any questions along the way. I had to chant him to silence too. Prattles on like a woman."

Shimmer was nuzzling the boy frantically, as Jain tried to back away, wary of the colt's temper when Jebe was in danger. Gareth saw the boy shake his head and the golden horse obediently stepped back.

"The lad talks to him," Jain said.

"Loose the boy's tongue, Edra."

Edra raised his hand and severed the bonds holding Jebe captive. For the first time in Sevenstins Jebe sighed. His eyes widened as the King approached.

Shimmer snorted and lunged between his master and Gareth, sending the King back on his heels. "Call your horse off, boy. I want to talk to you."

Go back, Shim.

Hurt Jebe.

No. He is the King. He is a good man.

Bad.

Go back.

The colt backed away.

"How did you command him?" Gareth asked, "I didn't hear you say anything."

Jebe's voice was hoarse as he replied, "In my head. We talk in my head."

"What's your name, boy?"

"Jebe."

"Where are you from, Jebe?"

"Lord Delran's hold."

"And this colt of yours. Where did you get him?"

"I was there when he was born. He's mine. Lord Jamus gived him to me."

"Lord Jamus?" Gareth asked, suddenly more interested in the boy than he'd intended. All he really wanted was the horse, but now, he wanted information. "And where did this Lord Jamus give you this horse?"

"Magiskeep," Jebe replied. When he saw the fury rise in Gareth's face, he regretted his words.

It was too late, the King gritted his teeth in rage. "Edra, you did not tell me this."

"I had no idea, Sire. We only met the boy at Delran's. No one ever mentioned the Keep."

Gareth turned back to Jebe. "I want your colt to be my warhorse. He is mine now."

"No!" Jebe cried, "Shim's mine. He won't do for nobody but me!" As if in reply Shimmer pawed the ground and shook his head, snorting.

"The boy's mother, Edra, is she at Delran's hold?" Gareth asked, keeping his eyes riveted on Jebe. When he saw the boy's eyes widen in fear, he knew the answer.

"She may well be, Sire. The Lord hid the women from us, all but one. We took our pleasure with her, but couldn't spare the time for the others. Some of my men can always ride back if you so desire."

"I might so desire, Edra," Gareth replied. "Jebe, do you love your mother?"

Jebe gulped and nodded.

"You wish her to be safe, do you not?"

Again the boy nodded.

"Do you love your colt more than you love your mother?"

Tears welled in Jebe's eyes as a sob caught in his throat. He shook his head, unable to speak in the face of such a terrible choice.

"If you love your mother, tell your colt he now belongs to me and must do as I tell him. If you don't, I will send Edra's men back to Telma to do with your mother as they please. They are hard me, Jebe. You, of all, know that. They will not tie your mother in a sack. Rather they will strip her naked and shame her until she can bear no more. Command your colt to be my warhorse and I will leave your mother alone."

Shim, I am sorry. You must obey the King.

Jebe hurt. Shim mad.

I know, Shim, I know. You must do this for me, for Mam.

Shim kill.

No, not now. You must obey him.

Shim love Jebe only.

I love you too. Obey the King for my sake.

Do now. Kill later.

The colt stepped forward and lowered his head to Gareth's outstretched hand.

"Is he broken to saddle?" Gareth asked, not offering to stroke Shimmer's nose.

"Jest started," Jebe said. "He's green, but a fast learner."

"Gant, fetch a saddle and bridle and tack this horse up for me. I am going to ride him now."

"Your Majesty, do you think that's wise?" Edra said. He had not brought the colt all this way for Gareth, but for himself. It was all he could to hide his disappointment. "The boy said he's green. You told me you needed a seasoned mount."

"Look at him, Edra. All gold and silver. See my standard? A gold and silver stallion on a field of red. When we slaughter our enemy and the field runs crimson with their blood, will I not fulfill my destiny by riding him across that red river? Can you not see it?"

Edra nodded numbly. Once again he had underestimated Gareth's ego.

Once Shimmer was tacked up, Gant gave the King a leg up as the colt stood perfectly still. Gareth nudged him with his heel and the horse walked obediently off. Soon they were trotting and cantering around in one of the empty paddocks.

"I will try him in the field," Gareth said, pulling Shimmer to a halt at the gate. "Call my Scarleteers, Edra. Tell them to dress in their formal uniforms. Find them all suitable mounts and have them meet me on the field. We will practice close order drill and maneuvers for the rest of the day. I am eager to see how my regiment looks."

"Shim ain't used ta being ridden that long, Sir King," Jebe protested. "Ya kin ruin a colt riding him too hard."

"He is a warhorse now," Gareth replied. "He'd best get used to being tired and sore. Forced marches and battle tolerate no weaklings. If he's bred of Magic, he'll survive. He is the King's mount, after all."

Shim strong. King's bottom get sore before Shim.

Jebe covered his mouth so Gareth would not see his grin. At least Shimmer was not worried.

"What do we do with the lad?" Jain asked, loosening his grip on Jebe now that the boy had found his legs.

"Throw him in the streets," Gareth replied. "I don't need him anymore. Perhaps a whore will take him in to play with." Then he dug his heels into to Shimer's sides and galloped out to the field to wait for his Scarleteers to make their debut.

Jain half dragged Jebe out the gate to the stableyard and shoved him into the street. "Glad to be rid of you," he said, shutting the gate behind the boy. "That damn sack was too heavy to lug around for another day."

Jebe didn't even make it to the second side street before he felt a gentle hand on his arm. He turned to meet two warm blue eyes.

"Come on, Jebe. You have friends waiting for you."

"Who are ya? How do ya know my name?"

"I'm Jyp. I was watching everything from the window up there," he pointed to the palace. "I'm sorry about your horse."

Jebe couldn't hold his tears back any longer. Sobbing he could hardly speak, "I dint want ta do it, but they said they'd hurt my Mam. I had to. I had to."

"I know, Jebe. It will be all right, I promise. Do you think you can you walk?"

The boy gulped and nodded, but then his legs gave out and he nearly fell. Jyp scooped him up in his arms. "Come on, I'll take you to Master Simen, he'll know what to do."

At them mention of Simen's name, Jebe stopped crying, "Master Simen? He's here?"

"Indeed he is, Jebe. He's the one who told me to keep watch for you. As soon as he saw your golden colt in with the herd Edra brought back, he knew you were here somewhere."

"Shim won't come nowhere without me. Leastwise not afore. He's the King's horse now."

"Tell you what, lad. Simen and I will do our best to make things right for you and Shimmer."

"Ma Mam...."

"We'll send men to protect your mother and all of Delran's hold. She'll come to no harm."

"Why dint Master Simen come hisself?

"Simen has to hide, Jebe. The King thinks he's dead. It would never do for him to show up so close to the palace. He's staying at an inn just down the way."

"I kin walk now," Jebe said.

"Tell you what. Let me Touch you and when I'm sure you feel a little better, I'll put you back down and we and walk to the inn together. A brave man like you wants to be on his feet, not carried about like a sack of garbage."

Jebe grinned weakly and nodded as Jyp set him down on a wooden crate in the alley. The young Magician cast a quick glance around to make sure no one was watching, and then laid his hands on the boy's head.

Exhaustion poured into his body and Jyp nearly collapsed himself under its weight. Then his stomach clenched with hunger, his mouth dried for lack of water, and his eyes strained to see through the dark weave of fabric imprisoning his body. He could not move his arms or legs for they were tightly bound and he could hardly breathe as his prison grew stifling with the heat of his own body. He wanted to move, to stretch, to stand, but he could not. Instead, he was forced into a little ball lying painfully on the hard ground.

The River surged to soothe his torment. Cool, refreshing, nourishing his hunger, easing the cramps in his limbs, loosening the bonds until, at last he could swim free in the golden water. His breathing eased, and his body relaxed, the air sweet and clean again.

Jebe sighed, and Jyp smiled. "So lad, I'll ask you again. Do you think you can walk?"

This time, Jebe nodded enthusiastically. "Aye, Sur"

They headed for the Crown and Thorn, a little inn nestled on a back street not far from the palace. Jyp walked slowly so as not to overtax Jebe, for even though he had Healed the worst of the boy's suffering, it would take time for him to recover his strength.

As soon as they got to the inn, Jebe rushed into Simen's waiting embrace, burying himself against the Follyman's chest, sobbing, "They put me in a sack, an' I had ta give Shim away. The King's got'em. They was gonna hurt ma Mam."

"S-h-h-h, Jebe," Simen soothed, stroking the trembling boy's back and kissing him on the head. "Slow down. Take some deep breaths and just don't say anything until you feel better." He looked up at Jyp, who was shaking his head helplessly. Simen hugged Jebe against his chest, letting his own gentle Magic reassure him, calming his sobs to sighs. "There, that's a little better, isn't it?"

Jada carried a tray over to the table. "I gots some broth fer the lad. Put some special herbs in it ta soothe his belly so he don't get sick from eating too much too soon. Got a nice cup o' warm keldherb wid honey here iffen 'e wants a drink."

Jebe let Simen put him in another chair by the table. "They din't feed me much," he said as he tore off a piece of bread and stuffed it in his mouth.

"I can see that," Simen told him. "Now, once you've had something to eat, you're going to tell us the whole story, Jebe. Everything that happened from the time Edra rode into Lord Delran's to the time Master Jyp found you in the street. Don't leave out any details. Take as much time as you want, we're here to listen."

By the time Jebe had finished his story, Weswin had turned. Except for an occasional question, his audience had simply sat, quietly listening. "And so, they throwed me out inta the street an' that's when Master Jyp finded me an' brung me here. I be real worried about Shimmer. He ain't no warhorse. Is he gonna be all right?"

Simen nodded. "If he is half the horse his father is, I'm sure he can take care of himself. You said he was a lot like Whim."

"Oh, he is. An' he's real smart too. He listens good ta me."

"Tell me, Jebe, can you Fartalk with Shimmer? Jamus told me some Beasttalkers can speak to their animals without being near them."

"I ain't never tried. I always bin right there with Shim. I kin try iffen ya wants me to."

"Not now," Simen said, noticing the boy's sagging shoulders. "I think right now what you need to to is go to bed for a good night's sleep. Jyp, can you show Jebe where his room is?"

When Jebe was safely tucked in for the night, discussion began in earnest.

"At least that explains why the Knights of the Hand have roused," Kala said. "I've gotten word from Grandisite that a contingent of Knights arrived there yesternight and will be coming to Aberdeen with four Masters. It seems one Seer is not enough to deal with these threats."

"Knights and Seers, legends come to life," Jyp said. "And all because one of the King's men raided a few villages."

"Jebe's account suggested more than a few, and a good number of Turan's citizens dead or injured along the way. These were not ordinary raids. They were done in the King's name."

"Ya think Gareth knowed?" Jada asked.

"Whether he knew or not," Kala replied, "he certainly didn't care. If he had, Edra would have been thrown in prison as soon as he set foot back in Aberdeen with those stolen horses. I would have been summoned to the palace for a judgment. Instead, our most noble King rode out to his beloved battlefield to prance around in his bright red Follyman's garb."

"Kala," Simen said, wagging his finger at her," I take exception to that insult to a fine profession. A proper Follyman would never wear something so ostentatious. We have far better taste."

"Ain't but thinking the frippery is hidin' somethin' a mite darker," Jada said. "This whole thing stinks o' Shadow."

"Unless I'm mistaken," Simen replied, "According to the Eldenlore, the Knights of the Hand only ride together against the Black Dragon.'

"So, the Shadows who've been killing here in Aberdal were signs of more to follow. Had I been able to Search Arista, I might have known," Kala said.

"We had no reason to suspect anything," Simen replied. Then he paused. "It's nearing Sowin's Change. I need to go to the mirror to see if Jamus is there. He needs to be know what's going on here."

He got up from the table and left.

"There must be a better way to communicate with Magiskeep," Jyp said. "Simen's been waiting at that mirror for days now."

"Cain't do much better," Jada said. "I be mistress o' the scrying pot an' alls I e'er managed ta do wid the talkin' from afar."

Kala started and jumped up out of her chair to pace the floor. "That's it, talking from afar. What did Simen call it? Fartalk?"

"He said something about Beasttalkers to Jebe."

"Look, I know it's no the most logical idea, but what if Jebe could Fartalk with Shimmer? Then, the colt could talk to Whim and Whim…."

"Could talk to Lord Jamus," Jyp finished for her. "It's a pretty far-fetched, but worth a try."

"Better'n a Swirlypot," Jada agreed, "as long as them horsies understand what they's s'posed ta say."

"We'll have to talk to Jebe about that," Kala said. "I don't quite think horses see the world the same way we do. It does present a bit of a problem. But we should be able to work it out."

Outside, the wind Changed and Norwin's turn sent the rest of Aberdeen to bed while the fires inside the Crown and Thorn still burned while Seer and Sorcerers talked until morning.

*****

Elyese took one final look at herself in the mirror, pushed a wisp of golden hair behind her ear, adjusted one lace on the bodice of her gown and then swept out of the room to greet her visitors. When she heard that a group of riders was spotted on the road to Landhold, she'd been indifferent. But then one of the Watch mentioned the great silver horse, and she immediately ordered the servants to make up the guest rooms and to prepare both welcoming refreshments and a special feast for evenmeal. She had hurried upstairs to dress in a soft blue shaenis gown, well cut to her slender body.

Now, as she stood at the door of the house, watching the group ride up, her heart took and extra bound when she saw Covane riding at Jamus' side. Seeing Magiskeep's Lord again was one thing, but seeing the love of her life with him was almost too much to bear. Not that Covane knew how she felt about him. Neither of them had ever discussed their relationship beyond the doors of the bedroom. Riders were not the most open about expressing their feeling with words, but his actions had always told her she was something more to him than just a sexual conquest.

Someday, she hoped they would share more, but for now, her longing to wrap herself into his embrace and make love would have to do.

She counted nineteen riders. Even with all the guest rooms in the house, there was not enough room. "Mirabel," said, calling her housekeeper. "We only have twelve beds. Send some of the men to bring cots from the stable quarters for the rest of our guests."

"Can't some of them take rooms down there, My Lady? A few of those men look to be ruffers."

"No one who comes to my Hold with Lord James and Rider Covane will be treated any less than their masters. All of them are guests in my house. See to the cots, and don't let them bring any with straw mats. We have some good ones stored up in the loft just for occasions like this. Use the good sheets and coverlets as well. I will not insult my visitors with rough linens."

"Aye, Mardel," Mirabel replied as she scooted off.

Five horse grooms waited at the gate to help with the horses as Covane, Jamus, Garv, and Moka dismounted and handed the reins over to the stablemen while the rest of the riders led their own horses to the barns.

"All of you come up to the house when you've finished settling your mounts in," Eleyse called from the porch. "I have refreshments ready and the rooms are being made up. You'll be staying here as my guests."

"Ever the proper hostess," Jamus said as he neared, offering Elyese a quick bow of respect. "Thank you for your hospitality."

"It's the least I can do," Elyese replied. "There are many debts still owed. You will be staying the night?"

"We will, My Lady," Covane answered, climbing the step to take her hand, kissing it lightly.

Jamus wasted no time with further formalities. He simply followed Elyese into the house, beckoning to the others. Once inside, he shook his head to a servant who offered him a cup of calidew. "We are here on serious business, Mardel. We have every reason to believe Tamor and his Shadows are planning another attack on Turan. I came for your help."

"My help? Surely a Mage of your power does not need much assistance from a fallen Cauge."

"I have learned a great deal since I left Arcula, Madam, and while my power is not the question, the Mages in my Keep are another matter. Magic flows in two Rivers, gold and silver" he said, not bothering to mention the White or Black. "My Master are experts in the gold, but the silver eludes them. Spellfire draws upon the Silver Magic and for a Golden Sorcerer, that poses certain challenges. When I was here before, Master Serenec helped me build my strength in the Silver so I could fight the Shadows. My Magicians need to be taught as well."

"Can't you do it yourself?"

Jamus shook his head. "Too many Mages, and too little time. I need teachers, Masters of the Silver Magic themselves."

"Lord Jamus has his Arculan Firecasters to go with him, My Mardel," Covane said. "And Warriors and Riders will be at his side."

"You are going with him, My Rider?"

"Aye, My Lady. Arcula and I owe Lord Jamus a great debt. I am grateful to be able to repay a part of it."

"Well, then," Elyese said, "I will send for Master Serenec and see that my bags are packed. We will leave tomorrow, if it suits. In the meantime, let us share the hospitality of Landhold."

It was not until well past Weswin that Elyese finally found herself able to have some private conversation with Jamus. He had left the main room to sit out on the porch away from the noisy gathering inside.

"You are thinking again, My Lord," she said, as she pulled up a chair alongside him. "When you are Arcula, thought denies you Magic."

"I don't need Magic all the time," Jamus replied. "As a matter of fact, I have found the greatest happiness in my life without any Magic at all."

"Your wife."

He nodded. "My wife and my son."

"A child? How wonderful." Elyese's hand dropped to her belly and she stroked it gently, as she sighed. "I have often wondered what it would be like to be a mother."

"I can't say you ever lacked trying," Jamus replied, his voice edged with bitterness.

"You still haven't forgiven me."

"I'm sorry," he replied. "That wasn't fair. Your world and mine have different beliefs. I have no right to condemn you for acting on yours. It's just that what I have with Salene is precious to me and I can't abide even thinking of anything that might jeopardize that."

"Will your Salene be there when we go to Magiskeep? I mean, will she want to meet me?"

"She will. I've told her everything, you know. We don't keep secrets between us."

Elyese leaned back in her chair. "I envy her, Jamus. To think of sharing so much with one person like that. She must be an amazing woman to have earned the love of such a man as you."

"I'm the fortunate one, to have earned her love," Jamus replied.

"Arcula has never afforded me such treasure."

Jamus leaned forward, and took her hand in his. Then, almost as soon as he did, he pulled away again, realizing the danger of his touch. "It could, Elyese, if you would just open your eyes to see how much your Rider loves you."

"Covane? He has never said…." She sat up again. "Has he said something to you?"

"Give him time, My Lady. It's not easy for a man like him, a Rider, to admit what's in his heart. I will not presume to speak for him, so all I ask is for you to be patient. Speak your heart, if you can, and perhaps he will learn to answer."

Jamus got up and left her alone in the early moonlight. Whatever the rest of the night was going to bring, at least for now, Elyese was content.

*****

Melthus bowed to Tamor and waited for the Dark Lord to give him permission to speak. Since gaining True Life, the Shadow had gained status, but Tamor was still the Master, second only in the Dark World to Blackwing himself.

"And how goes the campaign beyond the Rim?" Tamor asked as he peered in the mirror, looking for some sign of activity in Magiskeep.

"All is well, My Lord. The King will march whenever you declare it time. He has his cavalry now."

"Ah, yes, his red riders. Are they skilled warriors?"

"They ride well together, My Lord. As to battle skills? Most of them seem to be in the king's imagination. They will make a most impressive display if their horses can trample their foes. The regular army is better schooled, and I have recruited many to the Dark Ways. Among the sworn are Shadows too. They should do well in overcoming any mortals who dare defy them."

"And your plan?"

"We take the Provinces. Let the King ride on his mad quest to Magiskeep, out of the way. Once he leaves the city, we can take the palace and the streets. From their, our ranks can only grow in number and might. Gambel is near True Life himself, and as Dax, commander of the Royal Army, he can lead them to victory."

"I have Shadow forces to add to your numbers when the time comes. The Way of Mirrors has an endless supply of recruits and all are eager for freedom and thirsty for blood."

"And what of the Rivermaster, My Lord? We can kill thousands of mortals and still not Close the Circle if he lives."

"My plan will come to fruition soon. I will rid the world of his virtue in short order and Blackwing will reign again. Do your part to subdue Aberdeen and its vassals and I will take care of Magiskeep."

"It is time, then?"

"It is time."

*****

Natale was proving to be a perfect nanny, despite Sorra's frustration at finding it hard to actually be alone with Jarien. Even when Salene was gone, Rath had an annoying habit of appearing at the most unexpected times. And then, there was the dog.

Clouder, Jamus' big black dog had taken it upon himself to keep watch over Jarien himself. And he was proving quite protective whenever Sorra was near, sometimes even growling at her when she touched the baby.

"He makes me nervous," she told Salene after a Sevenstin of taking care of the child. "I don't think he likes me."

"Clouder's just a big bluff," Salene said. "He really is a sweetheart."

"He growls at me."

"That's strange. I've never heard him do that. I do like to have him here when Jamus is away. Maybe that's the problem. He might be upset because Jamus is gone. He can be quite protective, although I don't know why he'd bother you."

"I'm not really good with animals," Natale said, speaking more for Sorra than for herself. Sorra suspected the dog knew her true self. "Do you think you could take him out of the room when I'm here alone with the baby?"

Salene smiled. "Of course. I'll tell Jeanna to take care of him for you whenever I leave."

"That will ease my mind, My Lady. Thank you." One more obstacle out of the way. The Dragon was another problem. "Lady Rath...how long will she be staying on?"

"The Lady comes and goes as she pleases," Salene answered. "I cannot speak for her. I must admit, she can be a bit frightening at times."

"She is terrifying. I don't know how you've managed to deal with her for so long," Natale said.

"She is devoted to Jamus and to Jarien. We cannot do without her here, at least not for now."

"I don't know why. She's useless in caring for most of the baby's basic needs. About all she ever does is sing to him sometimes."

"She soothes him in ways you may never quite understand, Natale. Trust me in this if you can. We need her."

"Ah, well, I suppose I will just have to deal with her, then." Sorra's heart was not in the reply, but apparently she had no choice. It was a matter she needed to discuss with Tamor. Perhaps he could find a way to distract Rath long enough for her to do what was needed.

"I have to go see how Master Joria is doing with her new students," Salene said, pulling her long full sleeved blue shaenis robe on over her simple pale blue day gown. "Jarien will probably nap while I'm gone. Shall I send some food in for you?"

"I'll be fine," Natale replied. "Just go on about your business. Your son is in good hands."

Salene called Clouder and headed out into the hall. She went downstairs to the classroom hall to Joria's chambers. There, she found the Mistress of Illusion instructing a class of young PrePrentices in, as Jamus had called it, "Practical Magic."

Today the lesson appeared to be simple fire starting if the charred study tabes and books scattered about the room were any indication. When Joria saw Salene at the door, she dismissed her class, reminding them not to practice indoors unless there was an ample supply of water on hand. "They tend to get a little bit too enthusiastic when they learn a new skill," she said, restoring order to her classroom with a wave of her hand.

"Are they proving as adept as Jamus said they would?"

"Even better, actually. I've managed to tame their firecasting skills down from Spellfire to more natural flames, by encouraging them to smile when they cast. Your husband explained how the Silver Magic worked, but he didn't have a lot of useful explanations as to how to control it. It's been a matter of trial and error so far, but I seem to be getting better at it." She sat down on one of the student stools. "They are rather energetic for an old woman like me."

Salene laughed. "You are, My Dear Mistress, one of the youngest old women I have ever known. And it's quite clear you were the perfect choice to teach our little Magicians."

Joria smiled, spelling her grey scholar's robe into a simple, rose-colored gown. "I had forgotten how satisfying it was to instruct the little ones. I didn't think I'd missed it so much. After I lost that class to the fever circles ago, I didn't think I'd ever want to deal with children that young again. I was wrong. It's so rewarding when they finally learn something I'm trying to teach them."

"How old must a child be before he can learn to control the Silver River on his own?"

"Ah, you're asking about Jarien, aren't you."

Salene nodded. "Rath is keeping his Power under control now. That's all well and good, but having a Dragon around all the time does tend to upset some people."

"The Lady does tend to make some grand entrances. It would be easier if she didn't keep flying in and out of the windows."

"I've gotten so used to it I hardly notice anymore," Salene replied.

"Huge silver Dragons rarely go unnoticed by the rest of us," Joria said.

"Well, we do need her, at least until Jarien is old enough to control his power on his own."

"That might not be until he's past two circles," Joria said. "Then again, he is exceptional in how strong his power is. I don't see the same abilities in any of the other children. With the Rivermaster for a father, we can only hope he's precocious enough to learn much sooner. How old is he now?"

"Nearly ten months," Salene said. "I've nearly lost track of time. He's sitting up now and crawling about the room. I don't even want to think how soon he'll start walking. He'll be into everything when he does."

"It's time to start teaching him to behave, at least a little," Joria said. "It's a shame Becca had to leave. She knows how to raise children."

"Natale had a son," Salene said. "I would think she could advise me. If Jarien could understand even a little of what we tell him, we might at least help him gain some control. Then Rath won't have to constantly change her chantings on the River so often."

"It would be nice not to have her hovering over the Keep all the time," Joria said.

"There's more to it," Salene said. "You know she's warned us of Shadows. Jamus had told Sarn to be on guard, of course, Has he alerted the other Masters?"

Joria shrugged. "In passing, but nothing more than just a mention of it. He doesn't seem too alarmed."

"I knew I should have been more direct with him. I'm in a bit of a difficult situation as far as he's concerned. Jamus has left him in charge as Master, yet I am still Mistress here. Most of my dealings are with the running of the household and settling accounts. The defense of the Keep is his duty and apparently I know more about the danger than he does."

"It's really that serious?"

"Rath has seen Shadows in the mirror and insists she's heard the Black Dragon is planning an attack. That's why Jamus went to Arcula. We need defenses here and there is nowhere else to find warriors. Simen's been trying to contact him, to tell him about the trouble in Aberdeen…"

Joria was shaking her head in confusion. "Aberdeen? The King? What's been going on?"

"Gareth has taken the throne. The Shadows have been there already and now there's talk of war and rebellion."

"Does Jamus know about it?"

"Not yet. Simen's been trying to contact him through the Way, but since he's not been home since, there's no way to tell him. It's a mess, and apparently cleaning up at least this part of it falls to me. I need to talk to Sarn."

"I'll warn the other Masters, though I don't know how much good it will do. We are not warriors, nor masters of Spellfire. Without Jamus here, we're practically defenseless."

XXII

After a good night's sleep in a bed instead of a sack, Jebe was already feeling stronger. Simen's promise to protect his mother and get Shimmer back had given him the first hope he'd had since being kidnapped and with it came a renewed energy and a healthy appetite. By the time the adults were out of bed, he had already eaten a full plate of pancakes and was ready to finish off a thick slab of ham.

Simen was delighted to see him, ruffling his hair and giving him an affectionate hug before sitting down next to him at the table. "Looks like I have a bit of work to do to catch up to you as far as Firstmeal is concerned, lad. I see Jada's herbs did their work."

"Ain't had a good meal in forever," Jebe said. "This is almos' as good as ma Mam's cookin'."

"Lady Kala sent two Knights to Delran's after you went to bed. The Lord himself serves the Hand, so the men were eager to go to protect your mother. I'm sure, though, that he would not have left his Keep undefended."

"'E's a good master," Jebe said. "'E was always lookin' out for me an' Shim. Joss too. Ya say 'e's a Knight?"

Simen nodded. "One of their most important Captains. I'm sure he'll be here in Aberdeen soon. He'll be looking for you."

"Are we gonna stay here?"

"As long as it's safe. Some of my friends here in the city are Magicians too, and we've set wards around the Inn. It's going to be our headquarters in this part of the city. We'll protect you here."

"I wanna save Shim. I gotta do somethin'."

"Shim can take care of himself, for now," Simen said. "Trust me on that. As I said last night, he is his father's son. You know, you can always talk to him."

"I gotta see 'im ta do that."

"Have you ever tried to talk when you were far away?"

Jebe frowned and shook his head. "Never been far from 'im afore."

"Sometimes Lord Jamus talks to Whim when they aren't together. Do you think you could try to see if Shimmer would talk to you?"

Jebe shrugged. "What do I gotta do?"

Now, the puzzle. Simen had no idea how to answer. What was the secret of Fartalk? He didn't even know the first thing about talking to an animal when it was near. "When you talk to Shimmer, what's in your head, Jebe? What are you thinking about?"

"How much I wants to know what he's got to say," Jebe replied. "Then, I kinda believe he's gonna tell me, an' he does."

Of course. The First Rule. *Magic exists only if you believe.* It almost seemed too simple. Still, it was worth a try. "If I tell you it's possible to talk to Shimmer even when he's not here, do you think you can trust me enough to believe it?"

Jebe gulped and nodded. "Ya ain't ne'er lied ta me." He closed his eyes. "Shim," he said aloud. "Are you all right?"

Miss Jebe.

Jebe's eyes flew open. "I heard him! I did! Shim, did the King work you too hard? Are you tired?"

King bottom not last long. Shim all bouncy make sore. Happy in four walls now. Good food.

"He says he made the King's bottom sore," Jebe told Simen. "He likes the food."

"I hope he didn't get into the grain bins," Simen replied.

"I warned him about that a long time ago," Jebe said. "He knows it will make him sick. He had a bellyache onct and don't want another one."

"Do you think you can get him to do something for me?" Simen asked. "I need to know if he can talk to Whim."

"Shim, can you talk to the Silver Lord?" When Jebe saw Simen frown he said, "That's what the other horses call Whim."

He not listen much to little ones.

"It's important. Master Simen wants to tell him something."

Best One brother?

"Yes, Lord Jamus' brother. Do you think Whim will listen to him?"

Shim try. What tell?

"He said he'll try. What do you want him to say?"

"Tell Jamus I want to talk to him in the mirrors. He'll know when."

"He wants Best One to talk to him in the mirrors."

What be mirrors?

Jebe shook his head. "Shimmer don't know what a mirror is. Horses don't see the world the way we does."

What would a horse understand? Simen's mind was racing. Reflections, something that reflected—water. "Jebe, Shimmer must have a water bucket in his stall. If he looks in it, can he see his face? Can he see a reflection?"

"Probly not," Jebe said," but I see what yer gettin' at. Shim, where we goes out on the green path, there's a big water place. Sometimes, when the sun is big, ya can see yerself in it. Scairt ya the first time the sun come out, remember?"

Shiny water.

"That's it, the shiny water. Tell Whim Best One's brother wants to talk to him in the shiny water."

I tell now. All done.

"Already? So soon?"

Talk not take long time. Head closer than feet. Whim listen. Say Jamus hear. More talk?

"He says he's already told Whim and Jamus heard the message. He wants to know if you need to say anything more." Jebe said.

Simen shook his head in wonder, "That will be enough for now."

*****

Jamus wasn't sure how to react when he first heard Whim insisting that he had a message from Simen. As usual, at least a part of it needed translation.

Same in Blood need talk Best One in shiny water.

"Are you sure Shimmer told you this?"

Jebe talk. With Same in Blood. Place of tall walls. Far from home. Shiny water, he say.

Jamus sighed. The world was always full of riddles, but at least this one was easy to solve, as long as he thought like a horse. "Same in Blood" was Simen, his brother. He was the only relative he had. "Tall walls," was a city and, as far as he knew, Simen was in Aberdeen since he'd gone there with Kala "Shiny water," was the puzzle. Water reflecting the sun? Of course, since Simen wanted to talk to him, the only answer would be the Way of Mirrors.

He couldn't afford another day in Landhold waiting until Norwin to talk to his brother. It was going to take nearly two days to ride back to Magiskeep with his armed party and lifted strides were out of the question with such a large and diverse group of horses and riders. He needed to stay with them. How then, to contact Simen with no mirrors around?

Then he laughed. "Shiny waters." All he needed was a lake or pond on the trail back and he could use that as an entrance to the Way. It was riskier than using a mirror, but it would serve the purpose. For once the horses' language worked better than his own.

*****

Rebellion was brewing in Aberdeen's streets. Gareth's army was making a name for itself among the people and it was not good. The more drilling the men had done, the more they swaggered. The more praise heaped upon them by the King, the bolder they became. Soon, "In the King's Name" became more of a curse than an honor. They failed to pay bills in taverns, they cheated at gambling, they bedded honest women despite their--or their husbands'--protests. Street vendors lost goods to the quick hands of former thieves who now wore the King's colors, and pickpockets stripped even the common workers of their wages.

Pleas to Gareth went unheeded. And when one of his men was called to judgment on charges of a crime, he ignored Kala's decisions and offered only a stern reprimand and a one-day suspension of duty which only sent the culprit back to the streets for another day of acquiring goods "In the King's Name."

By the time the Four arrived from Grandisite accompanied by a squadron of twelve blue-tunicked Knights, armed citizens were wandering half- empty streets and nearly every door was locked tight. Torches burned in taverns late at night as local militia met to discuss defenses of their parts of town.

Worse, the murders, once few and far between, were escalating. Nearly every street in the city had at least one gruesome death, and the hushed word "Shadow" was no longer just a rumor as it took on a frightening reality. Except in Cuver Street, where Magic was well known, most of the city was edging near panic, for they knew Sorcery was the only way to defeat the dark enemies. Wizardchase and all its consequences were fast becoming a source of regret instead of pride.

When the Seers rode in from the south along with the Knights, a glimmer of hope caught fire. Word spread quickly through the inns and meeting places. "Only twelve?" someone asked.

"I saw a troop of Knights riding in from the north the other day," an innkeeper offered. "Some say the Great Bell tolled and they have been roused."

"How many for Aberdeen?" another asked. "And of that number, how many can cast fire? Even stelin blades cannot destroy a Shadow."

"The Hand blesses as the Hand needs."

"Pah, creed of the faithful, or belief of fools. What we need are some true Sorcerers."

"Ne'er thought I'd e'er hear a man of Turan say that out in the open."

"Why not? The King's got Sorcerers in the palace. It's about time we follow his lead, don't you think?"

The innkeeper put out another round of drinks and settled himself on a stool by the bar. "Kept it to meself for circles, but me brother, who owns a little inn down near the Course says there's been Sorcerers there for as long as he can remember."

"Healers and such," one the women said. "There's a Herbalist in the Gardens."

"More than that from what my brother says. After the first murders, they were out in the streets on patrol, every one of them armed with fire strong enough to do in a Shadow."

"Hope then," the man said. "If they are not too selfish to do for others."

"We can always petition them."

"How?"

"The Seers are here. Is it not their duty to serve the whole Kingdom? Perhaps they can convince the Sorcerers."

The woman laughed. "Listen to the lot of us! First we curse Wizardchase and now we expect Seers and Sorcerers to ally to save our pitiful lives. The Hand spins the Circle in curious ways, doesn't it? Who would have suspected such a day would ever be upon us?"

*****

"Will the King see us today?" Kestia asked as they dismounted from their horses in the stableyard. The palace would welcome the Four no matter what, but audience with the King was another matter.

"I will demand it," Kolea replied. As First of the Seers, she was one of the only people in all Turan who would dare command the King. If he refused, she could call a Council of Lords to challenge his right to the crown.

"A mighty undertaking, Madam," Klef said. "In all the Eldenlore only one rightful King has ever been challenged, and his accusers lost in the end."

"Perhaps we will make history then. I need no Sight to see this city is living in terror and it all stems from the King's army. I Visioned Shadows, though, and no matter where they come from, it is the King's duty to protect his city. If Gareth has been remiss, we need to deal with him."

Once they were in the palace, Corm greeted them as honored guest, making excuses for his Royal Master. "The King is in drill with his cavalry," he said. "If you would care to watch, there is a pleasant balcony overlooking the field just up the stairs."

"When will this drill be over?" Kolea asked. "Our business is pressing."

"By Sowin's turn, Madam Seer. The King is building up his stamina in the saddle and must ride at least a span more each day. You really should watch, it is a magnificent spectacle."

They made their way to the balcony, where it was apparent their visit had been anticipated. Four cushioned chairs were set by the railing affording a good view of the practice field below. There was a table with a tray of sweet and savory pastries and pitchers of calidew and surlep punch. Reluctantly, the Seers settled to watch the King and his cavalry.

For the display, Gareth had ordered formal uniforms, and the cluster of red-jacketed riders riding in close order was impressive. The King himself, riding a beautiful golden horse with a silver mane and tail, rode to the front for the parade into the field. Then as the drills progressed, he merged into the ranks, surrounded on all sides by his warriors whose sole duty, it seemed, was not so much to attack the enemy, but rather to protect their royal leader. He swung his sword overhead most dramatically as if directing a great chorus dancing around him in intricate patterns of march. This dance went on for some time. Then, they all broke rank to begin practice passes at some of the dummies set up along the circuit around the field.

One at a time, each rider would spur his horse into a gallop, leap over a hedge, fence, or ditch and make a pass at the target with a stroke of sword or ax. A good strike sent the dummy spinning, and it seemed the more spins, the better. All the while, King Gareth sat in the center of the circle, counting. "Twenty-eight," he cried more than once when a rider veered slightly off the proper line galloping for more than twenty-eight strides to the strike. Workmen had spent spans measuring the distance from jump to target with careful precision until it was quite possible, though extremely difficult, for a rider to ride exactly twenty-eight strides between each obstacle.

Some horses, longer-strided than others, had to be reined hard at the last minute to hit the required number. Others were spurred on, nearly crashing over the jumps to meet the goal. Even to the untrained horseman's eye, it was an ugly sight.

The King himself, whose golden mount had set the standard for the twenty-eight stride requirement, cantered the course easily, never missing the count, despite the fact that the King's skills with the ax were almost laughable. Each swing of the huge blade nearly unseated him from his mount, and it seemed the horse somehow managed to keep itself underneath him despite his horrific balance.

Kolea watched intensely as the King made his third pass, opening herself to Vision out of amazement at seeing Gareth still in the saddle after two disastrous strikes. "The horse is chanted, I'd swear it," she said.

Klef nodded. "He dissolves and reforms under the King every time he starts to fall off. It is fascinating."

"I thought I was seeing things at first," Kendil said. "I should have trusted my Vision, but it was so incredible, I simply couldn't. Where could Gareth get such a creature?"

"I seem to recall a silver stallion with similar skill," Kolea said. "I thought then he was the only one in the world."

"Lord Jamus' horse," Kestia said. "I wonder if they are related."

"The colt came from Magiskeep," Edra said from the door behind them. "He was at Lord Delran's Keep." He stepped out on the balcony and bowed respectfully to the Seers. "I am sorry I was not at the yard to meet you when you arrived. I was disciplining one of the King's riders when you arrived. I'm afraid it took a bit longer than I expected. It is always difficult when a man refuses to repent."

"Had he committed a crime?" Kolea asked.

"He argued with the King about the twenty-eight. He has been replaced in the Scarleteers."

"The twenty-eight?"

"Haven't you been watching? The King demands his riders take twenty-eight strides to each obstacle. To try is one thing, to defy another. Private Girad complained his horse was too short-strided to match the number. Bad enough to make excuses, but then he told the King it was a foolish demand, one no soldier could ever follow in a real battle."

Kestia nodded. "The private had a point. No man counts strides riding into war."

"The King's men will. It is his command."

'That's ridiculous," Klef said.

"It is the King's command," Edra repeated. "And so it shall be."

"So, Private Girad was dismissed."

"He is dead," Edra said with feigned sadness. "I'm afraid he was not able to bear his punishment. I did think twenty-eight lashes would satisfy the King, but when I miscounted and stroked twenty-nine, I had to add another twenty-seven to even the count again. The poor man's back was flayed to the bone, I fear."

"How could you do such a thing?" Kestia asked, shuddering at the thought of it. "There can be no reason to beat a man to death."

"Oh, yes. If we were to allow one man to question the King, where would it end? Gareth must command complete loyalty and obedience from his personal guards. And Scarleteers are his to do with as he pleases. They must be made to understand that."

"By the Hand, what kind of ruler can be so cruel?" Kendil said, shaking her head.

"I was First Hand of the Cuage in Arcula," Edra said proudly. "I know how to demand respect. I am proud now to serve a King with equal skill and wisdom in governing."

"This is not governing," Kolea said, "It is tyranny. A good King rules with justice, not terror."

"Ah, my dear Seer, you and the rest of Turan have lived in peace too long to understand the ways of war. We cannot afford those under us to question our decisions."

"We are not at war, Sur."

"I did not know your Vision made you blind to reality. Even now the Darkness is marching in our lands. Blood is running in the streets every night. The King must command. It is as simple as that."

Kolea got to her feet. "It is useless for us to talk to fools." She waved her hand over the battlefield, "This pageant is a mockery of war, a game played to entertain a man's ego while the enemy laughs. It's clear, even without the Sight, that we have come in vain to plead our case to the King, for it is the King himself who poses the greatest threat to Turan. We are done here."

The other Seers nodded in agreement and followed Kolea down the stairs to the courtyard.

The First Seer was visibly shaken. "He spoke so coldly of Girad's death. As if it were just a matter of course."

"And the twenty-eight, the King's obsession. It makes no sense at all."

"It was said Gailvarg went mad at the end. Could his son be so now?"

"With Shadows in the city, I would think he would have been leading patrols along the streets rather than performing for us," Kendil said. "Do we know where Jur Kala is now? If she'd been in residence at the palace, she would have met us instead of Edra."

"He is a Sorcerer, you know," Klef said. "I could not help but sift him."

"It is not his Sorcery that concerns me," Kolea replied. You saw the ring on his finger." The others nodded mutely. "He did not mention Shadows casually, and he did say they were marching 'in' the Kingdom, not against it."

"Seer's Art can be a curse," Klef said, "when we can interpret words so precisely. I fear your perception is keen, My Lady. The Darkness is the King's army, not its opponent."

"So what do we do?"

"We join the Knights and offer our services. They are the Light. It is our only defense."

Delaine, one of the Knights who had accompanied them to the palace, approached from the stable area. "The men are taking the horses to the stableyard at the Crown and Thorn Inn, Most Reverant Ones. Jur Kala has requested your presence there and has reserved rooms for each of you. It is but a short walk and we are here to protect you."

"Show us the way, Sir," Kolea said, gathering the skirts of her riding gown as she followed the Knight.

As promised, Kala was waiting for them at the inn, "Welcome, Masters," she said, ushering them in and locking the door behind them.

"For security?" Klef asked.

"Secrecy," Kala answered. "We do not want anyone to know of our meetings." She nodded to each of the other people in the room. "Mistress Jada of Counsel of Cuver Street, Master Jyp, our ears in the palace, Seymor and Jelda, also of the Counsel. The young man over there is Master Jebe, who has a personal stake in the royal cavalry, and here, is Lord Simen of Magiskeep."

Jolea studied Simen's face carefully before responding. "If I am not mistaken, you bear a striking resemblance to another Lord of the Keep."

"Jamus is my brother," Simen replied. "I am pleased to meet the First of Grandisite at last. He told me a great deal about his time with you."

"Are you his equal, My Lord? We could use a powerful hand here in Turan."

"No man is my brother's equal," Simen answered. "I am, however, a Magician of more than adequate skill and quite prepared to defend your city from its enemies."

"You have Spellfire, then, to defeat the Shadows."

"Enough, but as with all the Keepbred, I cannot sustain it for long. Using it drains Magicians of the Golden River."

"It does not drain the Knights," Kolea said. "When the Great Bell Tolls to call them, they ride together to the Ceremony where the

Magic is given to their hands. Our visit to the King was only one reason we came to Aberdeen."

"When does this all happen, and where?" Simen asked. "There isn't much time left. The Shadows are attacking people in the city every night now, and the numbers are increasing."

"Tomorrow night is Seremonth full moon, Light of the Spirits. The Knights will have gathered by then. It will be someplace where all their horses can be safely quartered."

"The Course," Jyp said. "It's the only place in Aberdeen with enough stalls. And the racing season is still on hiatus, so it's practically deserted."

"Tomorrow, then," Jada agreed. "We will leave here just past Sowin and stay at the Forgetful Friend until moonrise. It's the safest place in all the South Quarter."

They spent the rest of the day discussing the King's behavior, offering all kind of theories as to what he was planning. No matter how many times they twisted and turned the facts, they kept coming back to one disturbing conclusion. Gareth had allied himself with the Black Dragon.

"How else could Mistress Salene's spell be reversed?" Jyp asked. "I saw the weave. It was far too complex for Edra to unravel and there haven't been any other Sorcerers near him. Shadows, though, slip in and out in the darkness, unnoticed."

"It would not have been an ordinary spirit," Kestia said. "Only great power could undo a spell woven by a Seven Arts Mage of the Keep."

"Tamor," Simen said. "Blackwing's general, if you can call him that. He is the Dragon's voice and, I suspect, his power. He can walk the sky when he wants to."

"I have read of this in the Eldenlore," Kestia agreed. "Cloudwalking and suborning men in power to his cause, '*The call of the Dragon rings in the night, turning to darkness the forces of might. One is his voice, one is his hand, one turns the hearts with ebony band. Thus kings, queens, and princes by Blackwing are won, while virtue by evil's invention undone.*' A less than pleasant poem, I'm afraid, considering the circumstances."

"We saw the black ring on Edra's hand," Kolea said. "But we never saw the King. Perhaps we shouldn't have been so eager to hurry out of there before he granted us an audience."

"No matter," Jyp said. "I still have his confidence. Not as much, perhaps, since Edra returned. Still, enough to see his hand if that's what I need to do."

"You'll need to be careful," Kala said. "If the King has turned to the Darkness, he will be suspicious of everyone. It's never safe dealing with Shadows."

"I am armed with more wit than the King," Jyp replied. "All I need to do is keep sharp."

"What about Edra?"

"Edra bears watching, I'll admit. I've outsmarted him so far. All I can do is continue to be the man he thinks I am."

Jebe entertained the adults with tales of his own adventures in Magiskeep and of the exploits of his golden colt through most of Evenmeal before Jelda managed to bundle him off to bed, leaving the adults to finish off the night.

A span before Norwin's turn, Simen and Kala slipped upstairs to her chamber where the tall mirror waited. All they could do was hope Shimmer had somehow managed to Fartalk to Whim and, in turn, Jamus.

*****

The journey back to Magiskeep had been uneventful. They made camp the first night out in a grove of sheltering brellums near a small lake. Jamus waited until everyone had settled in, and headed out alone for the water.

Garv, on watch, noticed, and followed at a discreet distance, determined to give Jamus his protection, no matter how the Lord might protest. He knew the Sorcerer was confident in his ability to take care of himself, but he had a duty to defend his commander.

When Jamus waded into the lake, he sat down with his back to one of the trees and waited. The nearly full moon reflected silver like on the lake's still surface with hardly a ripple even as Jamus moved through the water. Then, he ducked under and Garv sat up, peering into the dim light, waiting for him to emerge again.

Moonlight filtered through the crystal waters, casting reflections all around. Jamus let himself sink into the beams, his feet soon hitting the sandy floor and the entrance to the Way of Mirrors. His Mastery of the images was complete as he sorted the watery images from the more solid reflections of passages into the endless corridors stretching through time and space in infinite directions. It took only a moment for him to orient himself as he headed west, seeking Aberdeen's room, beyond the Rim, past the heart of Turan.

He could not pass through the Rim's Magic from here, but he could see into the capital city where, if Whim's message was correct, Simen was waiting for him.

Instinct and a keen sense of the Way's trickery led him to a shimmering door.

"You challenge the Way, Kiselor," a voice said off to his right. "Is it wise in time of Shadows?"

"We wait. Tamor promises freedom when the Great Circle closes."

"Freedom," another voice whispered.

"True Life."

"Blood for blood."

"The time comes soon," the first voice said.

Jamus ignored them and pushed the door open. Inside, the walls were covered in mirrors, each visioning another place in Aberdeen. He spun slowly and finally, to the far right, he saw his brother, with Kala at his side. "Simen? You needed to talk to me?"

"Thank the Hand," Simen replied. "We weren't sure the horses could do it."

"Whim told me. How did you get word to him?"

"Through Jebe, and then Shimmer. It was an interesting experiment."

"Seems to have worked. What's going on?"

"Trouble," Kala said. "Gareth is King now and we think he's allied himself with the Shadows. The city's in turmoil, on the edge of rebellion. Gareth has a Black Sorcerer at his side and has raised an army. How many of them are Shadowsworn we don't know."

"Blackwing is awake and planning some kind of attack on Magiskeep," Jamus replied. "I'm on my way there now with Spellfire casters and my little band of warriors. It may not seem like much but if I can arm the Keep's mages with Spellfire too, we should be able to hold off the Dragon's forces. Arcula's in danger too, but they are hardened to war already and prepared to defend themselves"

"So it's what we feared then, the Dragon's move to close the Great Circle," Simen said. "That explains everything happening here."

"I can't come to help," Jamus told him. "You're not alone, are you?"

"By the blood, no," Simen replied. "We have Magicians of our own here. And Grandisite has been roused along with the Knights of the Hand."

"The Knights? So not a legend after all."

"No," Kala said. "Several hundred are rumored to be in the city by now, soon to be armed with Spellfire, as the old lore prophesized. If it's war Blackwing wants, war he shall have."

"On three fronts," Jamus said, Wolla's words clear in his head. "May the Hand protect us all."

"Take care, brother," Simen replied. "I want to see you again."

"Be safe, Jamus," Kala said. "We will take care of things here. You have a home to protect."

Jamus waved his hand in farewell and left the room, once again ignoring the voices calling to him.

"The Dragon rises."

"The Shadows feast."

"We will all walk the clouds and taste the blood of fools."

A dozen turnings later, Jamus returned to the corridor of the moonlit lake and he let himself float back to the surface.

Garv relaxed as soon as he saw Jamus' head emerge from the water. He had been under for less than a minute. All was well.

As Jamus made his way to shore, he saw Garv. "Keeping watch, my friend? I hope I wasn't gone too long."

"Jest a moment," Garv replied. "Whatcha doin' swimmin' this time o' night."

"I needed to clear my head," Jamus said, waving his hand down his body to dry himself off. "It's hard to explain, actually. Lakes and streams often connect to the Spring," he used the term for Magic's River he hoped Garv would understand.

"Aye, so I've heard. Warriors don't hold much ta the finer points o' the Mard. Whitefire serves us enow not ta bother wid much more. 'Tis a simple life that way."

Jamus sighed. "I wish I could make my life that simple. Every time I turn around there's some new complication. There's trouble across the Rim, too. Shadows attacking the city of Aberdeen. The Hand only knows what may be going on in other places."

"And all the Sorcerers here? What's ta be done?"

"My brother is there and your brothers too, unless I am mistaken."

Garv frowned. Then he nodded grimly. "So the Elds spoke true. The Warriors ain't alone after all. Seems we have a lot more in common than what's on the surface, eh? Ya onct told me the story of Wizardchase. Seems my clan was outcast from Turan proper too. Long afore the words was even writ down, I reckon. T'were onct a Citadel in the mountains, they say. An' all the clans were one. Then come the Rift an' the Wood Clan left. T'weren't no Rim then, an' no

Wall neither. All Turan were still one. Arcula were about as far from the Hand's tower as a man could get afore he drowned in the sea. Still hear the bell toll in me dreams, I does. The old ones say it's in the blood. Thought I heard it t'other day."

"It would explain a lot of the stories are true, Garv. I'm not an expert on the Knights of the Hand, though. Still from the little I know, your Warriors and they have a lot in common. I'd like to believe it. Allies like that against Tamor would be invaluable."

"Ya already knows ma men an' me kin fight them lightshifters, Milord. Jest a worry there be enow of us ta take 'em all on."

"That's why I need to all to help teach my Magicians. Then we'll have an army."

XXIII

The Knights gathered at the Course, making camp in the infield of the running track. There were nearly three hundred men of all ages and rank, united in the blue tunics and a common cause. Vows some had made circles before were coming to fruition, promises to be kept even if it cost them their lives. They had left farms and forges behind to follow the Way of the Hand and now, with the blessing of Grandisite, they were waiting to accept the power granted to them on the day they took the sword and swore to fight the Darkness in the Great Battle.

When Kolea and the other three Seers rode in, the men left their campfires and gathered on the track in front of the grandstand, swords in hand. Lord Delran and Lord Dale stood at the front. They had arrived with the Eastern contingent just a wind before and hadn't yet set up their tents. As soon as they saw Simen and Kala, they left the group to greet them.

Only the strict formality of the circumstances kept Dale from sweeping Kala into his arms to kiss her. Instead, he took her hand and kissed it, almost too properly. "My Lady Juris, I am pleased to see you well. We have had terrible news of violence in Aberdeen."

Kala's hand trembled at the touch of his lips as her heart lurched, longing for so much more. "And I am pleased to see you Lord Governor. The tunic suits you. And, my dear Lord Delran, you too honor the Hand with the colors. I should have suspected."

"The Knights have never proclaimed ourselves, My Lady. I am sure if you looked around you would see many faces you recognized," Delran said. "With Turan at peace, we kept our secrets."

"It's good to see you both," Simen said. "I must admit, I didn't quite expect this. And yet, knowing you both as well as I do, I'm not surprised. You have always been two of the most honorable men I have ever known."

"Speaking of honor," Delran said, "I have another promise to keep. I told Jebe's mother I would find him. Have you any word of the lad?"

"He is in good hands," Simen replied. "He went through a horrible ordeal after he was kidnapped, and, I'm afraid he's lost Shimmer in the process, but we have him safe and protected with our people in a small inn near the palace."

"Thank the Hand for that," Delran said, heaving a deep sigh of relief. He wiped a tear from his eye as he went on. "It nearly broke me when Edra took him, and all for that colt of his. You say he's lost him anyhow?"

Simen nodded. "The King took him as his warhorse. I can't think any good will come of it and I've told Jebe we'll get the colt back. I haven't quite figured out how."

"Times will change, Simen. When they do, we will all have answers. For now, we leave the King to his prattling and deal with the Shadows who follow him."

"And if he himself is in league with the Dragon?"

"Then he dies along with the rest," Delran replied.

Somewhere, in the distance a bell tolled as the moon reached its peak in the sky. Delran moved back to the front of the Knights and stood tall and proud as Kolea approached to stand at the foot of the grandstand, her arms raised to the sky.

"I call upon the great Scalewing, Master of Light, The time has come to bestow the Blessing upon those gathered here. Alrath, I call thee. Lord of Light, I call thee. Flame of Purity I ask of thee, Power to defeat the Darkness. Come, Master, come, Lord, come great Dragon, the moonbeam is thy road."

A great gust of wind blasted across the Course, blowing down tents, damping campfires, nearly knocking several of the nearer Knights off their feet. The Great White Dragon appeared, his wings on fire in the moonlight. His huge body took up half the track as he landed, his claws raking a huge furrow in the dirt. "I come," he said, his voice bellowing.

Kolea bowed. "We seek the Blessing. Blackwing rises. The time is near."

The huge creature swirled into a whirlwind, a blizzard of white sparks, spinning smaller and smaller as he transformed into another form, that of a tall, white-robed, white-haired man, his face glowing, a pure white aura surrounding him as he strode over to the Seer. He reached his hand out to her and as their fingers touched a jolt of power rocked her body. The same glowing aura surrounded her.

She stretched out her hand again to the heavens and this time a bolt of Spellfire shot from her fingers to challenge the stars themselves with its brilliance. "The Blessing," she said. "Those who seek, come forward. Receive it from the Dragon's hand. Accept the Gift due you by Vow upon your sword."

Delran approached Alrath and reached out his hand. He too was jolted back, surrounded by the glowing aura as his sword seemed to shine with a light of its own. Dale followed and then, one by one, each of the Knights stepped forward to accept the Gift of Power from the Dragon himself.

The moon had traveled in the sky by the time all three hundred Knights had been blessed. Then, Kolea brought Kendil, Klef, and Kestia forward. She beckoned to Kala as well and the four waited silently. Alrath spun again, his body growing with the whirlwind and soon he was once again the Great White Dragon. His glittering, whirling eyes fixed on the four Seers.

"Only those with true courage can take the Blessing," Kolea said. "If you dare approach the True Dragon, it is yours. If not, there is no fault. Choose."

Kendil and Kestia hesitated, but Klef stepped boldly forward, right up to the Dragon. Alrath lifted one sharp claw and touched the Seer's arm, cutting through the sleeve of his robe, to rake his skin. Klef cried out in pain as he started to bleed. Then, he too was surrounded in the white glow and he fell to his knees.

Kala started to go to him, but Simen held her arm. "Are you sure, Kala? Is it worth it?"

She shook free from his grip. "I must, Simen. Turan is my world too." She walked bravely up to Alrath and bared her arm. "No point in ruining my clothes, Master. I wish the Blessing."

Alrath through back his head and made a noise which might have been a laugh. Then he reached out and raked a gash along Kala's arm. She stood firm as the power enveloped her, the jolt charging through her shaking body. She reached down to help Klef to his feet as the blood dripped down her hand.

The Dragon peered at the other two Seers, who shook their heads and stepped back. Then, with one mighty flap of his wings he took off and soared back along the moon's beams into the sky and out of sight.

Simen rushed to Kala's side a stride ahead of Dale. He placed his hand on her arm and without asking, Healed the wound with a single thought. Dizzy, she fell back into Dale's waiting embrace. "It's still going to leave a scar," she said. And then, she fainted.

Kestia had bound Klef's wound with her scarf. "I couldn't do it," she said. "I was too afraid."

"No shame," Klef assured her. "You heard Kolea. You cannot use the fire if you fear it."

"May I Touch you, Master?" Simen asked. When Klef nodded, he Healed him as well, sealing the wound and doing his best to mend it. But, as Kala had said, there would still be a scar.

"The Mark of the Dragon," Klef said as he too swayed on his feet, working hard to stay conscious. "We are not of the Sworn as the Knights are. Alrath demands more from those who seek the Blessing without the Promise. The Gifting is a heavy burden."

"He didn't wound Kolea."

"The Mistress was long ago sworn in the Citadel. The Law decrees at least one Seer must be so in each Great Circle. She is the only one who can call the Dragon."

"My brother can," Simen replied.

"Ah, yes, but he is not here now, is he," Klef said. "Does the Rivermaster deny us?"

"I am his surrogate," Simen said. Then he thought better of it. "Blackwing is going to attack Magiskeep as well. Of all places in Turan, it is the least defended."

"All those Sorcerers and no defense?"

"The Keep practices peace, My Lord. It is all most of the Magicians there have ever known. The only defense against the Shadows is Spellfire, and for circles it has been denied in the Halls there. Few Mages even know how to cast it."

"What are they going to do?"

"Jamus has a plan. All he needs it time to put it into place. Until then we can only hope Tamor and his Shadows keep to the Norreaches."

*****

"Today, on the clouds," Tamor ordered to a dozen of his Shadow warriors. "Before the Rivermaster returns to his beloved Keep, you must strike."

"Do we feast, My Lord Master?" one of the Shadows asked.

"You are welcome to do as you please. The more fear you stir, the better. I cannot wait any longer to put my plans into action. The clouds will blot the sun for you, but know they have set watch."

"And the Silver Dragon?"

"My army is already attacking her homeland. She will fly to their defense as soon as she hears. Blackwing is already bragging on the winds. She will be gone by the time you get there."

The Shadows bowed and headed out to the cliff's edge where they stepped into the sky to walk the clouds to Magiskeep.

*****

Rath was rocking Jarien while Natale changed the sheets in his crib. Suddenly she cried out, "I must go! Take the kitling. Guard him well, the battle has begun." As soon as Jarien was in Natale's arms, she leapt to the window, transformed, and flew off in a gust of wind.

Sorra smiled. Salene had left the Keep to attend to some business in the village. She was, at last, alone with the baby. She wrapped him in a blanket, gathered a small bag including several bottles of milk, and stood by the window watching.

Outside the clouds were gathering quickly, sailing in from the north.

A watcher, posted on the north tower called out a warning. "They're coming!"

Joria, who had taken her little class outside to test their skills at firemaking looked up to see the darkening sky. "Run, children. Get to the front hall."

Instead of listening, the children froze, their eyes riveted on the heavy clouds above and on the even darker swirls of mist blowing in with them.

Then, one of the swirls snaked out a tendril at Jillia, the youngest student. She screamed as it lashed at her and threw up her hand, sending a blinding flash of Spellfire at the darkness. There was a screech of pain and the sky opened a bit, letting in a thin streak of sunshine.

The other students cheered, and before Joria could say another word, her young charges were sending deadly bolts of Spellfire into the sky. Uninhibited by Rule or Vow and still one with the Silver River, the children sent their Magic without thought or concern, shattering the Shadows into ashes, one after another.

As quickly as they had come, the invaders were destroyed as the sun burned the last of the clouds away.

Joria stood slack-mouthed and still as her students pounded each other on their backs, reveling in their success. "We done good, Mistress," Sandon said as he ran over to her. "They was bad things. One tried to hurt Jilli. We stopped 'em didn't we?"

Joria swallowed hard. "Indeed you did, Sandon. Indeed, you did." How easy for him it had all been. No thought, no effort, just the sheer liberty of Magic Unrestrained, untempered by the discipline of endless lessons learning how to control it. It had been a terrifying display and an exhilarating revelation."

"What did I just see?" Sarena asked as he hurried over to Joria's side. As soon as the watch had called she, along with the other Masters, had run to help but they never made it past the door of the Keep.

"The children," Joria said. "They have no scruples to stop them."

"Bless the Hand for that, or curse it," Sarena said. "Let us hope they never turn on us."

"They love us," Joria said. "But there is something more disturbing to think about. I counted but twelve attackers. Why? Do you see any more clouds on the horizon? Why would so few come and why now? It's broad daylight."

Soon Master Jorn was at their side. "Lord Sarn wants the children inside. He wants to place them in the northern tower rooms to stay with the watch."

"He'll risk them like that?"

"He saw what they did, Joria. To save the Keep, he will risk anything. He said you'd protest, so if you have anything more to say about it, he'll see you in the Dining Hall."

Joria called the excited children inside and sent them off with the Prentices, who were waiting to escort them to their new posts. Then, she headed to the Dining Room to speak her mind to the Lord of the Keep.

Outside, in the stables, Sorra finished tacking up Pebble, the only horse in the Keep who would tolerate her, and climbed into the saddle from a stacked up bale of straw. She had strapped a leather pack on her back with Jarien tucked safely inside. While all the commotion outside distracted everyone else, she rode out through the north gate of the paddocks and dug her heels into the pony's sides. Pebble broke into a quick canter and the disappeared into the cover of trees beyond.

*****

Silverwing fly.

"Rath?" Jamus asked when he heard Whim's voice.

Fly to home. Trouble.

"What kind of trouble?"

Darkones. Great many. Big fight. Must protect. Pebble run hard. Not happy.

"What's Pebble got to do with it?"

Not know. Just run. We run?

"Why? Is there danger? Is Magiskeep under attack?"

No danger now. Keep safe.

"Then we can't run, Whim. There are too many of us and I must make sure we stay together."

Dare he tell the others Arcula was under attack? They were too far away from Arcuse to do anything now, but it was there home. They had a right to know.

"Everyone, listen to me," he said waving for the troops to stop. "Blackwing's army is attacking Arcula, there in the north not far from Arcuse. Rath has flown to help, but I have no word as to how things are going. Any of you who want to go to the battle had best leave now. I must still ride to Magiskeep to defend my own home."

Of the band, only two riders turned their horses off the trail, the rest stood firm.

"We be sworn to the Rivermaster," Garv said. "For a Warrior a Vow made be a vow kept."

"I freely release you all from any Vow you ever made to me," Jamus replied. "No man is bonded to me by his word."

"Then we be bonded by love," Tobin said. "'T'ain't many a man what's willin' ta give his life fer another's homeland. I want ta be one meself." He stood up in his stirrups and called out to his companions, "What say ye all?"

"To Magiskeep," came a reply. And as one, the remaining Warriors, Riders and even the Sorceress herself, joined the chorus, "To Magiskeep!"

Jamus spun Whim around and set off at a brisk trot. The other horses had to canter to keep up.

*****

The coming of Weswin set Aberdeen's nerves on edge. It was always in the darkness when the Shadows struck, slithering in between the cracks in the shutters or even down chimneys. They were silent, deadly, and night by night coming in greater and greater numbers.

Some materialized wearing the King's colors, some were simply black figures, empty-eyed and terrible. Taverns refused service to the soldiers, and Gareth's name was poison on the lips. Hope was in short supply.

But now, word raced through the streets first as a rumor, then as reality. "The Knights of the Hand are coming!" Tall, proud riders dressed in pale blue tunics emblazoned with the crest of an eagle came riding out of the alleys, their eyes searching the heavens and the very windows and chimneys the people had learned to fear. Cheers greeted them on every corner as they spread throughout the city. Some were joined by Seers and Sorcerers, who, to be recognized, wore auras of silver light around themselves to let the people know they Touched the River.

Even Jada's companions, Keepbred and trained, had Spellfire in their hands, for long absence from the discipline of Magic's hold had freed them from their inhibitions and they had used Magic Unrestrained for so many circles it was natural to them.

As the Knights deployed, Simen, Kala, and Dale rode on to the palace. It no longer mattered if Gareth thought Simen was dead, for war changed the rules. It was his army attacking the city and he was responsible.

The King and his Scarleteers were out drilling on the field when they arrived. Corm tried to take them to the viewing balcony, but Kala brushed him aside. "Choose your allegiance, Corm," she said. "Either Turan or the King."

"They are one in the same," Corm replied, trying to keep his trembling knees from giving way.

"It is Gareth's army attacking the city. We have more than enough witnesses to prove it. Many are Shadowsworn and even those who are not have been raping and looting in the King's name. Even now, the Seers are going to the barracks to sort out the Darkness. Those who have not turned to Blackwing's side will be given the chance to choose, even as you are now. Every man, woman and child in the royal Keep will be questioned, and each Searched. So speak now, does your heart belong to the King or to Turan?"

Corm was quivering in fear. "Turan, of course," he replied as he felt Kala's Power boring into him. He shrank back. "I want my life, no matter whom I serve. If the King falls, I am yours."

"And if he wins?"

"I cannot lie, to you Madam, I know that. I have never been a warrior and have no skill with blade or Magic. I am at the mercy of whomever I serve. The King has been good to me, but so was his father. I have no more loyalty to give than that."

Kala nodded. "Your honesty protects you, Corm. It is, indeed, your only weapon. Swear on it now that you will do nothing to interfere on either side and Master Simen will let you live."

Corm nodded eagerly. "It's all I can ask."

"Go to your quarters and stay there. If the King thinks you are his ally, you will be safe from him. If you keep your word, you will be safe from us. Pray only that no Shadows find you, for their only sovereign is the feast."

Corm scurried off, his eyes darting back and forth to each dark corner as he passed.

"That was rather cruel, don't you think, Kala? The Shadows would never strike in the palace. The poor man was nearly fainting as it was," Dale said.

"Serves him right, he's been the King's lackey for far too long to trust completely. But I didn't lie to him. While it's not likely the Shadows would strike here, even we need to be careful." Kala said, "I have opened myself to the Light and should be able to sense the Darkness before it attacks, but when you are in the lair of the rimsnake, it always pays to be on guard."

"Which way to the field?" Simen asked, "I've never tried to actually go down there."

"Through the one of the west corridor doors would be the quickest," Kala replied. She led them along the vast maze of halls, stopping now and then to Search a cowering servant before hurrying on.

As soon as they reached the fence around the field, Gareth spotted them. He spurred Shimmer over and harshly reined him to a stop, cutting a furrow in the grass. "Do you like my horse? Isn't he a wonder?"

"He is not your horse," Simen replied, stepping forward.

"Lord Simen? Alive and well? How can this be? Is Magic at work in Aberdeen?"

Kala looked at the King's hands, but he was wearing riding gloves and she could not yet tell if he wore the ebony ring. "Magic has been in Aberdeen for a long time, Your Majesty. You know it as well as I do. The only question is, what color is it?"

"Why, only the best, Madam Juris. How can Magic that serves the King be any other."

"Problems, Sire?" Edra asked as he rode from the ranks to stand next to the King. "Master Jain and I are ever here to serve if you need assistance."

Simen looked past Edra to see another rider, playing the air with his fingers as he wove a spell of some sort around the squadron. If he was right, they were already too late to do much to control this part of the cavalry. He was sure Edra knew how to cast a protection against even Spellfire if given the chance. He sifted the air around the King and Sorcerer and knew he was right. This confrontation would never lead to any kind of victory. To even the odds, he wove his one spell around his allies before Edra noticed.

"It seems we are all of the same mind," Edra said, his brow arching in surprise. "Is is Seer's Vision or something more?"

"Magic cannot hide, Edra," Simen replied. "Sooner or later, though, a true Master can sort any weave."

"If he has time," Edra said. "My Lord King, if you plan to conquer Magiskeep, I would think now would be the best time to ride. Jain and I will supply provisions with our Magic."

"I am not ready," Gareth replied. "My boots need polishing, and my bottom is sore."

"Jain will see to your boots as well, Sire. As to your bottom, stand in the stirrups if you must. We can cushion your saddle a little more, but if you are to defeat the Sorcerers who tormented you, you must leave now. I cannot protect you if you stay."

"Why does the King need protection? We have an army?"

"You have a cavalry of twenty-eight, My Lord. The army is already under assault. Soon your palace will be overrun. See the tunic on this man?" He pointed at Dale. "He is an enemy to our Master."

"Blackwing's foe? Then slay him, Sorcerer." Gareth drew his sword and swung it uselessly in Dale's direction.

Kala did not flinch. "You are allied with the Shadows, Your Majesty?"

Gareth pulled off his left glove and proudly displayed the ebony ring. "I have been blessed by the Dragon. Ultimate honor to my throne, don't you think? Is it not beautiful? See how it glitters in the sun." He reached down and patted Shimmer on the neck, as the horse snorted and tossed his head when the ring touched him. "Not as pretty as my Gleam, of course." He frowned. "You did not tell me if you liked him. I did ask as I rode up. He strides the twenty-eight perfectly every time."

Edra moved his horse up next to the King. "Sire, it is time to go. Salene, the witch who cursed you, has been laughing again."

Gareth blinked his eyes, his face darkening. "Laughing? At me?"

"She does not even think of you," Simen interrupted quickly.

"Worse and worse," Edra said. "To think the King means to little to the witch."

Gareth looked down at his crotch and smiled. "I owe here a debt she denied me. This time, she will lie beneath me as I exact payment. Then I will kill her."

Kala shivered at his words. Madness and evil joined as one. A dangerous combination.

"The north passage across the Rim is open to you," Edra said. "Tamor's reinforcements will meet you on the way. Take you cavalry and ride now, My Lord. Ride to your revenge."

The King whirled Shimmer around and signaled to his troops. Obedience, born more of fear of retribution than any kind of loyalty, pulled the riders along with him. Jain, his enforcer, rode behind, keeping the men in their ranks seven ranks of four each to speed the march along.

Edra watched them go, his lips curling up in a satisfied smile. All the arrogance of Cauge registered in his demeanor as he turned back to Kala. "So, is this what they call a standoff, Madam Juris? It appears we are equals in power."

"Gareth will never conquer Magiskeep. You sent him on a fool's errand."

"What does it matter? He is useless here. At the very least, he will prove a distraction for your damned Rivermaster so Blackwing can gain advantage."

"The Shadows will lose here in Aberdeen."

Edra shrugged. "When the Great Circle closes, none of it will matter. Minds will shatter and all this will be forgotten. All your wisdom will flee and even you will be left to wallow in ignorance. But I, Blessed by the Dragon himself," he raised his hand to show off his ring, "will remember, and in times of your oblivion, I will remember and rule over all. Whether the King stands by me or not does not matter. My Cauge will live again." With that, he reined his horse around and rode off the field at a leisurely walk.

"Arrogant bocart," Dale cursed. "I should have cast them both on the spot."

"And it would have reflected back on you," Simen replied. "Jain and Edra had woven a spell of protection around them all. There was nothing your Spellfire could have done."

"So we can't do anything to him?"

"Not now. But he is only one man. Against our forces, he can do little for now. As long as our Knights and Magicians can contain the Shadows, we can win Aberdeen."

"But what about his threats to Magiskeep?"

"Hollow words from this side of the Rim," Simen answered. "Jamus already knows Blackwing plans to attack. If anyone can fight the Black Dragon, he can."

"Gareth has a Sorcerer with him."

"One of limited skill," Kala said. "Even I could See his weaving was slow and simple. Jamus would have cast a Sphere in the blink of an eye."

"He is still a Sorcerer."

"Worth a moment's thought to my brother, no more, though I doubt they will get that far. Even the northern pass through the Rim is difficult. But if what Edra said is true, and Gareth joins forced with more of Tamor's troops, it might be a different matter."

"Something we can't bother with now," Kala said. "Until Aberdeen is under our control it must be our main concern."

"Exactly what Tamor and his Dragon want," Simen said. "We focus our efforts here. Arcula defends itself, and in the middle, Jamus and Magiskeep are left alone and isolated."

"The most dangerous foe, alone?" Dale said. "There must be more to the plan. Jamus is not an easy mark even if he has no allies."

"There's nothing we can do from here," Simen replied. "The Rivermaster must take care of himself."

*****

Sorra pushed Pebble's gallop as long as she could, but even she knew better than to exhaust the pony. They were well away from the Keep and so far there was no sign of pursuit. The rocking motion of her mount's gait had put Jarien to sleep, and for the time being they could walk along the narrow trail, catching their breaths. The thrill of the abduction still burned in her belly, arousing a hunger for something more. Had she not been sworn to Tamor, she would have taken the child as a feast, but she knew the Dark Lord would kill her if she so much as touched him with anything more than perfect care.

"Bring him to me alive and unharmed," Tamor had ordered. "Wounded bait to my trap is useless. Kiselor will only come if he thinks he can save the brat."

"What of his mother?"

Tamor shrugged. "She would be a bonus, but we don't need her. Just bring the child and don't worry about the rest. I will provide a diversion when the time is right. Silverwing will fly to Arcula, and I will send Shadows to conceal your escape."

"Then I ride to the mountain with the boy."

Tamor smiled. "And the Rivermaster will follow."

Yet the mountains were still spans away and Sorra reckoned it would take her several days to reach Tamor's cave. She sighed, the Flesher skin another burden with its needs and weight. She and Tamor had labored to reach Blackwing's lair because of her skin and now it hindered this journey. Yet it was the way to True Life and she had learned to depend on it, as bothersome as it was.

Now she spied a small stream off the trail to the right. She dismounted and led Pebble to the water to drink while she squatted in the bushes to relieve herself.

Suddenly, the wind whipped up and the sun was blotted out completely by black clouds. She caught her breath and looked up to see a huge form with sharp claws bearing down on her. The talons closed around her, lifting her into the air, and before she could scream, she was carried off.

Below, Pebble bolted and raced back down the trail in panic as she fled the huge Black Dragon soaring off into the sky.

Sorra's heart had almost stopped pounding in her ears when she was set gently down at the entrance to Tamor's chambers. As Blackwing flew away, Tamor ran out and took her hand. Her white face must have betrayed her fear, for he pulled his towards him. "I am so sorry, Beloved One. I would have warned you the Master would come for you, but I could not risk seeing you before you abducted the child." He drew her into his arms and opened the top of the bag she wore on her back where Jarien still slept. "So this is what the spawn of the Rivermaster smells like."

"He needs changing," Sorra said.

"Changing into what?"

"His diaper. It's a cloth he wears to rid him of his waste. Haven't you ever seen a baby before?"

Tamor shook his head. "He is small and weak. I cannot be bothered with such things."

"You wanted him here."

"Bait to the trap, that's all. Does he need more attention than that?"

As if in answer, Jarien began to cry, his little fists beating as the sides of the bag, his feet kicking in a tantrum. Without Rath's chanting, the skies responded, thunder rolling in as clouds--not at Tamor's bidding--gathered.

The Dark Lord cursed. "Silver River, to his hand already. Stinking little brat." He threw a black net of his own Magic around the baby and outside the skies quieted, even as Jarien's little body shimmered with silver light.

"Change him and stop that squalling. It's getting on my nerves."

Sorra pulled the wriggling boy out of the bag and lay him on the fur rug on the floor. She stripped off his soggy diaper and pinned a new on in place as Jarien's tears melted to whimpers. She only had two bottles of milk, all she had managed to grab when they left the Keep. She shoved the nipple in his mouth and let him hold the bottle for himself as he suckled greedily "If he's here much longer than a day we'll need more milk."

"Where to you get that?"

"From his mother's breast," she answered.

"Then use yours," Tamor answered. "You are a woman."

"I have no milk," Sorra replied. "A woman must be a mother to nurse a child."

"You should have brought more if it would keep the brat quiet."

"I didn't know you needed to keep him alive. You didn't tell me all of the plan, My Lord."

Tamor sighed. "What else does he eat?"

"He's not yet weaned. He's like a foal to his mother."

"Then we need a mare." Tamor beckoned to one of his Shadow servants standing ever ready in the corner of the chamber. "Find a mare, pull her teats and fill a bucket. Then bring it to me."

Sorra picked Jarien up and rocked him in her arms as his eyes began to close. "He is a good lad, even if he is Magic's spawn."

"Don't be so tender, Dear One. He is the blood of our enemy and when we are done with him, we can feast together on his body."

"You do intend to slaughter him, then?"

"When he serves his purpose, I do not need him anymore."

"But you said I can only gain True Life from the blood of a Sorcerer if the Sorcerer lives."

"H-m-m-m. I hadn't thought of that. It matters little to me, but you, my Love, are another matter. You still just wear the skin, you are not yet the skin. Then let us hope he thrives on the mare's offering, at least until you have feasted twice to gain your immortality."

*****

As soon as Salene got back to the Keep, she ran to the Dining Hall to find Sarn. He was deep in conversation with Joria, maps of Magiskeep spread out all over the table.

"What's happened? I heard explosions and came back as soon as I could."

"The Shadows attacked the Keep," Sarn said.

"My children destroyed them," Joria added. "It was amazing to see. The little ones are uninhibited by Rule or Vow and use Spellfire quite naturally."

"We are already sending searcher to the villages to find any other children so Gifted in the Art who have not yet been tested. We have Joria's twelve and another ten or so already in the Keep. We think some of the First Year Prentices might not yet be disciplined by Rule to still have the talent to use the fire without consequence to them."

"Children," Salene said," defending the Keep. Jamus must have suspected something when he realize Jarien's effect on the Silver River. That's why he asked you to teach you class, Joria."

"I don't think either he or I quite expected this," Joria replied.

"We will put children at all the danger points," Sarn said, pointing to the maps.

"Jamus would never risk them like that," Salene replied. "Surely there must be another way."

"Jamus is not here, My Lady, and this is the very reason he left me in charge," Sarn said. "He knows I will dare anything to protect the Keep. Whether you agree does not matter. I am Lord here."

"Do as you will. I will have no part in it." Salene turned on her heel and hurried upstairs to her rooms.

Clouder was barking and scratching at the door. She reached down and stroked his silky head. "It's all right, boy. I'll let you in to see your little friend." She opened the door and cried out. The room was empty. No Natale, and no Jarien. Clouder trotted over to the cradle, sniffing and whimpering.

"Where are they, Clouder. Where is my baby?"

The dog looked at her, his big brown eyes meeting her gaze directly as if he were trying to tell her something. When she did not reply, he took her hand in his jaws and pulled her to the door. "You want me to follow you?" she asked. He let her go and barked again. Then he trotted out into the hall, looking back to make sure she was behind him.

He ran ahead of her, out to the stables, and there, sat beside the open door of Pebble's stall. The little mare's saddle and bridle were missing. Clouder spun around several times, barking again, then he put his nose to the ground and followed some scent to the stable's north door.

Salene wasted no time. She pulled Flax from her stall, slipped a bridle on her head and leapt up on her bareback. "Go Clouder, find Jarien." The dog ran out onto the path, with Salene riding on his heels.

In less than half a span and good speed, they were nearly trampled by Pebble, still running frantically back toward home. Salene slid to the ground and grabbed the bay pony's bridle. The little mare was lathered and blowing, the saddle slid to the side, one rein broken when she had stepped on it in her stampede. Salene did her best to calm her, pulling the saddle off and strapping it on Flax

instead. Then she set off Pebble's bridle and dropped it on the
ground. "Go home, little one. I have to go on."

Pebble stood in confusion for a moment, but then Clouder
barked again and she tossed her head and trotted off down the trail.
Salene remounted and nodded to the dog who took off again,
following the scent.

Another half span of hard riding brought them to the little
stream, and there the big black dog stopped and began circling, his
nose fixed on the ground. There was a large patch of earth raked by
Blackwing's claws and when he reached that, Clouder howled and
backed away, his ears flat his tail tucked between his legs. "What is
it, boy? What's happened here? Where is Jarien, can you find him?
Please!"

The dog sat on his haunches, his tongue lolling out his
mouth as he panted, his brown eyes once again fixed on Salene.

If only she had the gift of the Beasttalker, Salene thought,
but try as hard as she might, she could hear nothing of the dog's
thoughts. "There's no other way to go but north," she said. "I have to
keep looking. Go home. Find Jamus. Tell him where I am. He'll
know what to do."

The dog didn't budge.

"Jamus will be home soon, Clouder, I know it. Please, try to
understand me. Jarien was here, at least. I can only guess Natale was
with him. This is her scarf on Pebble's saddle. Go home. Wait for
Jamus. Show him the trail. With Lifted stride he can be here in a
breath. You have to tell him where I am."

With that, Clouder got to his feet and turned back down the
trail, heading back to Magiskeep to do her bidding.

Salene pushed Flax into an easy trot, letting her get her wind
back. North was the only way to go, and the mountains of the
Norreaches loomed in the distance. The Black Dragon's lair lay
hidden somewhere in the range. If he had taken her son, she would
search every cave if it took her lifetime.

One lone Shadow sat on a ledge above the trail, Tamor's spy
sent to Magiskeep. He had stopped along the way at a lonely little
farmhouse to feed, leaving two bloody corpses behind. The delay
had cost him, but now, as he watched the beautiful Mistress of Magic
riding toward the hills, he knew he had his reward. He reached up
and pulled one gray cloud toward him and stepped up on it, letting
the breath of Sowin push it along. When he finally stepped off, it was
at Tamor's doorstep.

"The Sorceress comes," he said, bowing to Tamor, who was
straddling Sorra, ready to make love.

Tamor swung his leg back and stood up, naked by the bed. "What Sorceress?"

"Kiselor's mate. I recognized her from the Keep. She is on the trail even now."

Tamor smiled. Without bothering to cover himself he strode to the large black caldron, bubbling over the fire on the hearth. He stared into the boiling liquid. "Master of All, Blackwing, Kesel, I call thee. Our enemy's woman is alone coming this way. The trap is already baited with the child, but the mother adds to the flavor. Bring her to us, if it is you Will. She can serve us well."

Blackwing screeched in triumph and took to the air.

*****

Tamor had left the attack on Arcula in Melthus's hands. "Keep to the high ground," had been the Master's only advice.

Trusting command to an untried warrior would have been foolish were it not for the fact that his army still had hardened survivors from their first encounter with Arcula's defenses.

This time the bulk of Shadows and Shadowsworn, managed to get within a half day's march of Arcuse, wreaking havoc on all the little villages and farms along the way. Until then, surprise had been on their side, few Firecasters roused to defense, and even fewer armed men to offer resistance. Once at the city's perimeter, however, the tide of battle changed. There the Arculans had had time to prepare and had set their Warriors and Firecasters on every strategic hill in the area.

Melthus and his warriors were under assault from all directions. Yet those of his army who did manage to reach the high ground themselves were able to make it an even match. Fire for fire between Shadows and Mages, and swords meeting swords on the lower ground where the mortal soldiers fought. The day ended in a deadlock, with neither army making any headway.

When Easwin broke the following day, Arcuse was again in peril. Under cover of darkness, the Shadows had surrounded most of the outposts and the city walls themselves, killing several Arculan Firecasters by striking from the dark clouds above. The capital was under siege, the citizens in panic, and with the loss of Spellfire's protection on two fronts, the army itself was in disarray.

Corbin, Master Rider, tried to rally his troops to attack the enemy's flank and was making his move when someone cried out, "Look to the sky! Silverwing is coming."

First just a shining spot on the Western horizon, Rath was flying towards the field, her great wings beating a steady rhythm, bending trees and stirring clouds of dust beneath them.

The Riders cheered as Shadows started to scatter, looking for cover from the Rain of Dragon flames bearing down on them. There was no escape and no defense against the Silver Dragon's rage as she swept to and fro across the plain, blasting her deadly fire into the Shadow's ranks. The Shadowsworn fell on their knees or fell prone on the ground fruitlessly covering their heads with their arms as the silver death rained upon them.

The screams were horrible, worse than the clash of arms and usual battle cried. Sparks seared men's skin to the bone if they were not mercifully killed outright.

With the main force broken, Riders and Firecasters rallied to clean out the nests of Darkness hiding in the positions they now occupied. All during the day, skirmishes raged as Rath soared above, keeping the remnants of Tamor's mighty force at bay. And this time, when night fell, there were not enough Shadows left to see the clouds let alone walk them.

XXIV

Salene had just crested a hill when a black shadow crossed her path. Flax stopped in her tracks and pawed the earth furiously, refusing to move and trying to spin back along the track they had come. Salene held the mare in place, her gaze searching the sky. It had been too dark to be just a cloud passing over the sun.

Then, from behind, a gust of wind swept up the slope. She turned, too late, to see the Black Dragon bearing down on her. She cast a quick blast of Spellfire, too badly aimed to do any damage as the monster's talons closed around her, pulling her out of the saddle. Flax trumpeted, rearing to strike out with her hooves at the mighty beast. She connected with the Dragon's slashing tail, sharp hooves and teeth tearing into armored scales, ripping one off as the creature flapped its leathery wings and sailed up into the clouds.

Salene struggled in its grip, but her arms were pinioned at her side as black coils of Magic twined around her, denying her Magic. She could barely breathe so tightly bound. All she could hear was the pounding force of the Dragon's wings against the air and the rush of wind past its great body as it flew.

At last, they landed and she was dumped on the cold stone ledge in front of Tamor's cave. Two Shadowed servants dragged her inside and deposited her next to the Dark Lord's bed where he lay naked atop a writhing woman who was moaning as he made love to her. Salene tried to turn her head away, but the bonds held her where she could see everything the couple was doing. All she could do was closed her eyes to block out the sight.

Then, she heard a baby cry and her eyes flew open, her body twisting in the black coils. "Jarien? My love, I'm here. Jarien?"

Her call attracted the man's attention and he pushed himself off his partner to get out of bed and squat next to Salene's head. He grabbed a hank of her blonde hair and pulled her head against his bare thigh. "Would you like some too, witch? Hah! I wouldn't dirty myself with you." He gestured crudely, then waved his hand, freeing her legs and arms, keeping her hands on two black leashes he held firmly in his grip. "Your brat is squalling again. He's either wet or hungry." He pulled out a black dagger and slit the front of her blouse, baring her breast. "Go, let him suckle. At least that will give me some peace and quiet." He yanked harshly on her bonds dragging her over to the fur rug by the fire where Jarien lay. "Be warned, shetark. Make one move to test your Magic and I will slit your spawn's belly and let my love drink his blood while you watch." He loosed the coil on her right hand to let her pull Jarien into her embrace.

Tears welled in Salene's eyes as Jarien found her nipple and began to suckle greedily. His little hands groped her breasts, then found a lock of her hair and latched on to it as he filled his belly.

The woman on the bed sat up. "I am pleased to see you, Madam," she said. "You make things much easier for us."

"Natale," Salene said hoarsely. "Why have you done this?"

"Call me by my rightful name and you will know. I am Sorra."

"Your name means nothing to me."

Sorra laughed. "It's been so long, I had forgotten. Let's try again, shall we? I am Shadow, born in the Way of Sonya's rage."

"Sonya?"

"Her sister, reflection of her hate for your husband," she spat. "The day he sent Sonya in shame from the Keep, I was born, and it is I who have found a way to repay him."

"How? By stealing our son and capturing me?"

"Bait to the trap," Tamor said, finally pulling on his robe.

Sorra didn't bother to dress as she slid over to the edge of the bed to glare at Salene. "Does it feel good to have him suckle?"

"What's wrong, Sorra?" Salene asked sharply as her courage started to return. The other woman's revelation had given her some hope there was a way out of all this. "Are you jealous of my body? Do you long for the life I own while you are yet a dim reflection of a pitiful, barren woman?"

Tamor moved back over to the bed and curled his hands around Sorra's breasts. "Ignore her, Loved One. These are as plump as hers and even more desireable. Look at her, like a brood mare nursing her foal. Slave to his hunger. You and I are free to couple while she is courted by a little squalling parasite. He got up and moved over to Salene, his dark eyes staring at her and the child. For one brief moment, something almost human tugged in his own chest and his glare softened. He frowned in confusion and sharpened his focus, honing it with his hatred for Jamus and the feeling subsided. "Beloved one, come here." He patted the rug at his side.

Sorra got up from the bed and walked over to him, sitting down next to him. She nestled against him, her knee digging painfully into Salene's side. "What do you want of me, My Lord?"

"How many feasts have you had?"

"Only two. One of this skin I wear, and the other in a small farmhouse far from the Keep. Oh, wait, make that three. I took the father and son there."

"She would make it eight," he said, nodding at Salene who tried to cower away, her moment of courage fleeing as he went on. "Of course, we cannot let her die. Sorcerer's blood is useless if the victim's life ends in the feast. Yet what harm could a taste do?" He drew his dagger again, pulled the coil tight on Salene's left arm, yanking it out straight from her side. With one quick stroke he slit her wrist. As the blood poured out, he nodded to Sorra, "Drink, My Love. Payment for bringing me the brat."

Salene cried out as Sorra began to drink. The world spun away as terror enveloped her. Jarien began to cry again and outside the thunder roared.

*****

Jamus grabbed the front of Sarn's green tunic and yanked him out of his chair. "Damn you, Sarn, where are Salene and Jarien? You were supposed to protect them."

"I was supposed to protect Magiskeep," Sarn protested, shoving himself free of Jamus' grip. "Your wife and son had a stinking Dragon to watch over them."

"Rath left," Joria said, hoping to calm Jamus at least a little. She could hear the thunder and lightning crashing outside already. If he lost his temper any more, the whole Keep might explode.

"By the Blood, I should have known," Jamus said, raking his fingers through his hair. "The attack on Arcula...he never wanted to conquer the city. All he wanted was Rath away from here. What has he done to Salene? My son. Where are they?"

"No one knows, My Lord," Joria answered. "Flax and Pebble are gone from the stables and no one has seen Natale either."

"Natale?"

"Jarien's nursemaid."

"Where's Becca? She never would have let anything happen to Jarien."

"She left days ago to be with her son. His wife's having a baby."

Damn the tapestry again. He'd saved Jeb only to have his child cost him his own. He dropped onto a chair, his head in his hands. For the first time in as long as he could remember, he had no idea what to do.

Dark one have pup. Flax say black flyer take One Love.

Jamus raised his head. Whose voice? "Clouder? Is that you?"

The big black dog burst through the door of the Dining Chamber and ran over to him, his eyes fixed on his Master's. *One Love say come. Say Best One know way. Into dark..*

Jamus leapt to his feet. Of course, Tamor's lair. Salene knew he'd been there before. He did know the way. "Did you see the dark, Clouder?"

Flax see. Pebble see. Clouder smell. Black dark. Best One go? One Love need. Pup need. Clouder come.

"No, Clouder, you must stay." He turned to Joria and Sarn. "I have to go to Salene and Jarien, they're in great danger."

Sarn got up. "Take your Warriors with you. We are fine here. We have our defenses set."

Jamus shook his head. "I can't. I need to lift Whim's strides to get there in time. I can't be worrying about anyone else." With that, he ran from the room, his mind racing. "Whim, I need you."

Whim know, here for Best One.

When he got to the stables, Josep was wrestling with Whim's reins as the stallion reared and plunged, refusing to let him untack him after the long ride back from Arcula. "Don' know what' got inta him, Milord. I gotta groom 'im an' 'e won't let me near."

"Never mind, Josep," Jamus replied as he snatched the reins himself. As soon as he did, Whim stood still so he could swing up into the saddle.

"Blood, Jamus, yer gonna kill yerself an' that horse iffen ya rides off agin widout restin'. Don't be a fool."

"Watch for Flax and Pebble," Jamus called over his shoulder as he trotted Whim for the gate. "They'll need some extra tending."

As soon as Whim's hoof hit the open trail, Jamus lifted the silver stallion's stride and they raced the wind on the way to Tamor's cave in the Norreaches.

*****

Edra strode across the bluestone floor of the palace's lower hall, searching for at least one ally. He was used to being self-sufficient, but the empty halls were unnerving. All the servants had either fled or were hiding in the quarters waiting for whatever King might emerge from the rebellion. Simen, Kala and Dale had not yet returned from the barracks or whatever other cleanup mission they had embarked on to finish off the last of Gareth's well trained army. Most of the men had deserted at the first sign of battle, leaving only the two hundred or so Shadowsworn who had no choice but to stand in defense of the Darkness. Most of them were now dead, with true Shadows burned to ashes by Spellfire and the rest cut down by Knights' swords.

Now, still well protected by his own Magic, Edra was alone.

"So, Caugeman, you are still here. I thought by the time I got here you would have fled."

"Erlik," Edra snarled as his fellow Arculan stepped out of the side hall. "I'd nearly forgotten you. Where's your pretty filly? I had my eye on her, you know. I still intend to teach her how a real man feels."

"You'll never get the chance," Erlik said, raising his had to send a bolt of Spellfire at his foe. The flame dropped harmlessly at Edra's feet.

Edra's own hand flew up to send a bolt back at Erlik only to see it fall short as well. "This is a dilemma now, isn't it." Edra said. "We could stand here and trade chanting forever and neither of us would get anywhere."

"I'll not let you leave this palace," Erlik replied. "So standing here forever would be just fine with me."

"Oh, don't play the hero, Erlik. I was Cauge, remember? I have always been your superior."

"I've learned a few things since I left Arcula, My Dear Mard. "Gold and Silver flow from my hand. If I need to chant you as prisoner here, I can. Yet I think we would both be more content if we settled matters once and for all."

"Spell for spell?" Edra asked.

Erlik shook his head and drew his sword. "Blade for blade."

Edra smiled. He was an expert swordsman. "And if I win?"

"Then I will be dead and whatever you decide to do will not matter to me."

"Let's go to it," Edra replied as he drew his own sword and squared off.

Erlik lunged, his sword meeting Edra's parry with a ringing clash of stelin. Caught off balance, he dodged to the side, barely escaping Edra's answering lunge.

Blow by blow, parry after parry the two men battled up and down the hall, Erlik matching Edra's better skills with quicker reactions, dancing away from the blade with practiced agility while still finding openings to strike himself.

Then Edra's sword drew blood, cutting into Erlik's thigh. Erlik stumbled. Edra pressed the advantage, diving into his opponent for the kill, but as Erlik fell back against a pillar, he raised his sword in feeble defense and Edra, unable to check himself, fell on the blade.

"Cheater," the Caugemen sputtered. "Shoulda known. I always was better." He collapsed, blood seeping from his nose and mouth.

Erlik pried his sword out from between Edra's ribs, letting the other Arculan fall lifeless to the floor. He clutched at his own leg as he sank down to the floor himself, exhausted.

He closed his eyes and never even saw Edra's body shrivel into a pile of useless ash at his feet.

Dale found him there a half span later when he returned to the palace to deal with Edra himself. He saw Erlik's bloody sword and Edra's loose one lying beside him. "So, you did my work for me, did you?" he said, pulling off his belt to tie around Erlik's thigh and stem the bleeding.

"I needed to. I owed it to Arcula to finish what I started there. I wanted to overthrow the Cauge, and now I've done it. A promise fulfilled."

"Can you walk?"

"I think so. I'm weak, though. I might need your arm."

"Come on then, Master. We'll get you into a bed somewhere near and have Lord Simen Heal you. Is your Lady in the city?"

"Talia? She should be at the Course. We were bringing racers back for the new season when the rebellion broke loose. Once I realized what was happening, I knew I had to confront Edra so I came here."

"You could have asked for help. We have spellcasters aplenty now. You didn't need to face him alone."

"Yes I did," Erlik answered. "It was the only way."

*****

Salene's breathing was shallow, her heart fluttering when Tamor finally pulled Sorra away. "You have had enough," he said.

Sorra's eyes were shining, her bloodied mouth smiling as she rocked back on her heels. "So sweet," she said, hugging herself with her arms. "I can feel the power surging through me."

"One more feast and you shall have your desire," Tamor said, leaning over Salene's pale body. He thrust a vial between her lips, "Drink," he commanded. She clenched her teeth and he pried her jaw open and poured the liquid down her throat, forcing her to choke or swallow. Almost at once, the potion revived her, so she could at least sit up. "You will live," he said, "and my Lady will feast on you another day. You will stay here, eat and grow strong until you have enough blood to drink again."

"Never," Salene said, "I will die first."

"And leave your son to take your place?"

Her eyes darted wildly when she realized Jarien was no longer in her arms. She saw him crawling to the edge of the fur rug, to sit, playing with the tassels on the table runner. "Jarien," she called, her voice weak. She tried to claw her way over to him, but her body betrayed her and she toppled over to lie helpless. Jarien giggled and crawled back over to her, plucking her hair.

"I could drink from him," Sorra said.

"No, he's too small. Let him grow." Then Tamor smiled again. He pulled Salene upright by her hair and shoved her against the edge of the fireplace. "I have hit upon a wonderful idea. Sorra will feed on you again, before the end of the Sevenstin. But she is not the only Shadow seeking True Life. I have thousands to free from the Way, an endless number of hungry souls thirsting to be free. You shall serve them all."

Salene cringed back from his dark gaze, shaking her head. "No…please."

"Fear is good," he said, stroking her ashen cheek with his lean fingers. "It makes the flavor so much better. I don't quite know why, but you and I will have plenty of time to figure it out. How long does a Sorcerer live? Forever? You shall be my fountain. I can heal your wounds over and over, and keep you alive with potions. And your son? He will grow, and when he is weaned from your breast, we will feed him our music and use him as we use you. Nurse mares to a thousand Shadows and then a thousand more."

"Jamus," she whispered.

"Kiselor will come. That's why I brought you here in the first place. Bait to catch a Rivermaster. He will be fodder to Blackwing when his heart breaks for you and his son. The Great Circle will close and you will sit here, drooling in your ignorance, serving me and offering the feast of life to all I bring to drink your bounty."

Sorra sidled up to Tamor, wiping the blood from her lips with the back of her hand. "A fitting end for the witch," she said, "and a perfect plan from a most perfect Master." She stood on tiptoe to kiss him passionately. "Come, My Lord. Take me. I am most in need of you. My loins ache for want of you."

Tamor lifted her into his arms and carried her over to the bed.

Jarien lay his little head on his mother's trembling stomach and fell asleep while Salene wept dry, heaving sobs.

*****

All the bells of Arcula rang out the triumph over Tamor's forces, The victory was complete and Rath perched on the city's highest tower, bellowing in tune as if she were singing.

The people stood in the streets below, hugging each other and cheering as Riders and Sorcerers marched into the city, driving before them the ragged remains of the dark horde, the few surviving mortal warriors who had sworn themselves to Blackwing's cause. They would be given fair trials under the just and merciful First Order. Some would be executed, some imprisoned and some, if able to prove they had been coerced, set free. Gaila promised justice to all who came to the Hall and prisoners of war were no exception. But all that was for another day. For now, the captured would be locked in the dungeons of the Cauge while the city celebrated.

Gaila climbed the long winding staircase to the main tower of the Hall where Rath sat preening her scales. Leaning out the little window, she addressed the Dragon, " My Silver Lady, I want to thank you on behalf of all Arcula. We will be having a feast to celebrate our victory. There is no room for you, though. If you wish to fly to one of the fields outside the city, we would be pleased to offer you whatever you desire as a reward for your great service to us."

"Feast?" Rath said. "Meat?"

"Why yes, we will have roasts of all kinds. We can bring you a cavel in the field if you wish."

"Rath like party. Join."

"We would love to welcome you, My Lady, but there is not enough room below."

Rath curled her head around to fix her whirling eyes on Gaila. "Rath come. You see." She spread her wings and glided down to the courtyard below, melting into a silver mist before she touched down. When she landed, she was already half transformed into a tall, slender, silver-haired woman.

Gaila mouth dropped open in surprise and she hurried back down the stairs to properly greet her newest guest. The people who had seen the Magical transformation stood agape as well, then moved aside, bowing as the silver-haired, silver-gowned lady made her way up the steps and into the hall.

She had learned much in Magiskeep and carried herself more now as a true lady of title than a Dragon transformed. She was gracious to those who spoke her and she nibbled at her plate of food, even though her eyes glittered when the first roast was carried in, still on the spit. Yet she had learned not to offend the more delicate appetites in the gathering, taking only two slabs of the rarest portion of the meat and then eating them slowly. She drank sparingly of the wine, all too aware of how erratic her flight could be if she let alcohol take hold of her small body. Experience had taught her that whatever she did in her human skin was always magnified when the resumed her true nature.

Gaila was pleasantly surprised to find the Dragon lady such a fine company and found herself at last alone with her at a small table by the window. "I must admit, Lady Rath, that I am delighted you were able to join us after all."

"Twoleg company pleases me sometimes."

"You have visited with people many times before?"

"In home of the Rivermaster, I keep time. Many months now. I watch for Shadows. Then Arcula called, so I came."

"We needed you. Without your fire, we would have lost the war. Is Blackwing truly driven from our land?"

"He will not return unless Kiselor fails. This I cannot know. Past the Great Circle, I cannot see."

"Then the battle for Magiskeep is not yet won."

"Neither won nor lost. It may never be. It is in Best One's hands now. He will decide the Circle's end, or not."

"We must pray for Jamus' victory, then."

"Pray if you wish, but it will little matter. What will be will be. His way is Turan's Way, there is no turning," Rath replied.

"Fate then, and nothing he can do about it."

Rath shook her head. "Do you not understand? The Rivermaster is Turan's Fate."

*****

Gareth pushed his cavalry on at brisk pace along the northern trail. Unaware of the losses his army had suffered in Aberdeen, he still pictured himself the magnificent general, leading a band of brave warriors against the forces of evil. He was sure that when he conquered Magiskeep and returned with the Sorceress in chains, he would be regaled as Turan's hero. He was already King.

The twenty-eight Scarleteers behind followed blindly, their eyes fixed on Jain, Gareth's second in command, not because of his worth as a leader. It was his Magic granting him status. More than one of the men had felt the sting of is fiery retribution for even the slightest disobedience and all knew about what had happened to

420   Blackwing Rising

Girad. His grisly death had taught them all to keep their mouths shut and obey orders no matter what. Now, they were riding off to who knows where to fight an unnamed foe while behind them, Aberdeen burned with the smell of Spellfire and blood.

"Master Jain," Gareth called from the front of the brigade. "There's a fallen tree up ahead. Clear it out of the way. I don't feel like jumping it."

Jain spurred his sturdy chestnut gelding to the lead and raised his hand. The men flinched as a bolt of red flame thundered from his hand to splinter the tree trunk into sawdust. Then, he turned back, flexing his hand and wrist casually, his dark eyes studying each man's face as he rode slowly to the back of the ranks again. He enjoyed reminding them all of the extent of his Magic and relished seeing the fear in their eyes. Gareth was King but he, like Edra, was the true master here. The King was merely a vehicle for his ambition, as ready and willing to do his bidding as every man riding with them. The only difference was that the King thought he was in charge.

The downed tree was only the first sign of a powerful storm that had recently struck the mountain trail. All along the way then noticed rock slides and washouts, slowing their progress to a cautious walk. As the day dragged on, Gareth grew more irritated and took to standing up in his stirrups for longer and longer periods of time. Shimmer grew restless under him, constantly shifting his balance to keep the King in the saddle even as harsh hands yanked on the reins to steer him around obstacles he had already avoided.

They rode in single file for a full span, adding to Gareth's annoyance, for a line of riders were not twenty-eight perfectly ranked, looking far less impressive than a well-ordered brigade. The fact that the landscape was deserted with no audience to admire him mattered little. To him the eyes of Turan were always on him, in all the imaginations of every loyal subject who worshipped their rightful sovereign.

At last, the trail opened into a wide, flat plain and the brigade was able to reform, lining up in perfect ranks where they stood awaiting Gareth's next command. He pointed to Dirk. "Scout on up ahead. The horses could use a gallop to stretch their legs. I need to know the terrain."

Dirk trotted his bay forward and rode on up the wide trail while the others waited at attention while Gareth rode past in review. At first, he said nothing. Then, he pointed to Jain. "Fill in that spot in Private Dirk's rank. I will not abide less than twenty-eight in perfect order."

Jain snapped his mouth shut to keep a protest from his lips and rode his horse into the empty spot. Once the twenty-eight were perfect again, Gareth resumed his inspection. "Private Ryce, is that dust on your boots?"

"Aye, Sir. We've been riding hard."

"Clean it off. I'll not have my men looking like dirt farmers. Corporal Cadan, button your tunic, you look like you're ready to bed a whore." Down the line he went criticizing each man for faults no one riding in the wilderness for so long could ever avoid. The mud on hs own breeches, or a twig caught in his collar, mattered little. After all, he was the King, and the King could do no wrong.

Dirk returned within the half span, his horse sweating from the gallop back. "Your Majesty, the trail is clear for at least a hundred strides, but then the bridge is out. There is a deep ravine blocking the way with no crossing."

"We can gallop then?" Gareth asked, ignoring the more important part of the message.

"With care, My Lord, and not at speed. There's a tree just shy of the crevice where we need to stop, though, It wouldn't be safe to go much farther without risking going over the edge."

"Ride on back then, and stand your mount at the marker," Gareth ordered. "That way we will know how far to go. Riders, prepare to gallop."

Dirk spurred his tired mount up the trail, hoping he was going to reach the stopping point before the rest of the cavalry overtook him Though all the horses were well trained, there was no guarantee they would all stop safely at the ravine's edge if they overshot the tree.

Hoofs thundered almost in unison. The cavalry had drilled for so many spans together the horses moved in almost perfect synchrony. Gareth kept Shimmer in the front, the golden colt's long fluid strides outdistancing the others with ease. Then, he spotted Dirk's lathered bay up ahead. Reluctantly he hauled on the reins, bringing his mount to a rough sliding stop a few yards beyond. Behind, the first rank saw him stop and reacted, shouting to the riders behind because the King had failed to issue the command to halt.

Horses collided as their riders tried to pull them down to a walk. The ranks broke into jumbled disarray and one or two of the cavalrymen tumbled from the saddles into the dirt in the turmoil.

Gareth was furious. "Scarleteers, stand to! Stand to at once!"

Somehow, order was restored and all but one of the fallen men managed to remount as the lines formed again. The rider on foot strove in vain to climb into the saddle, but the cinch had broken and as he put his foot in the stirrup, the saddle fell to the ground to be trampled by his shying horse. He hung on to the reins, his eyes wide with terror as the King rode over.

Gareth snapped his fingers to Jain. "Fix his tack," he said. "You are a lucky man, Private. Were we in Aberdeen, I would have you executed and replace you in a trice. I see no other soldiers here to take your place and I must have my twenty-eight." With that, he rode up the trail to look at the yawning ravine blocking their way.

Jain smiled, or rather leered at the fallen man. He waved his hand at the saddle, restoring it with and easy chanting. "Saddle him up yourself. I can't be bothered any more than that." Then he rode back to his accustomed spot at the back where he could watch the other riders while Dirk steered his horse back into the open slot in the ranks.

Gareth rode back from the ravine. "We can jump it," he said.

Dirk, who had seen the ravine on his first ride along the trail, dared to speak up. "Your Majesty, if I dare speak."

"What it, Private? I only allow you voice because you have done a service."

"I saw the ravine when I scouted the trail, It is very wide. Perhaps we can find a way around instead."

"And waste a day of travel?" The King replied. "No, we will jump and be on our way. First rank, move out."

None of the riders moved.

"Dare you defy me now? Master Jain, to the fore. Bring the men on as I command."

Jain rode forward. "My Lord, perhaps we should reconsider. Even I cannot condone taking such a risk."

To his surprise, Gareth laughed. "Cowards all. I would have hoped I had chosen better men." He yanked Shimmer's head around and pointed the colt towards the ravine. "Then I will lead as my crown demands. Watch and learn how easy it is." He spurred the golden colt forward into a gallop, straight for the cliff.

Shimmer's hoofs hit the edge and he soared into the air in a huge leap. It was clear from the moment he took off that he was going to clear the span with room to spare. But then halfway across, the golden colt faded into a shower of gold and silver sparks. The last thing the men saw was Gareth's terrified expression as he dropped screaming into the abyss, his hands clawing futilely at the air. The last thing the men heard was the sickening thud as his royal body shattered into a pile of blood and bone on the rocks below.

Jain trotted to the front of the brigade, his gaze fixed on the ravine's edge, "The King is dead." He raised his hand, illusioning a shining crown on the tips of his fingers. "Long live the King." Just as he was about to set the crown own head two swords pierced his body, one from behind, one from the left. His eyes widened in surprise, his hand falling empty at his side. Then he sagged and slid slowly off his horse to lie on the ground, blood soaking into the dusty earth. A few minutes more and his body, in the way of Sorcerers, dissolved into the dust and, caught by the shifting wind, blew away.

"The King is dead," Dirk said sheathing his bloody sword.

"Long live Turan," Cadin finished, wiping the blood off his blade with the hem of his bright red tunic.

Bart, the fallen rider, walked over to the edge of the ravine and looked down at Gareth's crumpled body far below. "Too deep to get it. Guess the tarks and rimhawks will have a feast."

"It would be nice to have a body to parade in the streets when we get back to Aberdeen," another soldier said.

"We could need proof," Ryce said.

As if in answer, Shimmer materialized in front of them, tossing his head and nickering as if quite pleased with himself.

"Do you think the King's mount would be proof enough?" Cadan asked.

"Think he'll stick with us on the ride home? Seems to me he has a bit of an independent attitude," Ryce said, laughing. Shimmer trotted over to him and nuzzled his arm, shoving his nose into the Ryce's pockets, looking for a treat while the private's own horse stood steady and calm, nuzzling the colt's withers. "I suppose you do deserve a reward," Ryce said, pulling out a crunchy surlep candy to give to the persistent colt.

Cadan, the only one among them with some rank, took charge. "We have two options as I see it. We can scatter, each to our own way, or we can stick together and risk going back to Aberdeen, Kingless and with no authority but our own. What say you?"

"We've been together all these months, Might well stick to it as far as I'm concerned," Bart said, swinging back into the saddle.

No one dissented. Dirk got off his horse, loosened the girth and pulled the saddle and bridle off. "You're a good fellow, Dice, but I'll not tax you further today." He looked up at Cadan. "He needs a rest. I'll ride Jain's horse back. Maybe Dice and the King's colt will tag along together if we keep a gentle pace."

"No reason to hurry," Cadan replied. "Whatever's happened in Aberdeen is over and done with, as it is here."

"Should we leave some kind of marker for the King?" one of the younger riders asked.

The Corporal shook off the suggestion with a Wave of his hand. Leave him to the scavengers. They'll pay him just tribute. Maybe one day we can ride back and collect his bones if there's a call for them. In the meantime, he doesn't deserve any more from us."

XXV

Jamus reined Whim to a stop beside the stream, his eyes searching the ground for some kind of clue. He saw the furrowed earth where Blackwing had landed, recognizing the Dragon spoor. At least part of what Clouder had told him made some sense now. Neither Jarien's kidnapper nor Salene had made it all the way to Lord Tamor's lair on foot. If the Black Dragon had carried off one, he had carried off both.

He knew the rest of the way, remembering with vivid clarity every turning of the rocky trail. He lifted two more strides and landed Whim on the ledge just below the entrance to the cave. "Don't try to go any closer, Whim. He has Salene and Jarien and now he'll have me. I don't want him to take you too. I love you too much for that."

Best One danger.

"I know. But my wife and son are up there. I have no choice."

Blackwing know.

"I understand." He gave the silver stallion a parting pat and climbed up the stony track to Tamor's chambers.

The Dark Lord was waiting for him just inside. "I wondered how long it would take you to get here," he said. "We've all been waiting."

As soon as his eyes adjusted to the dark interior, Jamus saw Salene leaning up against the fireplace, bare to the waist, her skin pallid, her eyes vacant. She was hardly breathing.

Jamus gritted his teeth, his Sphere of Protection sealing itself around his mind and body. "What did you do to her?"

"Ah, she has served my beloved one her first feast of Magic, and when she recovers enough, she shall feed her second. Your wife and I have a pact, Rivermaster. She will feed as many Shadows as there are numbers to count and in return, I will nourish her and your son."

"Jarien," Jamus said. Then he saw the baby curled up at Salene's side, fast asleep.

"We have agreed he too will serve the feast when he grows taller. Such a little thing. On sip and he'd be gone." Tamor snapped his fingers.

Unable to contain his rage, Jamus raised his hand, sending a bolt of Spellfire at the Dark Lord.

Tamor laughed as the chanting fell to the floor in a shower of white sparks. "Do you think your pitiful Magic and harm me? I have True Life. I am immortal."

"What do you want from me?"

"I want nothing. It is Blackwing, my great lord, who thirsts for your blood. He will be here soon. Why not share a cup with us while we wait?" He beckoned Sorra to the table. Dressed only in a filmy gown of transparent shaenis, her near-naked body swayed suggestively as she poured two goblets of wine.

Jamus took a step towards Salene, but Tamor raised a warning hand. "No touching. Never again, Kiselor. Her soft flesh is mine alone. You have no right to her."

"She is my wife. She needs my Touch, a Healing, at least."

"I will heal her, at my Will," Tamor replied, casting an encircling cage of black coils around Salene and Jarien.

She stirred as one of the tendrils touched her, startling her to consciousness. Her eyes focused, "Jamus? Is it really you?"

"I'm here, My Love. Don't be afraid."

"You will save us?"

"I will keep my Vows to you, no matter what happens. Trust me, I love you."

Sorra hooked her arm into Tamor's and rubbed her body up and down against him. "How precious. I am sorry now I never got to see the two of you in bed together in Magiskeep. I might have learned something to please my own lord."

"You...Natale," Jamus said, glaring at her. "You're the one who took my son."

"Payback," Sorra replied. "For Sonya's sake. You remember Sonya, don't you? I am her sister reflected in the Way."

"I threw her out of the Keep for her cruelty to the children in her care."

"Ah, so you do remember. It is well. It is not good for a man to die with a question on his lips.'

Tamor pulled her into his embrace, lifting her into his arms for a deep kiss.

Jamus raised his hand. Unbidden by reason, fueled only by his fury, another bolt of Spellfire shot out towards Tamor. The Dark Lord saw it a fraction too late and before he could throw Sorra safely aside, the fire struck her in the middle of her back. She let out a horrifying scream as the Magic seared into her skin, severing her spinal cord as it struck into her heart, collapsing her in Tamor's arms.

"I did love you," she gasped and then an oily, inky cloud of darkness surrounded her, wailing and screeching as it spun and vanished into the air.

Tamor threw back his head and cried out as the empty skin slipped through his fingers and dropped to the floor, a smoldering mass of bone and flesh already starting to stink with the smell of decay.

The Dark Lord reached out with his hand, parting the coils imprisoning Salene just enough for him to grab Jarien's little foot and pull the baby out to set him on the chair by the table.

Jamus started forward, his heart lurching, but another set of Tamor's coils lashed around his feet, rooting him in place. Before he could counter that spell, the Dark Lord smiled.

Jarien woke up and started to cry, waving his arms about looking for his mother's breast.

"He's hungry again," Tamor said. "Already I recognize the squall. Shall I feed him or put him out of his misery?"

"Leave him alone," Jamus commanded, but the black coils had done their work. He couldn't even defend his son.

Tamor's hand quivered in the air as a flicker of black flame danced on his fingertips.

"Leave him be, he's just a baby."

"Your baby," Tamor said as he sent the fire towards Jarien. The flame faltered a few inches from the child as a silver glow enveloped his body. Tamor spun to face Jamus, but he saw no casting from his foe. Even Jamus' face registered surprise at the failed attack. "So the brat has inherited some of his father's skill, has he? All the better. The more his Magic, the sweeter his blood. I can still imprison him as I imprison you now. He is still mine even if he lives."

Jamus had regained enough of his composure to shake off Tamor's bonds, Three Rivers answering his call. The Black Waters still defied him, their power at least the equal of the other three. Whether Tamor knew it or not, he had the upper hand, but as long as possible, Jamus he wouldn't let him know. Somehow he needed to free Salene.

Tamor kicked Natale's useless skin aside, his face dark, his shoulders slumped. There was an ache in his heart he could not understand.

All was short-lived, for in the next moment, the cave was plunged into an impenetrable darkness as Blackwing's huge form blocked the door. The great Dragon folded his wing and forced his way through the wide entrance to face his rival, Jamus, the Rivermaster, Turan's Way.

"Everendings ever be, time to pay the price to me.
Circle's Close in on thy head, this be where thy journey's led.

Everendings ever be, now your blood belongs to me.
I thirst, Rivermaster."

Jamus faced the Dragon, meeting its dark gaze with his own. "We meet again, Kesel." He thought he saw the creature wince at the mention of his true name.

"This time Kesel win. Have power over Rivermaster's heart. You pain before," the Dragon said, waving his scarred tentacle in Jamus' face. "Hurt again, I kill mate."

"And when you do, you lose the only advantage you have over me. Even if you kill me then, I will burn you with my fire over and over so your scars will never heal. Leave my wife and son alone, and I will not fight you."

"A bargain?"

"You know I am a man of my word," Jamus replied. "Let Salene and my son go free and I will not fight you."

"Life for life," Kesel said. "Only one, so say Rainbow brother."

"One is useless without the other," Jamus said calmly. "If the baby stays, the mother will not leave. If the mother stays the baby will not live without her milk. It is no bargain if he dies. He is small, insignificant in Turan's Way. When the Circle Closes what will two lives matter in trade?"

"Tamor,' Kesel said. "Set them free."

"They are mine, My Lord. I have great plans for them."

"I tell you what your plans will be. My Will, not thine. The Rivermaster is fair trade for their flesh. You have made a Vow to obey me. Set them free or forfeit."

Tamor cursed and chanted the coils away. Salene was still too weak to stand on her own. He yanked her to her feet, supporting her with one arm as he picked up Jarien by his leg and carried mother and son past Blackwing to the ledge beyond. Jamus followed, his eyes riveted on Salene.

"Jamus, no, please. Don't do this. We're not worth it," she pleaded as she sank to her knees on the cold stone, pulling Jarien into her lap.

"You are more than worth it, My Love," Jamus answered, then he spread his arms wide, surrendering to oblivion, the lesson of the final riddle racing through his mind.

Oblivion. The lesson he had half-learned in Naboth's cave. Surrender was the only way to breach the black barrier. Now, it was the only way to face the Dragon.

This was the way the Black River would be his, its mastery bought and paid for by his death. Losing his life, meeting death head on without reservation or fear, was the final sacrifice. He needed to embrace the end, welcome it, surrender. Surrender.

Oblivion.

He walked into the Black Dragon's waiting jaws.

Salene screamed as Blackwing's mouth snapped shut with a sickening crunch. She thought, for just a moment that she saw a flash of white light, as the Dragon swallowed. His great body lurched into the air and he began to spiral off the ledge, screaming in triumph before the wind caught his wings. She squeezed her eyes shut at the terrible sight, grief overcoming her frail body. She knelt there in the cold mountain air, trembling and weeping uncontrollably.

Then, she felt Tamor's hand on her shoulder. "Unlike your husband, I am not a man of my word," he said. "As I told my Master, I have plans for you."

"No, never," Salene cried, trying to crawl to the edge of the rock to throw herself over. Better to die than suffer the fate Tamor had in store for her.

The wind nearly blew her over, the sun blotted out again. Was Blackwing returning already?

The sun reflected silver. It was Rath, diving down from the higher mountaintops. Tamor threw up his arms for protection, but the silver fire from Rath's mouth was swift and deadly. The only power on all Turan able to destroy a Shadow fed with True Life—the furious fire of the Dragon's Tongue. It was Tamor who screamed in agony now, his flesh blackening, his eyes bulging out of his head, his hands groping the air. He plunged blindly forward, and his body toppled over the ledge, bouncing on a dozen sharp rocks on the way down as it broiled and smoked into a useless heap of black ash.

Rath touched Salene gently with her talon. "Too late. Rath come too late."

Salene gulped and nodded, too overwhelmed with anguish to speak.

"Hold kitling tight," Rath said as she carefully closed her talon around them. Then she flapped her wings and sailed out into the fading light of Weswin, heading for Magiskeep.

On the ledge below, Whim nickered mournfully as he slowly began to make his way down the mountain trail. His hoof sounded hollow on the stone.

*****

Simen's stomach twisted into a painful knot and he doubled over at the table. The small band was celebrating the victory of the Shadows and the successful purging of Gareth's army. For the first time in Sevenstins, Aberdeen was truly at peace. The lack of their King preyed on no one's mind, for Lord Dale had taken charge as the temporary Governor and already the work crews from Gareth's battlefield were repairing any damages the rebellion had caused.

Now, when all was finally quiet, Simen was near collapse. Jyp and Jada rushed to his side, but he managed to sit up, his teeth clenched. "Something's happened to Jamus," he said at last.

"What do you mean?" Kala asked, putting a cup of warm keldherb in his hand.

"I felt it, Kala. A part of me....a part of me died."

"Impossible."

"Is it? He had to meet the Black Dragon sooner or later. Think about everything's that's happened. I told you they wanted him alone and that's exactly what happened. Now, it's over. All our celebration is for nothing. The Darkness has won."

"Yet the Circle is not closed."

"If you're right, how long?" Jyp asked. "How long before the darkness overtakes us?"

Jada shook her head, "The Eld have ne'er writ of it. When the Circle do end, all knowin' end wid it. Man cain't write the history when 'e cain't write all. S'picion is the ignorance spreads kinda like plague, one village at a time. All depend on where it starts as ta how long takes."

"I intend to be back in Magiskeep," Simen said. "And all the rest of you need to go wherever you call home." He got up from the table, catching his breath against the pain. "Where's Jebe? I need to get him back to his mother."

"Lad's gone ta the royal stables agin. Heard a rumor the Scarleteers are on their way back ta the city," Jada said. "He keeps lookin' fer that golden colt o' his."

"I'll go get him," Jyp said. "Poor lad. Maybe the Circle's Close will ease his pain. Why, it could be he'll even forget he ever had a horse of his own."

"I don't want to forget everything I know, Kala sighed. "It's taken me too long to learn it all."

"Fresh start ain't so bad in the way o' things," Jada said. "Don't like tha loss o' he Healin' lore. Guess I'll put ma herb books and all ma notes someplace safe. That way iffen I ever learn ta read, an' write agin, I'll be able ta figger it all out."

Soon all the others were talking of ways to preserve their knowledge in the hopes of one day recovering all they had lost.

Simen headed upstairs to pack his bag. Kala followed him.

"Simen, are you sure? You're sure Jamus is dead?"

Even as she asked, the mirror in the room started to glow with the golden light of Magiskeep. Hope flared, but when the image appeared, it was not Jamus but Rath.

"My Lady," Simen said, "You have news."

"Kiselor is no more," she said. "Come, Salene needs you."

Kala clutched Simen's arm. "What happened?"

"Blackwing," Rath replied. "Rath come too late. It be over."

"So the Great Circle will close. You've been alive forever, Rath. Can you tell us how much time we have?"

"It be Turan's Way," she replied. "Dragon no count time."

"Can I get back to Magiskeep before I forget how?"

"Alrath bring. Faster than fourleg go. I tell. He come soon."

"I'll look for him."

As Rath's image faded from view, Simen strapped his pack to his shoulders."Well it looks as if I will be flying a Dragon now. Too bad I won't be able to remember it."

*****

As the Scarleteers rode into the city they greeted at first with jeers, but as the people began to notice the golden colt, riderless, the jeers quieted to excited whispers. Finally, at Dover Street, a woman, reached out and tugged at Cadan's leg. He halted the brigade and reined his own horse to face her. "What is it Mistress?"

"That's the King's horse, ain't it?"

"It is," Cadan replied.

"Then where be the King?"

"There was an accident on the trail," he said, taking a deep breath, "The King is dead."

The woman turned to the man behind her. "Ya hear?"

The man nodded. Then he climbed up on a nearby wagon and shouted to all who could hear, "The King is dead!"

To Cadan's and the other riders's relief, the streets erupted in cheers. Word spread throughout the city like Dragon flames. Soon every street the Scarleteers rode along was lined with cheering citizens, welcoming them back as heroes.

Gareth would have been pleased.

When they finally reached the royal stables, Shimmer broke from the group, cantering off to the gate, where Jebe waited for him. The boy burst into tears as his golden colt nearly knocked him off his feet, shoveling his head into Jebe's chest, searching for treats.

Shim happy, happy, happy.

"Where is the King, Shim?"

Hard hand soft body. Bad rider make big long fall. Land like dung. Plop.

"He fell?"

In big hole. Try make Shim jump. Shim do, then disappear.

"You vanished out from under him? Shim, you killed the King?"

Drop dung, drop King. Fall on bottom kill, not Shim.

Jebe hugged his colt around his neck, surprised to feel how broad and muscular it had become. As bad as losing him had been, the exercise and training had changed his golden colt into a powerful golden stallion, almost powerful enough to rival his father.

Jyp found the two together in the yard. "Jebe, you need to go home."

"I gots Shim back, Master Jyp."

"I can see that. I'm happy for you, lad. Lord Delran is riding back to his keep tonight. You need to go with him. You need to go home to your mother.

Jebe ride?

"Yes, Shim. I ride. Give me a boost up, will ya, Master Jyp. Shim's all growed up an' I ain't yet. Where be the Lord?"

"He'll be waiting for you at the Crown and Thorn. The Hand bless you, Jebe. Safe ride home."

As the boy trotted off, Jyp felt a catch in his throat. Of all the knowing he didn't want to lose, forgetting his friends was the hardest to think about.

He hurried back to the inn himself, determined to make the best of the time they had left.

*****

Rath's arrival back at Magiskeep with Salene, Jarien, and the terrible news of Jamus' death plunged their world into depths of grief no one had ever experienced before. The love nearly everyone had for him was intensified by the realization that he had been the only force holding off the Black Dragon's intent to close the Great Circle.

To a kingdom dependent on knowledge and learning, the thought of losing it all was even worse than losing the Lord they so loved. Maids wept in the hall, and men trying hard to pretend their eyes were dry hid their faces from each other as they too cried for their loss.

Sarena ran to Salene's chambers as soon as Rath carried her in. "Take care of Jarien first," Salene insisted, her voice raspy and slow as if even finding the right words to say was a struggle.

For his part, Jarien seemed fine, giggling happily as Sarena tried to feel his belly. He rolled over and crawled to the side of his crib and tried to climb out, failing only by a few inches. When he fell back on his bottom, he laughed again and clapped his hands together as if all the misery around him meant nothing at all in his world of joy.

"He's fine," Sarena said, moving back over to Salene. "What did Tamor do to you?"

Salene trembled again. She held up her arm so Sarena could see the freshly healed scar. "He used me for Sorra's feast."

"Sorra?"

"Natale, Jarien's nursemaid. That shetark in sheep's skin kidnaped my son to give him to that monster. She was Shadow, Sarena. Pure, evil Shadow."

"She drank your blood?"

"Feast for the Darkness, that's what I was. He said before he was through with me I would feed a thousand thousand Shadows. He was going to keep us there forever, Salene, imprisoned by his Magic, serving up our blood to his minions over and over."

"That's horrible," Sarena said, shivering herself at the thought. "Let me Touch you, Salene. I can ease your pain."

"The pain in my body, not the pain in my heart," Salene sobbed. "I saw him die, Sarena. He sacrificed himself for us, just walking into Blackwing's teeth without a word. He's dead, and it's all my fault."

"You didn't do anything wrong, Salene."

"I did, I did. I let them take Jarien and then I let them take me."

"No. See it for what it really was. Tamor sent Natale here to take Jarien. How could you ever know? She was Shadow, wearing a poor dead woman's skin. Senital tells me not even the wisest of Seers could penetrate such a well-wrought lie. She deceived us all, Salene. As for the rest, all you did was do what a mother who loves her son would do. You paid dearly for that love, I'm afraid."

"It hurts, Sarena. My heart hurts."

"I can't mend it." Sarena placed her hand on Salene's breast. *The River answered violently as if the waters were boiling. Their*

Master gone, all the dams Jamus had set were broken--gold, silver, white, and now black currents rushing into each other, colliding in absolute confusion.

Sarena's eyes searched for the Gold, the only force she truly understood, pushing away the darker waters. She touched a golden stream at last and drew it to her, letting her mind open at at last to Salene's pain.

Terror and revulsion took her breath away. She saw two naked bodies tangled in the rapture of lovemaking, while all around black coils swirled striking like rimsnakes, piercing her skin, their tongues licking up the blood. Her breasts ached, first with the heavy pressure of too much milk, then with too little as far away a baby cried at the top of its lungs, the sound of it beating into her head. Something sank its teeth into the tender flesh of her breast, biting hard until she whimpered, then it laughed, and yanked her up by her hair, throwing her against the sharp corner of bricks, bruising her back.

The foul odor of rotting flesh filled her nostrils, her stomach churned as she gagged. Something hot burned her tongue and made her throat raw when she swallowed. And all the while her legs and arms were frozen, bound in place, holding her prisoner forever.

Sarena pulled the River close, wrapping its cool, soothing currents around them both, using its energy to fill Salene's tortured body with its comfort. She willed blood to flow from heart to limbs and back again, its stream growing thicker and richer with each pass. Then at last, the Waters surrounding them quieted on their own and she pulled her hand away.

Sarena fell back in the chair, exhausted. Salene's breathing had eased. Her heartbeat was strong and steady. The terror and grief remained. No Healer in all of Turan could cure either.

She stayed beside Salene's bed for two spans, holding her hand, helping her to nurse Jarien when he was hungry, and trying to get her to eat at least a little more than broth and water.

"You need your strength, Salene, for Jarien's sake if not your own. Look at him. Don't you see Jamus in his face? He lives through his son, Salene, and through your love. He sacrificed everything trying to save you. Honor him by willing yourself to live."

"How? Without him, my life is empty. Do you know how much it hurts to love like that in the first place and how much more it hurts to lose it? It's like a great weight pressing down, suffocating me. Even taking a breath hurts."

'Think of Jarien. He needs you."

"He is the only thing keeping me here. Otherwise, I'd go back to that cliff and jump off the way I wanted to when Tamor told me he'd lied to Blackwing."

"And what would your son do without you? What would have become of him then?"

"He would have died too and been better off for it. Tamor broke me, Sarena. I never thought it could happen, but the sheer terror of becoming a fountain to his perversity broke me. Even when Jamus came, I hardly reacted." She burst into tears. "Sarena, I never even told him I loved him."

"He knew, Salene, he knew." She put her arms around Salene and tried in vain to comfort her. No words, no Touch, nothing could ever soothe such pain.

Rath alit on the windowsill, transforming herself to woman in a heartbeat. It was becoming easier and easier. "I will watch them now," she said, stepping into the room. "Dragons understand the deep loss. We have lived through many of our own. Go, get some rest."

Sarena got up. "She says she is broken."

"The world is broken, My Lady, yet the Dragon still flies. I will be here for her."

Salene met Sarn pacing the hall when she left the room.

"Is she all right?" he asked.

"Her body will heal. I don't know if her heart ever will."

"If there's anything I can do..."

"None of us can do anything," Sarena replied, moved by Sarn's concern.

"I never liked Jamus, you know that, but I respected him and I envied the love he and Salene shared. It made me regret so many things I had done to him and things I'd said. Still, he handed over the Rule of his Kingdom to me and in the end, I failed him."

"Magiskeep was saved, Sarn."

"And the Circle lost. I keep thinking it was as much my failure as anyone's. When those Shadows came, I forgot about Salene and Jarien. That was exactly what Natale wanted. She and Tamor played us fools and I was the biggest one of all. Jamus left me in charge to protect everyone here and I failed the two most important people in his life. There's no way to fix it."

"We all underestimated the enemy," Sarena said, "even Jamus. Joria told me what he said when he came back from Arcula, how the attacks there were just a distraction. He'd been tricked too, and by then it was already too late."

"By the blood, why did he have to die? This is his Kingdom, not mine. He should be here, with his wife, his child."

Sarena sighed. "We have more than that to worry about, Sarn. The prophecy says when Blackwing rises the Great Circle will close. We will forget all our knowledge, all the skills we have learned, and fall back into the dark age of ignorance. There's no telling how much time we have. Even Rath can't tell us. Somehow, we must protect as much as well can."

Given something to do, Sarn rallied. "The Library, the books. We need to put them somewhere safe. Get them off the shelves and lock them away. And your herbs and cures. Can we find some way to mark them so even a fool could figure out what they're used for?"

"Come on, let's find the other Masters. We'll send the Prentices to clear the books and take them to Senital's Vaults in the meantime. Then we can put our heads together and figure out something. At least we can spend our last spans before the Darkness trying to preserve our lives."

*****

Alrath carried Simen high above the Rim, passing through the mountains' highest illusions with True Sight, the purest Light of the White River. When he had landed in the streets of Aberdeen to get the Follyman, the people had fled in fear. He had simply laughed and sent a blanket of snow to cover their departure as a parting tribute to his passing. White was his color and he wanted everyone to remember him.

"I doubt they'll forget you, My Lord," Simen said as he settled himself on the Dragon's neck. "You made quite an impression when you arrived."

"When Circle close, men forget. Snow remember. Is gift of memory I leave behind. One small weapon against brother."

A gift. A trigger so men would remember something at least when ignorance descended on the world. "You are most wise, Lord Alrath."

"Love Rivermaster. Do for him. For him to I fly for you."

"Jamus would thank you if he were alive. I am honored to thank you on his behalf."

"Strange. Blackwing not brag yet."

"He's said nothing to you?"

"Only cry of triumph when swallow Kiselor. Then silence. Brood for Shadow loss? Many lose to gain one Rivermaster. Kesel never like lonely."

"He can always gain more allies," Simen replied. "the Way of Mirrors is infinite. I don't feel sorry for him."

"Sad. Once love brother. Now no more. Hate in heart, lust in belly. Cherish ignorance. We fly, he slither on ground, look up at Kiselor. Jealous burn Hate more."

Magiskeep's towers shimmered below, still glowing with Jamus' silver and blue. Simen felt a catch in his throat at the sight, memories flooding his mind. He owed everything to Jamus, and now there was no way to repay him.

They landed in the courtyard under cover of darkness, but it mattered little. Rath's constant comings and goings had made the Mages and villagers immune to Dragons.

Simen climbed down. "Do you want to visit longer? Your sister may be here."

"See Rath all time. No need now. Go, the Lady needs you." With that, Alrath stroked his wings once and flew off in the moonlight as Simen hurried into the Keep and ran up the stairs two at a time. He hesitated at Salene's door, took a deep breath, and pushed it open.

Rath was seated by the bed, rocking Jarien gently in her arms. She was so much less the Dragon now, he hardly recognized her. "My Lady," he said, bowing to her.

"Alrath fly fast. Is good." She got up from the chair, still holding Jarien and motioned for him to sit in her place. "Do not surprise her. She will see Jamus in your face. Tell her you are not before she wakes."

He sat and took Salene's hand in his. "Salene, it's Simen. I'm here. It's Simen," he repeated.

Her eyes fluttered open, "Simen. I'm sorry. I lost your brother."

"We all lost him, Salene. My heart is broken too. A part of me died with him."

"Your heart? Certainly not your wit, it was always so much better than his. He never could tell a good joke."

Simen smiled. If she was able to tease him now, even a little, he knew she was going to be all right.

"Jarien's grown even in the month or so I've been gone."

"He's going to be a fine man, the image of his father," she said, choking back a sob. "I'm sorry. Every time I think I have no more tears they flow again."

"That's the second time you've apologized and I've only been here a few minutes. I think it's time to stop."

"To stop apologizing or stop talking? Either way I lose again."

Simen laughed. "I thought you said I was the wit of the family."

"Half and half," she replied, managing a weak wink. "I feel better now that you're here."

Simen knew it was not his presence so much as his being a part of Jamus, his reflection, something she could cling to, easing her way along the journey of accepting Jamus' death. He hoped he could live up to her needs. "I'll sit with you all night if you want me to."

She shook her head. "Go see Jessa. Tell her you love her if you really do. I want to know there is some happiness in the Keep, even in my sorrow. Do it soon. If you wait until the Circle closes, you may forget." Simen leaned over, kissed her gently on the cheek and then left the room.

He knew Jessa would be waiting for him and he also knew Salene was right. Reaching for even a small bit of happiness would take away some of the sting of Jamus' death.

XXVI

For four long days, Magiskeep waited for the Great Circle to close. Masters, Mages, Apprentices, and servants bustled from room to room putting artifacts into cabinets labeled with child book pictures explaining what they were. Joria's little class of Firecasters proved invaluable. Since nearly all of them were too young to read much, they were officially dubbed "Testers of the Labels." Their job was to try to guess what each stored item was solely from the label placed on the drawer, door or box. When they guessed right the sign was accepted, but when they failed new signs were printed up and tested again until nearly everything stashed away could be identified by even the smallest child.

It was a massive project as Masters tried to sort through hundreds of collectibles, determined to save what was truly important and get rid of whatever had truly outlived its usefulness. Rooms that had not been cleaned in circles were suddenly dust free and organized to perfection.

Magic was used sparingly, as the labor of hands and minds became the order of the day until even those who thrived on Magic's impact felt little need to touch the River. Even Jiala and Siamel, whose mastery of Manipulation had lured many an unwary man to their beds, found themselves able to charm men into helping them move furniture or stack a box on a high shelf with sweet words and honest needs. It was a revelation to both of them to discover that their personalities and beauty alone was more than enough to bring men to their chambers to help and, for at least two of the days, spend the night.

By the end of the Sevenstin, Salene was strong enough to leave her bed. And though she was still always on the verge of tears, she managed to begin arranging some of the books and items in hers and Jamus' chamber. It was a tiresome task in many ways with so many books, but every now and then something would stop her, and she would sit, lost in memories. There was a flower pressed between the pages of a book, a bloom he had created as a child in Joria's classroom. The Mistress had kept it for circles and finally given it to Salene in secret, telling her the story of its creation. Then there was the little statue of a silver horse, which she put in a box along with a painting of a silver stallion that had hung in Jamus' boyhood room until she retrieved it to give to him on their first anniversary. One bell from Simen's original Follyman's tunic lay in a drawer, along with one of Whim's first horseshoes. The room was filled with Jamus. The only thing missing was the man himself.

Sarena had been right. Her heart would keep him alive.

Whim had wandered home that morning, and she had made her way to the stable to see him. The stallion had stood quietly while she rubbed his neck and sung softly to him stumbling over the words of an old song she had once heard Jamus singing to the horse as he was grooming him.

"A man and his horse are bonded e'er
Whenever they travel anywhere.
The horse on the bottom, the man up above
As man and woman when making love."

She laughed now to think of the absurdity of modest Jamus singing such a bawdy rhyme. How she had cherished his virtue. "He truly was Best One, wasn't he, Whim." The stallion nickered softly as if agreeing, and she let herself imagine he was trying to talk to her.

Clouder followed her everywhere, clinging to her side, growling if anyone dared say anything that seemed even remotely unkind or upsetting. He lay his head on her lap when she sat down and, when Jarien cried, he was the first to run over to him, anxious and hovering until someone tended to the baby's needs.

A few days later, just before Weswin's change, Salene had made her way to the garden. Rath was upstairs with Jarien again, giving her time to be alone to deal with her grief in her own way. The sun was low in the eastern sky, the clouds tinged with pink and purple.

Suddenly, the wind picked up. A cry went up from the north tower, "Dragon!" At first Salene ignored the shouts. Then her brain cleared when she realized Rath was already in the Keep.

She ran to the garden's north gate, and out to the courtyard where a small group of servants had gathered pointing up at the sky. She could just make out the dark silhouette of a huge dragon, its wings sweeping aside the clouds as it flew towards them.

"Blackwing," someone muttered. "The Circle closes."

Salene strained to see in the dim light, her eyes riveted on the dark form as it drew closer, looming larger and larger as it neared. She caught her breath as he heart began to pound wildly, fears born in Tamor's cave blotting out reason.

Then, there was a shimmer of rainbow light as the great creature dropped lower in the sky. Not Blackwing.

A great shining Rainbow Dragon, Kisel Master of all Dragons, and on his back, his master, Kiselor, the Rivermaster, her beloved Jamus, alive and well.

Kisel landed and lowered his huge head to let his rider slide to the ground. Jamus' tunic shimmered with the same rainbow colors of his mount, and his face was shining in the rays of the setting sun. He saw Salene and ran to her, sweeping her into his arms as she fainted. He picked her up and carried her into the Keep, barely nodding to the stunned servant and Mages who were running from all over to catch a glimpse of him. Simen met him as he started up the stairs. Neither man said a word as together they hurried to the private rooms above. Clouder was leaping joyously about, but once they got to the door and went inside, he stayed in the hall, keeping guard denying anyone else entrance.

Jamus lay Salene gently on the bed, before turning to his brother. "I don't think you were expecting me," he said, the first words out of his mouth since his dramatic arrival.

"I thought you were dead," Simen said when he finally found his voice. "I should have known...."

"You weren't wrong," Jamus replied. "I was."

"By the Blood, Jamus, where have you been? What's happened to you?"

Jamus placed his hand on Salene's head, sending his Magic into her. He no longer needed to reach for the River, for he was the River.

Rath seemed to purr as she moved to the window to leave.

Jamus saw her move, "Stay," he told her. "I want you here for now. You are too important to me. You and your brothers have given me my life."

"Always we have taken Turan's Way, Dragonlord," Rath replied. "It is a small matter."

"Not to me," Jamus replied. "Stay. We need you here for now."

"I obey," Rath answered. She sat on the window seat, her eyes spinning in Dragon whirls as she watched the others in the room.

Salene stirred on the bed as she woke and saw Jamus leaning over her. "I forgot to tell you I loved you," she said.

"You didn't have to," he answered, "I already knew." He bent and kissed her, then helped her sit up, propping the pillows behind her back. "You are still weak," he said. "I gave you another

Healing, but you still need time. I had no idea you were so close to dying in that cave."

"But you….I saw you die. This time I saw you die. How many times? How many times, Jamus? The Black Dragon ate you."

"He did, My Love. And I did die. I accepted oblivion and at that moment, he and I were bound together in the secret of the Black River. I had to let him win or we would have lost everything."

"You're not making much sense, Brother," Simen said. "At least not to me."

"The final riddle," Jamus replied, "was the secret of the Black River. Surrendering myself, offering my life a sacrifice, accepting oblivion--all were a part of it."

"And yet you are here."

"The rest of the Riddle, " Jamus said. "Spellfire. I cast it when Kesel grabbed me in his mouth. He had to spit me out, but before he did, he swallowed the flames. I fell onto the rocks in the water below. That's when I must have died."

"You don't know?"

"Oblivion is just that, Simen. How long? There is no time in the River. I can't remember anything because there is nothing to remember. It's only when I woke at Kisel's feet that I began to understand. 'Life for a life,' he said, but I had nothing to trade— except for Blackwing."

"Spellfire cannot kill a Dragon," Rath said. "Nothing can unless the Dragon chooses to die."

"It can make a slave of one if he fears the pain. Spellfire can only be purged from its victim by a greater Magic."

"And the only one with greater Magic than the Dragonlord, is the Great Dragon himself," Rath said, laughing. "My Dark brother must be furious."

"It doesn't matter," Jamus said, "As long as Kisel and I hold tight to his silver reins he must obey us."

"So Blackwing life was traded for your own," Simen said.

"The final riddle solved," Jamus replied, "and the Fourth River mastered."

"So the Circle will not close after all," Simen said. "All this work in the Keep for nothing."

"Not for nothing," Salene said. "The place needed a good Seremonth cleaning."

*****

The Keep was in an uproar over Jamus' return. Sorrow shattered into joy. Speculation as to what had happened and all kinds of rumors raced through halls and villages as far away as Tallridge with startling speed. Within the Sevenstin, nearly everyone knew the true Lord of the Keep was back and the Great Circle was safe.

Jamus' companions who had come with him from Arcula had been swept up in the drama as well, suffering the misery of the four days he was thought dead. Eleyse and Covane had lost themselves in their rooms in the South Tower, trying to sort out the tragedy without intruding on their host's grief. The rest of the group, settled in guest quarters on the lower floor, had helped with all the efforts to preserve the Keep's treasures and found themselves so integrated into the household they had nearly forgotten they had ever been strangers.

Now, as the Keep rejoiced, they were more than ready, willing and able to help plan and participate in all the celebrations suggested.

"Great feast in the hall," someone offered, and Moka started designing a menu with Ferna and the other cooks in the kitchens.

"A ball, with music and entertainment," another suggested. And soon after, Garv was sending Hobar and Carby back to Arcuse to invite Talia and her father to perform.

Jeamel found himself caught up in the enthusiasm, finally enlisting the aid of some of the Prentices to use their Magic to help decorate the Halls for the festivities.

Serenec had found Senital and the two of them starting working on a guest list, trying to decide who from Turan proper should be invited. "The Rim still poses a problem," Senital said. "Getting visitors safely across can be difficult."

"Well, we could ask the guest of honor to help us find safe passage through, but I'd like to think two old codgers like us, well versed the Eldenlore should be able to figure something out for ourselves."

"Jamus has better ways to spend his time right now," Senital said, laughing. "He hasn't been out of the bedroom in the two days since he came back."

"I hope we see him soon. The Keep is abuzz with so many versions of the story of what actually happened that my own head is spinning. I've been trying to write it all down, but I've filled up two scrolls already and I haven't told the half of it."

"Well, at least that explains why the Lore is always so voluminous and complicated. So many voices telling the same story in their own versions makes for a long tale."

Serenec sighed, "Maybe I should just give up and let things fall as they may. I can always write the rest later now that I have no fear of forgetting how."

Upstairs in the Great Library, Sarn was trying to be patient. Clouder and Rath had refused to let him talk to Jamus since his return. He, of all, felt he had the right to know what had actually happened. Two days of ignorance was far too long. He was grateful Jamus had managed to save him from an eternity of it.

"I've been looking for you," Simen said as he walked into the room.

"Ah, word from the Master? What took you so long? I'm not hard to find."

"I spent the first day with my brother and the second with Jessa. A man has to get his priorities straight," Simen replied.

"Seems to me they're a bit backward, actually," Sarn said. "Then again, I'm not sure Jamus would ever consent to spend a day with me. Come to think of it, neither would Jessa." He grinned. "So, does the temporary Lord of the Keep finally get to hear the true story?"

Simen sat down and told Sarn everything he knew, finishing with what had happened in Aberdeen.

"So Turan is without a King. Perhaps when I am deposed here, I could apply for the position?"

"I doubt they'd accept you despite your stellar qualifications. Lord Dale is acting as temporary Governor in the city and Kala seems to think Turan is done with Kings. The people want to have a say in their government. Erlik's headed back to Arcula to see how they've been managing with the New Order there. He may end up setting some kind of Council like in Aberdeen. The other Province will be free to choose what they want after that."

"And here in Magiskeep? Does Jamus have his own plans?"

"If he does, I haven't heard them yet. I think he's been too busy making amends with Salene to think about it. She suffered terribly because of him."

"It was as much my fault as it was his," Sarn said. "I was supposed to be keeping her and Jarien safe here while he was gone."

"Blame yourself if you want to, Sarn, but the truth of it all is that everything that happened was all a part of Turan's Way. Call it fate or destiny if you will. Jamus would tell you the story has already been written in tomorrow's Eldenlore. If he could find the right door in the Way or the right thread in one of his tapestries, he could step into the day when he could read the tale himself in some dusty tome.

The Great Circle is exactly that, Sarn. Its end meets its beginning and just goes on forever."

*****

When Jamus, Salene, and Jarien entered the Dining Hall at Evenmeal, they were greeted by a standing ovation. "Do I need to make a speech?" Jamus whispered to Salene.

"A short one might be in order," she whispered back. "This is the first time you've been seen in public since you came back. Just don't make a spectacle of yourself."

"I thought I'd already done that," he said laughing. He walked to the front of the Hall and raised his hand asking for quiet. "First, I am glad to be here, I won't tell you the whole story of all that's happened. It will spread around the Keep fast enough on its own." He waited until the laughter faded. "I do want to thank everyone here for all you've done to support my family and me during these hard times. Most importantly, I want to thank you all for your brave and unselfish defense of this Keep in times of trial and times of peace. Together, we have defeated the Shadows and their Master. For now and, I hope, for a long time to come, Magiskeep will be safe from the Darkness and the Great Circle will spin on. I have friends here, allies visiting from Arcula, our sister world of Magic. Looking around the room, I can see you have already welcomed them into our lives." There was a round of applause for this as Garv and the other Arculans stood at his acknowledgment.

"The Dark days are over. The Light dawns anew. I will call a Gathering tomorrow, and meet with the Seven Masters to choose the next course we will follow here. It is not fitting I do any of this alone, for we are all one here. Together we have preserved this Kingdom and together we will share its future."

With that he walked back over to Salene, gave her a quick kiss, and sat down at the dining table. "Perfect," she said. "But how could I expect any less from the Master of Four Rivers?"

Elyese and Covane, who had been waiting at the door while Jamus spoke, came to the table and sat down. "Most impressive, My Lord," Covane said. "I knew you were glib in the field. I never quite expected such skill from the throne."

"I have no throne, Covane."

"Just a turn of phrase, my friend. I think you could easily be crowned here if you ever wanted to, and unless I miss my guess in Arcula as well. It's a good thing you are not an ambitious man."

"Ambition has a dreadful price, I fear," Eleyse said. "I of all know it too well." She extended her hand over the table to Salene. "I am Mard Eleyse, Mistress Salene. I hope I am welcome at your table."

Salene smiled. "I should have known you would be beautiful. Most of the women attracted to my husband have been."

"How can you be so gracious to me? Surely you know what happened."

"I do. Jamus tells me everything. I certainly don't approve, but I am also aware that Arculan customs are foreign to me. I cannot condemn someone who does not believe as I do that the love of one man and one woman is a sacred thing, and more wonderful than I ever could have imagined."

Eleyse leaned back in her chair, closed her eyes for a moment and then sighing, answered, "I would like to believe one day I could find that kind of love. It was never something the Cauge encouraged. Now, though, the Cauge is gone and I am free to live as I choose."

Covane reached into the sleeve of her purple gown and took her hand in his, "I would like to be part of that life, My Mardel. Your one man, if you so choose."

All eyes at the table turned to Eleyse as the group waited to hear her answer.

She blushed, another new experience for the hardened woman who had served on the Cauge. "I would like that, My Rider. I would like that a great deal."

"That sounded suspiciously like a 'yes,' Covane," Jamus said, laughing. "I think you'd better kiss her now to seal the agreement before she says anything more."

He did as Jamus suggested and after a toast to honor the engagement, they enjoyed a good meal none of them would soon forget.

*****

The next day, Jamus met with Sarn in his study. "I have the right to be Master here, Sarn, and I intend to be so."

"I don't blame you after all the mistakes I made."

"You didn't make any mistakes," Jamus said. "Tamor outwitted us all. I'm the one who underestimated him."

"In the end you won."

"By the grace of a riddle and a tapestry," Jamus replied. "I'll tell you all about it one day."

"If you're still speaking to me."

"I'll have to. I need to be sure something like this never happens again. Magiskeep needs defenses, Sarn. The Mages need to learn how to use Spellfire, and training militias in the villages would help assure them protection. My Arculan Warriors have the skills to teach all this, but they don't exactly have the social graces good teachers need. They need supervision, leadership, and someone not afraid to speak his mind or to get what he wants from people around him. They need someone like you."

"You'd trust me with an army?"

"Not entirely, but I do trust the army. Garv and his men have all sworn oaths to me. The Warriors are an Elden race and their word is stelin. I'm sure they wouldn't let you do anything I wouldn't approve."

Sarn laughed. "Rivermaster and master of men. I envy you, Jamus. You are everything I should have been."

"I think Jebe and Lurela will be coming to the feast. Serenec and Senital have made quite a guest list and their names are on it. It might be time to try to make a few amends."

"I tried that once and failed."

"For all the wrong reasons. I'm working on clearing a safe passage through the Rim so everyone can travel from Turan to here. The road goes both ways, Sarn. Lurela has made a new life for herself—a home for Jebe. Delran's Keep is not so far away. Let it begin here and perhaps, one day, it can finish there."

Sarn nodded. "I'd like that," he said.

"Well then, come on with me. I've called the Gathering and we shouldn't keep the Masters waiting."

The Seven Masters were seated on the hearing platform in the Judgment Hall. The eighth chair, the one set aside for the Master of the Keep, was empty. Jamus motioned Sarn to sit in it since he had made no proclamation to claim it as his own. Instead, he stood as petitioner.

The galleries above in the balcony and below were filled to capacity by Mages and Apprentices all eager to hear whatever Jamus was willing to share in testimony.

Jorn, dressed in his formal green robe, spoke first. "Lord Jamus, you called the Gathering as is the right of all Masters in this Kingdom. We are aware of your claim to the Mastery of the Keep, yet you sit Sarn in your chair. Can you tell us why?"

"I have come to reclaim my title, but until I do, Master Sarn still has the right to sit with you. My question to you is whether you, as the wisest of counselors, believe I should. My world has expanded beyond Magiskeep's Halls to the west and east. I have conquered the Dragon in the Norreaches and have walked the desert to the south. Four Rivers now answer my call and three Dragons fly for me. The fourth scalewing is mine as well even though it does not please him. Magiskeep can no longer be my only priority. I will never desert her, never deny her, and never do her wrong, but Four Rivers flow to the Great Sea, and the world between is now as much my responsibility as Magsikeep is."

Joria and Sarena simply nodded, their decision made. Both agreed there was no true Master of Magiskeep except Jamus. Jiala and Jorn began whispering to each other while Jired leaned in to listen, his face registering his confusion.

Then Savel, Master of the Seventh Art, the skill to elevate even the most ordinary to precious value, spoke up. The others looked at him in surprise for he was always the last to express his opinion and had never made proclamation without hearing all sides of an argument. "Lord Jamus," he said. "You now claim Mastery of all Rivers?"

"I do," Jamus replied.

"Then is it no so that wherever you stand all the Waters converge? Does not your very presence call the Dragons at your will? If this be so, then whatever ground you walk the seat of power goes with you, be it here or on the Shores of Aberdeen. By no proclamation of ours, or of any man's the rule of Magiskeep must belong to you. How can there be any question?"

"Master Savel is right," Sarn said. "Magiskeep needs no other Master than Lord Jamus. Even a fool like me can wear the title and do what is needed to settle disputes or tend to the petty details day to day. It is the Magic itself that needs nurturing here, and there is no better man than The Rivermaster to do it. You all know the truth, no matter what your own ambitions may be. I know it, and I have always been the most ambitious of all." He got up from the chair, "Choose as you will, Masters. I, for one, gladly give this seat to the only man in all of Turan with the right to sit in it."

And so, as Sarn stepped down from the platform, order was restored in Magiskeep, The Kingdom Beyond the Rim.

XXVII

The guests were arriving daily for the Grand Celebration at Magiskeep. Senital and Serenec had whittled their guest list of invitees from beyond the Keep to a manageable number, at least according to Jeamel. As First Houseman, it was his job to find lodging for all the visitors and despite what often appeared an infinite number of rooms in the castle, there was a limit. Some of the residents in the main village opened their doors as well, and there were rooms in the local inns to fill. In the end, the two Mages were satisfied and everyone of importance would be welcomed.

For his part, Jamus didn't interfere with any of the plans, content to enjoy observing the special pleasure the servants and Mages in the Keep were having doing all the work themselves. Magic played a role in the preparations, of course, with many of the children delighting in being able to use the skills they had learned in Joria's classes to light fires for the cooks or fly decorations to the higher walls. There were some curiously crooked garlands here and there, but even Jiala, to whom appearance was everything, left them alone when she found out the littlest girls who had hung them thought they were just beautiful.

Despite Serenec's and Senital's best efforts, they had failed to find a way to open an easy trail through the Rim, so they had to ask Jamus for help. "My Lord, we didn't want to burden you with this, " Serenec said. "The illusions are simply too complex for us to Comprehend. We rode out yesterday, hoping to find an answer, but after Master Senital's horse nearly fell over a cliff, we decided we were in the River over our depth."

"Perhaps it is time to break the barrier between the rest of Turan and the Keep," Jamus said. "I took down the Wall to Arcula, of course, but those mountains are another matter. The weaves are ancient and far more complicated than even I can undo in even a month. I can open a passage, though. Where Cowltop lies in the center is a vast space free of Illusion. All I need to do is cast an open trail on either side."

That Sowin, he saddled Whim and rode out.

Windstep?

"Yes, Whim," and with that, he lifted the stallion's stride and reached the foot of the mountain range as soon as they landed.

Whim watch. We go through?

The horse had an uncanny perception of the Rim's illusions and had carried Jamus through safely many times. "Not this time, my friend. I am going to make a path where there are no illusions to sift."

No fun. Whim like have look. Make eye wake, not sleep. You make way sleepy then.

Jamus laughed. "So that explains why you are always to impatient to move on when we are out riding. You get bored. Sorry, my love, but most people like riding horses who are quiet and sleepy. This will make it so they can have good rides to come visit us whenever they want to."

No fun. Whim repeated as he lowered his head to graze while Jamus studied the mountains.

Sorem had created the range hundreds of circles past at the time of Wizardchase. Like the Wall of Arcula, it was intended to protect Magiskeep from the world beyond. Now, at last, it was time to forget the great divide between the mortal world and the Magic. The Knights of the Hand, the Seers, and the Sorcerers of Cuver Street had proven Magic's worth in the rebellion. The fact that Sorcery had been living and thriving in Aberdeen for so long without being noticed was even more proof the world was ready to unite again.

It also meant that Jamus' speech before the Gathering had more gravity than even Savel realized. Assuring Magic would never again threaten the rights of the people of Turan was a heavy responsibility. Opening the Rim was just the first step in accepting it.

As he sifted the weaves, he remembered how much had happened to him since he and the parents he had loved had wandered among these very peaks. Cowltop, the mountain where they died, no longer tormented him. Now it stood as a monument to their love for him. Here too was where Sagari found him, starting him on this very journey. Here, he fled from Sagari, and just on the other side, he met Kala. He never expected it would one day come to this.

He raised his hand, the Sifting complete. Here, Sorem had merged two Rivers, silver and gold, using a crude knowledge of the reflections of the Way of Mirrors to set the threads in place. It explained everything—why the illusions existed and why so few, even gifted with the Magic could pass through safely. For the

Rivermaster and the Master of the Way, it took only a simple casting to break the weave and open a clear trail even a mere mortal could follow.

Few mere mortals would use that trail to come to the Celebration, though. Instead, it was a caravan from Aberdeen with Dale and Kala in the lead. Kolea and Klef chose to come to represent Grandisite. Erlik promised Talia the horses would be well cared for at the Course by convincing several of the Sorcerers of Cuver Street to watch over them while they were away. Jyp ended up driving the carriage for Jada and Jelda when they insisted no one else could ever do the job as well. When they reached Delran's Keep in Telma, Lurela added to his passenger list.

Delran rode his charger, of course, with Jebe proudly mounted on Shimmer. Nobby rode one of Delran's well-trained cobs alongside Joss, who couldn't resist giving both boys riding lessons along the way.

When they reached the Host House a the base of the Rim, they set up camp for the night. Dale and Delran rode ahead into the mountains to check the trail ahead, armed with their Knights' perception to sift any illusions, but there was no need. Jamus had made clear passage all the way to Cowltop and they were confident the trail opened just as safely into Magiskeep beyond.

"We shouldn't have questioned you," Delran said to Kala when they got back from their scouting mission. "When you told us you'd spoken to Lord Jamus in the mirrors, I'll have to admit I was skeptical."

"Seers are sworn not to lie," Kala reminded him, "although we too can be deceived by our own blindness. Sometimes wanting something too much can darken even keenest Vision. I'm glad the trail is open."

"It will still take us two days to cross the mountains," Dale said. "One more camp at Cowltop and I'll be able to look forward to seeing the Keep myself. Is it truly as beautiful as I imagine?"

"At least three times larger than the King's Palace in Aberdeen," Kala said. "Towers, covered walks, grand halls, and wonderful gardens. I think you'll be impressed."

And indeed, when they crossed the range and came within sight of Magiskeep itself, Dale was most impressed. The castle seemed to shimmer in the late day sun, spirals of blue and silver adorning the bluestone walls. On the west side, were dozens of well-tended paddock and pastures with a huge stable complex. Even from afar, Talia could see the fine quality of the horses as they pranced about, tails high excited to see the visitors arriving.

"Ma Pap's the stablemaster," Joss said proudly as they rode into to the expansive yard. When Josep walked out to greet them, Joss jumped off his horse and ran into his father's arms.

"Welcome home, Lad," Josep said. 'I see ya brung your ol' Pap some extra work, eh?"

"Counting myself," Joss laughed, "I also brought three strong young horsemasters to help." He nodded to Jebe and Nobby, who hopped off their mounts and stood, waiting for orders.

"He brought an admirer too," Talia said, as she slid out of the saddle. "I am Talia, from the Course at Aberdeen. I would be honored if you would show me around your stables as soon as you have the time. I've trained horses all my life, but I've never seen any place quite like this."

"Magiskeep has a long history wid its horses, My Lady. I kin tell it ta ya after yer all settled in up the Keep. Jest come on back anytimes ya want. Wid these lads here ta take on ma duties for a while, I gots plenty o' time ta show ya around."

Joss laughed, "So much for a vacation. Come on, lads, let's git these animals cared for proper. No shortcuts in the Keep. Ma father taught me everythin' I knows an' I don't aim ta disappoint 'im."

Several other stableboys joined the three, taking all the horses into the barns while the guests headed into the Keep.

*****

Arcula's arrivals were fewer in number, mostly because those who had ridden in with Jamus earlier were still there. Gaila came, of course, with Corel at her side. With much pleading Dart and Emi managed to convince Densil to add them to his little carriage, though he refused to admit he'd already set aside room for both of them as long as they didn't sit between him and Wolla.

With Lord Sarkem riding up from the south with his wife and Delise and Mistress Jolene arriving from the Norreaches, the more formal list was complete.

Delegates from all Magiskeep's surrounding villages swelled the number, of course filling most of the available rooms in the Keep and inns.

Becca introduced her son, his wife, and their new daughter to the Keep with beaming pride. Yet the moment she saw little Jarien nestled in Rath's arms, she abandoned her own family to see him. "I sees ya finally learnt how to hold a twoleg kitling," she said.

"He wiggles a lot," Rath said. "And if I put him down and don't keep my eyes on him, he's likely to crawl off to get into some kind of mischief."

"Jest like 'is Pap," Becca said, winking when she realized Jamus was within earshot.

*****

The feast itself began on the last day of Seremonth, some three Sevenstins after Jamus' return. It would go on well into the night with celebrations spilling over into the Sevenstin beyond.

Jamus tried hard to enjoy every moment. Sharing his life with true friends like these was a gift beyond measure, but he longed for some quiet time with Salene and Jarien, and even more, time to be alone with his own thoughts.

Well after Norwin's Change, he went out to the balcony alone. The moon was near full, casting silver beams on the garden below, setting the fountains water to glimmering sparks. How many moons had passed since he first touched the River? How many lives had come and gone? In the room behind him were just a few of the people who had touched his life and here they were to celebrate him. It should have been the other way around.

The rustle of Salene's soft shaenis gown interrupted his thoughts, "Jamus, why are you out here? The party's still going on and everyone's been demanding another song from Talia and Simen."

"Better I stay out here, then," he said. "Otherwise they'll want me to join in. I'd really rather listen."

She let him take her in his arms, leaning her head on his chest. "Becca and Rath have been bickering all night about who should be holding Jarien."

"I'll put my money on Becca. She's twice as ferocious as a Dragon when it comes to children."

"She was your only solace as a child, wasn't she. I never quite understood that. If I had, maybe I wouldn't have left you here alone with Sagari."

"It was all a part of Turan's Way, Salene," he answered. "Whatever mistakes any of us made have long been mended."

"I'm glad," she said. "Now we can spend the rest of our lives together. I hope it won't be too boring for you."

"There's too much to do," Jamus answered, kissing her on the head. "We have to reorganize the Great Library, putting all the books back. Then there are the horses. I have all kinds of ideas for breeding and with the Rim and Wall open we can starts some real trade with both Turan and Arcula. Both lands know a fine horse when they see one. Then there are so many places to visit. We never really had a proper honeymoon, and I'd love to show Jarien the Sea. I haven't been to Arcula's shores yet either, and what about the Islands?"

"You're making me dizzy," she said, laughing.

Inside, Simen struck a chord on his lute and cleared his throat.

"My head is full of ideas, Salene. Bless the Hand Turan isn't going to have to start all over again. Instead, we can create a whole new age of learning, right here in Magiskeep."

Talia's clear voice rose above the buzz of the crowd, silencing the Hall behind Magiskeep's Master and his One Love.

On the winds fly the Dragons of Silver and White,
Dancing in moonbeams illuming the night.
Silver the Magic of heart's yearning song
Igniting the fire for righting the wrong.
White is the Magic of truth seeking light
Conquering all with the power of Sight.
O sing of the master who takes to their wings
O sing of the promise of freedom he brings.
O sing of the hope to the heart he does send
O sing of the day of the great journey's end.
Simen's strong baritone joined Talia in sweet harmony.
Then comes the Rainbow with gold in his eyes
Chasing the dark clouds away as he flies
Darkness is broken by his mighty call
Under his power, the Blackwing does fall.
O sing of the master who takes to their wings
O sing of the promise of freedom he brings.
O sing of the hope to the heart he does send
O sing of the day of the great journey's end.
Four be the Rivers that flow from his hand
Magic enveloping all of the land.
Circle of knowing, this circle of men
Now at its closing beginning again.
O sing of the master who takes to their wings
O sing of the promise of freedom he brings.
O sing of the hope to the heart he does send
O sing of the day of the great journey's end.
O sing of the master who takes to their wings
O sing of the promise of freedom he brings.
O sing of the hope to the heart he does send

O sing of the day of the great journey's end.
The music ended to rounds of applause.

Overhead, they saw the silhouette of a Great Dragon fly across the face of the moon.

Jamus smiled as he pulled Salene even closer in his embrace.

For now, it was enough.

www.ingramcontent.com/pod-product-compliance
Lightning Source LLC
Chambersburg PA
CBHW020631020726
47494CB00001B/139